I Sought Adventure But It Found Me

Reginald A Keeley-Osgood, MC

authorHOUSE®

AuthorHouse™ UK Ltd.
500 Avebury Boulevard
Central Milton Keynes, MK9 2BE
www.authorhouse.co.uk
Phone: 08001974150

First published by AuthorHouse 3/6/2011

ISBN: 978-1-45677-037-2 (sc)
ISBN: 978-1-45677-036-5 (hc)

This book is printed on acid-free paper.

I

SOUGHT

ADVENTURE,

BUT IT FOUND ME.

BY

REGINALD A KEELEY-OSGOOD, MC

Reginald A Keeley-Osgood

FOR RILY

WHO IS GOING THROUGH

A SERIES OF ADVENTURES

"DYING IS EASY; IT IS LIVING THAT IS HARD."

The Author in the 1960's

INTRODUCTION

This story is set in the late 50's and early 60's, and the middle 70's when the crime rate was low and work plentiful. It concerns two young men, who have been friends since childhood. The story is told through the eyes of one of the men.

After leaving school and getting employment in rather mundane jobs, they embark on a series of adventures, from joining the Merchant Navy to joining a Mercenary Force in the Belgian Congo, and after some excitement, enlisting in the British Army. They go through a series of conflicts until one leaves and re-joins a Mercenary Unit and the other after a period of time, joins the Security Service.

The part of the story that involves the Selection process of joining the Special Air Service Regiment is not told correctly, especially the interrogation procedure. If it was correct, those applying for Selection would know what to expect.

Bradbury Lines is now called Stirling Lines and the Main Gates are manned by armed Ministry of Defence Police, and quite rightly so.

Selection still takes place in the Brecon Beacons, but using a camp nearby, thus saving time and money. There is nothing worse than driving for three quarters of an hour and knowing that at the end of it, you have to start hoofing it. Further training is still carried out at another establishment near Pontrillas. The wastage rate is still high and so it should be.

Of a Selection of 140 all ranks, only approximately 10 will pass to go on to Continuation Training and even some of these will fail.

Once you have passed Selection, you will be handed that prized Beige Beret with the "Flaming Sword" badge, okay then, the Winged Dagger badge. Some will tell you, 'It is harder to keep than Selection.'

Words on an old sign which adorned the entrance to the old Training Wing comes to mind. "MANY ARE CALLED, BUT FEW ARE CHOSEN." I think that sums it up. The Regiment is now located at Credenhill a few miles outside Hereford town centre.

The book is not all about blood and thunder although there is a bit. There are some funny parts in this book as you will find out. If you want all gore etc. then there are other books written by well-known authors. Is this story true? Well, all I will say is read it and judge for yourself. To help you decide, I will give you a clue. I was one of those men.

CHAPTER ONE

'What are you thinking of doing when you leave school next week Dave?' asked John West, who was also leaving school at the same time.

'I don't really know at the moment John. I was toying with the idea of joining the Merchant Navy.'

'Hey! That's a great idea, we could join up together.'

The thought of us both joining had already crossed my mind. After all, we have been through our school days together, and, it would be a shame to break up a great friendship now.

'Wait and see mate, who knows what might happen, let us leave school first.'

The final day arrives and we both leave school. They say that your school days are the best days of your life. I do not believe that for one moment. The best days are yet to come.

I am lucky and find a job in a Wine Merchants as a trainee Assistant Manager, John finds a job as a milkman with a local Dairy. Both jobs are not up to much, but at least we are earning some money.

Over the next few weeks, I learn the finer points of wine management. It is pretty boring stuff, but, has to be learnt. My mind keeps wandering to other things. John's job with the Dairy is not going too well either. He is pretty pissed off with getting up at 4am in the morning to push a milk cart around the streets.

We meet up one evening and arrange to take the Wednesday off and go to Southampton to break the monotony.

'See you at 9am at the station in Fareham.' John said walking off home.

'I'll be there.' I reply.

Wednesday arrives and we meet up at the station in Fareham as arranged. We board the train for Southampton. The journey takes about an hour, as we had to change at Eastleigh. Once we arrive at Southampton station, we make our way to Dock Road and look for the offices of the Cunard Line. We find them nearly at the end of the road.

'Come on mate, let's go in and join the Merchant Navy?' John said opening the main door.

'Okay, let's do it.'

I follow him into the building and into a large office, which has a long counter. Sitting behind a desk is a withered old crone, who must be at least 200 years old.

'We want to join up love?' John said to the crone.

'Don't you call me LOVE,' she replied getting up from her desk. 'Fill this form in?' She said passing John a large form.

'We both want one Miss?'

'You both will get one in a minute, you cheeky pair of sods,' she replied placing another form in front of me.

We fill the forms in and hand them back to her.

'Your writing's not very good is it?' The crone said looking the forms over.

'What do you expect, we have only just left school, and they only teach you the basics,' said John smiling.

The crone smacks John round the head and walks off into another office, muttering under her breath that all kids of today were a bunch of illiterate twits.

'Funny woman.'

'I heard that,' said the crone.

'Bloody Hell mate, she's got a good pair of ears,' John whispers.

'Shoooosh, she will hear you,' I tell him.

After a few minutes, the crone reappears with some more forms.

'Fill these in and wait over there?' She said pointing to some wooden chairs by the wall.

'The doctor will see you in a few minutes.'

We fill the forms in. They are for our medical and ask questions about whether we have had any operations or infectious diseases.

I wonder what the medical will be like. Boy, are these chairs hard. After about 10 minutes, a rather old looking man in a white coat appears. I suppose this must be the doctor.

'What's your name?' He asked, pointing at John.

'John West.'

'Sounds like a tin of Tuna to me - and you must be Stubbs? - well, you had to be - follow me you two.'

We follow the doctor into a large room with doors leading off it. The room is bloody freezing.

'YOU!' the doctor said pointing to me. 'Sit down, and YOU,' pointing to John, 'Follow me.'

They leave me and disappear into one of the rooms. I pick up an ancient magazine to read whilst waiting for my turn with the doctor.

From the room that they have entered I hear, 'UP - DOWN -UP - DOWN - UP - DOWN, come on FASTER.'

Blimey! We are joining the Army, I say to myself just as John reappears carrying a large glass. Sweat is pouring from his brow.

'He told me to piss in this!' pointing to the glass.

'Will you have the energy, you look knackered.'

'It's your turn next mate,' John said opening one of the doors, which turns out to be a broom cupboard.

'Where's the bloody toilet?' John shouts.

'Try the next one.'

He opens the door and finds a room but it only has a chair and a window in it, no toilet.

'This will have to do,' he shouts from inside.

After a few minutes, John reappears carrying a large glass of urine.

'He will have to have a full glass as there isn't a toilet,' he said walking back into the doctor's office.

From the office I hear, 'What the bloody hell have you got there, when I said pee in the glass, I didn't mean you to fill it up, you dozy twit.'

Oh shit! I'm off. I say to myself, but before I can leave, John and the doctor come out of the office.

'You will do, park your arse down the corridor and wait for your mate.'

I get up and start to walk towards the office.

'Move yourself, I haven't got all day,' shouts the doctor.

I run into the office.

'Start running on the spot, I want to check your heart, come on, get moving, faster, UP - DOWN - UP - DOWN - UP - DOWN, let's get the blood flowing.'

After a few minutes he tells me to stop. The sweat is pouring from me. I'm knackered.

'Well, your heart is sound,' he says handing me a large glass. 'Pee in this? I want to see if you are a diabetic.'

I take the glass and go into the same room John used. He is right, there isn't a toilet. I fill the glass up and open the small window and throw three quarters of the urine out.

'Oi!' Someone shouts from below.

I don't wait to find out who has just received a bath of piss and return to the doctor.

After checking my sample, he tells me to drop my trousers.

'Cough?'

'I can't.'

'You will,' he replies grabbing hold of my testicles.

Yes, I did cough; well it was a sort of high pitched yelp really. Tears fill my eyes. Bloody hell! The doctor hands me a form with "FIT" stamped in red on it.

'Wait down the hall with your mate,' the doctor said opening the door for me.

I run off down the corridor and find John.

'Are you sure we have joined the Merchant Navy? That doctor's a poof, he grabbed my balls!'

'Quiet, walls have ears,' whispered John.

After sitting for what seemed like hours, a smartly dressed man comes out of an office and says, 'Come in?'

We enter a very plush and warm office. What no wooden chairs.

'Sit down you two,' the man said pointing to two arm chairs.

'I understand you want to join the Merchant Marine, my name is Timms, I am the Shipping Manager, and I hire and fire. I see from your applications, you wish to join the Merchant Marine as Officer Cadets. I also notice you have not put what branch of the service you wish to be trained in. Have you a preference?'

'Radio,' we both tell him.

'That is a very hard course, but I expect you will pass it. I will put you down for the Telecommunication Course which starts in about a month's time.'

He then tells us about the history of the Cunard Line, which is quite interesting.

'Have you any questions about anything I have said so far.'

'What pay will we get Sir?' I ask.

'Your pay will be £11.10.6d (£11.52p) a fortnight, all your food and accommodation whilst at sea will be free.'

'Does that include our stay at the College whilst we are under training Sir?' John asked.

'Of course it does.' Timms replied.

'Well, if you have no more questions, it only remains for me to say, welcome to Cunard.'

He gets up from his desk and holds out his hand. We shake his hand and start to leave his office.

'You should get joining instructions in a week's time, good luck.'

We both thank him and leave the office.

'Did you notice his hand shake, it was like a limp fish, perhaps he is a poof, just like that doctor.'

We leave the building after saying good bye to the Crone. If looks could kill, we would be stone dead. What a lovely lady she is.

The train to Fareham is delayed, so we have a sandwich in the buffet shop.

'I think we have done the right thing Dave.' John said with a mouth full of lettuce sandwich.

'I hope you are right mate.' I reply.

The train finally comes and we make our way back to Gosport.

'Are you going to tell your parents Dave?'

'You have got to be joking; they won't let me join the Merchant Navy.'

'I won't tell my mum then.' John said waving good bye.

'See you tomorrow after work?' I shout after him.

I have always wanted to join the Merchant Navy. My parents had friends in it and they always told me stories about the foreign places that they had visited. And not only that, the places they went to had plenty of sun.

The days go by and I wait for the letter that will tell me when to join the college as a trainee Wireless Officer. Nothing is going right at work. Old Yates is moaning about the shop not doing well, and John is moaning about his 4am starts. I wish the letter would hurry up and arrive.

As I am about to leave for work one morning, the letter finally arrives. I tear it open and read:

"YOU ARE TO REPORT TO THE PURSER ON BOARD THE CUNARD SHIP "SOUTHERN FOX" WHICH IS DOCKED AT JETTY No 2 SOUTHAMPTON DOCKS, BY 1200hrs ON MONDAY THE 23rd OF OCTOBER. PLEASE BRING WITH YOU YOUR MEDICAL CARDS AND P45 FROM YOUR LAST EMPLOYER. DETAILS OF YOUR TRAINING WILL BE NOTIFIED TO YOU BY THE CAPTAIN. WELCOME TO CUNARD."

Blimey! I'm going straight to sea, what has happened to the College. The doorbell rings and I find John standing there.

'I have taken the day off; you got your letter then?'

'Yes, but it doesn't give much away does it.'

'Perhaps we will be trained at sea instead,' said John.

I am not very happy about this surely we should at least get some sort of training before we go to sea.

I also don't go to work and we both go to the Dive Cafe at Gosport Ferry to discuss how we are going to leave without telling our parents.

At work next morning, Mr Yates asks where I had been yesterday. I tell him that I have found another job and that I would be leaving at the end of the week.

'I will be sorry to see you go Dave, but if that is what you want to do, I won't stand in your way. I will keep your job open just in case it doesn't work out.'

I will be glad to leave, this job is very boring and it doesn't tax your brain. I haven't told Yates that I am joining the Merchant Navy, the less people know, the better at this stage.

The end of the week finally arrives and I pick up my P45 and a week's pay. I say goodbye and make my way home. I have already packed my suitcase and hidden it in my wardrobe. I spend the weekend between John's house and mine. I can't wait to get going.

At last Monday is here and I wait for my mother to go over to her friend's house across the road. The coast is clear and I grab my suitcase and make my way to the bus stop in Brockhurst Road. John is waiting.

'You have just made it.' John said waving a bus down.

The bus arrives in Fareham just in time for us to get the train to Southampton.

The journey to Southampton is boring and instead of walking, we get a bus to Dock Gate 10, which is the nearest to Jetty No 2. On entering the gate, we are stopped by 2 Policemen.

'Where do you think you two are going?' One asked.

'Papers?' demanded the other Policeman.

We show him the letters we had received, which he reads and passes back to us laughing. He gives us the directions to the Jetty where the ship is moored and returns to his cubby hole still laughing.

'I wonder what's tickled him.' John said.

'No idea mate,' I reply, 'must be the air or something.'

'Air - My arse.' John replies.

We follow the Policeman's directions, and finally arrive at Jetty No 2. Moored there, is the biggest bloody ship we have ever seen.

'Bloody Heck, It's huge.' John exclaimed.

All I can see is a huge expanse of white ship with the words "Southern Fox" painted on the bows.

'This is ours.' I say out loud.

Walking up the gang way we and are greeted by a very smartly dressed man in dark blue uniform.

'Can I help you?' He asked.

'We are the new recruits we have to report to the Purser by 1200hrs.' I tell him.

'Wait here please.' He replied, and walked off into the innards of the ship.

A few minutes go by when he returns with two rough looking men.

'Go with these two, they will show you where your cabin is and where to stow your gear.'

We follow the two rough necks down into the ship. Our cabin is well below the water line. I don't like this at all, if the ship sinks, it will be a heck of a job getting to the surface. What grim thoughts. We enter a very tiny cabin with 4 bunks in it.

'These are yours.' Fat man said, pointing to two top bunks.

'And these are ours.' Said ugly pointing to two bottom ones.

I don't like these two there is something about them that I just can't put my finger on. I could see from John's face that he was thinking the same. They show us a small locker that we can put our clothing in. Small really isn't the word to use, Atom size would be more appropriate. They leave us to unpack.

Having packed our clothes away we look round the ship. It looks as if it is about to sail, as people are starting to leave down the gang way. As we are returning to our cabin a weasel faced man tells us that the Captain wants to see us.

We follow like obedient lap dogs and arrive at a door with the words "CAPTAINS OFFICE" written on it.

Weasel face knocked the door and walked off.

'WAIT!' Shout's someone inside.

After a few minutes a blonde girl opens the door doing up the buttons of her blouse.

'He's all yours now,' she said walking off along the corridor.

'ENTER!' The Captain shouts.

Entering the office we see someone who can only be described as Captain Birdseye. He can see we are scared.

'Now that's how I like you, SCARED.' He said laughing.

'We aren't scared of you; we have just left school, after that nothing, scares US.' Said John flippantly.

'Don't get smart with me sonny, I can make your life sweet or misery. I have the upper hand and don't you forget it.'

John apologises and I'm glad he has, this guy could really screw us up.

The Captain outlines the training we are expected to carry out. He is sorry that we have not attended the College first, but as the ship was sailing on its maiden voyage it had to have a full crew. It would be good training for us first hand. We are to obey every order from senior personnel. When the Captain said "Senior Personnel," that meant everyone above us. We will be at everyone's beck and call. I don't like this one little bit.

This prat seems to be enjoying himself, the bastard.

'Have you any questions?' He asked.

We are too numb to ask anything and reply, 'NO.'

'Right, get back to your cabin, we are sailing in a few minutes, I will call you when I want you.'

We leave the office and wander back to our cabin.

'The prat didn't even welcome us on board.' I say to John as I open the cabin door.

I don't like the hours we will be working, no one said we had to work a 19 hour day. I've heard the saying, "You make your bed and you lie in it," but this was ridiculous. Have you ever had that feeling that you shouldn't have done something, well, I have that feeling now?

From the short look round the ship we have had, it looks absolutely massive. All I hope is that we have made the right choice in joining.

After about half an hour the ship sets sail.

'It's moving,' exclaims John.

'Damned right, what is the first port of call, any idea?'

John starts to turn a bright shade of green and rushes to a porthole. He flings it open and spews up his insides. Boy! Am I glad he got his head through it?

The night is non-eventful. John is still throwing up. Sleep is virtually impossible as John is running back and forth to the porthole.

'You are obviously not a sailor.'

'Fuck off, you bastard, can't you see I'm ill.'

Morning comes and John looks absolutely ill. He is a lovely shade of green. The two bottom bunkers come into the cabin and peer over John.

'What do you want? Sod off,' John replies.

'We will leave you to it, mind you; we have some lovely things in store for you later.' Said the ugly one.

'Bollocks.' John shouts at them as they leave.

We have been at sea now for a day and a half and we haven't yet been sent for by the Captain. I spend my time walking around the ship as John is still in his pit feeling sorry for himself.

Returning to our cabin, I find John is getting up.

'How do you feel now mate?' I ask him.

'A lot better thanks, those two bastards are up to something? We haven't seen them sleep in here yet, have we? I wonder what they get up to.'

Thinking about this disturbs me.

'You know, I reckon we have got a couple of poufs bunking with us.'

'You could be right mate, they certainly do seem odd, and did you see the way the ugly bastard was hovering over me?'

Were they poofs or was our imagination running wild, I wonder. If they were poofs, then we had better sort it out very quickly or we will be in deep shit, to coin a phrase. John suggests that we take turns in staying awake, just in case. I think this is a bit drastic, but agree with him.

Over the next few days we are given tasks to perform by the Purser and the Captains Mate. Funny sort of training this is. I have just taken a message to the Radio Officer when I meet up with John.

'What's up mate, you look agitated?'

'I have just overheard some guys talking; they are going to get us tonight.'

'No chance, we will lock the cabin door.' I tell him.

'We can't do that! Those bastards live in the cabin with us.'

'Tough! They will have to find somewhere else to sleep till we can think up something else, so sod them.'

That night the ship sails into Las Palmas and docks at No 5 Jetty.

'I'm off this ship tonight Dave, are you coming with me?'

'Too right I am mate.' I reply.

I make my way back to the cabin whilst John picks up our empty cases from the baggage store. We then lock ourselves in the cabin. Having packed our suitcases, we wait for the passengers to go to dinner.

Now that no one is about, we leave the cabin and make our way down the gang way to the Dock area.

'Now what.' I ask him.

'Who cares, let's get going, I want to be as far away from this ship as I can. No one, and I mean no one, is going up my arse.'

We walk out of the Dock and see a sign that tells us we are about a mile away from the centre of the town. I rephrase that, it is not a town but more like a shopping precinct. Finding a small Cafe, I order 2 cups of coffee in extremely broken Spanish and then we discuss what we are going to do. We are miles from home in a foreign land and we have very little money. The Cafe owner hears us and comes over, thank goodness he speaks very good English and I ask him if he knows of any place that we can get a room for the night.

'You can rent a room here, I have some rooms at the back of the Cafe,' he tells us.

We follow him through the Cafe to the rear and he shows us a double room with two beds in it. We thank him and get undressed and get our heads down. It has been a bloody long day.

Next morning, we enter the Cafe and have breakfast. The radio is blaring out some sort of message in Spanish.

'What's it saying?' I ask the Cafe owner.

He replies that two men have jumped ship and the Police are treating them as illegal immigrants. He looks at us with his head to one side. He is obviously convinced that we are the two men, but don't say anything.

'Poor sods, how much do we owe you for the room and breakfast?'

Thank goodness we had the sense to change some money to Pesetas with the Ships Exchange before we left. We pay him what he asks and then leave.

'I'm sure that guy thinks we are the two men Dave.'

'He'd be right then, wouldn't he, come on let's get out of here.'

The events over the next few days are nothing to write home about. We hitch lifts with various vehicles and carts and finally arrive at Calais, unwashed, tired, starving and really pissed off, and, just enough money to pay for the tickets to Dover.

'You know what mate? The Merchant Navy is not for me.'

'I second that, in fact, NO NAVY, is for me.' I reply. We finally arrive back in Gosport after being away for nearly 4 weeks.

'Oh well, it is face the music time.'

John is not looking forward to facing his mother. I ring the doorbell of my front door and my mother answers it.

'Where in the name of hell have you two been? We have been worried sick. Your father rang the Police and everyone has been out looking for you both, get in here!'

'We haven't done anything wrong mum, we joined the Merchant Navy, but found that we didn't like it, so we left.'

'Wait till your father comes home, you will cop it, I can assure you. I think you should get home to your mum John, she is worried sick.'

John isn't looking forward to this.

'Come with me Dave, you know what she is like. I need moral support, please.'

'Shit! Do I have to?' I reply knowing full well what she is like. She is a right cow, and that is being polite.

I tell my mother that I am going with John and will be back later. She is about to speak but walks off into the kitchen. I go with John to his house.

As we enter the garden, his mother opens the front door.

'Where in the bloody hell have you been? I've been worried sick, you have no thoughts for your mother John,' she shouts at him.

'I've been sick too mum.' John replied.

At this, I start to laugh, because I knew what John meant.

'This is no laughing matter Dave Stubbs.' Tina West shouts at me, and storms back into the house.

'Do you think she is mad at us Dave?'

'Just a little bit mate,' I reply.

We follow his mother into the house. She is throwing things around the kitchen.

'It's your entire fault Dave Stubbs, you lead my John astray.' She shouts at me.

ME lead HIM astray, he was the one who said, "Lets join up." There is no point trying to talk to her in this mood, she wouldn't listen if I tried. I tell John that I will see him later and make my way home. Bloody heck! I don't need this agro. I arrive back home and guess who is waiting to see me. YES..........my DAD!!!!!

My father never hit any of his children, he believed that shouting did the trick much better than belting, though; my mother wasn't adverse to giving us a belt round the ears when the mood took her.

I try to explain the reasons why I joined the Merchant Navy without telling them. My father didn't seem to understand that I had now left school and should be able to stand on my own two feet, and look after myself.

Over the next few weeks, things start to get back to normal, well, as normal as things could be. I still see John and we still get into scrapes with his mother, though, it is all minor stuff.

Our short brush with homosexuality, though we were unwilling to participate, showed us that we will have to be on our guard at all times. It is strange, but I later find out that "Homos," were rife in the Merchant Navy, especially amongst the Deck Hands and Stewards. I don't think I would ever had stayed in the Merchant Navy, the hours were terrible and the time off was non-existent. The Captain was a right bastard and could only think of getting his end away with the woman purser. I just don't know how people could stay in it for so long; I suppose the perks were good, though I never saw any in the 4 weeks we were in the Merchant Navy.

I suppose we will have to tell them we have quit, though I'm not relishing doing it. We will have to go to Southampton and get it over with. I wonder if they will do anything to us for jumping ship.

I hope John don't get any more stupid ideas; I don't think I could bear another of his hair brained schemes. And I definitely won't be joining the regular navy; they go to sea as well. I don't need any more experiences like that, bad for the nerves.

It's Monday morning and I go to the wine Shop to see Mr Yates. He is glad to see me.

'I heard that you had joined the Merchant Navy Dave? I didn't think you would stay. Too many funny people in it, do you want your old job back, if so, let's get to work.'

I thank him and confirm everything he has said about the Merchant Navy. This job may be boring, but at least I am earning some money, and that's the main thing at the moment. Our little adventure had cleaned me out, so the coffers have to be replenished.

As I am cleaning the front of the shop, a girl walks by. I have seen her on occasions walking to the Coop across the road with her mother.

'Hello,' I say to her. 'What's your name then?'

She looks at me as if I have 6 heads.

'Kathy actually.' she replied.

'My names Dave, I have seen you quite often up here, fancy going to the pictures tonight Kathy actually?'

'You are a fast worker, we have only just met and the name is just Kathy.'

'Well, just Kathy, you are a long time dead, and time waits for no man.'

'My Name is K-A-T-H-Y, KATHY.'

'Well, Kathy, are you coming with me to the pictures?'

'Be round my house at 6.30pm and we shall see.'

She gives me her address and walks off to the Coop. Boy! A date, John will be upset.

I complete all the days' tasks and Mr Yates tells me to go off home. Roll on 6.30. I tell my mother that I will be going out to the pictures with a girl I have just met, so that she won't worry about me if I come home late.

Dead on 6.30, I enter Kathy's garden and knock the door. Her mother opens it.

'You must be Dave? Kathy, that boy is here.'

Blimey! What a frosty reception, what have I done to deserve this, I wonder. Still, no matter, I'm not going out with her mother.

Kathy comes down the stairs, she looks great and I tell her so.

'Don't be late in Kathy, you have school in the morning,' said her mother.

'We won't be mum; we are only going to the pictures.' Kathy replied.

We catch the bus to the Criterion Picture House in Forton Road and buy seats at the rear of the cinema. The film is pretty boring and not much action.

'Shall we go to the Cafe at the Ferry?' I ask her.

'Crumbs, this film is terrible, okay, let's get out of here.' She replies.

We leave the cinema and walk the mile or so to the Town.

I find out that she will be leaving school soon and taking up a job in the office of the Coop opposite the Wine Shop.

'That will be nice; I could see you every day.' I say to her.

'I won't be able to see you every night during the week Dave, my mother is a stickler for me staying in on school days, I'm sorry.'

'Don't worry about it, as long as I can see you at weekends, it won't matter so much, we are seeing each other again, aren't we?'

'Yes, I think I would like to see you again.' she replied.

I tell her about the adventure me and John had in the Merchant Navy and the reason why we left. She finds it quite funny and starts laughing. I can see the funny side of it now and laugh with her. She is great to be with and I like her a lot. I'm sure she likes me too. I look at my watch and see it is coming up to 10pm.

'Come on, I had better get you home, I don't want to get in your mums bad books.'

We catch the bus home and I walk her to her gate. The front door opens and her mother shouts, 'Come on in Kathy, you know you have got school in the morning.'

I say goodnight and she runs into the house. God! What a dragon for a mother. Shit! I forgot to ask her for another date, I hope I see her during the week so that I can ask her. Mind you, the way her mother acted, I very much doubt if I will see her again. Who needs a mother like hers? Ug!

The next day I see Kathy walking to the Coop and ask her if she would like to go to a dance on Friday at Bury Hall.

'That would be lovely, what time are you going to pick me up?'

'About 7pm providing I'm not struck by lightning or your mum shoots me in the meantime.'

'Silly sod, see you Friday.'

I suppose now you could say she is my girlfriend, she was certainly keen for another date.

John comes round in the evening and tells me he is back at the Dairy. I tell him about Kathy.

'Hey! That's great, I'm going out with a girl called Sonia, let's make a foursome and go to the dance at Bury Hall.'

'You kept her quiet, you randy sod, where did you meet this Sonia?'

'In a Cafe in Fareham the other day, she's great, you will like her.'

Friday comes and I pick Kathy up from her house.

'And where are you two going this time?' asked her mother.

'I'm taking her to a dance at Bury Hall with some friends, we won't be late back.'

'See that you aren't.' replied her mother.

Stone the crows this women is the pits.

Kathy comes down the stairs, 'Mum it is Friday, I haven't any school tomorrow, and surely I can be a little bit late tonight?'

Her mother has to have the last say. 'Just don't make it too late; I think 1030 is late enough.'

We walk out the gate and I ask her, 'Is your mum always like that or is it me?'

'She is alright really, she gets very protective at times, but she means well.'

I wonder what her father is like, I haven't met him yet, I hope he has a better outlook on things.

We arrive at Bury Hall and meet up with John. He introduces us to Sonia. She is rather tall and thin, just like John. We all have a great time, as there is a live Band performing. The evening is a great success.

I walk Kathy home as she didn't want to get the bus. We talk about things in general and I suddenly say to her, 'I really like you a lot Kathy.'

'What made you say that?' She asked.

'I don't know it is probably the way I feel about you I suppose.'

'Well, you can stop worrying, because I like you a lot as well.'

I make a date for the following evening, and we walk along with our arms round each other.

We reach her gate and guess what, Yes; her mother is waiting on the doorstep.

'Say goodnight and come straight in Kathy,' her mother shouted for all to hear.

The woman's a Bitch! I kiss Kathy on the cheek.

'That was nice.'

'I thought it was the right thing to do.'

Her mother comes back out. 'Come on in Kathy.'

Kathy kisses her hand and puts it on my lips, smiles, and then walks off into the house.

I walk off home in a very happy mood. I open our front door whistling.

'Christ, He's in a good mood, must have got his end away.' Said my brother going up the stairs.

'Piss Off.' I tell him.

The months go by and boredom sets in. I feel totally cheesed off with life.

One Saturday morning I am having a lie in. The doorbell rings and my mother answer's it.

'Is he up yet?'

'John is here.' My mother shouts.

'Tell him to bugger off mum I'm having a lie in.'

'Come on get up we have things to do.'

I get up and go to the bathroom.

'What's all the rush about?' I shout from the bathroom.

'I will tell you later, any tea going Mrs Stubbs?'

I'm sure this is another one of his hair brained schemes.

We get the bus to the Ferry and take the boat to Portsmouth. Whilst on the Ferry, John shows me a torn piece of paper.

'Read that!' He said pointing to an advert.

I start to read, "Is your sex life...!"

'Not that, THIS,' pointing to a very peculiar advert. I look at the advert he is pointing to, and read:

"DO YOU NEED ADVENTURE? WE ARE LOOKING FOR FIT YOUNG MEN WHO ARE SEEKING ADVENTURE WITH THE POSSIBILITY OF EARNING LARGE SUMS OF MONEY. IF YOU THINK YOU FIT THIS BILL, THEN RING THE FOLLOWING NUMBER 041-346-456732 AND ASK FOR EXTN 25. YOU WILL NOT BE DISAPPOINTED, FINANCIAL GAIN IS DEFINITELY GUARANTEED, SO RING NOW. WE ARE WAITING FOR YOUR CALL, IF YOU USE A CALL BOX, WE WILL RING YOU BACK. RING NOW!!!!"

'This sounds very interesting, don't it?' I tell him.

'Let's ring the number and find out what it is all about.' John suggests.

We arrive at Portsmouth and make our way up the ramp. I go to the call box by the rail station and ring the operator and ask her where the 041 code is.

'Scotland.' she replied.

'Mate, that number is in Scotland, it will cost us a fortune to ring it.'

'I'm sure this is just what we want Dave, let me ring the number, the advert said they would ring us back.'

I must admit, my job is getting me down and I know John hates getting up at 4am to push a milk cart around.

'Ring it.' I tell him.

John dialled the number and a man answered.

'Are you in a call box?'

'Yes.' John replied.

'I'll ring you back, give me the number?'

John gives him the number and we wait by the telephone box. We wait and wait and still no call. I stop a little old lady from using the telephone by saying my mother is ringing straight back.

She isn't very pleased and walks off muttering something unintelligible.

'Ring you bastard.' John shouts.

John has a habit of calling everything a bastard when he is agitated.

At last, the phone rings. John leaps up from the pavement where he had been sitting and grabs the phone.

'Yes, this is John West speaking, (It does sound like a tin of Tuna, doesn't it) Yes, my mate Dave Stubbs, wants the details as well.'

'What's he saying John?' I ask.

'Hang on Dave. My address is 24, Denby Road and my mates, 61, Cherry Road, both in Gosport, Hampshire, okay, I look forward to hearing from you, bye for now.'

John puts the phone down and looks at me.

'He is going to send us a letter in a few days' time with tickets to go to London for an interview.'

'Did he say what the job was?'

'No, he just said he would send us details.'

'John, it sounds really weird.'

'We will have to wait and see then, won't we.' said John walking towards the Harbour Cafe.

'You can buy the teas?'

'I buy the teas, I ALWAYS buy the teas.' I shout after him.

In the evening, I go out with Kathy. We have a great time. I do believe that I am in love with her. She is great fun to be with. We are walking along the road and she turns her head towards me. I take the opportunity and kiss her full on the lips.

'You should have kissed me ages ago.'

'I didn't want you to think I was being too forward.'

'You wouldn't have been.'

'Kathy, I think I love you?'

'Now isn't that a coincidence because, my darling Dave, I love you too.'

Monday morning, and no letter, is it a hoax I wonder. Wednesday morning and a letter arrives it has a Scottish stamp on it. Ha, Ha! The letter I have been waiting for has arrived.

I open it and find a new £5 note and a letter telling me to attend an interview at the Dorchester Hotel, London on the 28th November at 1230pm. I would be met at Waterloo station; there was no mention of what the job was or the pay. Most strange, I wonder what the job is.

DING, DONG! The doorbell rings. John is standing at the door.

'Shouldn't you be at work?'

'Stuff work, did you get your letter?'

'Yes, it doesn't tell us much does it.'

'Well, it isn't going to cost us anything to find out is it; they have sent us the fare to London.'

'I suppose so mate, and I am rather pissed off with the job at the shop.'

'Do you think I like walking the streets at 4am each morning pulling a milk cart?' John replied.

'Are you going to tell your parents about this Dave?'

'You have got to be kidding; I'll wait and see what the job is about before I do that.'

'Okay mate, I won't say anything to my mum either.'

I wonder what the job is; it must be good, for them to send us the fare money. All I hope is that it is nothing illegal. Oh well, we'll soon find out.

Over the next few days, I keep thinking about what the job will be, I make stupid mistakes at work and get old Yates annoyed.

'Come on Dave; keep your mind on the job.'

I only wish I could, but I can't. I don't sleep at night because of thinking about it. What can it be? I don't tell Kathy about it either. I don't want her alarmed; it is bad enough me worrying about it let alone her.

The day of the interview is slowly approaching and sleep at night is near impossible. I just cannot believe that worrying over an interview could do this to me. I get up and go down stairs and make a cup of tea. I'm sitting in the dining room when my mother comes in.

'You look as if you have been up all night son, what's the matter?'

I now tell her why. 'I have applied for a job mum and I am a bit worried about the interview, I have to go up to London on Friday.'

'Don't lose any sleep over that son; after all, it is only a job.'

It's easy for her to say, she doesn't know all the details, come to think of it, nor do I.

At last Friday arrives and John, like the proverbial bad penny, arrives on the door step very early.

'Stone the Crows mate! Its only 7am, can't you sleep?'

'I haven't slept for a couple of days.' John replied.

I know how he feels. I get dressed and even put a tie on. As I am coming down the stairs, my mother is going up.

'Who's the girl then?' She asked.

'It isn't a girl mum; I'm off to that interview today.'

'Good luck Son.' she said disappearing into a bedroom.

We catch the 9.20am train from Portsmouth harbour station and arrive in London an hour and twenty minutes later.

As we get off the train, I notice a man holding a card with our names on it.

'That's us sport.' I tell him.

'Great, follow me, I have a car to take you to the Hotel.' He said throwing the card into a bin.

We follow him out of the station and get into a green Rover, which then speeds out of the station car park.

'Blimey! What's the hurry?' John asks him.

After about 40 minutes, we arrive at the Dorchester Hotel.

'Follow me.' The driver tells us.

We enter the hotel and make straight for the lift. The lift door closes, the driver pushes a button and a few seconds later the lift door reopens. We walk out of the lift but the driver stays put.

'The room you want is down the passage to the right, number 236.' He says as the lift door closes.

'We are on our own now mate.' John said.

We walk along the passage until we find door number 236.

'This is it, in for a penny, in for a pound.'

I knock the door, my hand is sweating and I wipe it on my trousers. The door is opened by a smartly dressed man.

'Ah! You must be Mr Stubbs and Mr West do come in?'

In the room sitting behind a desk are two more smartly dressed men. They look rather military to me, my grandfather was a Brigadier and he dressed like them.

'Please sit down gentlemen?' The man that showed us in walks behind the desk and sits down. We seem low in the chairs; they seem to tower over us.

'I want to apologise for the cloak and dagger secrecy, but our organisation is rather secret in this country and the less people know about us the better. Please smoke if you wish, though I think it is a dirty habit. But then, that is my opinion.'

'We don't smoke.'

'Good for you,' he replies, 'now, before we start, let me introduce ourselves. I am Colonel Hoare, this gentleman on my left is Major Thomas and the gentleman on my right is Captain Richards. Please tell me your ages?'

'18.' we both replied.

'Good, have you any idea what this interview is about?'

We both replied, 'No.'

'Okay, we are all members of an elite Mercenary Unit in the Belgian Congo. We are here to recruit people for that unit. So you can appreciate the secrecy. Are you interested in adventure and lots of money?'

John not being adverse to flippancy replied, 'Too right we are pal.'

I look at John and mouth at him "Prat." Colonel Hoare smiled.

The Colonel then went on to explain the reasons behind the Mercenary Force being in the Congo. (I must find out where that is)

'The President of Katanga, Moise Tshombe, is having problems with neighbouring Province Leaders since he broke away from the main country, and because his Province is the richest, needs help in controlling the Province. Katanga is now independent. You will be serving with Katanga Army personnel at times. Our main job is to protect the white population which is mainly Belgian, and to keep the rebels in check. To do this, we can use any force that is considered necessary to complete the job. Your training will last 4 weeks and you will have to successfully complete it before you can actually serve in the Congo. Any questions so far?'

We ask a lot of questions and get really good answers to them.

'Okay, let us break for a cup of coffee before we carry on.' said the Colonel.

'Sounds okay so far Dave,' whispers John picking up a coffee cup.

We drink our coffee and return to our chairs.

'How do you feel about us so far?' asked Major Thomas.

'Fine.' We tell him.

'Good, you are interested then?'

'What pay will we get and how long will the contract be for?' I ask.

'I was wondering when you would get round to money.' Said Colonel Hoare smiling.

'Your pay will be £140 a month, paid into any bank account in any country you wish, and whilst you are under training, you will be paid £35 a week. It is doubtful that you will spend any of this money as everything is free to my troops. At the end of your contract, which is for a year in the first instance, with an option to extend, you will be paid a Bounty of £1500, an insurance agreement will be taken out for you to the value of £30,000, which will be paid to your next of kin should you be killed in action. If you sign up today, you will be paid from today and put on immediate leave until you join us in Africa. How does that grab you both?'

My mind is in a whirl, £35 a week, that's more than my dad, earns, and he has got a damned good job earning £21 a week. I look at John who must be thinking the same as me.

'Let's have another cup of coffee, and you can talk it over.' Said Colonel Hoare.

Over coffee, I whisper to John, 'It don't sound too bad does it and the money is out of this world, what do you think mate?'

'We are rich, let's go for it.'

This is just up my street, adventure and plenty of money and of course, sunshine. England is not the best place to get a good tan, and £35 a week is better than £2.13.4d a week (£2.82p) Mr Yates, you can stick your job where the monkey stuck his nuts.

We sit back down and it seems as if we are now all at the same level, funny that.

'Well! What have you decided?' Colonel Hoare asked.

'We accept your offer.' I tell him.

'I don't think you will regret it boys, you have really impressed us with the questions you have both asked, fill these forms in?' He hands us both a form.

We fill in the forms and both come to the same question. "Date of Birth."

'Make a date that just puts you over 18.' John mouths.

I fill in a date that makes me 18 and 3 days and then complete the rest of the form and hand it back to the Colonel.

He reads through the form, 'You don't look 18?'

I quickly tell him that all my family look younger than their age, even my mother.

'Sign this?' Major Thomas said handing us a slip of paper. On it in words and figures is the sum £140.

'That is a month's pay and expenses.'

My hand starts to shake and I scribble a signature of sorts on the line indicated. Major Thomas then counts out £140 in £5 notes for each of us.

'Sorry it is all fivers, but that is all the Embassy could get at short notice.'

I look across at John who is staring at the 2 piles of £5 notes, "I'm RICH," I want to scream out loud.

'You can now consider yourselves members of the 25th Airborne Regiment of 4 Commando. You are both on official leave until you join us in Africa. You should get your joining instructions in about 5 weeks, in the meantime, welcome to the Regiment.' Said the Colonel getting up from his chair and holding his hand out.

We shake hands with him and the other two guys.

'The driver will take you back to Waterloo, good luck; see you in about 5 weeks.' Captain Richards said opening the door for us.

Outside the room is the driver.

'Right lads, back to Waterloo, let's go.'

We are both very quiet on the journey to the station. The driver drops us off and as he speeds away, he shouts, 'See you in the Congo.' (I later find out that he is the Colonels Bodyguard)

We board the train to Portsmouth harbour station. We are 17 years old and have just joined a Mercenary Unit.

The journey back is in silence. As we arrive at Portsmouth, John shouts, 'We are bloody nuts, what in the name of hell have we done, and what am I going to tell my mum, she will kill me.'

'Nuts we may be John - but rich, we certainly are - and anyway - it might be fun fighting for some black twat who can't look after his country.'

We walk out of the station and make our way to the ferry for Gosport and the bus home.

'We are MAD, MAD, and MAD!' We say together laughing.

CHAPTER TWO

Neither of us has ever had so much money. As we approach my house I say to John, 'How are we going to play this, and explain all the money.'

'Play it my way Dave, by ear.'

I open the door and notice that my dad is home from work. That is funny; he is usually not home until gone 7pm on a Friday.

'Hi dad, what are you doing home?'

'There wasn't anything doing, so I thought I would finish early.'

We watch him carry out the same thing he has been doing for years, putting certain amounts of money in his wooden box to pay the bills. He works ruddy hard for his £21.16.8d (£21.84p) a week. Seeing him do this makes me flip. I pull from my pocket the money I have been given and throw it onto the table in front of him. It goes everywhere.

'What in God's name have you done this time?' He screams at me.

'Nothing dad, that's a month's pay and expenses, we have just come back from that interview in London. We've signed a contract for a year, and we are now on holiday with full pay until they send for us in about 5 weeks' time, great isn't it.'

My dad looks at John,

'You got the same?'

'Yep, sure have,' John replied.

He looks at all the money and shakes his head.

'Well, what job are you doing then, to get that sort of money?'

'It's a security job with an African Company,' I tell him with my fingers crossed behind my back. 'They have come over here to recruit people because they can't trust the Africans to do the job.'

'What's the name of this Company then?'

'Star and Company,' I tell him.

'They must be a Mining Company to pay that sort of wage; you don't have to go down the mines, do you?'

'No dad, that's not our job.'

My father is looking at the pile of notes.

'I could do with a job like that,' he said picking up some of the notes. 'Have you got to do any training for this job?'

'Yes, we have to carry out 4 weeks training before we are allowed to do the job. They have put us on holiday with full pay. The training is pretty awful, but they said we could get to enjoy it.'

'And they have put you on holiday with full pay?'

'They sure have, it's great isn't it,' said John smiling at me.

"Pillock." I mouth at him.

'I don't know what your mother is going to say about this Dave?' remarked my dad getting up from his chair.

'Mother going to say about what?' Said my mother coming into the dining room.

'Your son and his mate have just been paid £140 each for a month's holiday,' he tells her picking up a handful of the fivers.

My mother looks at me and then at John.

'That true?'

'Sure is Mrs Stubbs, we have just signed a contract for a year in South Africa at £140 a month.'

My mother's eyes are wide open.

'When do you have to go?'

'We should hear in about 4 weeks' time, they will send us the air tickets and all the other details, but until then, we can enjoy a great holiday at the expense of the African Government.' I tell her.

I can see she is not happy with this and she makes her feelings known.

'I don't know why you have to take a job abroad; you have a good job now, why do you want to change it.'

How in the name of hell can I tell her that her son has become a Mercenary at the age of 17 and will be fighting in the Congo, (I definitely must find out where that is) for some Black guy who probably has too much money and no brains. She will never understand. My parents have agreed to let me go. Though, having signed a contract, it would probably be hard for them not to. I don't somehow think that they believed us about the job. How do I know! My mother has taken my dad into the front room and is talking to him.

'Find out more about it Frank?' I heard my mother say to him.

'Come on John; let's get out of here quick.'

As we make for the door, my dad comes out of the front room.

'Where are you two going?' He asked.

'We have got to see John's mother and tell her the news, see you later, Oh! By the way, help yourselves to some of that money if you want to, bye for now.'

We run off down the road and make for John's house.

'Bloody hell that was close.' I say to him.

'Now we have got to face the Gorgon.' John said bitterly, 'I know exactly what she will say. Have you stolen it, I will call the Police.'

We arrive at John's house and find his mother putting the kettle on the gas.

'I saw you both coming, so thought you might like a cupper.' Said Tina West putting a light to the gas, 'Well how did you get on?'

'Not bad mum, we signed a contract for a year and they have paid us a month's pay in advance and have put us on holiday until we get our air tickets, which should be in about 4 weeks' time.'

'So you have already signed a contract, what type of job is it then?'

'It's a Security job.'

He has his fingers crossed behind his back. Now where have I seen that done before?

'How much did they pay you for this month's holiday?'

John pulls out the £140 and throws it onto the kitchen table.

Tina West looks at him and screams, 'You have stolen it, I'll tell the Police.'

'I told you she would say that, didn't I,' John shouts at me.

'Mother, I didn't steal it, it is a month's pay and expenses, what's the matter, and don't you trust me?'

'I'm sorry son; it's just that I have never seen so much money, your dad would have been proud of you for getting such a highly paid job.'

'Oh no, he wouldn't.' I say to myself. He would have bloody well killed him for sure if he knew what he was up to.

'Hold on a minute! Did you say - air tickets?'

'Err, yes mum, the jobs in Africa.'

Tears well up in her eyes, the old girl is human after all.

John tells her that we will only be gone for a year and stuffs some of the money into her hand.

'Go to Bingo with Dave's mum, she would love to go with you.'

Tina West kisses John on the cheek.

'Come off it mum, stop being silly.'

We leave her to get ready to go to Bingo.

'Want to go to the dance at Bury Hall tonight Dave?'

'Why not, I'll go and call for Kathy and you get Sonia, how's that grab you?'

I go back to my house and receive a very frosty reception. I'm sure they don't believe us.

'John's mother is coming round in a few minutes mum she wants you to go to Bingo with her.'

'Oh, thanks son, I could do with getting out for a change.'

I make myself some tea and then I go to see Kathy.

Her mother is still in a funny mood with me. I can't think what I have done wrong. Perhaps she is going round the bend. I don't even get shown into the lounge; I have to wait for Kathy in the passage. Her mother is a funny bloody woman.

Kathy comes down the stairs.

'Hello darling, where are we going?'

'To the dance,' I tell her.

She kisses me on the lips, her mother coughs.

'Don't be late in will you?'

We meet up with John and Sonia. There is a live Band called the "Clyde Valley Stompers," performing tonight. They should be good.

Once inside, we find some seats and sit down. Across from us are some old school pals. They come over to us.

'How you two doing? We haven't seen you for ages, what have you been up to?' Terry asked.

'Not much, we had a stint in the Merchant Navy, but now we have pissed poor jobs,' said John.

'I know how you feel, my jobs crap,' Said Mike.

'I haven't got one yet,' said Pete.

'What are you doing Terry?' I ask him.

'I'm working for a builder, labouring, the pays rubbish, but the job isn't too bad.'

'Right, who is buying the drinks this time?' Kathy asks.

'I'll get them,' Replied John.

'Ruddy Heck! Check if there is a blue moon out there, JOHN WEST IS BUYING,' I shout for all to hear.

'I've turned over a new leaf,' John said getting up from his chair.

'I'll give you a hand,' Said Kathy, walking with him towards the canteen.

'I think she fancies him?' Pete said,

'Don't be a prat, she goes out with me, and, I can assure you, she does not fancy John.'

'Sorry Dave, I didn't know you and Kathy were an item.'

I tell them that I have been going out with her for some weeks and that her mother was a right dragon.

'Well, you know what St George did to dragons.' Terry said, laughing.

'I must put some more pins in that doll.' I say to myself just as John and Kathy return with the drinks.

'You had better get a shovel mate, the snow has piled up at the door, and we won't be able to get home.' I say to John laughing.

He comes over to me and whispers "BOLLOCKS" in my ear.

'What did he say,' Asked Kathy.

'I told him that I knew what kept his ears apart.' John replied.

We both laugh. Kathy doesn't see the funny side of the joke. She will learn.

'Sonia and John make a nice couple, don't they? Both tall and thin.' Kathy said, holding my hand.

I look at my watch, the time is 1015pm.

'Come on Kathy, we have to go, otherwise her in doors will start moaning.'

'Do we have to?'

'I'm afraid we do, let's go.'

We say goodbye to everyone on our table and leave. At her gate I kiss her goodnight. And yes, you have guessed right, mummy opens the door.

'Kathy it is late, come in now.'

Kathy kisses me and walks off into the house. Why can't the dragon lady leave us alone?

Over the weekend, I see Kathy for a few hours. Her mother is always about. What is wrong with her? I am more in love with Kathy than ever. I want to be with her every minute of the day. She is going to be really hurt when I tell her that I am going away. Damn! Damn! Damn! Why did I have to fall in love?

Working in the Wine Shop is becoming a pain. I make so many mistakes with the pricing of bottles, Mr Yates sends me home.

'Come back when you can keep your mind on the job.'

I take a few days off from the shop and mope around the house. My mother tells me to buck my ideas up and to stop getting under her feet. I really am, bored.

Friday comes, and what date is it, yes! Friday the 13th. The post arrives and a letter drops on the mat. My mother picks it up.

'It's for you Dave,' she said passing me the letter.

I open it, it is from Colonel Hoare. In it is £15 in five pound notes and an air ticket. I have to report to Heathrow on Wednesday the 20th December for the 1230pm flight to Ndjili, with a stop off in Durban. Shit! Just when things are going right for me, I have to leave. I won't be here for Christmas or my mum's birthday. She isn't going to be very pleased about this.

'Son, is it bad news?' She asked.

'Yes and No mum, this letter is the one I have been waiting for, it's the joining instruction for that job. The only thing is, I have to leave before Christmas, and I won't be home for your birthday, I'm sorry mum.'

She looks hurt and tears appear in her eyes. This will be the first time that I have missed a family gathering. Damn, Damn, Damn. I put my arm around her and try to comfort her. She tells me that it will be alright. I know she is only saying this to make me feel better.

The doorbell rings. I open the door and find John standing there.

'You've got your letter then? I can see from your face. Hello, Mrs Stubbs.'

'It doesn't leave us much time does it?' I say to him.

'No, It don't, and I was just getting to know Sonia a bit better too.' he replied. 'Still, we will see the girls when we get back.'

'IF, we get back.' I reply.

My mother looks at us both with a puzzled look on her face.

'What do you mean by that?' She asked.

'Well, we might stay on for another year, that's all.'

She looks at us again and walks off.

Now we have a date, I have to buck up courage to tell Kathy I'm going. She is not going to like this at all. Her mother will though. I tell John we will have to tell the girls tonight at the dance.

So far, we have been paid £155, and haven't done a thing. I wonder how long this will last. We are sitting in the lounge having a cup of coffee when the doorbell rings. I go to the door and find a telegram boy standing there.

'I have a Telegram for Mr David Stubbs?'

'That's me.'

'Sign here please?' he said pointing to a line in his pad.

I open the telegram and read:

"FLIGHT 405 ON 20th DECEMBER STOP CANCELLED STOP NEW DATE IS 4th OF JANUARY STOP INFORM WEST ABOUT THIS CHANGE STOP DESTROY AIR TICKETS STOP COLLECT NEW TICKETS AT THE AFRICAN AIRWAYS FLIGHT DESK HEATHROW STOP SEE YOU SOON STOP HAVE A HAPPY XMAS AND BEST WISHES FOR THE NEW YEAR STOP HOARE."

'Any reply Sir?'

'No, thank you,'

I give him a sixpence (2½p) tip and he leaves. I scream out. My mother and John run to me.

'What's up?' They both ask.

'It's okay mum! We don't have to leave now until the 4th of January, I will be home for Christmas and your birthday.'

This is the best news I have had. We still have to tell the girls though they have a right to know what's happening.

I will ask Kathy if she would like to come to my mother's birthday party. We always have a great time, plenty to eat and drink and lots of fun. Perhaps she will come to terms with me going away. I hope so.

I go round to Kathy's house and knock the door. Her mother answers it.

'She isn't home from school yet, what do you want?'

'Will you please tell her that I will pick her up at 6.30 instead of 7pm?'

'I'll think about it.' She replied.

At this I lose my rag. Enough is enough.

'Listen you, don't fuck me about, I don't need this hassle from you. I haven't done anything wrong, yet you hassle me and Kathryn on every occasion, what's the matter with you? Don't you want your daughter to be happy? Tell her I will be round early, do you understand what I am saying?'

Kathy's mother goes red in the face. She tries to speak but can't. Blimey! I think she is going to blow a gasket; I've overdone it this time. I apologize to her for swearing and walk out of the gate and back home. God! That woman gets to me.

I arrive back home just as John is leaving. 'Strewth! What's wrong mate?' He asks.

I tell him that I have just had an up and downer with Kathryn's mother.

'Oh! Boy.' He replies.

'I expect I have blown my chances with Kathy now. Her mother will see to that.'

I calm down and then go down to the wine shop to see old Yates. I tell him I will be leaving again as I have found a job abroad.

'It's not the Merchant Navy again is it?'

'Bloody hell, no.' I tell him.

'I hope it is the right one this time Dave.'

'Yes, I think it is, I've signed a contract for a year, and, it's in the sun.'

'I will be sorry to lose you, wait a minute and I'll get your pay made up.'

He gives me a week's pay and I say goodbye to him. He isn't bad really.

6.30pm and I call for Kathy. She comes to the door ready to go.

'What on earth did you say to my mum when you came round earlier? She won't speak to anyone. She told me you would be round early and that was it.'

'I swore at her and told her to stop giving us hassle. I don't think anyone has spoken to her like that before, in fact, I have never spoken like that before. I did apologize for swearing though.'

'You should do it more often?' Kathy said taking my hand and laughing.

'I know she is a pain at times, but she means well.'

'I can't see it,' I tell her.

We meet up with John and Sonia at the dance. No live Band tonight, only a Disc Jockey. Kathy tells me that she will be leaving school in a week's time and will start her job on the 5th of January. I just haven't the heart to tell her that I start a new job in January as well, but abroad.

Kathy senses something is up and keeps asking me what is wrong.

'Don't you want to go out with me now?' She asked.

'Of course I do Kathy; it is just that I have something on my mind at the moment.'

'It's not that agro with my mother is it?'

'No darling, it isn't.'

We have a few dances and I tell John that I am taking Kathy home as I want to tell her about going away.

'See you later mate, good luck.' He replied.

I take Kathy home and at her gate I am about to kiss her when her mother opens the door. She must spend all her time looking out for us. I reckon I am now about to get it in the neck for what I said this afternoon.

'Would you like to come in for coffee Dave?'

I look at Kathy who is looking at me.

'Err, yes please Mrs Grey.'

I follow Kathy into the lounge. Watching TV is Mr Grey.

'Well done lad, whatever you said has done us a favour,' he whispers.

I thank him but can't understand why she is so nice to me. Kathy's mum comes into the lounge carrying a tray full of cups and cakes.

'Sit down Dave.' She said handing me a cup of coffee.

I'm now worried, why is she being so nice.

'I think we got off to a bad start Dave, I am very sorry,' she said handing me a plate with a cake on it.

Both hands are now full. Kathy plants a kiss on my lips and whispers in my ear, 'You've cracked it darling, I love you lots.'

Mr Grey asks me what I do for a living. I tell him that I use to work in a wine merchants learning management.

'Use to work?' Mr Grey asked.

'Yes, I quit this afternoon, it was only a stop gap, and I had another offer.'

'Have you something else lined up then?' Kathy's mum asked.

'Well, yes I have actually; I start a new job in the New Year.' I tell her.

'Doing what?' She asked.

'I'm working for a Security Company.'

'Is it local?'

'Oh! Come off it mum, stop asking so many questions.' Said Kathy.

'I was only being polite Kathryn, no need to get up tight,' said her mother handing me another cake.

'I don't mind really, Kathy.'

'Anyway, you never told me you had got another job Dave?'

'I was going to tell you tonight.'

'Is - it, local?' Kathryn asked.

Here goes!

'Well, no, the jobs in South Africa.' I tell her.

Kathy looks at me as if she has been pole-axed.

'SOUTH AFRICA!' she shouts.

'Err, yes,' I reply.

'How am I going to see you, if you are in bloody South Africa?' She screamed at me.

'Now steady on girl, there is no need to swear, it is not the end of the world.' Said her father trying to calm her down.

'It might as well be,' she shouts running out of the lounge.

'I think I have upset her,' I say to her parents.

'She will calm down in a minute or two,' said Mr Grey.

Her mother being the nosy sort, asked, 'How much will they pay you then Dave, for doing this job?'

'I get £140 a month; they have already paid me £155.' I tell her.

Kathy returns to the lounge wiping her eyes.

'Did you say £140 a month? What have you got to do, kill people?'

She couldn't be nearer the truth, if she tried, but I wasn't going to tell her.

'Kathy, we have been going out with each other for some time now, and I know you love me, and I love you.'

I pull a small box from my pocket, and hand it to her.

'Open it?'

She opens the box and a diamond ring is staring at her.

'I want us to get engaged, what do you say?'

'Oh Dave, It's lovely, yes, I would love to get engaged, look mum?'

Kathy showed her mum the ring. I look at her mother; I can see she is thinking pounds, shillings and pence.

'It's very nice, I bet that cost a pretty penny Dave?'

'Put it on my finger darling,' Said Kathy taking the ring out of its box.

I put the ring on her finger and her father says, 'Well done lad, welcome to the family, they make a fine couple, don't they Elsie?'

I can see her mother isn't very pleased, but she doesn't say anything. She has met her match and knows I won't stand for her interfering.

Over the next few days, I see a lot of Kathy. We are inseparable, and very much in Love. Although we are both under 18, we know what we are doing. We are not too young to get engaged. I don't intend to get married for at least 3 years.

To announce the engagement, we have a party round at Kathy's house. John and Sonia come, and are pleased for us.

'Bit sudden mate, isn't it?' John whispers. 'She's not in the club is she?'

'No! She isn't,' I tell him, 'I have never touched her.'

Sonia comes over to me.

'Congratulations Dave, she is a smashing girl and I don't think she will mind if I give you a kiss.'

It is a great party, and I meet quite a few members of Kathy's family. One of her Aunties is a right "piss head," and I get on great with her.

'I understand you put old Elsie in her place? Well done, she needed that doing,' said a drunken Aunty Barbara.

I remember Terry's words at the dance. "You know what St George did to dragons." I feel like St George, I've vanquished the Dragon at last. At least, I hope so.

Christmas comes and I spend it between Kathy's house and mine. We have a great time. I buy her a Black Woollen Jumper with a Rose motif on it, which she has always wanted. Kathy bought me a Cigarette Case with my initials engraved on it as I have just started smoking. I do love this girl.

I invite her to my mother's Birthday Party. The whole family are there. I introduce her to my brothers and sister and my aunties and uncles. They all like her a lot.

'You are not thinking of getting married yet, are you Dave?' asked my Uncle Bert.

'NO, not for at least 3 years.' I tell him.

I take Kathy into the kitchen so that we can be alone. She is a little tipsy.

'You haven't told me when you have to start your new job darling,' she said trying to stuff a sausage roll into my mouth.

'I have to be at Heathrow in three days' time.'

'Oh!' she replied, tears in her eyes.

'Make love to me Dave?'

'NO, Kathy, I can't do that.'

'Don't you love me enough?'

'Of course I do, I love you very much, but I think we should wait and not do it because I am going away.'

She looks away tears are rolling down her face. I comfort her knowing that she feels rejected. It's not that, I don't have any Johnnies, and I don't want any little David's waiting for my return. I cuddle and kiss her and tell her that I love her very, very, much. She is very quiet.

"Let's get on that damn plane." I say to myself.

John finally tells Sonia that he will be leaving with me for South Africa and will be flying off soon.

'When are you going?' she asks.

'Well, in three days' time.' He replied.

Sonia calls him all the pigs under the sun and that he is only using her.

'That's not true, I love you.' He replied with one hand up her skirt. 'I really love you.'

'Sod Off.' She replies, but don't take his hand away. She is obviously enjoying it. I cough and walk in on them.

'You seem to be enjoying the party?' I tell them.

John slowly takes his hand from between her thighs.

'You can sod off as well.' She shouts, pointing at me.

Kathy comes into the room.

'What's wrong? I heard you shouting Sonia.'

'Nothing much, John has just told her he is leaving with me.'

'You call that nothing much? You insensitive sod, how do you think I felt when you told me?'

'Sorry love.' I tell her.

The girls walk back into the kitchen crying.

'Another fine mess you have got me into.' I tell him.

'Well you told me it had to be done mate.' John said, filling his gob with food.

I spend as much time with Kathy as I can over the next few days. I tell her that I will write every day and she shouldn't worry, I also tell her that they may give us leave half way through the contract. I don't think she believed me.

The fateful day finally arrives. I borrow a suitcase from our next door neighbour. I don't tell her that she won't get it back for at least a year. I say goodbye to my mum and dad and get the bus to the ferry. John is waiting for me at the ticket office.

We board the ferry for Portsmouth. As we get off of the boat, I see the girls waiting for us.

'We have come to see you off.' Kathy said taking my hand.

'What time is the train?' Sonia asked.

'8.20am.' I tell her as we walk up the ramp to the station.

We go to platform 2 and stand by the train that is waiting there. I pull Kathy to me and kiss her.

'Why?' she asked.

'It is something I have to do, I was bored with the job in the wine shop, I need something better, something with adventure in it, and I think I will get it with this job.'

I know she will never understand that I don't want a dull life. I again tell her that I love her and pull her onto the train. I undo the buttons of her coat and place my hand on her breast, she unbuttons her blouse. I put my hand in her blouse, she isn't wearing a bra. I caress her right breast; she lets out a soft moan.

'You don't know how long I have wanted you to do that; you should have made love to me?' She said, tears streaming down her face.

'I know.' I reply.

'Oh Dave, I do love you.'

A guard shouts, "ALL ABOARD," and Kathy re-buttons her blouse and coat. I kiss her for the last time and she gets down onto the platform.

'Write to me every day.' She cries.

I don't answer. The train gives a lurch forward and the guard blows his whistle.

'I love you.' Kathy shouts.

'I love you too.' I shout back.

The train starts to move off and Kathy and Sonia are waving like mad. I can see tears streaming down their faces. I will miss her like mad.

We move along the train and find some empty seats.

'This is it mate, we are on our way.'

Yes, this is indeed it, the start of a new adventure. I wonder what it will be like in Africa, but who cares, it beats the cold any day of the week.

'AFRICA! Here we come............!'

CHAPTER THREE

We arrive at Heathrow Airport, collect our tickets from the South African Airways desk and go through the boarding procedure to get on the plane.

'I've never flown before?' John said handing his suitcase to a very pretty girl at the desk.

'There is nothing to worry about, it is quite safe flying, and I'm sure you will enjoy the experience.' She replied.

I haven't flown before either, but I wasn't going to tell her that. I'd feel a twit. I hand her my case and she puts it on the scales.

'You are just within the weight allowance.' she tells me.

'I must have packed too much this time.' I tell her.

'Packed too much this time, what are you on about?'

'Shut up mate, she will hear you; I don't want her to know I haven't flown before.'

We go into the departure lounge and have a cup of tea and a sandwich.

'This isn't bad is it mate, comfy seats and plenty of tea and bickies.'

'This is home from home!' I reply.

We are called to board the plane and proceed down the corridor, handing our boarding passes to another pretty girl.

The flight is quite boring, nothing to do but read and drink. I taste my first gin and tonic, it is quite refreshing. John is chatting up a stewardess. He has just left his girlfriend and can't wait to get off with someone else.

'Leave your dick in your trousers mate, remember that girl you left behind?' I tell him.

'Sorry mate, I forgot, it must be the lack of air.'

'Bollocks.' I reply.

Thirteen and a half hours tick by when suddenly a sign lights up and a stewardess says:

"RETURN YOUR SEATS TO THE UPRIGHT POSITION
AND
FASTEN YOUR SEAT BELTS. WE ARE ABOUT TO LAND."

Over the aircraft speakers a man is telling us that we will be landing in a few minutes and hoped that we had enjoyed our flight.

On landing a set of stairs are placed at the exit. The door opens and the first thing that hits us is a belt of heat.

'Bloody Hell!' I say to John, 'It's hot out there.'

We both remove the coats we had put on.

Having walked down the stairs we board a bus that is waiting to take us to the flight for Ndjili, another eight hours away.

On arrival at Ndjili we hear the Customs say to each passenger, 'Have you anything to declare, how long are you staying, is it business or pleasure.'

We collect our suitcases and are about to go through Customs when we are stopped by a man in green uniform.

'Are you Dave Stubbs and John West?'

'That's us.' I reply.

'Follow me; you do not have to go through Customs and Immigration.'

We follow him out of the lounge into the heat, to a beaten up wreck of a jeep.

'Chuck your cases in the back; I'm Lieutenant Davey, your training officer, I'm taking you to the Transit Base we have set up, before we fly on to the Training Camp.'

The trip to the Transit Base takes five hours over the worst tracks and roads I have ever been on. We bounce about so much; my arse begins to hurt like hell.

'Christ! Is it all like this?'

'We will hit a good stretch of road in a few minutes.' Davey informs us.

'Thank goodness for that.' John said, holding onto the side of the jeep. 'I now know how scrambled eggs feel.'

We finally arrive at the Transit Base completely covered in yellow dust. If I didn't know better, I would have thought John was a native.

'Don't unpack anything, we will be here for one hour only, and then we will fly out to the Training Camp near the border.' Davey informs us.

The Training Camp is a further 800 miles, but, thank goodness, we will be flying to it. I don't think my arse would take kindly to being bumped about for hours on end.

After what seemed hours, a little black fellow appears like magic. He hands us some packets of sandwiches and a flask of water each.

'So you will not go hungry on your trip.' He said smiling.

'Well! We won't starve.'

'Boy! Could I do with a wash?' I say to John, and, as if by magic, the little guy re-appears carrying some towels and a large bowl of hot water.

'You wash dust off.' The little guy says handing me a towel.

We thank the little guy and quickly wash.

'That's better; I wonder what is going to happen now? Christ! It's hot here.'

'You wanted to be in the sun Dave, so stop moaning. You will have a tan in no time at all.' John said sarcastically.

'I could do with a change of shirt mate?' I reply.

'Right, let's go.' Davey said getting back into the jeep.

'I thought we were flying?' John asks.

'We are,' Davey replied, 'the airfield is down the track a couple of miles.'

Davey puts the jeep into gear with a real grinding sound. 'No synchromesh on these gears.' He said laughing.

We speed off in the direction of the setting sun and after about 10 minutes, we arrive at a makeshift airfield. I see the oldest plane I have ever seen in my life.

Before I can say anything, Davey remarks, 'It's a Dak (Dakota), we use it to ferry people about and also to carry out parachute training.'

I look at John and mouth "PARACHUTE TRAINING." John has lost his colour.

Davey went on, 'The 25th Regiment is an Airborne one, we parachute into a trouble spot with our vehicles, no one walks in the 25th without a very good reason, believe me, at least, not intentionally.'

We climb into the Dak, there are no seats.

'You will have to sit on the floor and hold on the best you can.' The pilot informs us.

'HOLD ON, HOLD ON TO WHAT? THERE ISN'T ANYTHING TO BLOODY HOLD ON TO.' I shout at him.

There is a sound of engines being revved up and we suddenly shoot forward. The engines get louder and louder and we leave the ground. I grab hold of a small bolt that has appeared from the fuselage just as we bank over to the right. It stops me from being thrown about. John isn't so lucky; he falls over and hits his face on the side of the plane.

'Ouch! That bloody hurt.' He shouts.

We hit an air pocket and my stomach reaches my mouth. I don't like this one little bit. This is worse than the trip in the jeep; at least we had a seat in that. The plane levels out and Davey makes his way back towards us from the cabin.

'Sorry about that, here, put these straps round you and put them through these holes.' He said pointing to some slits in the fuselage, 'It will stop you being thrown about.'

'Now he gives them to us.' John said caressing his face.

We put the straps around us and also our cases. It is a lot better and we settle down for the flight. John has a large bruise on the side of his face where he hit the side of the plane.

'We are not there yet, and already I'm bruised, sod this.' He retorts

John falls asleep, how he can do that, I will never know. The noise in the plane is deafening. After what seemed like eternity, we start to lose height. I kick John on the ankle and he wakes up.

'What did you do that for?' He asked.

'I think we are coming in to land mate.'

'Bloody Hell! More bruises.' he shouts.

'HANG ON.' Davey shouts from the cabin.

CRUNCH, we hit the ground and take off into the air again and come down with a bump.

'Remind me in future to go by train.' John shouts trying to stop his case from taking his head off.

I don't say a word. I am only too glad to be on the ground again. Davey comes down the plane and opens the hatch door. A blast of very hot air greets us.

Davey looks at our faces and laughs, 'you will get use to the heat soon enough.'

He jumps out of the Dak and is greeted by Major Thomas. I'm 17 years old and feel like 60. We alight from the plane and Major Thomas shakes our hands.

'Welcome to Camp Forest.'

I look around and see that the Camp is completely ringed with razor sharp barbed wire.

'Sgt Jones!' Shouts Thomas, 'Take our newest recruits to Billet No 2 and get them kitted out ready for tomorrow.'

'Will do Guv.' said Jones, 'Come with me lads, it isn't far.'

'Be at Force HQ at 2000hrs tonight for a briefing.' Thomas shouts after us.

We follow Jones through the Camp until we come to a long hut.

'This is yours, I'll show you your beds and then we will go and get your kit.'

'Your home for the next 6 weeks,' Jones said pointing to our beds. 'Chuck your cases on your beds and then we will go and get your kit. Don't worry; no one will touch your stuff.'

I put my case on my bed which is made up, and follow Jones out of the hut and into the heat.

'Strewth! It must be at least 90 degrees.' John comments.

'Actually, it is 104 in the shade today.' Jones replies.

As we pass a green building, Jones tells us that it is Force HQ.

'That is where you have to be at 2000hrs tonight.'

The store is another wooden hut. I hope they don't have wood worm out here. We all go inside, it is lovely and cool. There is a long counter with two guys dressed in green uniform behind it.

'Who have we here then?' A guy with upside down tapes on his arm asks.

I think he is a corporal, but I'm not sure.

'Two recruits to kit out.' Jones tells him.

'Right Sirs, my name is Cyril and this is Pongo, welcome to the Regiment. The kit we are about to give you is free. That is, if you lose any of it, it will be replaced free of charge. You don't sign for anything. If you require any special equipment and we haven't got it, it will be got for you, okay?'

That's a relief, my brother is in the Army and he lost a cap and had to pay for it out of his pay.

'By the way what are your names?'

'I'm Dave and this is John.'

Cyril hands us both a large canvas bag.

'Right, let's get started:'

'4 pairs of Green Trousers, what size waists are you?'

We tell him.

'4 Green Jackets, What's your chest sizes?'

We tell him.

'2 red Berets, What's your head size?'

We tell him the sizes.

'4 complete camouflage suits with emblems.'

'2 pairs of Jungle Boots. What are your shoe sizes?'

We tell him.

'6 Cammy shirts, what are your neck sizes?'

We tell him.

'2 belts for holding up your trousers.'

'10 pairs of green socks.'

'1 Field Dressing.'

'1 Water sterilizing kit.'

'1 set of waterproofs; it rains like mad out here.'

'1 Map case and pencils.'

'1 Compass.'

'1 knife with sheath.'

'1 Patch 6ER Parachute.'

We look at each other!!!!!

'1 x 18 foot Oscillator reserve Chute.'

'Bloody Hell! Doesn't the first one work then?' I ask him. Cyril laughs.

'1 set of 48 pattern webbing.'

'1 FN Rifle.'

'8 FN Magazines fully loaded'

'1 .45 Automatic pistol.'

'6 Pistol Magazines fully loaded.'

'1 pair of Zeiss Binoculars.'

'Now have I left anything out?' Cyril said scratching his head. 'Oh Yes! One little Cyanide pill in plastic case.'

My heart speeds up, what we want that for, I wonder. Cyril must be reading my mind.

'The people you will be fighting are real animals, they will torture you and then hack you to pieces, that pill will help you along.'

'Great! That's put my mind at rest.' said John looking at me.

'Don't worry yourselves over this, you will never be on your own in the bush, there will always be help at hand, believe me.' said Cyril trying to calm us down.

'I believe you, I think.' stammered John. I don't say a word. I'm speechless.

'Remember what I said, if you need any extra equipment, just ask. The President of this God forsaken country has said that we will want for nothing. And we haven't.'

'That's nice to know.' I tell him stuffing everything into the canvas bag.

It all fits in except the FN, which I carry over my shoulder, and we return to our billet, sweat pouring from us. The heat is unbearable. I drop everything onto my bed. I'm knackered and we have only walked a couple of hundred yards.

'What's the grub like Sgt Jones?' I ask.

'It's like being in the Ritz Hotel.' He replies, 'It is nearly grub time now, come on, I'll show you where the mess halls are.'

We follow him through the camp until we come to three long wooden huts.

'The end hut is yours.'

We follow him inside and see that all the tables are laid up with cutlery and table clothes.

'We in the right place mate?' asked John.

Jones then informed us that it is waiter service, and that we should treat the waiters in the same way that we would back in England.

As there isn't anyone in the mess, we sit at a table near the window.

'Just because we are a Mercenary Regiment, doesn't mean we have to lower our standards.'

After a few minutes, a waiter comes to our table and gives each of us a menu. I notice that there are three main courses. I order the roast beef; John orders the Curry and Jones the fowl. I wonder if Jones was mucking about when he said it was like the Ritz. The food is indeed excellent, Jones wasn't mucking about after all. I later find out that the cook or chef as he likes to be called actually worked for the Dorchester.

'Don't forget to be at Force HQ at 2000hrs.' said Jones leaving us to get sorted out.

There are a lot of beds in the room but no other people. We unpack our cases and put our clothes in the small lockers by our beds. I lay on my bed and think of Kathy. I suppose I had better write her a letter when I come back from the briefing.

It is 1955hrs and we make our way to Force HQ.

'Come in gentlemen.' Said a Captain in full camouflage dress.

We enter the large office and are shown some seats.

'The Colonel isn't here yet, my name is Tony Blythe, and I'm the Adjutant of the Regiment.'

We shake hands and introduce ourselves. After a few minutes, Major Thomas and Captain Richards together with Lt Davey enter the room.

'Isn't the Colonel here yet?' Thomas asks.

'I am now.' Colonel Hoare replied, entering the room.

We all stand up and the Colonel shakes our hands.

'What's wrong with your face John?' The Colonel asks pointing to the large bruise.

'Collided with the side of the Dak on take-off Colonel, I think the pilot was a learner driver.'

The Colonel looks away smiling.

'Right, let's get down to business,' Said Colonel Hoare, 'I want to bring you both up to date since we last met in England. I have decided, and the others agree, that you both should train as Troop Officers, how do you feel about this?'

'Fine.' We both tell him.

'Good, once you have finished your training, you will be in charge of a Troop of 12 men each. The situation has changed drastically. The President, Moise Tshombe, has asked the UN to help him quell the riots that are happening daily in and around Elizabethville. He has also asked for help from Belgium and troops are arriving daily. There is a slight problem with a load of mutineers who have been killing white folk and looting shops. We will be leaving most of this to the Belgian troops. This way, we will be able to concentrate on the Rebels in the bush. Leopoldville is under attack and we may be asked to assist there. At the moment there is a lot of political argument going on, which we will not get involved in. Our main job is to protect the white civilians on the farms out in the bush. I should tell you, we had 4 men killed yesterday in an ambush. We got sucked into a situation which won't happen again.'

We listen intently to what the Colonel is telling us, he certainly seems to look after his men.

'Any questions?' the Colonel asks.

We reply to the negative.

'Just remember, once you are Officers, your men will look up to you and they will rely on your decisions, they will not stand for idiots, I know you will do well and not let me down, good luck with your training, I will see you later.'

'Okay lads! Get some sleep, you will need it, reveille is at 0500hrs, sweet dreams!' Davey said, rubbing his hands together.

We return to our billet and find it full of men.

'Hello.' said a small guy with a Birmingham accent, 'You must be the Officer recruits? My name is Paul and I come from Birmingham as you can probably tell.'

We introduce ourselves to him and he in turn introduces us to the rest of the people in the room.

'This is Peter, Jack, George, Gerald, Albert, Fritz we call him Fred, Alan, Mick and Sefton.' Paul said, pointing to each in turn, 'Welcome to Deaths Head Troop.'

'We arrived yesterday and immediately started training.' Albert said as he folded some kit.

We talk for an hour or so swapping stories etc., when a Corporal enters the hut. His name is "Bright"; he is the Troop Corporal and always has a smile on his face.

'I think you lot should get your heads down, it is going to be a hard day tomorrow. I understand that the temperature will be 108 in the shade, night, night.'

He switches off the lights and leaves the hut. I climb into bed and dream of Kathy. 0500hrs.....'

'Get Up and on your feet.' Corporal Bright shouts, throwing a bucket down the middle of the hut. It makes a hell of a racket. John leaps out of bed.

'Are we being attacked?' he asks.

'Good morning Mr West and how are you today? I trust you had a good sleep. NOW MOVE YOURSELF, we haven't got all day. Outside everyone at the double, that means RUN.'

We run out of the hut and parade in front of the entrance. Some of the men are with boots un-done, some with shirts on, some trying to get into trousers and some with no trousers on at all. Lt Davey arrives smiling.

'Good morning gentlemen, we are going for a short run just to get rid of the cobwebs, some of you will give up and some of you will throw up, but get used to it as it will happen every morning from now on. I want you all to be dressed the same for these runs. No top and green trousers and boots. Right, back in your hut and all get your boots and trousers on.'

Back we go into hut and change and parade outside again.

'Form two lines, turn to the right and double march, that's RUN.' screams Bright.

We all turn to the right and start to run. It is nice and cool, but we soon start to sweat. Some of the guys stop and throw up.

'Keep running.' shouts Davey.

After about 20 minutes, which seems like 20 hours, Davey calls us to a halt. Peter and Sefton collapse onto the road, heaving for breath. Davey approaches and towers over them.

'What's the matter lads?' He said smiling.

'Not yet use to it Sir.' Peter replied trying to get his breath.

'Right, get on your feet you two.' Bright shouts.

'That was only a warm up, it gets harder.' Davey said, smiling.

They get up and return to the ranks. We move off again, what a shambles. Some start with the left foot others with the right. Total shambles. We finally arrive back at the hut.

'Now you know what to expect tomorrow morning.' Shouts Davey.

'Get showered and changed into full camouflage dress and be outside the hut in one hours' time, move your selves.' Shouts Bright.

We rush into the hut, grab our washing kit and run to the ablutions hut. I dive under a shower and turn on the water. I leap back out. 'Fucking Hell, this water is freezing.' I shout.

If the runs don't get us the showers will. I gingerly try and get use to the coldness. John has turned blue and I start to laugh.

'Don't take any notice of this git; he has a warped sense of humour.' John shouts pointing at me.

'Oh Shit!' Fred shouts, 'My dick has disappeared with the cold.'

We all laugh at his dilemma. I look at mine, it's vanished too.

Back in the hut, we change into cammy kit and put on our berets. What a sight. We parade outside looking like Dads Army.

'I trust the water has woken you up? Now, take off those berets, I will show you how to shrink them this evening after classes.' said Bright looking to the heavens.

Lt Davey arrives.

'Okay, we will now march to breakfast. What I mean by March, is that everyone will start off together with the same foot, the left one. I want to see all left feet together and all right feet together, understand?'

Bright shouts, 'Form two ranks and listen to what I am saying. When I say, move to the right, I want you to come to attention, that is, bring your left foot into your right foot and stand still feet together and shout "ONE STOP." Then, turn to the right by swivelling on your right heel and left toes and bring your feet together and shout "TWO STOP." When I say "QUICK MARCH," move your left foot forward and then your right and keep marching, shouting "LEFT, RIGHT, LEFT, RIGHT," okay, let's practice it. Troop, move to the right, QUIIICK MAAARCH.'

We all move off together, I can't believe it. It must be the cold water.

'Brilliant.' Davey shouts, 'Keep the step going, LEFT, RIGHT, LEFT, RIGHT.'

As we are marching along, Bright comes along side us.

'Listen to what I am going to say, we are going to halt, we do this in the following way, on the command "TROOP HALT," halt will come on your left foot, you will immediately shout "CHECK" on your right foot and then move your left foot forward and shout "ONE" then move your right foot forward and shout "TWO," bring your left foot to your right and shout "STOP," you will now be at attention, stand by.'

We continue marching and are approaching the mess halls when suddenly, Cpl Bright shouts, 'TROOOOP - HALT.'

We shout, "CHECK, ONE, TWO, STOP." Would you believe it? Perfect.

'Well done, that was a good effort.' Said Davey, 'Right in and get your breakfast.'

John, Paul and I rush to the end mess hall, the rest go into the middle one. We sit at a table near the window. A cool breeze is coming through it. A waiter arrives and asks us if we want the full breakfast.

'What's that?' asked John.

The waiter replies, 'Eggs, Bacon, Fried bread, beans or tomatoes, fruit juice, toast and coffee.'

'That's for us.' We all tell him.

After a few minutes the waiter returns with our breakfasts and we eat ravenously.

Breakfast over; we form up again outside the mess hall.

'I hope you enjoyed your breakfast gentlemen, we are now going to walk it off.' Bright shouts with his ever smiling face. 'Turn to the right, QUICK MAAARCH, LEFT, RIGHT, LEFT, RIGHT, keep it going.'

I am sure we were told that no one walks in the Regiment, or have I got it wrong. We arrive at another large wooden hut.

'Troop - HALT.'

He catches us unawares and we make a right cock up.

'Get inside.' Shouts Bright.

We go into the hut and are met by Major Reynolds, who is our Squadron Commander.

'Welcome to the Regiment gentlemen, when you have finished your training, you will all come to Simba Squadron. The Squadron is 100 men strong, made up of 4 Strike Troops and 4 Support Troops. We are the best there is out here and don't any of you forget it. Since coming to the Congo, we have had the most kills on the Rebels and have lost only 4 men. I want to keep that record. On completion of your training, you Mr West will take over "A" Troop, you Mr Stubbs, "B" Troop and you Mr Garth (pointing to Paul) will take charge of "C" Troop until an Officer is appointed. This could take some time so you will be given the acting rank of Lieutenant, if you do well you will keep it. The rest of you will be slotted into Troops and any promotions will depend on your own ability. I expect my men to be loyal to me, the Squadron, the Colonel and the Regiment in that order. Don't let me down, have you any questions?' There were none.

'Carry on Mr Davey.'

We split up into pairs for weapon training. We are taught the fundamentals of the FN Automatic Rifle and the .45 Calibre Pistol. We are taught how the weapons operate and what each is used for and how. We have to carry out stripping the weapons until we can do it blindfolded. After a few times, it becomes second nature. I enjoy the lessons and can't wait to get on the range. Now that we have mastered these weapons, we are taught the .5 machine gun. It is a formidable weapon, belt fed instead of magazine. The weapon is used on our jeeps. I like this weapon, the fire power is tremendous.

We keep at it until we can name each individual part of the weapon taken from a pile blindfolded, and say which weapon it came from. The rate at which we are learning is earth shattering. At times my head swims with all the things I have to take in. There is no let up to the training, it has to be completed quickly and everything must be learnt parrot fashion. After dinner this evening, we are being taught the Compass and Map Reading. This should be a good lesson. We break off for 10 minutes.

'Christ!' Cries Gerald. 'It's like being back in the Army, only worse.'

Gerald had done 6 years with the Staffordshire Regiment.

'It should come easy then, to you Gerry.' John said.

'Well it bloody well don't, I can assure you.' Gerald replied.

We return to the weapon training and continue until dinner time.

'Okay you lot, break for dinner.' Davey tell us.

We walk to the mess hall and discuss all the things we have learnt.

'I like the .5 machine gun.' I tell them.

'You would, it makes the biggest holes.' said John laughing.

I order the roast pork and John and Paul order the duck. The food is really good. I must write to Kathy tonight if I can.

We return to the lecture room and are taught the art of reading a map and compass. It is very interesting and we all soon master it. The lessons over, and we return to the hut.

'I'm for bed Dave.'

'Me too mate, it has been a long day.'

It looks as if I will not be writing to Kathy after all. I'm far too whacked.

0500hrs.....It comes round far too quickly. In flies the bucket, we leap out of bed, and parade outside for the daily run round the camp. Everyone this time is dressed the same.

'Well done.' Said Cpl Bright, 'We will make soldiers of you yet.'

We've been here 3 days and it seems like 3 months.

'Now gentlemen, turn to the right, QUICK, MAARCH, as you were, DOUBLE MAAARCH.'

We double round the camp which is 2 miles round. It feels like 10. Some of the guys throw up, but it is getting better, even the freezing water of the showers is becoming invigorating. After breakfast, we parade outside the mess hall.

'All of you, report at the MT Park in 15 minutes.' Davey shouts.

No one knows where the MT Park is and we find it by accident. Davey and Bright are waiting.

'Get on the truck you lot.' Shouts Bright.

We all pile onto the truck and within seconds it is driving out of the camp. After about 30 minutes over the bumpiest roads, I mean tracks, the worse I have ever been on, we come to a disused mine.

'All of you off the truck.' Shouts Davey.

We form up alongside the vehicle. Bright is removing some dark green boxes.

'I never saw them.' said Sefton.

'What are they?' Albert asks.

'Hand grenades.' Davey said.

'Bloody Hell!' I say in return.

'Today we will teach you all about the grenade and how to throw it. Please pay attention to everything I tell you, if you don't, we could all be killed. You will also be taught how to prime the grenade. Remember, safety is the prime element in grenade throwing. The grenade is a very powerful weapon, it can be your friend or enemy, it is up to you. Treat it with love and affection and it will be your friend. These grenades have a 7 second fuse, you have plenty of time. Do not prime the grenade until told to do so, and when priming, hold the detonator by the middle of the cloth bit, not the metal, it could explode in your hand otherwise. Are there any questions?'

None were forthcoming.

We practice on some inert ones until we get it right. The priming is simplicity itself; you undo a plate in the bottom of the grenade, slip in the detonator and re-screw the plate. It's simple. John is the first to throw.

'Okay John.' Said Bright, 'Prime your grenade and check that the pin is still in and not bent over. On the command "READY," I want you to pull the pin with your left a hand, check that the grenade is still in your right hand with your fingers covering the lever. Extend your left arm and your right arm. On the command "THROW," I want you to lob the grenade into the mine shaft. Make sure you see the grenade land before getting your head down. I would hate for the grenade to land just in front of us. Okay, any questions?'

John replied, 'No.'

'READY!'

John pulls the pin and checks everything is okay.

'THROW!'

John lobs the grenade into the mine shaft and gets his head down behind the mound of earth he is hiding behind.

BOOM!

'Well done John.'

'NEXT!'

I run over to the mound.

'Right, you have seen what John had done, you do the same.'

I lob the grenade into the mine shaft.

BOOM!

A piece of grenade flies over our heads.

'That was the base plate.'

'I don't like grenades.' I tell him.

Bright, smiles as usual. Fucking sadist.

After we have chucked about 10, my arm begins to ache. I still don't like them. We carry on until all the Mills grenades are used up.

'It's now onto Phosphor grenades, which are used to flush out bunkers and for smoke screening. Do not touch any of the white burning substance, or get it on your clothing or skin, it will burn even under water. This is one of the most dangerous grenades you will ever throw.'

He throws the grenade into a pit. The only sound heard, is a loud pop, and then an eruption of white particles, which fall to the ground and sizzle causing huge amounts of smoke. Yuck! I don't like this grenade.

'I trust you are now familiar with the types of grenade we have. Just remember that they are your friends if used properly and your enemy if you don't. Right, get on the truck.' Shouts Davey.

We move off and return to Camp covered in yellow dust.

'Tonight, you will be taught camouflage and concealment, don't be late.'

We all rush into the hut and collect our washing kit. The water of the showers is still freezing. I'd have thought that it would have been hot by now with the sun beating down on it. I later find out that the water comes from an underground spring. No wonder it is freezing. We return to the hut and Peter and Fred are complaining of a headache.

'Here, catch.' I say throwing them some aspirins.

'Thanks mate.' they both reply.

We all go off the dinner which is again excellent. Afterwards we go to the lecture room.

'Blend in with the Terrain.' Bright informs us.

We watch a film on the subject of Camouflage and Concealment made by the British Army for use in the 2nd World War. We will be practicing this in the daytime in the bush sometime during the week, we are told.

Once the lecture is over we return to our hut totally exhausted. Can we keep this pace up, I wonder. There isn't enough hours in the day, I'm afraid letter writing will have to go by the board tonight. Perhaps one day I will be able to write. I fall asleep fully clothed on my bed.

0500hrs......OH NO!!!!

The runs are now becoming easier and we are getting fitter. Today we are going to be taught the Rocket Launcher and Identification of the Enemy. The training is now starting to hot up, the pace has increased. Will we learn it all, I wonder.

Two weeks have passed and I haven't written two paragraphs of a letter to Kathy. I think of her and wonder what she is doing. She can't even write to me, I haven't sent her the address. By the time I have finished in the evening, I am too knackered to write. I really must find the time though.

I get the address of the camp from the Post Corporal who tells me that it takes 12 weeks for a letter to get to the UK and about 6 weeks for it to come back. They must be using Wells Fargo.

We are now into the 4th week of training, and, yes, you have guessed it, the dreaded parachute training is about to start. We are taken to a large area which has towers of different heights dotted about it; some are over 60 feet high.

'Now gentlemen, we start your Parachute Training.'

A Sgt who I have never seen before, says, 'This will sort the men from the boys. Before you can jump from a plane you will be required to carry out ground training. I will be teaching you how to roll when you hit the ground and what to do if you have a malfunction with the parachute. You will be jumping from the different towers so that you can feel what it is like landing before you actually do the jump. Don't worry about your chute not working. If it doesn't open, take it back to the store for a new one.'

John whispers, 'Sadistic bastard.'

I don't think I am going to like this part of the training. We form a circle and the Sgt shows us how the parachute is made up. He points out the canopy, rigging lines, the harness and bag. He shows us the rip cord which is in fact made of wire and the reserve chute. He explains how to use the reserve when the main chute fails. OH Shit! We split up into groups of 4 and another load of instructors arrive. These people only attend to instruct recruits in Parachute Training. They are not part of the main Regiment.

We start by being shown how to roll. It hurts like hell, and takes some mastering, but we finally get it right. It's then on to the towers and we start leaping off them. The first one is 15 feet above the ground. When you are on top they look higher. I'm sure my backside is black and blue; I seem to land on it enough times. At last I have got it right, I'm not a 100% happy with the technique, and I would rather stand up when I land. I understand that the chutes we have been issued, will allow us to do that.

The last tower is over 50 feet high and has a winch on it. The Sgt is in charge of this tower. I gingerly, climb up to the top. Bloody Hell! It looks a long way down. The Sgt straps me into the harness.

'Are you ready?' He asks. 'As ready as I will ever be.'

'Okay now JUMP!'

I leap off of the tower and plummet to the ground. The winch takes most of the speed out of the jump but I still land with a thump. I roll over as taught to brake the fall. It was a shambles.

'Get up here and do it again.' The Sgt shouts.

I follow John up the ladder to the top of the tower. John is strapped into the harness and leaps off of the tower. His fall is just as bad as mine.

'Back up here.' The Sgt shouts.

'Right Mr Stubbs, let's see if we can get it right this time?'

I fasten myself into the harness and jump off of the tower. I control the landing better this time.

'That was much, better.' The Sgt shouts from the top of the tower.

I'm pleased he is pleased, can't we go home. I unbuckle the harness and it is hoisted up to John. He straps himself into it and leaps off.

'Keep your bloody feet together Mr West.' shouts the man on high.

The rest of the group have the same problems as us, so we don't feel too bad.

'We will continue the ground training tomorrow. If you are good enough we may make a plane jump, but we shall see.'

'My arse is ruddy sore.' Sefton said, rubbing his bum.

'Mine too.' I tell him.

We return to the camp and wash and change for dinner. There are no lectures tonight thank goodness; I should really finish the letter to Kathy. The evening is spent asleep on my bed, whilst the rest of the lads are pissing it up in the canteen.

0500hrs - another run, it is really easy now. We return to the Para Training and continue jumping from the tower. After about 2 hours the Sgt tells us we will be making our first jump from a Barrage Balloon in the afternoon. He is hoping to get at least 10 jumps each in, if time allows. Once we have completed them, we will jump from the Dak.

'Anyone wants to drop out?' said the Sgt.

No one answers.

We have a light lunch of a sandwich and a wrinkled apple, washed down with jet black coffee.

'How high is the Balloon Sgt?' Albert asks.

'You are about 1000 feet up.' He replied, 'Don't worry, the jumps will be by static line, that is, the rip cord will be pulled automatically for you, so that you can concentrate on your position in the air.'

I don't think Albert is convinced.

Now we have another day to think about it. The lesson we return to is unarmed combat. At least we have another evening off. I really must get this letter to Kathy finished. Dinner is another scrumptious affair, plenty of meat, well cooked and good company. Everyone is talking about the parachute training.

'I didn't like those ruddy towers much, did you Dave,' said Paul.

'No I damn well didn't, and nor did my bum, I landed on it enough times.'

The dreaded 0500hrs arrives too quickly. We go for the usual run followed by a bloody freezing shower, but a smashing breakfast. Not many of the guys are having breakfast, I wonder why. Ha! Ha! Of course, the balloon jump, they don't want to be sick. I now begin to wonder if I have done the right thing by having breakfast. Oh well! It is too late now.

We parade outside the mess hall and are then marched to the airfield. Someone did say we never walked in the Regiment. He certainly was a good liar. As we approach the airfield we see a grey Barrage Balloon with a basket underneath it. Bloody heck! The basket looks small.

The Sgt who was training us yesterday turns up.

'Right gentlemen, this will be your first real jump, remember all you were taught yesterday and nothing will go wrong, in fact, you may get to like the experience.'

Who is he kidding!

'You lot,' pointing to me, John, Paul and Sefton,

'Here goes nothing.' said Sefton.

We put our chutes on and check each other to see if we have got them on correctly, and climb into the basket. It certainly is very cramped. The Sgt waves his hand and the Balloon suddenly floats up into the air. I look out of the basket, shit! We are a long way up. All of a sudden we come to a grinding halt with a jolt.

'We are now at a thousand feet, let's have a look at you; I wouldn't want your chutes to come off in mid decent, now would I. Right who's first out of the basket?'

'You can go first.' I say to John.

'No after you.' He replies.

'Enough of this shit.' The Sergeant said throwing me out of the basket.

I shoot down head first then all of a sudden I am pulled upright. I keep falling and there is a loud pop above me.

'Keep your fucking legs together.' The Sgt shouts.

I check that the rigging lines are not tangled and before I know it, the ground is rushing up to me.

THUMP!

I hit the ground and roll over. I am on the ground thank goodness, and I'm still alive. John has followed me down and lands 30 yards away. I see him kiss the ground. Sefton lands 20 feet from me. I can see he is pleased to be down as he too kisses the ground. I look up and see Paul has his rigging lines tangled and is frantically trying to free them. All of a sudden they free and his canopy opens and he floats to the ground and lands with a bump 50 yards away. I bet he shit himself.

The Balloon is winched down and the rest of the guys have their go.

We do this 9 more times each and funny enough, I get to enjoy it. It wasn't as bad as I thought. Mind you, anyone who leaves a perfectly good Balloon to jump out with a bit of cloth above them has got to be mad. The plane is next....!

We throw all the used chutes onto the vehicle and it takes them away to be repacked. The Sergeant calls us all together and gives us a talk on what he noticed whilst we were jumping. He said that we would get better as we carry out more jumps. Once we have got our wings, we would have to carry out 2 jumps a month. It is too late to do a jump from the Dak and we return to camp - in transport - we didn't have to march.

'You haven't got out of the plane jump.' The Sergeant said, 'We will be doing that tomorrow.'

'Shit! I thought we got out of it.' Albert said.

I will ask the Sergeant if he will show us how to pack a parachute, after all, we may need to do our own at some stage, and anyway, it will help to pass the time away instead of jumping out of planes. I hope.

We have got another evening off. I get down to writing the letter to Kathy and my parents. I tell Kathy that I am in the Congo with a Mercenary Unit and not to worry etc. etc. I must have fallen asleep because the lights come on and the bucket is thrown down the middle of the hut. Bloody hell! It is 0500hrs.

I don't bother with breakfast this morning, we are jumping from the plane and I don't want to bring it up as I come down, so to speak.

We arrive at the airfield and are met by the Sergeant. He must be reading my mind, because he shows us how to pack a Para Patch 6ER Parachute.

'This chute is one of the best there is, it is easily steered and you will be able to stand up on landing, you can control the speed of decent so that you can land softly. As you can see, the rigging lines are folded and kept together with very thin elastic bands. ON NO ACCOUNT, USE THICK BANDS, because if you do, you will die. They will not let the lines release, and you will then have a disastrous malfunction. Be Warned!'

We practice the packing of a chute, I'm sure we will have to do it at some stage in our training.

'Okay - let's do a jump from the Dak. Said the Sergeant counting us off into a stick.

We gingerly climb aboard the Dakota and sit along the fuselage. Once everyone is on board the plane starts to move and it takes off and climbs to 6000 feet.

'Now remember all that I have taught you - all stand up - clip your static line cords to the centre wire above you.' He shouts, pointing to a length of wire running down the middle of the fuselage above our heads.

We clip onto the wire and stand ready. A red light is on above the door which is now open. The roar of the wind is tremendous. The red light changes to green.

'GO.'

One after another we leap out, arms folded across our reserve chutes. One by one the chutes open and we drift slowly to the ground.

We are far enough up to see all around us. The view is fantastic. Suddenly the ground rush's up. I control the rate of decent with my toggles and slow the chute right down and land on my feet.

'That was great.' I shout to no one in particular. The guys are landing all around me. All say the same thing - "SMASHING."

The plane lands and taxi's towards us. The Sergeant leaps out and walks towards us.

'You have now done your first jump from a plane, I am only required to get you to do one jump, but, if anyone wants to have another go, pack your chute as you have been taught and get back on board.'

We all want to do it again. I must be mad, why leap out of a perfectly flyable plane. Our chutes are repacked under the Sergeants supervision. If they don't open - we only have ourselves to blame.

All of us carry out 4 more jumps and then return to camp. I really enjoyed today. It wasn't as bad as I thought it would be. Another evening off, training must be coming to an end. The Troop Corporal enters the hut and reads out a list of names. These people will be Passing Out on Friday and John and I are told to attend. I don't know why, we have still got two weeks training left.

I am writing to Kathy when the parachute Sergeant enters the hut. He points to me, John, and Paul.

'How would you three like to do some Free Fall Parachuting with me tomorrow?'

'I'm game, what do we have to do?' John and Paul nod their heads

'Good - be at the airfield at 0800hrs, I will clear it with Lt Davey.'

I pack up writing the letter and climb into bed. I WILL get this letter to Kathy finished one day.

0500hrs - Bloody hell! Not another run. I have breakfast as I found that it was better to have something inside you. We have been given permission to go to the airfield and meet up with Sgt Allen. He explains what we have to do and said we would do static lines first so that he could check our position in the air. Once the correct position is mastered, we will do full Free Fall.

We carry out 5 static line jumps and then get a briefing on Free Falling. Our chutes must be open before we reach the 1500 feet point on our altimeters. The first jump will be from 6000 feet and we will be falling at 120 mph. I am a bit apprehensive but am looking forward to it.

'I'm hoping to get a couple of jumps in at 8000 feet, if time permits. Now remember what I have told you - enjoy it - people pay lots of money to do what you are doing for free.' Sergeant Allen said walking off.

We all climb aboard the plane and it takes us up to 6000 feet. I leap out and adopt the frog position (now called the Star position) as taught. I am coming down at a right old rate of knots. I check the altimeter and it reads 3000 feet. I pull the rip cord and check that the chute has been pulled from its bag. "POP," and the chute billows open. I check the rigging lines and everything is okay. I steer towards the drop zone and land on my bum. I forgot to toggle back for the landing, what a prat. John is just behind me and lands upright 6 feet away. Paul has just left the plane and is in free fall. We watch him pull his chute - there is something wrong - it is still billowing out above him. He pulls his reserve, and thank goodness, it opens. He can't steer the oscillator and he lands 200 yards away. We both run over to him and see that he is okay.

'Fucking Hell - that was a nasty few minutes - the bloody thing failed to open.' He said rather shaken.

The plane lands and Sgt Allen rushes over.

'What happened?'

'I don't know.' Paul replied.

Sgt Allen checks the chute and finds that the pilot chute had come away from the main canopy.

'You were just unlucky; I have never seen this happen before.'

'What caused it Sarge?' I asked.

'Haven't a clue, repack your chutes and let's get back up.'

Paul uses another chute which Sgt Allen has brought with him. This time we all jump out together and link up in the air. It is a marvellous experience - the 4 of us are falling to earth at 120mph. We break away and each in turn opens his chute -we all land safely. It is now getting late and we carry out a few more jumps before returning to camp. I thank Sgt Allen for allowing us to do Free Fall - it is an experience I will never forget.

As we enter the camp, we are called to Major Thomas's office.

'You are nearing the end of your training and will soon start the admin side of being an Officer. You both will attend the Passing Out parade on Friday where you will be presented with your wings by the President, Moise Tshombe. So get your best kit ready, and put these on.' Thomas said handing us some cloth badges.

They are Lieutenants Insignia.

'But we haven't finished training yet Sir?'

'Colonel Mike has said that you are to be given your rank now, are you going to argue with his orders?'

'Not bloody likely Sir.'

We go back to our hut and sew - well sort of sew - the badges to our shoulder straps of our uniform. The guys return to the hut from dinner - which we had missed because we were parachuting.

'Stone the Crows, we have got full blown Officers billeted with us.'

'Oh well, we can't all be perfect.' Albert said laughing.

'Do we call you, "Sir" now?' George asks.

'Bollocks.' said John, 'We have been through a lot together, I am still John to you lot.'

'And I am still Dave.'

'Well you lot can call me, SIR.' Paul said laughing.

We all throw kit at him. Being an Officer, won't make much difference between us, we have become very attached to each other after going through some very strenuous training and relying on each other for support.

Friday comes and we are on parade with the rest of the trainees. We are called to attention and are inspected by the Colonel and the President. They shake our hands and the President presents each of us with a pair of Wings.

'Thank you for coming to my country to help.' He said to each man in turn. The Colonel winks at me and John. I like Colonel Mike, he is very genuine, a real smashing person. I would follow him anywhere and he knows it.

After the parade, we go to the Officers Mess and are introduced to the rest of the Officers.

'Here - have a drink?' said Lt Davey - passing me a glass full of clear liquid.

Thinking it is water, I take a great gulp. My throat is on fire, the liquid is neat Vodka.

'Bloody Heck!' I squeak.

We get talking and I find out about the President of Katanga.

His full name is Moise Kapendu (Beloved Moses) Tshombe. He was born in 1919 at Masumba, the tribal capital of Katanga. He was the eldest of 6 sons and was educated at an American Mission and trained as a Teacher and an Accountant. At one stage in his life, he worked for his father, an influential businessman in Elizabethville. Tshombe went bankrupt 3 times and had to be bailed out by his father on each occasion. One time he was arrested for passing dud cheques. He married the daughter of the Chief of the powerful Lunda tribe and through her connections, got appointed to the Council in Elizabethville. He has a talent for survival, especially in politics. This man will certainly plunge the Congo into Civil War. You could say that Tshombe was the White Man's - Black Man.

Tony Davey shows us to a room each in the Mess.

'This is where you stay from now on, welcome to the Club.'

We return to the hut to collect our things. None of the lads are there. We lug our gear across to the Mess and stow it away. Luxury, we have our own wash basins. I turn the tap on and boiling water pours out.

'HOT WATER AT LAST.' I shout. Things are looking up.......!

CHAPTER FOUR

My training completed, I take over "B" Troop. The Troop Sergeant is a guy called Alistair Green, who comes from Chichester. I introduce myself to him and he in turn introduces me to the Troop. 'This is Lt Stubbs, he is our Troop Commander.'

I am 17 years old and feel like 30. I speak to each of the men in turn and learn something about each one. I have 3 men from Essex, 3 from Portsmouth, 2 from Scotland and 2 from Yorkshire. They are all seasoned mercenaries having been out in the Congo for over 13 months.

I am shown round the Troop Lines and have a look at our vehicles and kit. Everything is okay and in good order. The guys themselves seem a great bunch. They are always laughing and seem to get on well together. For this I am glad. Alistair tells me that it was our Squadron that got zapped in an ambush and lost 4 men.

'Yes, Major Reynolds has told me about that.'

'It won't happen again Sir.' Alistair replied.

'I hope it don't either.' I tell him.

After lunch, I am called to the Colonels office.

'Hello Dave, settled in? – you have a great bunch of lads in "B" Troop and a very good Sergeant, he should really be an Officer, but he doesn't want to be one, try and persuade him if you can. What I want you for is this, "D" Troop have found some dead bodies in the bush, we haven't killed them, so they will have to be investigated, bearing in mind the ambush when we lost four men, we are going to treat this with caution. I want you to liaise with the Troop Commander, Jeremy Wilkins, and patrol the area. Please be very careful.'

Colonel Mike shows me a map and points to the area concerned. I make a few notes on my pad.

'Is this how they ambushed us last time Colonel?'

'Yes, so be very careful, I do not want anyone on our side getting killed.'

I salute and return to the Troop Lines.

'What's up Guv?' Asked Alistair.

'We have got a patrol to do with "D" Troop; they have found some bodies in the bush some 10 miles east of here.'

'Oh heck - that's how they zapped us last time out.' Alistair replied.

'Well, they won't do it this time Alistair.'

I get the Troop together and explain the situation to them. I tell them that any information I get from high will be passed to them immediately as I feel that they should know what is going on at all times.

'Get the vehicles packed, and Frank, check that the radios work, okay.'

'Will do Guv.' He replied.

20 minutes after I told them, we are ready to roll. They are raring to go into action.

'Remember lads, I don't want any heroes.'

'You aren't going to get any.' said Jock Hines.

I smile to myself. 'Okay let's move out.'

We drive out of camp in the direction of Albertville. After about 30 minutes, the radio kicks in.

'B Troop this is D Troop how do you read – Over.'

'This is B Troop - loud and clear - Over.'

'We are about half a mile ahead of you – Over.'

'We will be with you in about 5 minutes - Over.'

'Roger - Out.'

I ask Alistair why he joined up.

'My wife was having another baby, the money was tight, I saw an advert in a magazine, went for an interview, and here I am. I haven't regretted it one little bit. My wife doesn't like it though.'

I got to know Alistair very well and I liked him a lot. I put the point about becoming an Officer to him.

He replied, 'The Colonel has been on at me for ages to become an Officer. But I like it with the lads too much.'

I can see his point and don't push the subject. The radio crackles into life again. 'B Troop this is D Troop, you are about 300 yards from us - Over.'

'Roger - Out.'

'They are just up ahead Guv.' said Frank.

'Thanks mate.'

We pull up alongside their two jeeps and the Troop Commander; Jeremy Wilkins gets out and walks over to me.

'Hi - I'm Jeremy, welcome to the arse end of the world.' He said holding his hand out.

I shake his hand and tell him my name.

'What's the situation then Jeremy?'

'We found five bodies, pretty badly mutilated, about six hundred yards down that track. I think it could be an ambush. The same thing happened a few days ago. You take the left flank and proceed up the side of the track and we will come in from the right.'

We remount our vehicles and proceed slowly forward.

BANG - BANG - BANG! Shots are fired at us.

'DISMOUNT!' shouts Alistair.

The vehicle immediately comes to a halt and we all dive for cover. I take up cover behind the front wheel as that is the safest place to be at the moment. Bullets take a long time to get through an engine block. Alistair joins me. Bullets are hitting the ground all around us. A rocket explodes about 40 yards out. Over the radio, Jeremy informs me he is coming in at the rear of the rebels.

BANG - BANG - BANG! - The sound of an FN on auto. A loud scream is heard. I hope it is one of theirs. BANG - BANG -BANG! - Another burst of automatic fire, another scream. From the bushes in front of us, three men appear carrying rifles. They look like beggars. I fire a burst at them and they fall to the ground screaming loudly. Alistair kills the remaining rebel with a well-aimed shot from his pistol.

'Watch yourselves there is bound to be more of them in a minute.'

Before Alistair could stop speaking, five rebels run at us from the left. Jock, Frank and Colin fire a hail of lead at them - the rebels fall in a heap - all dead. Three more appear from the right. I throw a grenade at them. The rebels are killed instantly. Christ! This is dangerous. I hear the sound of a .5 Machine Gun and everything goes quiet. The radio crackles back into life.

'Dave, I think we have got them all, come up the track about 200 yards.'

We re-mount our vehicles and drive up the track until we see "D" Troop. Jeremy comes towards me.

'The little buggers nearly got me that time,' he said wiping blood away from above his left eye.

We check the dead - there are 18 of them. I pick up a funny looking weapon. The writing on it is in Russian. Frank looks at it.

'It's an AK47, I haven't seen one for ages.'

I asked him what was so special about this type of weapon.

'It's more reliable than ours; it uses the short round 7.62 and is accurate for at least 600yds can I have it Guv?'

'It's yours mate.' I said handing him the weapon.

'Let's move on.' Jeremy said.

We remove the assorted weapons and leave the bodies to rot in the sun. There won't be much left after the scavengers have finished with them. We re-mount our vehicles and Jeremy takes the lead.

'Keep about 200yds apart.' He said as his vehicle moves off.

After about 5 minutes, the radio comes to life.

'We have found some rebels in a wadi about 400yds ahead, dismount your vehicles.'

I check the map and see that we can get ahead of them as the wadi turns off right about 500yds further on. These rebels must be some of the ones that got away from the fire fight. We dismount and move to cut them off. Sure enough, six ragged men appear. They are slowly walking along the bottom of the wadi.

'Use grenades.' I whisper.

Eight grenades wing their way into the wadi, right at their feet. They all explode within milliseconds of each other. There is no screaming and everything goes quiet. After a few minutes we all climb down into the wadi and I see that two men have no heads, two have no arms and legs and the sides of their heads missing and two have so much damage done to their bodies, they are hardly recognisable as human beings. One of the bodies looks like it is only 12 years old and probably is. Why do they do it, I will never know - they can't win - they haven't the weaponry we have, nor the fire power. Will they ever learn? The portable radio bursts into life.

'SITREP, SITREP, this is Sunray, Over.'

Frank, who is carrying it comes over and hands me the microphone.

'Sunray this is Sunray B Troop, 24 rebels killed, no casualties on our side, and no prisoners taken either, over.'

'Return to base, over.'

'Roger, Wilco, Out.'

I feel dejected, this is the first time I have killed anyone - and it troubles me greatly.

We remount our vehicles and meet up with "D" Troop and drive back to base in silence. I'm dropped off at the Officers Mess and go inside.

'How did it go mate?' John asks.

'I killed my first human beings today John, it happened so fast, it was instinctive.'

'That's what we joined up to do mate, it's them or us.' He said putting his arm round my shoulder.

'I hope I don't get to like it John.'

The Colonel enters the Mess.

'I have just bumped into your Troop Sergeant Dave. You did well in your first action. He said you took to it like a duck takes to water. Keep it up, I'm proud of you.'

I felt as if I had the world on my shoulders.

'Will you excuse me Colonel?' I said walking out of the Mess. I had to be alone for a while. I had just killed someone and felt sick.

Major Thomas is coming towards me.

'I've just heard you have been in action? Well done, how many were killed?'

'We killed 24 Sir.'

'I know how you feel son, it is always like that at first, come on, I'll buy you a drink.'

'I hope I don't get to like it Sir, the killing I mean.'

'As long as you feel something, you will be okay - remember - a human will kill for no reason at all, only animals kill for something.'

I don't understand what he has said, but don't push the subject.

We return to the Mess and I apologise to the Colonel, who puts his arm round my shoulders.

'If you didn't feel the way you do at this moment, I would think there is something wrong with you, I won't say you will get used to it, but it does come easier. Always remember, they will kill you in a horrific way if they can, the rebels may be human beings, they don't act like them, does that make sense to you.'

'Yes I think it does Sir.'

I go into dinner and then go to my room. I try and write a few lines to Kathy, but give up after a couple of minutes. I think what happened this afternoon has something to do with it. I am sure Kathy must be worrying where I am.

Over the next few weeks, the Troop is sent out to different areas to deal with the armed rebels. We kill loads of them. They are a ragged army of misinformed people who don't know when to stop. John has his first encounter with a band of rebels and narrowly missed being killed by a homemade grenade. He has a few cuts across his back but nothing serious.

I receive information that the rebels will be using a train to get out of a village. UN soldiers are seen on the train, so this must mean that they are taking sides. The President has said that he will pay 10 shillings for every rebel killed. I go and see John and tell him the news.

'Bloody heck mate, we could get extremely rich.'

I tell him about the UN helping the rebels. 'Can't we do something about it Dave?'

'Yes, I think we can.' I explain my plan to him.

'Let's do it.' He replies.

Both of us go to the stores and pick up a .5 machine gun and 5 boxes of ammunition. I grab Alistair and 4 of the Troop and drive out of the camp.

'Where we going Guv?' asked Frank.

'We are going to get rich and blast some rebels, check the radio works.'

After an hour, we arrive at the rail junction going into Elizabethville.

'Set the machine gun up on the water tower.' I tell John,

'The rest of you take cover behind that mound and wait for the fireworks.'

There is a good line of fire from the tower and I sit down and wait. 20 minutes go by when I hear a whistle.

'The fun is about to begin.' I tell John, 'I'm sure the UN would never escort rebels.'

I look through my bino's and see UN soldiers on the flat beds.

'What are they doing, outside the carriages?'

I put a burst of fire into the train - the engine immediately comes to a stop. The UN soldiers leap off of the flat beds and hide on the opposite side to us. Strange, they haven't returned fire. I put another burst into a carriage and it explodes.

'The bastards are carrying explosives.' Shouts John.

A few rebels now return fire at us, but it is pretty ineffective. I put another burst into a carriage. That explodes as well. If those guys down there are UN, I'll eat my hat. I fire at the flat beds and kill a few men with blue helmets on. They start running up a bank to get away from us. I put a burst into them and kill six more. There are about 40 bodies scattered about on the ground. Nothing is moving. I remove the .5 from the tower, it is pretty hot to handle.

'I want to check the bodies of those UN soldiers.'

We cautiously move forward to the train. The first body I look at has UN insignia on its jacket arm.

'I was right, these sods are rebels.'

John helps me to pick up a body and put it into our jeep.

'That thing is evidence.' I tell the lads.

We return to camp and I take the body over to the Intelligence Section.

'Ah! Ha!' said the Intelligence Officer, 'He must be one of the little shits who killed that UN Patrol last week, where did you get him?'

I tell him that we zapped a train which was carrying explosives and the dead man was one of about 40 who were on it.

'Well done Dave, I'll inform Colonel Mike, he will get in touch with the UN Commander in Albertville, good work. Hey, they might give you a medal for this.'

We go and get some grub and Colonel Mike comes into the Mess.

'Good news and bad news, which do you, want first?'

'You may as well give us the bad news first Sir.'

'The President has withdrawn his statement concerning the 10 bob a head for each rebel killed.'

'Oh Shit - I was, going to be rich.' John said, kicking over a chair.

'Temper - Temper.' said the Colonel.

'And the good news?'

'You have all been given a UN medal by the UN Commander for your actions concerning the train.'

Our first medals and they come from the UN, how nice.

The days go by and we are involved in more and more shoot outs. I am sitting in the Mess when the Ops Room runner comes looking for me.

'Sir, you are wanted urgently over in the Ops Room.'

I rush to the Ops Room and am told that a farm is being attacked about 25 miles due east of the camp.

'Get your Troop together and get out there as fast as you can and see what can be done.' said the Ops Officer. 'And don't get killed.'

I run to the Troop Lines and get hold of Alistair.

'Get the men together; we have an urgent job to do.'

Having briefed them on the situation we pile into the jeeps and roar out of camp. Colin, who is my bodyguard, hands me my maps. The radio crackles into life.

'B Troop this is A Troop. We are coming as well, over.'

Before I can answer – 'B Troop this is C Troop, us too.'

Three Troops for the operation must mean it is pretty serious.

We arrive at the farm and see dead bodies everywhere. As they haven't been removed, it means that the rebels are still around.

'Fan out and be careful, I don't want any casualties.'

A window opens in the farm house and we hit the ground. A voice shouts.

'The bastards are still here somewhere, so watch out.'

It is the farm owner, an Ex Parachute Regiment major. We get up off the ground and start to creep forward to an outhouse. BANG! Colin is hit in the throat and falls to the ground. I see who has fired the shot and put a burst of 7.62 into him. He dies instantly. I bend down and see blood pouring out of the wound in Colin's throat. I remove my beret and stuff it into the wound.

'Jock!' I shout, 'Get over here with your medical kit – hurry. Frank - get on the radio, I want a chopper here ASP, if not sooner.'

Jock shouts that he is pinned down by a sniper. I look at Colin and tell him everything will be alright. Frank is screaming into the mike giving map references of our position. I pick Colin up and drag him towards the farm house door. Bullets hit the ground all around me. I kick it in and lay Colin on the kitchen floor and shout to Jock to get to me fast.

'Fuck it.' I hear Jock shout.

There is a burst of fire as Jock tries to run towards the house. Bullets are whistling around him, and he has to hit the deck.

'Hang on!' he shouts.

I sit on the floor and cradle Colin's head in my lap.

'Help is on the way mate, you will be okay.'

Colin looks up at me and blood spurts from his mouth. He tries to say something and dies. I'm covered in his blood and lay his head down. Tears form in my eyes. Damn! Fucking Damn! Why Colin. He was my mate and a darn good mate at that. I take off my jacket and lay it over his face. Jock flies through the door and stops dead.

'Oh, No!'

'He died in my arms Jock.'

'I'm real sorry Dave, I couldn't move because of that bloody sniper, had I got here sooner, perhaps I could have saved him.'

'You wouldn't have been able to do anything Jock, his throat was blown away.'

Firing is still going on outside. "A" Troop has found a bunch of rebels holed up in some outhouses. "C" Troop is engaged in a battle with some rebels on the north side of the farm. My own Troop is mopping up south of the farm. The owner comes down from upstairs and sees the body on the floor.

'I am sorry; the man who killed your friend was my servant. I didn't know he was a rebel.'

'No one knows who is, nowadays.' I tell him.

The chopper arrives and takes Colin's body back to base. The shooting stops and we check out the whole area. We have killed 40 rebels. The owner of the farm thanks us for our help and again apologises for the death of Colin. As we are about to leave, fire is directed at us from some trees.

'I thought the area was secure?' I shout.

36 men and three .5 machine guns return a hail of lead nothing could live through. The rebels are completely cut to shreds.

'Don't fuck with us you bastards.' John shouts.

I receive another call on the radio. We have to get to another farm about 3 miles away. Rebels have attacked and are burning the house. We speed off and arrive 20 minutes later. There are no dead bodies about. The farm house is in flames.

'Where are the occupants?' Jerry asks.

A check of the area finds the farmer and his family tied to trees. Their bodies had been mutilated and it could be seen that the women had been raped - semen was running down between their legs. They even raped a little girl who couldn't be more than 5 years old. These people are bastards. I remember Cyril's words, when we first arrived. I must get a grip of myself; otherwise I could make the wrong decisions.

'Cut them down and give them a decent burial, see if you can find out who they were Jonesy, I'll need to have the information for handing in when we get back to base.'

'Will do Guv.' he replies.

God - I hate this place - call these people civilized - they are out and out scum bags.

We continue to patrol the area and find a band of rebels holed up in a disused mine. They give up without a fight and we take them prisoner.

'Shoot them.' said John, 'They are not worth taking back.'

I tell him that if we did that, we would be lowering ourselves to their level. He nods in agreement. The rebel's hands are tied behind their backs and they are then thrown face down into the back of one of the jeeps.

One of the rebels starts talking. He tells us that they were a skirmishing party ahead of the main force.

'How many men are coming?' I ask him.

He doesn't reply.

'Pull him out, and tie one hand to that tree there, and the other to the vehicle.'

Frank knows what I am about to do and stems a laugh. The rebel looks frightened.

'What are you going to do man?' the rebel screamed.

'If you don't tell me what I want to know, I'm going to pull you apart and feed your heart to the hyenas.'

The rebel's eyes open wide and there is a stench of shit in the air as he craps himself. He tells us everything we want to know, in fact, we can't stop him talking he is so scared. I radio the information back to base so that reinforcements can be sent to the area. One of the rebels still in the jeep shouts something at the man in his native tongue.

'Pull that man out?'

Frank drags the man out of the vehicle and throws him onto the ground.

'What did you say to him?' I demand, pointing to the chap who has shit himself.

The man spits on the floor. How I don't kill this man, I will never know, especially after seeing the atrocities his comrades had committed on the farmer and his family.

We put the man back onto the vehicle and make our way back to base. On the way we meet up with some Belgian troops. I relay what the rebels have told us and hand them over to the Platoon Commander who said he would take them back to Albertville for further questioning. I very much doubt if the rebels will ever get to Albertville alive, but then, who cares. We return to base and together with John and Jeremy go to the Ops Room for debrief, and then on to the Officers Mess. It has been a long day and I need a drink.

I am just walking into the Mess when I am summoned back to the Ops Room. I have to go back out on patrol. This time I am to lead 4 Troops of men.

'Blimey - What's going on?' I ask.

I'm told that a farmer has just sent in details of a band of rebels who have taken 4 Nuns prisoner and have holed up in a quarry. I get the map reference and go to find Alistair.

'Not another job Dave? We have only just got back.'

We leave the base in single file. I pity the guys at the back, covered in dust. We have about 36 miles to cover. Unfortunately the track is rather dusty so we may be seen coming. It can't be helped. After what seemed like days, I halt the convoy. I call the Troop Commanders over.

'We are about 500yds from the quarry. We will leave a few men here to watch the vehicles and then proceed on foot. The rebels will kill the women if they see us and I want to avoid that. John take half of Paul's men and covers the rim. Jeremy, you take the rest of the men and lay ambushes on all the tracks leading out of the quarry. I don't want any of them escaping to fight another day. Be careful, I don't want any casualties on our side. My guys will give us covering fire when we go in and get the women out. John I want you to cause as much noise as possible, to divert their attention.'

'Who is going into the camp to get the women out then?' asked Jeremy.

'Me and Alistair.'

'When did I volunteer for this?' Alistair asked.

'Just now.'

'Cheers mate.'

The men take up their positions around the quarry. So far so good, we haven't been seen. Me and Alistair move down into the quarry and I suddenly see the women. They don't look as if they have been harmed yet. They are guarded by what looks like a small boy with a spear.

'Forget his age Alistair; take him out when I tell you.'

Alistair nods and screws a silencer to his .45 pistol. I now wait for John to cause the diversion.

All of a sudden, I hear shouting. The rebels run towards the sound.

'Take him out.'

Alistair shoots the kid in the head and he falls to the ground without uttering a sound. We run towards the women and whisper to them not to make a noise if they wanted to get out alive. I tell them to follow Alistair; I stay behind to cover them. Once they are clear I return to the safety of the rocks. John sees me get the women out and then starts to rain fire onto the rebels. There is total confusion and the rebels start shooting each other in fear. Many of the rebels die without knowing what is going on. After a time, everything is quiet. We don't bother to check to see if they are dead or not and make our way back to our vehicles.

Once safely in a jeep, I ask the women if they are alright.

'Yes.' they reply.

They are Nuns from the Mission.

'Did the rebels harm any of you?' I asked them.

'I think they were about to when you turned up, God thanks you.'

I radio base and inform Sunray that we have got the women and are returning.

'Well done, Sunray Out.'

On arrival back at base, I take the Nuns to our medical room for a check-up and then we report to the Ops Room for debrief.

'Congratulations Dave, I wouldn't have done what you did, and I have been out here over 2 years.' Said Steve.

'Good on you.' Paul said. John comes over. 'You are fucking nuts mate,' he said shaking my hand. I don't know what the fuss is about; I had the best men in the world with me. I see Major Reynolds and I tell him how Alistair helped me and that I was recommending Alistair for a medal. He agrees to forward the request to the proper authorities.

After the debrief I go to the Mess and get the Mess Steward to take over to the Troop lines 12 cases of beer, they deserved it. I still haven't written to Kathy or my parents. I know John still hasn't written to his mum either. We are stood down for a day and John and I lounge about in the Mess. A runner enters.

'Are Mr Stubbs and Mr West here?'

'Yes,' we answer.

'You are both wanted in the CO's office.'

We thank him and report to Colonel Mike.

'You want to see us Sir?' I ask him.

'Yes, come in and shut the door both of you.'

We stand by his desk.

'Sit down the pair of you.'

We sit in the arm chairs and wait for him to finish what he is writing.

He looks up and says, 'I understand that you both have not told your parents what you are doing?'

'We tried writing but with all the training and then the operations we have been on, there hasn't been much time, why Sir?'

I look at John and he looks at me.

'I had a letter from your father Dave, he informed me that you are both under 18, is that correct?'

'Yes Sir.' We tell him.

'Damn.' he replies.

This is the first time I have ever heard Mike Hoare swear.

'You know I will have to send you both home, don't you? I can't have you out here now.'

'We will be 18 soon.' I tell him.

'I have made my decision, you are relieved of your commands immediately and confined to the Mess, you may go.'

I try to talk to him, but he won't listen. We leave his office and return to the Mess.

'Well - we had a good bash, didn't we mate,' said John.

We have been in the Congo 11 months and now we were being sent home - Blast. I was really enjoying being a Troop Commander, I will miss the lads. This is the first time that I have really been content in a job, and now it's over. Shit - Shit - Shit! Major Reynolds enters the mess.

'The Colonel has just told me about you two - I'm sorry to lose you - especially after the great job you did rescuing those Nuns - your lads think highly of you as well - good luck.'

He holds out his hand and in turn we shake it.

We have dinner and Major Thomas comes over to our table.

'I am sorry to see you go, you have done a damn good job since coming out here. I have asked the Colonel if he would reconsider his decision, but he won't and I will not try and change his mind again. By the way, Dave, you have been awarded a medal for Brave Conduct in the Field. The President is making the Citation out at this very moment, congratulations.'

'I'm not interested in me Sir; I hope Alistair has got a medal for his part in the operation, because he sure enough deserves one.'

'I can put your mind at rest; he will also be getting the same medal.'

'Thanks Sir.'

'Alistair will be taking over your Troop, and he has now accepted the rank of Lieutenant.'

'I'm very pleased, he is a great guy and the lads think a lot of him.'

'I'll see you before you go.' Thomas said leaving us to get on with our dinner.

I return to my room pretty dejected. Jeremy bangs on the door and enters.

'I have just heard the news, I'm going to miss having you around, we have had some pretty hair raising times together haven't we?'

I shake his hand and offer him a drink from a bottle I have kept in a drawer.

'Your very good health old friend, and the best of luck.'

Morning arrives and we have got to go to the pay office to collect our final pay and air tickets. We are both given £200 in English currency and a ticket back to the UK.

As we are about to leave the office a clerk comes up to us and hands each of us an envelope.

'The CO said to give this to you.'

I open my envelope and find inside £1500.

'The Colonel has paid you your Bounty.' The clerk said shaking our hands.

'Stone the crows we didn't even complete the year.'

We have to leave the camp straight away. Outside the pay office, a jeep is waiting to take us to the airport. Frank is the driver. He gets out of the jeep and walks towards us.

'I'm going to miss you Dave, we had some damn good times didn't we.'

We drive over to the Mess and get our things. I'm going to miss being a Mercenary.

As we are about to drive out of the camp gate, Major Thomas stops us.

'This is yours Dave.' He said, handing me a small box and a large envelope.

I open the box and find a medal. It is the highest award that can be given to a foreigner by the President.

'You deserve it, good luck.'

Alistair runs over to us.

'Thank Christ I have caught you, I just want to say, It's been a pleasure working with you, good luck in Blighty, keep your head down mate, I'll miss you, you too John. I hate saying goodbyes, see you.'

He then runs off without looking back. I'll miss him as well.

Frank drives us to the airport and we board the plane to Johannesburg. The flight is 13 hours long. Nothing like the trip we made in the Dak. The Colonel never saw us off, nor did he say goodbye. I do know he would be thinking of us though. Mike Hoare is one the finest men I had ever known, I will miss him greatly.

This episode in my life has turned me into a man. I will take no shit from anyone ever again. As the plane leaves the ground we say goodbye to the Congo. We will miss it and the friends we had made. Be safe old friends. The journey is in silence. On arriving in Johannesburg we have to wait 2 hours for the flight to Durban.

Nothing is said between us and we read magazines that are scattered about. Finally, we board the plane for Durban and the journey is again in silence. On arrival in Durban we get the Swiss Air flight to Heathrow. As the plane leaves the ground, we wave goodbye to Africa and all the friends we made whilst serving with the best mercenary unit in the world.

CHAPTER FIVE

We have returned to England and are about to board the train to Portsmouth. Everyone is looking as us because we have got the deepest tan for miles around.

'Cor blimey mate, where you been?' A small boy asks pulling a suitcase on wheels.

'Brighton!' John replied.

Having settled down in a carriage, I start to read the "Weekend," which I had just bought at W H Smiths. John is reading a book he has bought. I can't see the title because he keeps it in his lap.

'I see here, that on the 24th July, 24 passengers took the first trip on the Hovercraft service between Rhyl and Wallesey.'

'Uh!' replied John not looking up from his book.

'Here's a snippet, Stirling Moss is recovering from his 110 mile an hour crash which he had at Goodwood on the 23rd April, he must have lost concentration, because he is a bloody good driver.'

'Uh - Uh!' replied John still not looking up from his book. John starts giggling to himself, and I continue to read the "Weekend." Every now and then, John starts laughing.

'What's so funny?' I ask him.

'It's this guy keeps getting his leg over.'

I take the book out of his hands. It is Lady Chatterley's Lover.

'Dirty Sod.'

He grabs the book and continues reading and giggling to himself.

The train finally arrive at Portsmouth harbour station, and we lug our suitcases down the ramp to the ferry for Gosport.

'I'll get the tickets.' John said walking to the ticket kiosk.

'Bloody Hell!' He exclaimed, 'They have put the price up to 3d (1½p), the price of oil must have gone up.'

That is a 100% rise in under a year, why I don't know, hundreds of people use the ferry every day of the week, 364 days a year.

The boat arrives at Gosport, and we go up the ramp to the bus station.

'Sod this.' I exclaim, 'Let's get a taxi we can afford it.'

We move towards a taxi and the driver gets out and opens the vehicles boot for us to put the cases in.

'Strewth! Where did you get that tan?'

'Brighton.' I tell him.

He looks at us with a puzzled look.

'Where do you want to go?'

'61, Cherry Road, we'll tell you when to stop.' I tell him.

As we drive off, the driver starts asking questions about where we have been. I tell him that we have just come back from a couple of weeks in Brighton.

'I didn't think it was that hot. I was there last week and it pissed down with rain the whole time I was there.'

'Just drive sport and no more questions.' John tells him.

This guy is a typical taxi driver, wants to know the ins and outs of a donkeys arse.

We discuss what we are going to do now that we are back.

'I suppose I will try and get my old job back at the dairy if they will have me, if not, the dole I suppose.' John replied.

'I'm not going back to that wine shop, I will have to find something else to do, but what, I don't know.'

I want to see Kathy as soon as possible, to explain to her about not writing any letters. Perhaps if I give her the unfinished letter I have in my pocket, she will understand. I hope so.

The taxi enters Mill Lane we are only 5 minutes away from home. I am not looking forward to meeting my mum and dad and I know John is not looking forward to seeing his mother. The sparks are about to fly.

The taxi enters Cherry Road.

'Drop us here.' I tell the driver.

He stops and we get out. The driver takes our cases out of the boot.

'That will be 3 bob (15p).'

I hand him a £5 note and tell him to keep the change. His eyes open wide and he stammers,

'Th-Tha-Thank you, Sir.'

He gets back into the taxi and roars off down the road. That made his day, that tip was probably half his weeks wage.

'This is it, face the music time, again.' We say together.

We walk up the path and I ring the bell. My dad comes to the door.

'You are home then, your mum is in the front room John.'

We follow my dad into the house and John goes into the front room. My mum rushes up and hugs me.

'We have got a lot to talk about son.' My dad said.

John and his mother come out of the front room.

'We are going Molly, I will see you later.' Tina West said with her arm round John. My dad opens the door for them and they leave. I notice, John has forgotten his case and I shout after him.

'I'll pick it up tomorrow mate.' He replies, and they walk off arm in arm.

I walk back into the lounge just as my brother comes in the back door.

'Ah! Ha! The wanderer returns.' He said pouring some milk into a cup.

'Bollocks.' I reply.

'That's enough of that.'

My mother said handing me a cup of tea. It tastes real good, this is the first cup of tea I have had since going away. We only had coffee out there. I am not sure what to make of my mum and dad, because they haven't exploded. I drink my tea and my dad asked, 'Why didn't you tell us you were going away to be a Mercenary.'

'Come off it dad! Would you have allowed me to go if I had told you?'

'Possibly not.' he replied.

'Well, there you are then, that is why I never told you, in fact I didn't tell anyone what I was doing, no one knew.'

He did not reply at first and then said, 'We were worried, we hadn't heard anything from you and it took till last month to track you down.'

'How did you find out where we were?'

'John's mum found a magazine under his bed with an advert torn out, I rang the publishers and they told me about the advert, they knew who placed the advert but not the address, we saw in the daily paper that a Colonel Hoare was running a Mercenary Force in the Congo, so I wrote to him, he obviously got the letter, as you are now home.'

Trust John to cock it up again.

'We didn't have time to write, we were so busy with the training.'

'Well - did you kill anyone then?' my brother asked smiling. He was enjoying this.

I look at him with hate in my eyes.

'You bloody arsehole, Yes, I did kill people out there, that was what I was paid to do, I'm not proud of it, and it is nothing to boast about, wait till you have to do it, then you will know all about how it feels, you stupid sod.'

I am so angry with him.

'Calm down son, he didn't mean anything by it.' said my dad.

'I'm not sorry I went, in fact, had you not wrote to Colonel Mike, I would still be there, I enjoyed the adventure and the comradeship of the guys under me, do you know, I was the youngest Officer they ever had, and I was respected by everyone. I had guys who would lay down their lives for me, and one did. People depended on my decisions, NO! I'm not sorry I went, I'm not proud of the killings, it was them or us. I had one of my men die in my arms, his blood was all over me, and he gave his life protecting me.'

I go to my suitcase and pull out the medal and Citation.

'Here, this is the highest award you can get out there.'

My brother reads it and is apologetic. He passes it to my dad who then passes it to my mother. She has tears in her eyes.

'Can I frame it son?' Asked my father.

'Do what you like with it dad, it is of no use to me, here, you may as well have the medal as well.'

My mother gets up from the table and leaves the room. I can see she is upset and my dad follows her out. I hear him speaking to her.

'There, there, he is back now.'

My brother picks up the medal.

'I'm sorry; it must have been hell out there.'

'You don't know the half of it, those blacks were utter bastards.'

I remember Colin and the bodies tied to the tree and the little girl. My eyes start to water. "I won't forget you Colin." I say to myself.

Things gradually get back to normal and I go round to see Kathy. I knock and her brother Jim answers the door.

'Yeh.' he asked.

'Hello Jim, is Kathy in?'

Jim looks at me puzzled, then exclaims, 'Bloody roll on - It's you Dave - I didn't recognise you with that tan - Christ! You really look black - come on in.'

I go into the house.

'Kathy! There is someone here to see you.' He shouts up the stairs.

'Who is it?' She asks.

'Get your fat arse down here and see.'

She comes down the stairs and looks at me.

'Can I, Oh my God, David, where in the bloody hell have you been? I have been worried out of my mind, I haven't had any letters from you, I went and saw your mum and dad every week and they hadn't heard from you either, where in the name of hell have you been?'

'Calm down and I will tell you everything.'

Before I can speak, she flings her arms round my neck and kisses me.

'I love you; I have missed you like mad.'

'I've missed you too darling.'

'You have a lovely tan Dave, you look like a nigger.'

'I don't know whether to take that as a compliment.' I tell her.

I then explain to her that I had joined a Mercenary Force in the Congo and that I tried to write to her, but did not have much time. I hand her the unfinished letter.

'Perhaps after reading this letter, you will understand that I was, telling you what I was doing.'

She opens the envelope and starts to read:

"My dearest Kathy,

Sorry I haven't written before, but I have been very busy. It is hard to tell you this, but, I have joined a Mercenary Force in the Congo. I know darling that I should have told you before I left, but I was worried just in case you let it slip to my parents. As you know, I will be out here for a year. The training is pretty hard, but I am enjoying it, I think. I finish late at night so it doesn't give me much time to write as I have to get up at 5am. Guess what, I am training as an officer and will soon command a Troop of 12 men. Tomorrow we are going parachuting, as the unit I have joined is an airborne one. I love you very much. I must close now, as the time is getting on. I will write tomorrow. 24th - Hello again darling, I'm really tired today. We have been jumping off of ruddy high towers all day and my back and bum hurt like mad. The food is great, and there is plenty of it. The pay is very good as well. We should have a tidy sum by the time I come home, as we get everything free here. The camp is rather dusty and the heat is at times unbearable. I'm getting a great tan, I look like a native. I will close now and try and write some more tomorrow. I love you. 30th - Hello again, write to the address at the top of the letter darling exactly the way it is written. It takes about

6 weeks for a letter to get here. Damn, I will have to stop as I am required for a lecture. I love you very much. I will write some more when I get back"

She puts the unfinished letter back in the envelope and looks straight at me.

'This has taken you nearly a year to write; couldn't you trust me not to say anything? I am your fiancé, I wouldn't have told your parents.'

'But you wouldn't have wanted me to go, now would you?' I tell her.

'You could have been killed and I would never have known.' She cried.

I could see things seem to have changed between us, and I get up to go.

'Where are you going now?' She asked. 'You have only just got back.'

'I didn't think you wanted me here.'

'Oh darling, of course I want you here, Oh Dave, I have missed you.'

Tears are falling down her face.

'Don't cry darling, everything is okay now.'

I tell her that I have been paid my Bounty of £1500 and that we can do what we like now. I am rich. (£1500 then, is about £15000 now) Jim has overheard everything.

'They have paid you what?' He exclaims.

'You heard right mate.'

'Bugger me!' He replied dropping a cup onto the floor and smashing it.

Kathy kisses me full on the lips and her eyes light up.

'Oh Dave, I love you lots.'

Does she love me or my money? I stay talking with her till late in the evening as her parents are away for the day.

I haven't seen John for a few days and decide to go and see him. As I walk up his path, he comes out of the house.

'Hi mate, what are you up to?' I ask.

'I thought I would look for a job.'

We are walking down the road when he suddenly says, 'Sod it lets go for a drink.'

We walk along Ann's Hill Road and into the Foresters Arms.

'Two pints of bitter barman.'

'Where have you two been to get a tan like that?'

'Brighton.'

'Get out of it, I was in Brighton last week and it was pouring with rain.'

We pick up our drinks and go over to the Gaming Machine.

'What's up mate?' John asked.

'I can't stand pricks like him, questions, questions and more bloody questions.'

'Have you been to see Kathy yet?'

'Yes, I went round to see her yesterday, you seen Sonia?'

'No, I think I had better go and see her, instead of looking for a job, come on drink up and let's go.'

John goes off to see Sonia and I walk off home. On the way I stop and buy a daily paper. I read that a Mercenary Force had killed a load of people in Chad, and they are calling them the "Dogs of War."

So Chad has flared up now, can't these wogs get their act together. Well at least we never had that title when I was in the Congo. We committed no atrocities and definitely never raped anyone like it says in this paper about the Chad Mercs. They must be led by a right prat. I know Colonel Mike would never have allowed that to happen. He treated his Regiment just like one in the British Army. Why are they decrying Mercs, it was an honourable profession and had been around for hundreds of years. (Today it is a different story) I enjoyed my time as a Merc; we did a good job for good pay. We helped a man rid his country of a rebel faction or at least tried to. I return home and throw the paper in the bin. Bloody biased paper, what do they know about Mercenaries. Unless you have been one, or served with them, you will only get a clouded view. Most of what is written in the papers is lies anyway.

It is Friday night and the dance is on at Bury Hall. I am not seeing Kathy because she has gone to see her aunty in Portsmouth. Sanity at last.

John comes round and says he has seen Sonia.

'That's just what you wanted wasn't it?'

'Well, Yes.'

'Come on mate, what's wrong?'

'I went round to where she was living and when I knocked the door; this bloke opened it dressed in only a towel. I asked him if Sonia was in and he told me to sod off as she was his girl. I saw red and smacked him in the mouth and took his towel and threw it over the next doors wall. He wasn't very big, if you know what I mean. The bitch couldn't even wait for me.'

'There are plenty more fish in the sea mate.'

'How are you getting on with Kathy?'

'Don't ask, it is, I WANT, I WANT, I WANT, that's all she can say, she is becoming a pain in the arse, it's not the same anymore, it was great when I first met her, but now, well.'

'I think I am going off women Dave.'

'Christ! You aren't turning are you?' I say to him laughing, 'Let's go to the dance?'

At the dance there is a live band called, "The Clyde Valley Stompers." I remember seeing them before I went away; they are a great Jazz Band. I bump into a girl I have seen in the paper shop, who is with her friend.

'Hello girls, I'm Dave and that (pointing over to the bar) is John.'

'Jesus! Where did you get that tan?'

'Brighton.'

'Pull the other one, Brighton my arse.'

She is called Jane and her friend is called Maureen. John returns with our drinks.

'Hello girls.'

'This is Jane and Maureen.' I tell him.

I can see John is taken with Maureen. I ask Jane for a dance and we leave John to get acquainted with Maureen. I find out that Jane doesn't have a boyfriend and only comes to the dances that have live bands.

'You work in the paper shop at the top of my road, how come you are not in there every day?'

'I usually work in the office at the back; I only help out in the shop if old Moggs is short staffed.'

'That explains it,' I tell her.

'Is it true that you are engaged to that stuck up cow Kathy?'

'Yes I am, but we are not getting on at the moment.'

'Really, you want to ditch her and come out with me, if you don't get on, what is the point staying together?'

'And what makes you think I want to go out with you?'

'I can see you are interested.'

Jane has a point, we haven't got on since I returned from the Congo, and the sparkle has gone out of our relationship. I don't mean sexually. I haven't had intercourse with her, and the only time I have touched her was on the train before I went away, so Jane could be right, I should seriously think about our relationship.

I look at John and Maureen, they are deep in conversation.

'They have hit is off, haven't they?'

'Are you going to tell me where you really got that tan Dave? Your Kathy has told everyone that you had gone to work for some Security Company in Africa. Is that where you have been?'

'I was a Mercenary in the Congo with John.'

She looks at me with her eyes and mouth wide open.

'Bloody Heck! Did you kill anyone?'

'I don't want to talk about it Jane, so please, don't ask any more questions.'

I excuse myself and go to the toilet. Jane rushes over to John and asks him about us being Mercenaries. On my return she is looking at me goggle eyed.

'What's the matter?' I ask her.

'So you are a hero? John has just told me what you did.'

I look at John and he replies, 'I thought you told her mate, sorry.'

'You are a devious little girl, aren't you, you deserve a spanking.'

'Oh, yes please.' She replies.

Jane is very easy to talk to, she has a bubbly personality and full of life, whereas Kathy is just the opposite. If it wasn't for Kathy, I could really fall for her.

'Was it as bad as they said it was in the papers, Dave?'

'You know, I don't have any idea what the papers said, we didn't get any, except the African ones. It was pretty dangerous at times. But, we had some pretty boring times as well. John nearly got killed by a grenade once, but, as you can see, he survived. Anything else you want to know?'

'I want you to tell me everything.' She replied.

'On your bike.' I tell her.

'Dave, can I ask you something?'

'Go ahead.'

'Do you like me?'

'Yes, of course I like you, why?'

'Is it enough to go out with me?'

'I'm engaged, I can't go out with you.'

'Chuck her Dave?'

'Enough of this Jane, if you carry on, I will go, you have to remember, I am, engaged to Kathy.'

'She is a gold digging bitch, you said so yourself, you will be better off without her.'

'Shut your mouth, not another word.' I tell her.

'Come on mate, she is only winding you up, she didn't mean anything.' John said coming over to the table.

I get up to go, Jane stops me.

'I'm sorry if I upset you Dave, I didn't mean to, it's just that, I quite fancy going out with you. But I know I can't.'

I can't believe what I am hearing, I have only seen the girl a couple of times in the shop, and though I thought she was nice, I didn't think too seriously about it.

'I have seen you with Kathy at the Coop on quite a few occasions and I knew you use to work in the Wine Merchants, so when you told me how your relationship with Kathy was going, it made me buck up the courage to tell you. I'm sorry if I have upset you.' said Jane with tears in her eyes.

'You haven't upset him Jane, if you had, you would be flat on your back holding a sore jaw.' said John.

'I don't hit girls, you know that John.' I replied.

'It has calmed you down though hasn't it?'

I start laughing.

'Are we still friends then Dave?' asked Jane.

I kiss her on the nose.

'Yes dear - we are still friends.'

'Thank goodness for that.' Maureen said.

We have a few dances and then leave. The girls are walked to the bus stop and we then walk off home.

'Well, that's an eye opener Dave, fancy Jane saying that, how could she fancy a git like you?'

'On yer bike John, it came as quite a bombshell when she dropped that in my lap.'

'What are you going to do about Kathy?'

'I don't know. Have you ever had that feeling you want to be with someone yet when you are with them, you want to get away? I have that feeling when I'm with Kathy, I love her lots, but, I can't stand being with her. I know I have to sort it out, but someone is going to get hurt whichever way it goes.'

'See you tomorrow mate, I hope you work it out.'

'You and me both John, see you mate.'

On the way home, I decide to end it with Kathy. She should be, back home now. I go round to her house and knock the door. Kathy answers it.

'Hello Dave, what are you doing round this late? We have just got back. Mum and dad have gone to bed, so be quiet.'

'I want to talk to you about us? It can't wait.'

'You had better come in then.'

I follow her into the lounge.

'As you know, we haven't been getting on lately and always seem to argue about things. I don't like arguing and it is beginning to upset me a bit. I think we should break off our engagement?'

She looks at me and takes the ring off of her finger and says, 'Ever since you went to Africa, I have been wondering whether we did the right thing. I didn't have the courage to say anything. I want to still go out with you, but I think you are right, we should break off the engagement.'

I then tell her, 'I think we should stop seeing each other as well.'

She looks as if she has been pole-axed and tears fill her eyes.

'Are you sure this is what you want to do, is there someone else?'

'There isn't anyone else I just can't stand the arguing we do. Perhaps we will feel differently after a break, I hope so, because I still love you and I know you still love me.'

'Dave, please go.'

'I'm sorry.'

I get up and kiss her on the cheek and leave. I close the front door behind me. I know I have hurt her, but it had to be done. I walk down the road and as I turn the corner, I hit out at a fence, smashing a panel right out. What did I do that for! Kathy was my first girlfriend and my first love. I will always have a soft spot for her in my heart.

It is Saturday and John comes round.

'I quite fancy that Maureen mate, when are you going to tell Kathy that you are going to finish with her?'

'How did you know I was going to?' I ask him.

'Dave, I have known you for hundreds of years, I know when you are going to do something.'

'I told her last night, she still wants us to go out together, but I said we had to finish completely.'

'I think it is for the best mate, you weren't the same guy, and she really must have fucked you up.'

'As I said last night, I love her, I want to be with her, but when I am, I want her to go. John, it is hard to explain.'

'Look mate, I understand, and anyway, there's Jane to think of now.'

I clip him round the head and go and make us some tea.

I don't want to think about girls yet, I have just finished with one I don't need another yet. We go to the pictures and watch the worst horror film we have ever seen.

'Well, that has really insulted my intelligence.'

'I didn't know it was going to be like that mate?'

We walk to the pub and have a few drinks, and then go home to bed. I still think of Kathy. I must get her out of my mind, but I can't.

Monday arrives and I find a job with a building merchant making sheds. The job doesn't seem too bad, but the pay is piss poor. Still I am earning something even if it is a pittance. I come home every day covered in wood dust. My mother isn't very pleased as it always falls on the floor when I take my coat off. How long I will stay with this firm, I just don't know. I will look for something better in a few weeks' time.

The week flies by and it is Saturday. I don't have any work, so I have a lie in. The doorbell rings and my mother answer's it.

'It's John for you Dave?' She shouts up to me.

'Tell him to bugger off; I'm having a lie in.'

He comes up the stairs and pulls the blankets off of me.

'Now What.' I ask him.

'Come on mate, get up, we have things to do and places to go.'

'Where are we going then?'

'Portsmouth!' He replied.

Oh No! Whenever we go to Portsmouth, something happens - like trouble. I remember the last time we went to Portsmouth we telephoned a number and ended up as Mercenaries. What hair brained scheme has he thought up this time.

I get up and wash. My mother has cooked me breakfast, which John is slowly eating.

'Do you want breakfast John?' asked my mother.

'No, it is okay Mrs Stubbs; I'll help Dave eat his.'

The cheeky sod.

'Well - what have you got lined up then?'

'I'll tell you when we are outside.'

My mother overhears what he has just said. 'I hope you are not planning something without telling your father and me David?'

'Don't worry mum, I'll tell you this time, but I don't know what this bugger has thought up yet.'

'It's alright Mrs S - It's nothing bad this time.'

'I hope you are right, what is it then?'

'It's a secret at the moment Mrs S, I don't know yet if we will be able to do it.'

Very sinister, what has the guy got up his sleeve this time?

We catch the bus to the ferry and the boat to Portsmouth.

'Okay mate, what have you got in mind?' I ask him.

'You know I have always wanted to join the Royal Marines, well, I want to find out all about them, because I have decided to join up.'

You could have knocked me down with a feather.

'You never mentioned you wanted to join the Marines to me.'

'Didn't I, I thought I did.'

Bloody hell! He really has flipped his lid this time.

'Why the Royal Marines they are a right loony bunch of people, they do daft dangerous things.'

'Then they should be the right outfit for us mate shouldn't they.'

Oh my God, he's finally cracked. I'm now 18 years old and have done things a 40 years old hasn't done, what in the name of hell do I want to join the Royal Marines for.

I didn't think Recruiting Offices were open on a Saturday, but they are. We walk into the Naval Recruiting Office in Commercial Road and up the large flight of steps to the office. In the office is a Chief Petty Officer in the Royal Navy. I know his rank because my cousin is one.

'Can I help you lads?' He asked.

'I would like to know about the Royal Marines?' John said.

'Right, hang about and I will get the Marines Colour Sergeant.'

He gets up from his desk and walks off into another office. After a few moments he returns with the biggest bloke I have ever seen.

'I understand you want to know about the Royal Marines?'

'We sure do.' John replies.

'Please sit down both of you.'

We sit in the chairs indicated and he explains the training, which will take from start to finish about 2 years. The depot training will take about 12 weeks and then on to Lympstone and Portsmouth. The pay is quite good as what you get in your hand is yours. Food is free and so is the accommodation. He hands us some forms.

'These have to be filled in by your parents?'

Ah! Ha! Saved at last, mine won't sign them.

We leave the Recruiting Office and the Chief Petty Officer asks us where we got our tans from. "The Congo," we both tell him walking down the stairs into the street leaving them looking at each other.

In the evening we go to the pub. We both haven't got a girlfriend anymore. We get absolutely plastered. John stays the night as he can't stand up. The piss head, at least I could just about walk. I had to carry him into the house.

Sunday morning - and can I have a lay in - you must be joking, West is snoring louder than a fog horn on a ship. I throw a pillow at him and shout, 'QUIET,' but it doesn't make any difference, so I get up and go down stairs. My mother is making breakfast.

'Do you want some Dave?' She asked.

'No thanks mum, I couldn't face it.'

'What did you do yesterday?' My mother asked.

'You are not going to believe this, but John wants us to join the Royal Marines.'

'Don't tell me you are thinking of joining up?'

'I don't know mum, It's a big step, they gave us some forms to fill in which you have to sign, that is, if we decide to join up.'

My brother had joined the Army, so I don't somehow think she will be very pleased with me wanting to join up as well. John comes down just in time for lunch. We all discuss the possibilities of joining the Royal Marines with my dad. He isn't exactly pleased with the idea, and said so.

He put forward the pros and cons and then said, 'I suppose, if you do join up, at least we will know where you are, the Royals are a real tough outfit, you may find the training too hard.'

'Dad, I've had the hardest training in my life in the Congo, so this shouldn't worry me none.'

'Well if you have made up your mind, I won't stand in your way, give us the forms and I'll sign them.'

I can see my mum isn't too pleased. We have now to convince John's mum that joining up is the right thing to do. The mind boggles. I don't really know yet whether I want to join up, and if I do, should it be the Royal Marines. I just don't know.

Monday morning and John is on the door early. He has convinced his mother to sign the forms.

'I have to think about this mate, I'm not sure I want to join up.'

'Well, I'm going to join up; I've had it with being every ones dogsbody.' John replied.

'I'll listen again to what they have to say and then decide.' I tell him.

We arrive at the Recruiting Office and ask for the Colour Sergeant. We hand him our forms and he reads through them.

'I notice you haven't put your last job down, why is that?'

'We were Mercenaries in the Congo.'

'I damn well knew it. I said to Sam, I thought you were Ex Mercs.'

We are given some tests to do which we pass with flying colours. I still don't know if I will join yet. The Colour Sergeant outlines the procedures for entry.

As we had got very high marks, he tells us that we should be able to do any job we liked in the Royal Marines. He then went into greater detail about the training we would be getting. It seemed pretty hard but nothing I couldn't handle, IF, I joined. I ask a load of questions concerning pay etc., which he answers fully.

'Well Dave, are you coming with me?' asked John.

'Yes mate, I'm with you.' I reply.

'That's great.'

There is no problem with the medical and our forms are stamped **"FIT FOR SERVICE IN HER MAJESTY"S FORCES."** We get dressed and return to the Colour Sergeants Office. CSgt Read informs us that the Major won't be in until 2 o'clock, so we will have to come back then to get sworn in.

Instead of waiting, we go to the pub and get rat arsed. I look at my watch and tell John we should get going as we have to be back at the Recruiting Office at 2pm. We leave the pub and wander down the road until we finally enter the Recruiting Office.

'I'm sure we went up some stairs John.' I say to him in slightly slurred speech.

'You sure mate, how many Recruiting Offices have they got in Portsmouth?' He replies in just the same slurred speech.

'I don't know, but I don't think this is the right one, I'm sure we went up some stairs.'

'Of course this is it, come on mate.' He replied.

We enter the Recruiting Office and speak to a chap in dark green uniform.

'We have to get sworn in; we signed all the papers and had the medical this morning.'

'Strewth, what did you do, celebrate?' He asked.

'We sure did,' we say together.

The man takes us into a room which has a desk with crossed flags behind it. A uniformed chap with a crown on each shoulder comes into the room and walks behind the desk. I presume this is the Major. He reads out a statement, which we repeat in turn. It is the oath of allegiance to the Queen. Once we have repeated the oath the Major hands each of us a shilling (5p), and shakes our hands.

'You should get your movement orders for Winchester in a couple of days; collect your Rail Warrants from the Sergeant in reception, good luck.'

I look at John and say to the major, 'Excuse me Sir, but we are supposed to be going to Deal, not Winchester.'

'There is no Army Training Centre in Deal that I know of, the only one there is for the Royal Marines.'

'That's correct Sir, we signed on for the Royal Marines, not the Army.'

'I'm afraid you have just enlisted in the Green Jackets, not the Royal Marines.'

'But we can't have, this is the Naval Recruiting Office, isn't it?'

'I'm afraid not, that's in Commercial Road, this is the Army Recruiting Office.'

'You bloody twit John, what is my old man going to say about this, he expects me to go to Deal, I told you this was the wrong bloody Recruiting office.'

'Never mind about your old man, what's my mum going to say, she hates the Army.'

'Bloody Hell! Can't you do something about this Sir; we took all the tests in the Naval Recruiting Office, including the medical.'

'You have taken the oath and received the Queens shilling, I'm afraid you are in the Army, I'll contact the Ministry of Defence on your behalf, and see what they say about it, until then, you are in the Army.'

'Trust you to make another cock up, why I get involved with you, I will never know.'

As we leave, I ask the guy in the green uniform which Regiment we have joined.

'Why mine of course, the 2nd Green Jackets.'

'Fucking hell, we have joined the fastest marching Regiment in the world, you daft bastard.'

'Sorry mate.'

On returning home my dad asks, 'How did you get on then son?'

'Don't ask dad, we have made right balls up.'

'What do you mean?'

'Well, we went to the Naval Recruiting Office and did all the tests and the medical, then went for a drink and ended up in the Army Recruiting Office, where we were given the oath and a shilling, so we are now in the Army instead of the Royal Marines, we tried to get out of it, but at the moment, we are in the Army, thanks to John.'

My mother comes into the room.

'You have joined the what?'

'The Army mum.'

'Oh my God!'

'I'm hoping it will be reversed, the Major is going to contact us about it.'

'Well son, you have made your bed, now you must lie in it.'

'I'll kill John, you see if I don't.'

I know one thing though, whichever one gets us, we can't get out of joining up.

I can't sleep through thinking about what had happened, John has a lot to answer for, mind you we both were as bad as one another, and we should never have gone on the beer.

Morning finally comes and I mope about the house. I'm just having a sandwich for lunch when the doorbell rings.

'If that is John, tell him to sod off.' I tell my mother as she answers the door.

'I have a Telegram for D Stubbs?'

'That's me.' I tell the Telegram Boy.

I tear open the Telegram and read that I am in the Army and not the Royal Marines, and have to report to Winchester as stated in the joining instruction that would follow. I tell the Telegram Boy there is no reply and close the door. I'll kill the bastard, I really will. This will teach me to stay away from beer, it never did agree with me.

A few days later I receive my joining instructions and meet John.

'I should kick your arse from here to bloody China, you Pillock; I'm in the fucking Army and can't get out of it.'

'I know it's my fault Dave, but we can make a go of it, okay, it's not the Royal Marines, but let's see how we go, you never know, we might like it.'

'You should have heard my mother; she flew through the air without her broomstick.'

'What a bloody mess, it does tell us one thing though.'

'What's that mate?'

'We leave the booze alone when we make decisions.'

'I'll agree with that.'

The dreaded day arrives and we make our way to Winchester. We don't speak much, I'm still sore about the cock up. Secretly, I think I'm to blame as much as John, but I don't tell him, I let him stew, it will be good for his soul.

We have joined the 43rd and 52nd Oxfordshire and Buckinghamshire Light Infantry, better known as the 1st Battalion Green Jackets, and not the 2nd Green Jackets as the Sgt had told us. The Regiment is based at present in Malaya. Our training will last 12 weeks. Boy! Oh Boy! Oh Boy.……..!

CHAPTER SIX

The train arrives at Winchester and we are met by a chap with a mini bus. 'All recruits for Bushfield Camp follow me.' he shouts. We pile into the back of the mini bus with our cases and proceed out of the town to a hutted camp on a hill.

'These bring back memories Dave?' asked John.

'They sure do – another bloody hutted camp.'

'You were in huts before then?' asked a pimpled faced youth, with a London accent.

'We sure have.' I tell him.

'Where was that then?'

'Africa.' I tell him.

'Oh.' He replied.

Well, "Oh" was better than, "Where's that then?"

After about 2 minutes, pimple face suddenly says, 'Ear! You was Mercenaries, I've heard about you lot.'

Before we can say anything the mini bus stops and the back door is opened.

'You lot, out.'

A guy with 2 stripes on his arm shouts, 'Parade in front of the Guard room with your cases, and answer your name when it is called.'

He's got to be a Corporal.

He reads our names out.

'Follow me and I will show you where your huts are, West, Stubbs and Riley, you are in Hut No 2, which is the last hut on the left down this path, the rest of you are in Hut No 4, which is the 2nd to last hut on the right of this path, dinner will be at 1700hrs, parade outside your huts at 1800hrs for the issue of bedding, DO NOT BE LATE, you are not in civvy street now, everything in the Army is dead on time, you have been warned.'

'What's 1700hrs?' Riley asks.

'5 o'clock, you stupid prat.' Said the Corporal.

Into the hut we go, which is nice and warm thank goodness. Inside we meet the rest of the Platoon. There are 22 of us in the hut, which has 11 beds along the length of each wall with a locker in between each bed.

We introduce ourselves. The Platoon is made up of men from Hampshire, Essex, Liverpool, Wales, London and Newcastle. The Corporal comes into the hut.

'Right, pick a bed and stand by it, I am about to give each of you a number, memorise it, it is yours for life.'

My number is 525625. It is a funny number, because my brothers started with 237. I ask the Corporal why we have different numbers than the rest of the Army.

'We in the Green Jackets have personal numbers issued by HQ and not by the MOD; does that answer your question?'

'Thank you Corporal.' I reply.

The Corporal eyes me and John up and down; he can see that we are a bit different than the rest of the Platoon.

'You two, been in the Services before?' The Corporal asks.

Pimple face shouts, 'They are Ex Mercenaries.'

'Who spoke to you, arsehole, speak only when spoken to, is that clear?'

'Yes Corporal.' Pimple face whimpers.

'Good, remember it. Is what the arsehole said true?'

'Yes Corporal, we were both Lieutenants in the 25th Airborne Regiment under Colonel Hoare in the Congo.'

'Were you now, I heard they were the best out there, did you see much action?'

'Yes Corporal, quite a lot.' I tell him.

'You don't give much away, do you Stubbs, just remember, you are in the British Army now and you do what we tell you, is that understood?'

'Of course, Corporal.'

'That's alright then.'

'Right, get over to the cookhouse for your dinner, and remember, be outside on parade at 1800hrs.'

We leave the hut and make our way to the cookhouse.

'I think we have got trouble with that Corporal, Dave.' John said.

'I think you are right mate.' I reply.

The dinner is absolutely revolting. I bloody well hope we don't have to eat this shit throughout our training. I don't know where the cooks were trained, but they want to send them back for more training. I bet the food was edible before they got their grubby mitts on it.

'I think I will stick to orange squash in future Dave, the tea is disgusting, have you tried it?'

'No, I saw your face when you tasted yours, so I left it alone.'

'Wise man,' said Arthur Peel.

'Can we do anything about this?' Tony Hatcher asked.

'I very much doubt it, but, we can try I suppose.' said Robbie Taylor.

Having returned to the hut we wait for 1800hrs. We pack our stuff away in our lockers and put the suitcases on top of it. I don't know whether this is right or not, but I'm sure the Corporal will enlighten us.

1800hrs arrives and we sort of march to the Bedding Stores. Inside the store we sign for everything. Each of us are given a mattress, mattress cover, 2 pillows, 2 pillow slips, 2 sheets, 4 blankets and a bed cover.

'Carry that lot back to your hut and I will show you how to make up a bed, Army style.' Said Cpl Sykes.

We cart the bedding back to the hut. Half the guys loose bits and pieces and have to go back for them. You can see that they are not use to Service life. We are shown the right way to make a bed.

'This is called a Bed Pack; your bed is to be made this way every morning before you come on parade. You can make your bed down, after you have finished training at about 1700hrs each day.'

I make my bed, and I can see that John is going to have fun, the bed is 6 foot long and John is 6 foot 4 inches tall. His problem, thank goodness and not mine. The Corporal then tells us that Reveille is at 0500hrs each morning. This must be the magic time that all Armies around the world use, and I bet there is a run as well.

'Once you have been kitted out, we will start the early morning runs.'

There! What did I tell you?

The Corporal leaves the hut and returns with a Sergeant.

'My name is Sgt Blacker, I am your Platoon Sergeant whilst you are under training, I have a staff of 3 Corporal, your Platoon Commander is 2nd Lt Soames who you will meet later, you have already met Cpl Sykes, the other two, Cpl's Hunt and Davis you will meet tomorrow, have you any questions?'

'Yes Sergeant, who do we make complaints to about the food in the Cookhouse?' Said Tony.

'Stone the Crows! You have only had one meal and you are moaning already, what's wrong with the food?'

'It was not cooked and the tea tasted like tar, everyone left their meal.' said Arthur.

'I will make a note of your complaint and pass it on to the Cook Sergeant, any other complaints?'

None were forthcoming.

'Thank God for that, you lot need toughening up. At 2000hrs you are to parade at the Bedding Stores for the issue of your personal kit. This kit is to be marked with your last 4 numbers, I will show you where to put the numbers on your kit once you are all kitted out, any questions?'

No one answered.

'Right, the rest of the evening is yours, make the most of it.'

'Let's go to the Canteen and have a drink.' Said Tony.

We all follow him over to the Canteen. On the wall in lights is the word "NAAFI." I wonder what that stands for. As we enter, I ask one of the recruits.

'It stands for Navy, Army and Air Force Institute, but we call it, NO AMBITION AND FUCK ALL INTERESTED.' Said the recruit, who is in the last few weeks of his training.

The Canteen is full of recruits in different stages of training. They all seem to be enjoying themselves. We have a few drinks and then at 2000hrs we collect our kit from the stores.

0500hrs - The magic hour. The lights come on and Corporal Sykes shouts for us all to get up. He is a good alarm clock, no batteries to run down.

'Get washed and shaved and parade outside, MOVE YOURSELVES.'

This is getting to be a nightmare. The Platoon parades and we are then walked around the Camp and shown places that we will need to know.

'At 0800hrs you will parade at the MI Room for jabs, at 1000hrs you will parade at the Admin Office for documentation, and at 1200hrs you will parade at the Hairdressers for an Army haircut, do not be late for any of these parades, because if you are, you will be charged for being late for a duty, you have been warned.'

Christ! This place is getting to be like a Concentration Camp. After breakfast we parade at the MI Room. I hope I don't get the blunt needle. It takes ages, as we have to have three injections each. 1000hrs - Admin Block parade, we go in, in alphabetical order. I finally go into the office.

'Who are you?' Demands a LCpl.

'525625 Rfn Stubbs, Lance Corporal.'

'Hang on here Rifleman.' He replies and goes off into another office.

After a few minutes he returns.

'You are to see the CO.'

I follow him down a corridor and the Lance Corporal knocks a door.

'Come in.'

It reminds me of when I was in the merchant navy and had to see the Captain.

We march into the office and stand to attention. The Lance Corporal salutes.

'Rfn Stubbs for interview Sir.'

'Thank you LCpl Brown.' Brown salutes and leaves.

'Stand at ease Stubbs, this is for you from a dear friend of mine.' He says, handing me a letter. 'He has told me all about your exploits in the Congo and that you were awarded the highest decoration a foreigner could be given by the President of Katanga. You are something of a hero by all accounts.'

'I don't class myself as a hero Sir; I did what anyone would do in the circumstances.'

'From what Colonel Hoare has told me, I doubt that very much, I shall be looking for bigger things from you in the future Stubbs.'

The CO picks up his telephone and speaks into it.

'Ask Sgt Blacker to come to my office?'

After a few minutes, Blacker knocks and enters.

'You wanted me Sir?'

'Yes Sgt Blacker, Stubbs and West are being sent to Mons Officer Cadet School. They will be promoted to Lance Corporals in the last week of training. HQ has decided that they should be given the chance to show what they can do. Stubbs was awarded a very high decoration by the President of Katanga for heroism in the field, look after him; he has friends in high places.'

'I don't understand Sir?' said Sgt Blacker.

'Stubbs and West are special people, it has been agreed that they are to be given every opportunity whilst in training to carry out leadership duties, have you any questions Sgt.'

'No Sir, it is, rather strange though.'

'Ours is not the reason why Sgt.' said the Colonel.

'No Sir.' Sgt Blacker replied.

'Right, you may go Stubbs; I will see you again later.'

I leave the CO's Office, my mind in a whirl. I join the Army and now

I'm going to be an Officer. Bloody hell! It's a strange world. I don't see anything of John; he must have gone in for documentation.

I wait with the rest of the lads outside the Admin Office, 20 minutes later John appears and stands beside me and whispers, 'Did you get put on Officer Training Dave?'

'Yes.'

Sgt Blacker comes out and calls us to attention.

'That's, your feet together.' Blacker shouts.

'Gentlemen, we have 2 Officer Cadets with the Platoon, they both have a wide range of experiences, and they will be helping me to get the Best Platoon Cup, won't you.' He says looking at me and John.

'If you say so Sergeant.' we reply.

'That is exactly what I say.'

I can see he is about to tell the Platoon about my award.

'Can I see you in private Sergeant?' I ask him.

'Come with me?' he replies.

I follow him to the edge of the parade ground.

'What do you want?'

'I would be grateful if you didn't tell the Platoon about my medal Sergeant.'

'If that is what you want, so be it.'

I thank him and we return to the Platoon.

'What did you say to him Dave?' John asks.

'I'll tell you later.'

We march to the barbers shop and the barber gives us all a Regimental Haircut, which is bloody short. We are all nearly bald. Arthur tries to bribe the barber to let him keep most of his hair, but ends up getting the shortest haircut he has ever had in his life.

The Platoon is told to fall out for lunch. I hope the food is better today, breakfast wasn't too bad, now let's see what lunch is like. We have the afternoon off to get our kit sorted out. John and I are called to the Adjutants office. We knock the door and he tells us to enter.

'I want to go over a few things with you both, before you actually start your training, from the records I have here, you were both Officers in a Mercenary Regiment under Colonel Mike Hoare and that you Stubbs, were awarded the President of Katanga's Citation, what is that?'

'It is the highest award that a foreigner can get for brave conduct in the field Sir.'

'I see, a hero, eh!'

'I don't class myself as a hero Sir anyone would have done what I did.'

'Very modestly put, but it still doesn't change anything, I understand that you both applied to join the Royal Marines and ended up in the Army, well it looks like the Marines loss and the Armies gain, how did this come about?'

We tell him what had happened and he bursts out laughing. I didn't think it was funny.

The Adjutant then explained that we would be going to Mons at the end of our training for 6 months Officer Training. We would have the rank of unpaid Lance Corporals. He went on to say that he expected a high standard from us and that we were not to let the Green Jacket Brigade down.

'Have you any questions?'

We both replied 'No', and leave his office.

'This is getting out of hand Dave, that's two interviews we have had and we have only been here a couple of days, I don't like it.'

'Nor do I John, and I don't trust that Sgt Blacker either, I can see we may have some problems with him.'

We return to the hut.

'Do you think we stand a chance of winning Blacker that Cup Dave?' Gordon asks.

'I don't see why not, as long as we pull together and work as a team.'

The week flies by, we are gradually shown what life is like in the Army. We get use to the fact that we have to get up early and carry out tedious minor routines. It is all pretty boring stuff, but the training starts in earnest on Monday.

Friday arrives and we are told that we can go home for the weekend. Sgt Blacker hands out leave passes which we fill in and he takes away to be signed and stamped. We finally meet 2Lt Soames, who is a right prick. Talk about a Hooray Henry, this prat really does take the biscuit. He has only just left Sandhurst and we are his first Platoon.

'I hope we will all get on together and make this Platoon the best in the Depot.' he said with a very high pitched voice.

Definitely suspect for a bandit.

Sgt Blacker returns with our leave passes and hands them out.

'Make sure you are all back in the depot by MIDNIGHT Sunday, I do not want ANYONE going absent, is that clear?'

'Yes Sergeant.' we all say together.

'Right, fall out and go on your way, have a nice weekend and return ready to start your training.'

Joe Bell comes over to me.

'Do you mind me asking Dave, but what was it like as a Mercenary?'

'It was very adventurous at first. The training was sheer murder, and we had to do parachute jumps. When I took over my Troop, we had many battles with the rebels they committed the most horrible atrocities that you could ever imagine a human being could commit. They were absolute bastards. In fact, they weren't human, because no human being would do what they did. In the end it got extremely dangerous and we were lucky to leave the Congo without being injured. John was nearly killed by a rebel grenade, and was lucky in that he only got a load of scratches to his back. I suppose I was really lucky, in not getting a scratch. My bodyguard was shot and he died in my arms, but I enjoyed the life. The Colonel was a smashing guy, and so were the lads in my Troop. Don't believe everything you hear and read about Mercenaries, not everyone acted like those arseholes in Chad.'

'You certainly seem to have led an adventurous life so far, what made you join the Army?'

'Now that Joe is another story, I think you should ask John about that.'

Joe goes over to John, and I presume, asked him about what I had just said. After about 10 minutes, Joe comes back with a smile on his face. It is obvious that John had told him about the cock up.

'You don't need enemies when you have John for a friend Dave.' I laugh and tell him I agree.

Having packed our cases we make our way to the Guard Room and show the Guard Commander our passes. A mini bus is waiting to take us to the station.

'Service with a smile.' Said the driver as we climb aboard.

We arrive at Winchester station and wait for the train to Fareham. It is delayed for half an hour, so we go to the buffet.

'Well, what do you think so far Dave?' John asks.

'I haven't a clue mate, we have only been doing the admin bit all week, and I'll save judgement till we start the training.'

The train arrives for Fareham and we climb aboard.

'Are you going to the dance tonight Dave?'

'I may as well you never know who might be there.'

'I hope that Maureen is, I fancy getting into her knickers. She really turns me on.'

'Sex starved maniac, is that all you can think of?'

'It's enough for starters mate.'

From my pocket I pull out the letter the CO had given me.

'I forgot this; it is a letter from Mike Hoare. The CO gave it to me on my first interview.'

'What has he got to say?'

'If you hang on a minute, I'll tell you, I haven't read it yet. I forgot all about it till now.' I open the letter and read:

"Dear Dave,

I am sorry that I did not see you off at the airport. I was too upset at you going. You did a great job out here, for which I am truly grateful. We will miss you. I hope the payment of the Bounty went a long way to helping you get back to normality and that you enjoyed spending it. By the time you get this letter, you will have already joined the Army. Colonel Miles is a very good friend of mine and has been for 25 years. I chuckled when I heard about the Royal Marines mix up, so unlike you. Trust John to do something like that! Don't ask how I found out about it. It is getting very bad out here. The left hand doesn't know what the right hand is doing. They have arrested Moise Tshombe for treason and we are hoping that they will let us get out of the country shortly, without harm. Must close, keep in touch via James Mills; he will know where I can be contacted. Keep up the good work. Give my regards to John. Bye for now,

Yours aye,

Mike."

I hand John the letter.

'How did he find out about us joining the Army?'

'I have no idea; he probably has friends in the MOD, or something like that.'

The train arrives at Fareham and we get the bus home. We have arranged to meet at the Dance in the evening. It is nice to be back home after living in a barrack room. There is nothing like a bit of privacy and you can only get that, if, you have your own room.

I go to the shops and bump into Kathy.

'Hello! How are you getting on?'

'I'm okay, I started a new job in town, I have still got your ring. Do you want it back?'

'No Kathy, that ring is yours, I bought it for you, put it on another finger, but please keep it.'

'Are you seeing anyone else?' She asked.

'Not at the moment, did you know I have joined the Army.'

'Good grief! When did you do that?'

'It is a long story and you certainly don't want to hear about it.'

'Can I ask you something Dave?'

'Go ahead.'

'Did you stop going out with me because you found someone else?'

'No, I wasn't seeing anyone else, in fact, I had the offer of going out with someone the night you went to your Aunties, but refused, I told the girl that I was engaged to you, No, it wasn't because of someone else, as much as I love you, I just felt that I couldn't be with you, it is hard to explain.'

'I see, well, I must go now, my mother is waiting for this shopping, I hope I see you again, and good luck with the Army, Bye.'

It was nice seeing her again, but I still feel the same way about her. Perhaps it is better that we stay this way I would hate to upset her again. She didn't deserve it really. GOD! What am I saying, I left her because I couldn't stand being with her, I can't start weakening now.

I meet John at the dance. They have got Acker Bilk tonight. How they can afford him, I will never know. Jane and Maureen wave to us to come and sit at their table. We go over to them.

'Hi! How are you doing? I heard that you have broken off your engagement to Kathy Dave, is it true?' Jane asks.

'News travels fast in Gosport, yes, it is true.'

'Oh goody, you can go out with me now?'

'Don't get any ideas. I have enough to worry about being in the Army.'

'In the WHAT!'

'You heard right, we have joined the Army.'

'Bloody Hell! Things must be bad.' Said Maureen, 'Haven't you had enough adventure?'

'Obviously not,' said Jane, 'I'm sorry it didn't work out with you and Kathy.'

'Thanks Jane, but I think it was for the best. But deep down, I bet you are pleased, you minx.'

'David! How could you say such a thing?' Jane said with what looked like a wicked gleam in her eyes.

John takes Maureen onto the dance floor and I talk to Jane.

'What made you join the Army then Dave?'

'It's a long story, and if you have a few hours, I'll tell you about it.'

'I'm all ears.' She replies.

I then tell her about the cock up we had and how we came to be in the Army. She bursts out laughing.

'I don't think it's funny.' I tell her.

'I do.' She replies with tears, streaming down her cheeks.

'Trust me to sit next to a girl who is a fruit cake and one with a warped sense of humour as well.'

She gets up and plants a kiss on my lips.

'You really are a treasure.'

'Thank you, that was nice.'

'What the kiss or what I said?'

'Both.' I tell her.

'Then let's do it again, how would you like to go to a party tomorrow night?'

'Whose party?'

'Maureen's.'

'Okay, count me in.'

'Good, pick me up at 7pm.'

She gives me her address just as John and Maureen return to the table.

'Why don't you take Dave for a dance, I'm sure he would like that, Jane.'

'Stop match making Maureen, I don't want to dance.'

'Match make - who - little old me.'

The dance is soon over and we walk the girls to the bus stop.

'Aren't you going to walk me home Dave?' Jane asks.

'Only if you want me to.'

'I do.'

'Right, we'll see you guys later then, me and Maureen are getting the bus.' John said.

We say goodnight and leave them at the bus stop and walk off down Whitworth Road.

Jane is so easy to talk to, there are no airs and graces with her, she is quite pretty in a funny sort of way. I like her a lot, but I don't think I will get serious about her. I still think too much about Kathy, and I shouldn't, but I can't help it, I'm all mixed up. Women!

We arrive at Jane's gate and chat. I don't know why, but I kiss her on the lips. She looks at me puzzled.

'Why did you do that? I didn't think you wanted to get involved.'

'I haven't a bloody clue Jane, it just felt right.'

'Ah! Ha! He fancies me after all.' She said laughing.

'I'll see you tomorrow, let's play it one day at a time and see how it pans out.' I tell her.

'If you say so, but I am sure you will fall for me.' She replies.

'Sod off to bed.' I tell her.

She kisses me on the nose and runs in doors. She really is quite a nice person, cheeky, but nice with it.

I walk off home in a very happy mood. Do I really want to go out with Jane, or is it a rebound from Kathy. I'm really mixed up. Oh, bloody heck!

Saturday morning and I am definitely going to have a lay in. I hear the doorbell go, I hope it isn't John because all I want to do is lie in, please don't let it be John.

It isn't, it is the old girl from across the road. I must have dozed off, because my mother is shaking me and saying that it is midday. I get up and shave and go down stairs.

'Well, Well, Well, the soldier has decided to get up,' my dad said. 'Here!' Throwing me a tea towel, 'Wipe these up?'

'I met a nice girl last night dad. I'm seeing her tonight, her name is Jane and she lives at the top of our road.'

'I thought you were going out with Kathryn.'

'We finished dad, we just didn't get on.'

'Does anyone get on with women?' He replied.

I go up to the paper shop and buy the Weekend and again bump into Kathy. This has got to stop if I am ever going to stay sane.

'Why hello Dave fancy seeing you.'

'Hello Kathy, what are you up to?'

'Jim wanted a paper, so I said I would get it for him. Mum has been giving him a hard time lately; he met some girl and put her in the family way. I came out to get away from it all.'

'I know how you feel.'

We chat for a few more minutes and I collect my Weekend and return home. I'm glad I am not here during the week, especially as I keep bumping into her. I must get her out of my mind, but it is hard to do. I don't think I will ever really get over her, she was my first real love, and I will always have a soft spot for her.

It is 7pm and I knock on Jane's door. A bald headed man answers it.

'You must be David? Come on in, Jane will be down in a minute or two, you know what women are like when it comes to getting ready.'

I follow him into the lounge. A rather big woman with glasses is sitting in a chair.

'This is Jane's boyfriend mother?' Bald head said.

'Hello love, sit down, Jane won't be long.'

I hate cats and there is one sleeping on the chair. I pick it up and it turns on me. "Ouch!" The cat scratches me on the hand. Lucky Bald Head is watching, otherwise, the cat would be dead.

'What's wrong with him? Silly cat, he has never done that before.' Bald head said.

Who knows, but if I get hold of it, it is dead.

Jane comes into the lounge, she looks a million dollars, and I tell her so.

'Why, thank you kind Sir, I might be a bit late dad, you know what Maureen's parties are like.' She grabs my hand and we leave.

'Well, what do you think of my mum and dad then?'

'They seem all right to me.' I tell her.

We walk hand in hand and 10 minutes later we are knocking on Maureen's door. The worst noise in the world is coming from a thing called a record player.

'What's that bloody noise?' I ask Maureen as she opens the door.

'That is in the top 10 at No 4.' She enlightens me.

'It is obvious the guy who made the record didn't know he couldn't sing.' I say to her.

'You are just jealous.'

How the hell a record like that got in the charts, I will never know. I must be getting old.

I'm introduced to everyone at the party, and they seem a really nice bunch of people. I take Jane into the kitchen and give her a lingering kiss.

'You will fall in love with me if you carry on like this.' She says holding me tight.

'I'm trying not to, but you could be right.'

'Well, don't fight it you know I have always fancied you. I told you a couple of weeks ago.'

'Yes I know, but I couldn't do anything about it then.'

I kiss her again and we return to the lounge for a drink.

We have a great time, I have enjoyed being with her.

'Are you going to see me again?' She whispers in my ear.

'I would like to very much, but I haven't a clue when my next weekend off is, but as soon as I know, I will let you know.'

'Okay dear.'

I walk her home and get invited in for a cup of coffee. I never got that when I went out with Kathy, well, not until the end.

Jane takes me into the lounge and her parents are still up.

'Did you have a good time,' her dad asks.

'We sure did, Dave didn't like the music though. He's a square.'

'I'll make some coffee.' Said her mother.

I can't see the cat anywhere; it is probably hiding, ready to pounce on me. I have news for it; its nine lives are up.

Jane's dad asks me what I do for a living and I tell him that I am in the Army.

'I served in the Army during the war, I was in the Tank Corps, and it was the best years of my life. When the war finished, I signed on for the full 22 years.'

I think her dad likes me, we have something in common. Jane winks at me and pouts her lips. She is teasing me and she knows it. I look at my watch, it 1am.

'I must be going; perhaps I will see you again soon.'

I get up and Jane follows me to the door.

'Thanks for a smashing time Dave.'

'It's me who should be thanking you, I had a great time.'

'When will you be home next?'

'I honestly don't know Jane, it will depend on what training we will be getting, but if I am able to get home, I will come round for you, that's a promise.'

'Can I say that you are now my boyfriend?'

'Your dad has already said that to your mum, so I suppose I am.'

I give her a kiss and walk off home. Shit! I have done it again, will I ever learn not to get involved.

Sunday evening comes round far too quickly and John is round ready to go back to Camp.

'Looking forward to going back mate.' he asked.

'Not really John, I had a great time with Jane.'

'I had a better time with Maureen, she has got the most gorgeous tits I have ever touched, I didn't have it off with her though, she said we should wait a few weeks, I can certainly wait to get into her knickers.'

'You randy old sod.' I tell him.

'Less of the OLD.' He replies.

We arrive back at Bushfield Camp just before midnight and hand in our leave passes to the Guard Commander. On entering our hut, we find that everyone is up as they have only just got in as well.

'Have a good weekend you two.' Asked Dave Turner.

'Smashing, thanks.' I tell him.

'I had the best pair of tits in my hand you have ever seen.' Said John.

'Lucky bastard.' said Denny Morris.

One of the Fire Picket comes in, 'Lights out you guys.' He shouts.

We all get undressed and get our heads down. Who do I dream about tonight - Jane or Kathryn?

0500hrs – 'WAKEY, WAKEY!' Shouts Corporal Sykes, 'Get dressed into PT kit and parade outside, AT THE DOUBLE.'

We leap out of bed and get dressed in vest and shorts and parade outside.

'RIGHT, we will now go for a short run around the Camp, just to wake you up.'

We run around the square and after 10 minutes, the Corporal tells us to walk. Just as we start walking, John keels over and screams with pain. I run over to him and see that he is holding his right side. His face is screwed up and I can see that he is in agony.

'I think it is your appendix mate, hang on.'

'Stop slacking you two, come on move yourselves.' the Corporal shouts.

'Bollocks! West is in pain, I think it is his appendix; help me get him to the MI Room.' I shout back.

Joe Bell helps me get John up.

'You a Fucking Doctor?' sneers the Corporal.

'No, but I have had some medical training in the Congo, so less of your chatter and help me get him over to the orderly.'

At the Medical Centre I wake an orderly from his sleep.

'Bugger off.' He replies.

I grab him by the throat and pull him out of bed.

'Listen arsehole, there is a friend of mine out there with a suspected appendicitis, get moving and arrange an ambulance for him NOW!'

'Let me have a look at him.' The orderly said pulling on his trousers.

He checks John who is sweating profusely. He puts his hand into John's right groin and John screams with pain.

'Kill him Dave!'

I look vehemently at the orderly, if looks could kill!!!

An ambulance is called and about 6 minutes later arrives at the MI Room. I leap into the ambulance and go with John to the hospital. I'll worry about the consequences later.

At the hospital, John is rushed to the Operating Theatre, and I sit in the waiting room. After about 2 hours, a Doctor comes and tells me that he is okay and stable.

'Thank Christ for that, his mother would have killed me if anything had happened to him.' I tell the Doctor.

'He was lucky to have you around, another 10 minutes and he would have been a goner.'

'Bloody Hell! That doesn't bear thinking about.'

I make my way back to Camp and report to Sgt Blacker. He has already been appraised of the incident by Cpl Sykes.

'You did a good job Stubbs, even if you did break every rule in the Military Law Book.'

Oh Balls! In the shit again.

I am about to go to the Canteen for a cup of tea when Cpl Tribe tells me I'm wanted in the Admin Office. It didn't take them long to find out. I report to the office and am told that I will be on CO's Orders at 1100hrs.

'What do I wear Corp?' I asked the Lance Corporal in charge of the office.

'See your Sergeant, he will tell you.'

I report back to Sgt Blacker who tells me that I have to wear fatigue shirt and trousers. I'm beginning to hate the Army.

1100hrs - I am waiting outside the CO's Office with Sgt Blacker. My name is called out by the RSM and I'm walked into the office. Had I been in training longer, I would have been marched in.

'We meet again Stubbs; do you know why you are here?' The Colonel asked.

'No Sir, not unless it is because I shouted at Cpl Sykes.'

'I didn't know about that, but no, it isn't that. I understand that your quick actions saved the life of Rfn West; you are being put forward for a commendation for your actions. Well done, you are upholding the traditions of the Green Jackets, your friend and mine will be proud of you.'

'Thank you Sir, but anyone with my training would have done the same.'

'Sgt Blacker, Stubbs is to be given a long weekend.'

'I'll make a note of it for this weekend Sir.'

This is great; I'll be able to see Jane.

'Is it possible to visit West in hospital Sir?' I ask the CO.

'Sgt Blacker, make sure Stubbs has a night leave pass every other night whilst West is in hospital.'

'Will do Sir.'

Blacker does not like this one little bit. Tough Shit.

'Okay Stubbs, you may go.'

I return to the hut and the guys ask me how John is.

'He's okay now.' I tell them.

Sykes comes into the hut.

'I want to see you Stubbs?'

I follow Sykes into the Sgt's office.

'Close the door. How is West?'

'He will be okay Corp.' I reply.

'I'm glad, I want to apologise for not acting sooner this morning. It is a good job you recognised the symptoms. Where did you learn First Aid?'

'In the Congo when I was a Mercenary. I learnt all about how to recognise certain diseases. How to mash roots that could be found in the bush to help combat infections, even how to do minor surgery with a penknife. I also learnt how to deal with major and minor injuries and how to patch up bullet wounds. Perhaps the Platoon could be taught First Aid.'

'I will put it to the Sergeant, and if he agrees, maybe you could teach us. Anyway that was what I wanted you for, you can go back to your room now.'

I return to the lads, we have got Marching Practice on the square. Yuk!

What a laugh, everyone is out of step, it is utter chaos. Guys are bumping into each other etc. etc. After 2 hours of marching, we finally get it right.

'AT LAST.' Shouts Cpl Ridge, he looks to the heavens and says, 'WHY ME!'

The afternoon brings Weapon Training. The SLR is nearly the same as the FN, except the FN could be switched to automatic. This lesson is dead easy for me and I fly through it. The lads can't believe how quick I can strip and reassemble the weapon.

'You have done this before Dave, haven't you?' Rick said.

'I used an FN out in the Congo, this is virtually the same.'

Having completed the day's lessons we return to our billet.

'I can't wait for grub time, I'm starving.' Said Joe rubbing his stomach.

Off to the cookhouse we go, the food has improved slightly. I have a quick meal and get changed to go to the hospital.

At the entrance to the hospital I meet Mrs West.

'How are you?' I ask her.

'Oh Dave, thanks for looking after my John. If it hadn't been for you, he would have died. Thank you for what you did.'

'He would have done the same for me, come on let's go and see how he is.'

We go down a corridor and find Ward "C."

John is chatting up a nurse.

'I might have known it, chatting up the birds again.' I say to him.

'Hello mum, Hi yah mate, I owe you one.'

'Cobblers.' I tell him shaking his hand.

'I'll go and get a couple of chairs and leave you to talk for a few minutes.'

After about 10 minutes, I return to the Ward and tell John how we are getting on with the training.

'We will be in our 3rd week when you get out of here, I expect they will back squad you mate, and you know what the CO said.'

'I have an idea, if I do the training I have lost at night, perhaps I can get up to the stage you are and that way, stop myself from being Back Squaded, what do you think?'

'You have got to get out of here first, but it is a good idea, and worth considering.'

Visiting time comes to an end and we say goodbye to him.

'I'll see you day after tomorrow mate they have given me a night pass for every other night whilst you are in hospital.'

'Look forward to you coming mate, bye for now, and thanks mate.'

'Just don't give me any more scares, okay, see yah.'

As we are walking down the corridor, Mrs West says, 'Keep an eye on him for me please Dave. I really worry about him, and please call me Tina, not Mrs West.'

'He's a big boy now, he can look after himself, and anyway, he would have done the same for me if I was in the same situation.'

I kiss her on the cheek and walk her to the station. Her train arrives and I wave her goodbye.

On returning to camp, I hand my leave pass into the guardroom.

'Stand Still!' Someone shouts.

I look round and see a Lance Corporal in the Regimental Police walking towards me.

'Who do you think you are, lounging about the guardroom; get your feet together, what's your name.'

I come to attention and tell him my name and that I have just returned from seeing someone in hospital.

'I don't care if you have been seeing the Queen of Sheba.' He shouts.

I haven't a clue what I have done and why he is shouting at me.

'Lance Corporal, if you don't stop shouting at me, I am going to tear your head off of your shoulders, I don't know what I have done, so please enlighten me?' I tell him.

Before he can speak, the Duty Sergeant comes out of the Guardroom.

'What's all the commotion about?'

'It's this Rifleman Sergeant; he has just threatened me because I balled him out.'

'Is that true Rifleman?' asked the Sergeant.

'In a way Sergeant, the LCpl shouted at me, I don't know what for and he wasn't prepared to tell me. I handed my leave pass in and was just walking away when he started shouting. I told him to stop and said I would do something about it if he didn't. I'm sorry if it caused offence, I don't want any trouble.'

'What's your name son?'

'Stubbs, Sergeant.'

'I've heard about you, on your way son, I'll sort this out.'

'Thank you Sergeant, goodnight.'

I leave the Guardroom and hear the Sergeant screaming abuse at the Lance Corporal. Oh well, another enemy made.

I arrive back at the billet and Wally Hicks asks how John is. I tell him that I caught him chatting up a nurse and that he would be in hospital for at least a week.

'He'll get Back Squaded then Dave.'

I tell him what John had said about training in the evening.

'It could be done if we all pull together, what do you think lads?'

'I reckon old Blacker will go for it, he wants that Cup desperately.' Arthur said.

Alan Roper comes in and walks up to me.

'I hear you have just had a run in with Don Simms at the Guardroom Stubbs, be on your guard that bastard will try and get his own back.'

'I'll remember it, thanks mate.'

Roper is a real head case. He is a loner and doesn't get involved with any of us. He keeps to himself and only does the bare minimum. He will later go down in history as a murderer, who killed a policeman in Epping Forest.

'He's a strange fellow.' I say to Arthur.

'You can say that again Dave, he didn't want to join the Army, he was made to by a Judge. It was join or go to prison. He has a record as long as your arm for different violent crimes.'

That's all I need, a raving nutter with me, but it was nice of him to let me know about Simms.

Over the next few weeks, we carry out all the different types of training that is required of an Infantryman. Some of it is pretty hard, but most of it, is the same as I had already done in the Congo.

Friday morning and we are getting ready to go on weekend leave.

'Hi everyone, I'm back!' Said John walking into the hut.

'Well, Well, Well.' Said Wally, 'Look what the cat has dragged in.'

'You never told me you were coming out?' I said shaking his hand.

'I thought I would surprise you mate.'

'Well, you certainly did that.'

'You are wanted in the Platoon Commanders Office West?' said Cpl Ridge coming into the hut.

John leaves and heads for Soames office.

'Let's hope he don't get Back Squaded.' Rick said.

'I hope he doesn't either.' I tell him.

John returns and tells us that Lt Soames and Sgt Blacker have bought the idea that we should train in the evenings to get him up to scratch. We are all pleased, because it would be a shame if we lost him now. The Platoon has got some good marks so far towards the Best Platoon Cup, and it would be great if we could achieve it with a full Platoon.

We work like slaves in the evenings to get John up to standard. Sometimes it is 4am before we finish, but everyone, including Roper agrees that we had to do it. John is up to standard, and passes the tests with flying colours. He has come up to our standard of training in 9 evenings. We can now relax and have a few evenings off.

On our weekends off, I see quite a lot of Jane. We go out together on every possible occasion. She is a great girl to be with. John also sees a lot of Maureen in more ways than one, if you know what I mean. All I hope is that he doesn't, get her in the club. They are just like rabbits, at it all the time.

Back at camp, we are told that we will be spending 2 weeks at a training camp at Yockster in Devon. Whilst we are there, we will be doing numerous night exercises and carrying out live firing. All I hope is that it doesn't snow, at least not for the two weeks we are there. It has just started to snow in Winchester.

Now that we have completed 9 weeks training, and as soon as we have got the exercises over with in Yockster, we will start preparing for our Passing out Parade. I must admit, I'm looking forward to it. We are neck and neck with another platoon at the moment for the Best Platoon Cup; it all hangs on the exercises and shooting at Yockster.

I ring Jane up and tell her that I won't be home for a few weekends as I'll be on exercise in Devon and that she can come to our Passing out Parade if she wanted.

'Are your mum and dad going? If so, I'll come with them, is that alright darling?'

'Of course it is, see you later, and love you.'

We arrive at Yockster and the snow is about 3 inches deep and still coming down. Blacker gets out of the front vehicle and tells us to dismount. Each Platoon is allocated a hut.

The hut we are allocated has a large black stove.

'My! Oh! My! I see we have got central heating.' Cpl Ridge enters the hut behind us.

'Get a fire going in that stove before you do anything else? It is the only means of warming the place up, be at the bedding stores at 1500hrs.'

Cpl Ridge is right; the hut is freezing and feels quite damp.

'I'll get the fire going,' said Arthur, 'I saw some coal down by the main gate as we came into the camp.'

1500hrs - and we go to the store to collect our bedding. The snow is coming down quite heavy. The store man is a really big guy with a funny accent.

'Right my darlins, let's be having yer, pick up one of them there covers and fill it with this straw, now don't put too much in as you won't be able to sleep on eh.'

'What's he saying Dave?' Rick asked.

'I think he wants us to fill the covers.'

'You mean we are going to sleep on them, where's the mattress?'

'That's, it mate.'

'I bet he says we don't get sheets either.'

'Sheets are for poofs my darlin - blankets is for men - take two each and two pillows.'

'Don't we get pillow slips?'

'You been pampered far too long my darlin.' The store man tells him.

'Then I want to be a poof.' Rick said laughing.

We fill the bags with straw and carry them back to the hut. Some of the guys have overfilled and others have under filled them. Mine looks like a large flat sausage. The room is just starting to get warm.

'Make sure we have plenty of coal for the stove, so that we don't have to go out at night.' Said Roper.

Sgt Blacker opens the door, and a blast of cold air hits the room.

'Stubbs - with effect from now - you are the Platoon Commander - pick a Sergeant and two Corporals and give me their names at dinner.'

'Fuck in hell, he could have come into the hut and closed the door behind him, it was just getting warm in here.' Tony remarks.

Bloody hell!

'John, you are now a Sergeant.'

'Oh good, three stripes at last.'

'Arthur and Rick, you are Corporals. Anyone disagree?'

I look out of the window; the snow is really coming down now. We could be snowed in by morning. I hate snow. Dinner is at 1730hrs and we are all looking forward to it. I must admit, I'm pretty starving, so I hope the grub is good.

Sgt Blacker asks me for the names of the people I have picked for the job as NCOs. I tell him who they are and he replies, 'I would have picked the same, you are doing okay at the moment Stubbs, so keep it up.'

It looks as if I have done something right after all. Let's hope I can keep doing it. Perhaps they will cancel the exercises if the snow gets too bad.

The food looks and tastes like the stuff you would find in a swill bin, it is disgusting. I have never tasted such revolting grub in all my life. Everyone shouts at the Cook, and asks him where he learnt to ruin food. He screams abuse at everyone and storms off into the innards of the Cookhouse.

'I think we have upset him.' Rick said throwing his plate of mush into a bin.

God Almighty! Do we have to eat this shit all the time we are here. I must see if I can get to the shop in the village we passed coming in.

Our first exercise in the field is one of collecting information and acting on it. John will take out a Section and collect the information required and then it's up to me. Interesting! The snow is about 6 inches deep as we set out for the training area. The vehicles can only make it so far and we have to hoof it with all the kit.

'I now know how a pack mule feels.' Wally said dropping kit all over the place.

'You and me both.' Arthur said.

The area we have been given is out of bounds to the enemy and we pitch the tents ready for the start of the exercise. John's Section patrol has collected the required information on the whereabouts of the enemy. I am to get a prisoner from within their camp without being seen. I gather the guys together and brief them.

It is 2200hrs and the exercise begins in earnest. John has taken up a defensive position. I and 5 of the Platoon start to move off towards the enemy camp. From the information I have, the enemy should have men along the tree line 600yds ahead. Suddenly Rick, who is on point duty stops. I move forward to him.

'There is a chap just under that tree in front of us, he hasn't seen us yet.' He whispers.

How the hell Rick saw him in this heavy snow beats me. I would have walked right over him.

'We won't hang about we'll grab this one and get back to camp.' I tell him.

Everyone is lying in the snow. Christ! We had better start moving otherwise we will all freeze. Thank goodness the enemy don't seem to be very interested. They must be as pissed off as we are.

We move to the left and come in on the man from his left side. Roper pounces on the man and puts his hand over the guy's mouth. Whack! Whack!

'He will be easier to handle now.' Roper said pulling the guy over his shoulder.

'Bloody Henry, did you have to hit him so hard, He's out like a light.' Arthur said.

Roper shrugs and carries the man back to our camp.

Once in the camp, I check to see if the guy is okay. He is quite unconscious; the blow Roper had given him has really knocked him out. After a few minutes the man starts to come round and Roper stands him up.

'Well, Well, Well, if it isn't Mr Simms our friendly Policeman.'

'What did you hit me for? That's not allowed you know, you are not allowed to use force. I could have you all on a charge for this.' Simms shouted.

The snow is really coming down now and it is about 9 degrees below.

'Shut him up will you.' I say to Roper.

'With pleasure.' Roper replies smacking Simms on the jaw and laying him out again.

'Not like that, I meant gag him.'

'Oh!' Roper replied.

'You had better bring him round.'

Roper opens his water bottle and pours freezing cold water over Simms head, which revives him immediately.

'What the Fuck are you playing at? You daft bastard that water, is freezing.' Simms cried.

'Any more noise out of you prat and I will strip you of your clothes and leave you to die in the snow.' Roper said menacingly.

'Now Mr Simms, I would like you to give me information which you have concerning your positions in the woods, please answer my questions immediately or I will tell Roper to carry out his threat of relieving you of your clothes. If you are lucky, someone will find you, if not, frozen Simms.'

'Fuck off bastard.' Simms shouts.

'Strip him.' I tell Roper.

He moves towards Simms and Simms starts to whimper.

'What is the Password you are using tonight?'

'Wild Willie.' He answers, looking away.

'How many men are out of the camp in ambush position?'

'6 men, they are about 50 yards north of the camp.'

'What flares are there?'

'Only on the west and south side in banks of two.'

'Where is the command centre and who is in charge?'

'It is by the large tree, Sgt Dart is in charge.'

'Thanks you.'

What prat thought up Wild Willy, the mind boggles?

This information will be very useful when we attack the camp.

'You're that fucking mercenary; trust me to end up with a fruit cake.' Simms said, getting cocky.

I don't like the man; he is arrogant and shouldn't be an NCO.

'You wait till this exercise is over. We'll see who has the upper hand. Your card is marked.'

Roper being Roper clouts Simms alongside his head.

'Shut up cretin, you are on borrowed time with me.'

I can see that they hate each other. Roper ties Simms up and puts him in a tent with a blanket over him to stop him getting cold.

Sgt Blacker is informed that we have captured a prisoner. I am informed that we are to return to the drop off point with all our kit. The exercise has been called off for the time being. We are to leave the tents in situ.

'Okay guys, let's move out, the sooner we get to the drop off point the quicker we will be back to a nice warm room.'

It takes us over 20 minutes to arrive. The snow is pretty deep in places. Sgt Blacker is waiting for us.

'Where's your prisoner.' Blacker asked.

I look round; Simms is nowhere to be seen.

'Oh shit, we have left Simms in the tent.'

'I'll go and get him; I bet he is nearly stiff by now.' Rick said.

'Have you left LCpl Simms out there in the freezing cold, Oh dear.' said Blacker laughing. He obviously didn't like the prat either.

The Platoon climbs on the waiting truck to shelter from the snow. After about 40 minutes, Rick returns with a very het up Simms.

'These bastards tried to kill me Sarge.'

'What do you mean - tried to kill you - are you making an official complaint against this Platoon?' Blacker asked.

'They really meant to kill me Sarge.'

'Crap you Pillock, get on the truck, tried to kill you indeed, what a moron.' Blacker said winking at me.

The journey back to the camp is pretty hairy; I hope they cancel all the exercises. The Platoon is dropped off at the Armoury and we clean our weapons and hand them in. By the time we get into bed it is 0400hrs. Our wet clothing is put around the stove to dry.

At 0600, Wally wakes up and shouts, 'The bloody kit is on fire.'

'Good.' Someone replies, 'It will keep the hut warm.'

'Oh, Yeh.' Said Wally who goes back to sleep.

I leap out of bed and grab the fire bucket. It is empty. Rick had used the water to shave in before going on the exercise. I grab the clothing which is well alight and throw it out of the door. Fucking hell! It's freezing out there. I jump back into bed, not one of the sods has woken up. We could have all been burned alive and they wouldn't have known anything about it.

Sometime during the early morning, Tom wakes and goes to get his trousers from near the stove.

'Hey! Some bastard has pinched my trousers.' He shouts.

The rest of the Platoon wakes up at this, and a few walk to the stove.

'My shirt's gone.' Alex shouts.

Wally goes to the fire place. 'So are my trousers.'

I get up and inform them that their kit is out the door where I threw it.

'Why did you do that Dave?' asked Tony.

'Because the bloody stuff was on fire, that's why.'

Sgt Blacker comes into the hut.

'What's all that burnt clothing doing outside the door?'

'Small accident, Sarge, nothing to worry about.' I tell him.

'Make sure the mess is cleaned up.' Blacker said, leaving.

'It's your fault I couldn't put the fire out Rick, you used the water to shave remember.'

'Sorry Dave, it won't happen again.' he replied.

John wakes up.

'What's all the noise about? I'm trying to get some sleep.'

Eight pillows, wing their way in his direction. John has slept through the whole incident.

At 1200hrs we are all washed and shaved and waiting for Sgt Blacker. We should be starting the second phase of the exercise, unless it is cancelled. No such luck. Blacker informs us that the next stage will carry on providing the snow doesn't get any deeper. Damn! Our God must be on holiday.

After lunch, we get all the kit together and move out to the tents we left behind last night. The journey is horrendous. The tents are covered in snow and we leave them like it. It should make them warmer inside. After all, Eskimos live in igloos. This part of the exercise is for us to defend our position from the attacking enemy. As LCpl Simms is still with the enemy, I tell Roper not to be too hard with him if he is captured again.

'Who me? As if, I would.' He replies with a sneer.

This guy is really weird, I can't fathom him out.

I take Tony with me and we lay out a pattern of three flares all around our camp. I have overlapped them so that nothing can get at us without being seen. I position the Bren gun so that its arc of fire is across a gap in the trees.

'They will come through that, you mark my words.'

Roper asks if he can be the Platoon cook.

'Be my guest mate.' I tell him. Strange man, I never took him to be a cook.

The weather starts to turn nasty. It's snowing again and the temperature is starting to go down fast.

'Put on some more clothing guys, and get into the tents and keep warm. We will take it in turns to stand guard, Wally, take the first watch.'

'Do you think they will come now?' he asks.

'You never know mate.'

After about half an hour, Roper brings me a mug of tea.

'You will need this to keep the cold out.'

'Thanks mate, I appreciate the thought.'

My, he's a strange bird. Stan takes the next watch as Wally comes in to my tent half frozen.

'It's getting worse by the minute Dave.'

'Yes I know Wally, but there isn't a lot we do about it, is there?'

'No I suppose not.'

We have now been in the snow for 6 hours and I open the envelope that Blacker had given me. The enemy will start their attack at 2100hrs. I think they may be early because of the conditions. I stand to, half of the Platoon whilst the other half keeps warm.

'We will change at 15 minute intervals until something starts to happen.' I tell them.

I hate snow.

Wally starts banging his foot on the ground.

'What's the problem Wally?' I ask him.

'My foot has started to go numb.'

'Get your boot off quick and start massaging your toes, or else frostbite will set in.'

Wally quickly unties his boot and does as I tell him.

'That's better Dave, thank mate.'

'No problem, we don't want to lose you now, do we.'

Rick pokes his head into the tent and shows me what he has done to some thunder flashes.

'Bloody Hell!' I exclaim, 'they are going to make a right old bang.'

It is coming up to 2045hrs and I gather the Platoon together.

'We will rely on a system of finger clicks to let each other know if the enemy is in sight, no loud voices, okay, right let's get stood to, they will be here in a few minutes.'

Rick starts to click his fingers and I creep over to his position.

'There are 4 men crawling towards us about 50 yds out.' He whispers.

I train my binoculars in the direction he is pointing and sure enough, I see 4 trails in the snow. It is so deep I haven't seen the men yet.

'Wait until they are about 15yds out, and then lob those thunder flashes of yours at them.'

'Boy will they have a headache.' He quietly laughs.

BOOM!

The nearest of the 4 men leaps up from the snow and drops his rifle on the ground, trying to cover his ears.

'Fucking Aida! I've gone deaf.' He shouts.

The nearest man to him is rolling in the snow, also holding his ears. The other two sit up in the snow, totally bewildered.

'I suppose you could say we have just killed 4 of the enemy.' Said Rick with a smirk.

'Yes, they are dead.' Said an umpire, who came from nowhere.

'Where did he come from?' Wally asks.

I must admit, I didn't know. He must have been watching us all the time.

'Keep watching your front lads, I think things are about to hot up.' shouts John from the left side of the camp.

The enemy try to get to our position throughout the next 2 hours, but thanks to the way we have positioned the flares, they are seen every time. They try a consorted attack and the Bren gun starts working overtime.

'I've only got 2 mags left Dave.' Tommy shouts.

A man leaps the perimeter and Tommy puts a burst straight at him.

Unfortunately the man is too close and his combat clothing is riddled with wood splinters from the bulleted blanks.

'You fucking bastard!' The man shouts falling to the ground.

'Sorry sport!' Tommy said with a smile on his face.

The man concerned is none other than LCpl Simms. Oh dear!

The exercise is a success. We have learnt a good lesson, don't use ammo willy nilly, or you run out, and don't fire bulleted blanks at close range, you get splinters. A whistle blows and the exercise is over.

We pack up the camp and take the kit back to the trucks that are waiting for us.

'Clean your weapons and hand them into the armoury, before getting your breakfast and then you can get your heads down, parade again at 1400hrs.' Said Sgt Blacker.

The weapons are cleaned and handed in and we head off for breakfast. Holy Moses! The cook has excelled himself, the grub is excellent.

After breakfast, we return to the hut and get our heads down. There is no fear of not being able to sleep, as once my head hits the pillow, I'm gone.

I wake at 1300hrs and find that the water in the taps is only just warm, something must be wrong with the boiler. I inform Sgt Blacker of the situation.

'Keep this to yourself Stubbs, we are to carry out a live firing exercise and then we will be returning to Winchester early, the conditions here are too dangerous for recruits.'

'Mum's the word Sarge.'

The Platoon parades at 1400hrs and is told that there will be an exercise using live rounds starting at 1430hrs. We have to draw 50 rounds of live ammunition each for this phase of the exercise, this is going to be fun - believe me - except for me and John, and I don't think anyone in the Platoon has ever shot a live round before. We collect our weapons and ammunition and parade at the trucks.

'What I am about to say, you will inwardly digest, YOU ARE NOT TO PUT A MAGAZINE OF LIVE ROUNDS ON YOUR WEAPONS UNTIL TOLD TO, AND ONCE THE MAGAZINE IS ON THE WEAPON IT IS TO BE POINTED DOWN THE RANGE AT ALL TIMES, IS THAT CLEAR?' The Sergeant shouts.

'Yes Sarge.' We reply.

'Good, I don't want any accidental discharges and I don't want to see any weapons being pointed in any direction except the front, failure to carry out this order will result in the person concerned being Courts Martialed, okay, on the trucks.'

Once at the range area we fill our magazines with the 50 rounds, and split into teams of five men.

'Right, listen in, each 5 man team, will in turn advance down the range. At certain places, targets will pop up. You are to fire 2 rounds at each target. On the command "Cease Firing," you are to unload your weapons and make them safe before putting a further magazine on the weapon, is that clear?'

'Yes Sarge.' We all say together.

'Right, the first 5 men load your weapons and make ready, safety catches on.'

John is in the first team to go.

'ADVANCE.' Shouts Blacker.

A target pops up in front of John. BANG, BANG! Two hits. The rest of the team do the same, until all ammo is expended. Now it is my teams turn. I have Roper in my team and I'm not sure I like having him with a loaded weapon. We follow the same paths as the previous teams and I get maximum hits.

The walk down is completed and the Platoon has 714 hits out of 800.

'Well done lads. That is going to take some beating. We are definitely in with a bloody good chance of winning the Cup.' Blacker says happily.

I hope he is right.

The rest of the exercises are cancelled and we pack up to return to camp.

'Before we get on the trucks, I want you to line up in one line. Empty your pouches and cock your weapons holding your magazines alongside your weapon so that I can see into the chamber and the head of the magazine. You will say in a loud voice, "NO LIVE ROUNDS OR EMPTY CASES IN MY POSSESSION SIR," as I come to you in turn. If after this declaration you are found to have any rounds or cases you will be charged. It is a Courts Martial offence to leave this range with rounds, is that clear?'

'YES SERGEANT!' We all shout.

No one has any, thank goodness, and we pile onto the trucks and head back to camp. On arrival we are told to clean our weapons and put them in the armoury.

After a couple of hours, Blacker tells us that we will be returning to

Winchester as the rest of the exercises have been cancelled due to the bad weather. Everyone is elated; Yockster isn't the best of places in winter. Everyone starts running round like headless chickens getting the placed squared up so that we can get the hell out of here.

Our return to Winchester is greatly appreciated by the publicans in the area. All though they don't rely on the trade from the Army, it is appreciated, even if there is the odd punch up to put up with.

John and I together with Wally and Rick, go to the Bakers Arms for an evening out.

John chats up a girl but is soon stopped by her boyfriend who is 6 foot 6 inches tall and just as wide.

'Piss off squaddie and leave my girl alone.' the big guys says menacingly.

'The bigger you are the harder you fall.' John replies.

Oh shit! Not another fight, and what he has just said, well, isn't really true.

The big guy throws a punch at John and misses, but John lands a round house straight on the guy's jaw, which immediately knocks him cold.

'See! No contest.' John said.

'Fluke.' Said I.

'Get out of my pub you lot, I don't want any trouble.' The publican said, picking up a pick helve.

It is now time to move on. The girl kicks her boyfriend with her shoe and starts calling him a big wimp. We leave before he comes round.

'What's that landlord moaning about, he is always having punch ups in his pub, it's renowned for them?' Rick said pocketing the money that fell out of the big guys pocket when he hit the deck. 'Drinks are on him, I think.'

'I didn't like the beer in there anyway.' Wally said as we walk along the street.

We visit a few more pubs and then walk back to camp.

'Do you think we have got that cup Dave?' Asked Wally.

'We will soon find out mate, we have only got a week to go before we Pass Out. Blacker seems confident enough, we will just have to wait and see. Mind you, if we haven't got it, our lives will be made a misery.'

The Platoon spends the rest of the week on the Firing Range to get our classification for when we join our Regiments. The platoon has 9 marksmen and 7 first class shots. The rest are 2nd class shots. Not bad at all. Friday comes and we are given the weekend off. I am looking forward to seeing Jane again. I know John is definitely looking forward to seeing Maureen. The train ride to Fareham is pretty boring and it doesn't look as if the snow has laid much compared with Devon.

I arrange to meet John at the Dance tonight and head for home.

'How did your exercise go?' asked my dad.

'Most of them got cancelled due to the amount of snow we had in Devon. At one stage we had about 14 inches and it was pretty damn cold I can tell you.'

Having unpacked my kit and put it away I then go round to Jane's house. As I walk up the path, I'm met by her dad.

'Hello Dave, nice to see you again, I'll tell Jane you are here, she is round at a neighbour's house, I won't be a tick, go on in and make yourself at home.'

I park myself in an arm chair and wait. The cat sees me and scarpers, lucky for him he did, I remember the scratch it gave me last time we met, and I want to get my own back with a size 9 up its arse.

Jane runs into the lounge.

'Hi sweetie, how you been?' She said, putting her arms round my neck.

'Cold and miserable.' I tell her.

She whispers in my ear, 'I can warm you up.'

'Naughty, Naughty!' I whisper back. 'Are we going to the dance tonight?'

Maureen is looking forward to seeing John. I think she has been reading the Karma Sutra all week.

'I have already arranged with John to meet him and Maureen at the dance - I've missed you.'

'I've missed you too It's boring without you around.'

Jane goes off to get ready and I talk to her dad.

'How's the training going Dave?'

'Next week is the final week and then we Pass Out on the Friday.'

'Will you be getting any leave before you join your Regiment?'

'I get the weekend off and then I have to report to the Officers College at Aldershot.'

'Blimey! An Officer in the family. You know, Jane is always talking about you, she seems lost when you're not around.'

'I miss her as well when I am away.'

Jane comes back into the lounge and looks great.

'Ready?' she said putting on her coat.

We catch the bus to Bury Hall and meet up with John and Maureen.

'I understand you have been reading the Karma Sutra all week Maureen?' I say to her.

She colours up and puts her hands over her eyes.

'Ha! Ha! It's true then?'

John looks puzzled.

'Have I missed something?' He asks.

'Just a little joke.' I tell him.

'What's this about the Karma Sutra Maureen?' John asks.

'It's a book of love positions I've been reading, that's all.'

'Bloody Hell! I thought you knew them all already.' John said laughing.

Maureen thumps him on the arm, 'Shoooosh, someone might hear.'

'Now we know what you two get up to when we are not around.' I tell them.

The dance is pretty crowded and we only get on the floor a few times.

'You coming to our Passing Out parade next Friday girls?' John asked.

'I'm going with Dave's mum and dad, I've already been invited.' Jane said.

'You can come with my mum, Maureen; I'll arrange it with her, okay.'

After the dance I take Jane home and we kiss at her gate.

'Do you want to come in for a coffee?' She asks.

'Thanks, I'd like that.'

We go into the house. Her parents have gone to bed.

'If you listen you will hear them grunting and groaning, its nooky night for my oldies.'

'Jane how could you?'

She laughs and makes two cups of coffee.

We drink our coffee and have a kiss and a cuddle on the couch.

'Can we talk openly darling?' She asks.

'Of course, why.'

'It's just; that you have never once made a sexual pass at me Dave, why is that?'

'Jane I think a lot of you, when the time is right, perhaps I will do something about it. I'm not like John, who wants his oats with every girl he meets. It is hard for me to explain, I'm not sexually experienced. I have never touched a girl intimately except I once caressed one of Kathy's breasts, and that was only for a very short time and by mistake really. It was when she saw me off at the station when I left for the Congo.'

'You can caress mine if you like?'

Jane unbuttons her top and pulls it off. She is wearing a white flowery bra which she unclips and drops to the floor. She has very pert breasts.

'They are all yours.' She murmurs.

'Please don't get upset, but will you put your top back on.'

Jane picks her bra and top up and puts them back on.

As she is doing up the buttons she says, 'I wanted to see if you would do anything, I knew you wouldn't.'

'I'm sorry Jane, you are not going to believe this, but I'm scared to do anything. I do love you and I want to make love to you, just as John does with Maureen, but I can't, I'm sorry.'

'You really are a dear; I've never met anyone like you before Dave.'

'And probably never will again, I'm afraid it is my upbringing, I was taught that sex was for marriage, and not before, can you understand what I am saying?'

'Yes, I understand, but don't expect me to like it. I accept the way you have been brought up and I will try not to badger you. But don't be cross with me if I slip now and then. I'm missing out; you do realize that, don't you.'

'I suppose so.' I reply.

Things could have got out of hand then, but I'm glad she didn't press the matter, had she done so, I'm 100% sure I would have made love to her, I'm glad she didn't realize.

'Look, it's late, I must go, I'll see you tomorrow, and by the way, you have got lovely breasts.' I tell her.

'You shouldn't have looked. You should have closed your eyes.'

I kiss her goodnight and walk off home. I wonder what made her bring up sex. It must have been Maureen asking her if she had done it yet, I bet. There is more to life than getting your end away, I don't want any kids yet, and I have a lot of living to do before I'm ready to settle down.

I'm looking forward to going to Mons and joining my Regiment. My Battalion is at present in Malaya operating in the jungle. I miss the adventure - I wonder what Mike Hoare is up to at this moment in time - I hope he is okay - I must drop him a line.

The weekend is soon over and I return to camp with John. Snow is falling pretty steadily and it looks like it is going to lay. The weather forecasters have said that we may get a white Christmas. I hope not, I hate snow.

Over the next few days, we carry out drill and more drill ready for the Friday Passing out Parade. Some of the Platoon has been selected to give a Gym display for our guests. I'm glad I wasn't selected, John was though. He has to descend from a rope head first. I'm glad it is him and not me.

It will be nice to have the girls see us Pass Out. I'm sure they will enjoy it. I know my mum and dad will. All I hope is that that the weather is kind to us.

The day of our Passing Out Parade finally comes and we parade on the square ready for Inspection by the Lord Lieutenant of Hampshire. It is freezing and starts to rain. I'm not very happy with rain pouring down my neck. Still the Inspection will soon be over. I can see the girls waving out of the corner of my left eye. Sgt Blacker is presented with the Best Platoon Cup; it makes us all feel good. The Inspection over, we march past in quick and double time. Those chosen, change into PE kit for a demonstration of Physical Training. I go off with the rest of the Platoon to get the hut ready for our visitors to see where we sleep.

Now that the demonstrations are over we take our guests over to the NAAFI for tea. Jane is clinging to one arm and my mother to the other. We enter the NAAFI and sit at one of the decorated tables.

'This is a nice place son? Is this where you spend most of your time?' My mother asks.

'Sometimes, mum, but mostly we go down to the town and sit in one of the pubs.'

After tea we take them all round the camp and show off our accommodation.

'Christ! Is this where you sleep? Look how many beds are in here.' Jane exclaims.

'You get used to it after a while.' I tell her.

The platoon is given a week's leave, except for me and John; we have to be back in camp on Tuesday, because we are off to Aldershot for Officer Training at Mons. At least I will get some time with Jane and I'm sure I will get leave during my time at Mons, I hope so anyway.

It is nice not to go back to camp on a Sunday night. I take Jane all over the place, and see things that we have never seen before, like Nelson's Flagship, the Museum at Portsea. It is strange really we have these things on our doorstep and never see them.

I am really looking forward to going to Mons, I have read a bit about the place and it seems okay. I don't know how John will take the place, but we shall see.

He is with Maureen all the time, in fact, I don't think they get out of his bed, and if they do, it is only to eat or piss. He is a right randy bastard. Lucky his mum is away at her sisters, she wouldn't have stood for it, that's for sure.

Jane keeps pestering me about sex, she is either jealous of Maureen or she is a little prick teaser. I'm sure she doesn't want to make love really. I don't want to be tied down with kids yet, and anyway, I have heard from different people that the rubbers on the market aren't very reliable. (Note: This is in the 1960's, today's Contraceptives are much more reliable)

'Do you love me Dave?' Jane asked.

'I think so, why? Forget it; we are not getting in the sack.' I tell her.

She laughs and hugs me.

'I'm only teasing darling, I know how you feel.' She said with a glint in her eye.

'I bet you do, you little hussy, you deserve your bottom spanked.'

'Oh please Mr Soldier, please spank my bum!'

I gently smack her on the rear end.

'More, more, please Mr Soldier.'

What in the name of hell am I going to do with her?

Our few days are soon over and back to camp we go. We are both summoned to the Adjutants office.

'Remember you two, you are representing the Regiment, don't let it or us down, good luck to you both.'

We shake hands with the Adjutant and proceed on our way to Mons.

On arrival at Mons we are taken by surprise, more wooden huts, surely the Army doesn't revolve round "Wooden Huts." Well, at least we are used to them. I think I have been in huts all my life, well, it feels like it.

The training is pretty stiff and we have to bull everything. Our boots have to be immaculate as well as our uniforms. The man management part is very good and we adapt to it easily, especially as we were once officers anyway and use to dealing with men.

The weapon training comes as second nature, but the runs are still murder. We have to pitch ourselves to the limit. The rest of the squad we are in, seem to find it hard and we help them out as and when we can. John cracks a rib on the confidence course but never reports it. He went to a local doctor and had it strapped up, so that the powers that be wouldn't send him back to the Depot.

We have to go on exercises of differing magnitudes, some are really horrendous, but we just about cope. We do stacks of work in the evenings learning Staff Duties in the Field and how to look after soldiers who have problems; you have to be a mum and dad to some of them. Who'd be an officer?

One weekend is all we are getting off throughout the course and thank goodness it is coming up soon. The RSM and training Staff are very good and nothing like what we are used to. It is strange being called Mr all the time, instead of STUBBS and WEST. I must admit I am looking forward to commanding a Platoon.

The weeks go by and the training becomes easier. I spend our only weekend off with Jane. We have a great time and she is now getting used to having a boyfriend who is an officer. Maureen don't seem to have come to terms with it though, she is giving John stick.

At last, the day has finally come for our Passing out Parade at Mons. The Inspecting Officer is Sir Roderick Mountbatten, the Permanent under Secretary of State for Defence. He seems a right prat. He presents each of us with our 2nd Lieutenants scroll and shakes our hands in turn, wishing us well in the Regiments that we are going to.

The Parade goes off quite smoothly, we have to do a March Past in normal time, which isn't too well done, but who cares. The inspecting officer is probably in a hurry to get a Gin and Tonic down his neck to worry about straight lines anyway.

I am now a 2nd Lieutenant in the 43rd and 52nd Oxfordshire and Buckinghamshire Light Infantry or better known as the 1st Battalion, Green jackets. John unfortunately has been commissioned in the Kings Royal Rifle Corps, better known as the 2nd Battalion, Green Jackets.

This will be the first time we have been separated since we left school. Perhaps he will be able to get a transfer, or I can.

We wear our uniforms home, with one new black star on each epaulette.

'It's going to be great Dave we have made it at last.' John said caressing one of the new stars, 'This is going to be our greatest adventure, you mark my words.'

'I hope so John, at least, it won't be boring.'

'Boring! We won't have time to get bored; we will be running a Platoon.'

CHAPTER SEVEN

It's nice to have some long leave. Both of us have been given 2 weeks off before reporting for duty with our respective Battalions. My Battalion is at present in Malaya and John's is in Colchester. I intend to see a lot of Jane over this period as I will be away for quite some time in the near future.

One evening whilst going to visit Jane, I bump into Kathy.

'How are you?' I ask, 'Are you going out with anyone yet?'

'Not at the moment.' She replied, 'I did go out with a boy for a time but he wasn't for me, are you still seeing Jane?'

'Yes, I'm just off to see her now, though it isn't the same as being with you. Did you know I'm a 2nd Lieutenant now, I have just passed out from Mons Officers School?'

'So now you are an Officer, I bet Jane is pleased?'

'It's nothing to write home about really, though it means more money, I still miss you like blazes Kathy.'

'And I miss you, but I'm not going to do anything about it, you were right, it wouldn't have worked out between us, as much as I love you.'

'You know I will always love you Kathy.'

'Of course, and I won't stop loving you, no matter what, after all you were my first love and I yours, it is only right that we should feel this way.'

I say goodbye to her and walk on to Jane's house. I don't think I will ever get over Kathryn but it won't stop me from going out with other girls, mainly Jane at the moment. I will never understand women, and if the truth is known, no one else will either.

Having arrived at Jane's house, she takes me into the front room so that we can be alone. We discuss our future together.

'Are you still going to go out with me now that you have become an officer Dave?' She asked.

'Of course I am, but unfortunately, my Battalion is in Malaya until the end of next year, so we won't be seeing much of each other. I understand that I can apply for leave in the UK after being out there for 6 months, so it won't be too long before I am home again will it. And there is certainly one thing in its favour. I won't be able to go out with anyone else all the time I am out there, because we are in the jungle.'

'So you want me to wait for you?'

'Yes I do, will you?'

'Yes Dave, I will. I won't go out with anyone else, I promise.'

We kiss and cuddle. Things could get out of hand here. I had better take her out.

'Come on, let's go down the pub.'

Jane collects her coat and we walk hand in hand to the Ship Public House. If I had stayed in the house, I don't think I could have kept my hands off of her, and I think she thought the same. If, I had started anything, I don't think she would have stopped me.

The day comes when I have to leave for the airport.

'Can I come and see you off Dave.' Jane asked.

'I would love for you to come and see me off, but, don't you think it is a long way to come just for a few minutes?'

'I still would like to see you off darling. After all, you will be gone for such a long time.'

We arrive at Heathrow airport. I remember the last time I came here. It was to go to Africa. Now it's Malaya. My flight has been delayed for some reason. I look at the flight screen and see that all Army personnel are to report to security.

'I wonder what that is about.' I say to Jane.

'You had better go and find out darling.' She replied.

I go to the security office and find that there are about 10 other different ranks in the office.

'I'm Lt Stubbs, What's the problem?'

A Major arrives and informs us that all Army personnel are being sent to Aden as there is an emergency on. Individual units will be informed. I tell the Major that I should be on my way to Malaya, as they also have an emergency on.

'Mr Stubbs, your commanding officer has already been informed and you are now in command of these men. You are to report to Air Movements on arrival in Aden, they are expecting you, I'm afraid things have got a bit out of hand in Aden at the moment, and they need all the men they can get.'

I go back to where I left Jane.

'Sorry sweetheart, but I'm now off to Aden, and God knows when I will see you again. It looks as if I have been commandeered to do some other job, bloody nuisance isn't it.'

'I don't know darling, it might not be for so long.' She replied.

A Warrant Officer comes up to me.

'I understand Sir that you are in charge of the men going to Aden, my name is Taylor and I'm from the Cheshire Regiment, do you need any help?'

'Thanks Mr Taylor, I would appreciate it. Do you know how many men we will have with us?'

'You will have to check the flight lists with movements Sir, do you want me to come with you?' He replied.

'I certainly do Sarn't Major

I leave Jane having a cup of coffee and we both go off to the movement office. All in all, there are 25 men due to fly out to different locations around the world, and all are now under my command.

I feel strange having so many men relying on me to give the right decisions. I gather the men together and explain to them that I know as much as they do about what was going on. They seemed to understand.

'Have any of you been to Aden before?'

No one replied.

'Then we are all in the same boat, so try not to worry too much about it.'

Whether they believed me or not, I just don't know.

I again return to where I left Jane. I find that she is being chatted up by a soldier from the Movements Section.

'Have you got a boyfriend then?' he asks her.

'Actually, I have and he is right behind you.' She replied.

The soldier turns round and stammers, 'SSSSSorry Sir, I didn't know the lady was with you.'

I laugh as he walks swiftly away.

'Oh darling, you have spoilt my fun, he was just about to ask me out.'

'Trust you to lead him on, you deserve a spanking.'

'Yes please. Mr Officer' she replied laughing.

A call comes over the tannoy for me to attend the Movements Office. I take CSM Taylor with me. We are told that our aircraft is waiting at Gate No 3 and that we should make our way to the plane.

I return to Jane and kiss her goodbye.

'I'll write as soon as I can darling, I'll miss you heaps.'

'Me too, I love you.'

I gather the men together and we make our way to the aircraft at gate Number 3.

'Put your suitcases on that truck.' Said a uniformed airport employee.

We load the cases on the truck and board the aircraft.

Once on board, we are told that the flight will be in 2 stages, with a stop off in Malta. Meals would be served during the flight. I haven't flown with the RAF before, so I have no idea what it will be like. I wonder what we will be doing in Aden. The stop off in Malta wasn't too bad. It was quite hot and very humid. We are not allowed to leave the airport lounge. The aircraft is refuelled and we re-board and take off for Aden.

After what seemed like hours and hours we finally land at Khormaksar airfield. Boy is it hot.

We collect our cases and report to the Movements Office.

'Welcome to Aden.' said a Captain in sandy coloured clothing. 'Are you in charge?' He asks me.

I salute and tell him that I have been given that unenviable task.

'Come with me?' he replied.

We walk off into a large office.

'You are now under command of 43 Commando at Al Milah, they will be sending some trucks for you shortly, I'm afraid I don't know any more than that. Good luck.'

I return to the men and inform them what the Captain had just told me.

'It looks as if we will be taking orders from the Navy from now on.' Said a Lance Corporal from the DLI.

After about 20 minutes, the trucks arrive. They are covered in yellow dust.

'Okay lads, get aboard and we will be on our way.' The driver of the leading truck said.

We throw our cases on and climb aboard the trucks.

The journey is a dusty one and we soon arrive at 43 Commando Brigade.

'Come with me Sergeant Major.'

We enter a large tent, and speak to a clerk sitting at a typewriter.

'My name is Lt Stubbs and this is CSM Taylor, we have just arrived from the UK, do you know anything about us?'

'One moment Sir, I'll get the Adjutant, he knows all about you coming here.'

We sit in some chairs and wait. After about 5 minutes the clerk returns and tells us that the Adjutant would be along shortly.

'Funny how no one is available to greet us, especially as we have come such a long way to meet everyone.' I say to CSM Taylor.

The clerk just stares.

'I've worked with the Royal Marines before Sir, funny outfit; they always seem to get the best trouble spots if I remember correctly.'

A Captain enters the tent.

'Welcome to 43 Commando Brigade, I trust you had a pleasant journey. Now your job whilst you are here will be to patrol the highway north of Al Milah. We have a problem with the natives; they seem to want to kill us for some reason or other. Your first patrol will start at 1600hrs tonight. I'll see that you and your men are kitted out and shown where to sleep. Unfortunately, we are only a tented camp and it does get dusty at times. Make sure once you have been issued with weapons that you keep them with you at all times. There will be a briefing at 1500hrs in the Ops Tent which is 6 tents down from this one. Cpl Tonks, show Lt Stubbs' men where their tents are. You and Mr Taylor will be sharing a tent in the Officers Lines. Your tent is 9 tents down from the Ops Tent; your names are on a board outside it. Take your cases to your tent and come back here and I will take you to get your kit.'

We both salute and lug our cases down the row of tents until we find ours.

'Not another bloody tent, one day I will get away from them, they are a fucking nightmare.' I say out loud.

'You been billeted in tents before then Sir?' Taylor asked.

'It's a long story, which bed do you want?'

'This one will do.'

'It's yours.'

Having unpacked our cases and stowed our belongings in the lockers provided, we then return to the Adjutant.

We are taken to a large tent which has sandbags all around it to a height of 6 feet.

'Just in case, we are attacked.' The adjutant said, 'And don't worry, it hasn't happened yet.'

'Famous last words come to mind.' Said CSM Taylor.

Now kitted out we return to our tent.

'Get the men together Mr Taylor and I will give them a briefing as to what is going on so far.'

'Will do, Sir.'

He leaves the tent and goes off to find the men. After a few minutes I follow after him. I inform the guys that they are not to leave their weapons unattended and they must be carried at all times even to the shower and toilet.

'Are we in the shit then Sir?' asked a private in the Devon and Dorset's.

'I don't think so, but I have been informed by their Adjutant that the natives are not very friendly towards us, so we can't be too careful.'

I leave the men to get their kit together and go off to the briefing.

'Welcome to Aden Mr Stubbs, I trust you have settled in. How many men have you brought with you,' asked Lt Colonel Carter, the Commanding Officer of 43 Commando, Royal Marines.

'I have 1 CSM, 1 Sgt and 23 assorted other ranks Sir.'

'Not really enough, but it will have to do. Your job will be to patrol the north of the camp for about 25 miles along the road to Thurmier. (Pointing to a spot on a map) Do not go further than here (again pointing to a map) or you will encounter very heavy mortar fire. I do not want any casualties, at least not yet.'

I write down everything the Colonel has said. It's not looking very good.

The Colonel outlines the situation and details each officer in turn to a specific task.

'Any questions?' The Colonel asks.

'Just one Sir, what support do I have if we come under fire?'

'You will have fighter and bomber support from the RAF, as and when you require it, just radio them and they will do the rest. At least I think they will. Just remember, you have to give the grid reference first before they will assist you. They have been very good lately, giving us enormous support, use them.'

I'm cheered up no end, and I'm sure the lads will be as well.

The briefing is over. I return to our tent.

'Mr Taylor, I want to let the lads know what is going on.'

CSM Taylor rounds the men up and I inform them of the patrols we have to do. We have been allocated 5 vehicles. The patrol will last about 4 hours and we should be back in camp by at least 2215hrs. I then start to detail off drivers and Signallers.

'Right - let's see who we have got for each vehicle - Mr Taylor - you take Privates Saunders and Hayes, Sappers Howard and Stokes - Sgt Woods you will take Privates Jones, Donald, Wales and Sapper French - Cpl Souter you will take Sappers O'Neill, Cunnliffe, Brownlow and Private Davies - LCpl Walsh you will take Privates Hind and Maitland, Sapper Walsh and Trooper Smith - I will take Privates Dunland, Joshua, Hope and Guardsman Ford - Drivers will be, Saunders, French, Davies, Hind and Ford, Signallers are Howard, Jones, Brownlow, Walsh and Dunland. Collect the vehicles and radios in 20 minutes from the Stores Section, the rest of you are to collect the ammunition, ration packs and water - drivers make sure you have plenty of fuel and spare Jerri cans - signallers plenty of spare batteries, any questions?' None were forthcoming.

'Right - let's get to it.'

The vehicles are collected and all equipment stowed on them. The men are keen to get going, I am as well, and I don't like tented camps.

'Check comms with HQ.' I tell each operator.

'All okay.' They each inform me.

'Well Mr Taylor, if everything is okay, let's get going. Inform the drivers will you, to keep about 20yds from the vehicle in front of them, I don't pity the vehicle at the rear in these dusty conditions, it's going to be absolutely covered. Also tell them to keep their eyes peeled; we don't want to get caught unawares. At the first sign of trouble, dismount and take up firing positions, but don't return fire unless you have a target. I don't want any indiscriminate shooting, let's move out.'

We proceed out of the camp in single file, each vehicle 20 yards apart. I hope we don't run into anything on our first day in Aden. I must try and write to Jane tonight and let her know what is going on.

The patrol has been out for nearly 3 hours and all we have seen are some dirty Arabs selling their wares at the side of the road. I suppose we are doing a good job letting the population see the Army is around. We hear gun fire in the distance, but it is out of our area, thank goodness.

The patrol over, we start making our way back to camp. I inform HQ that the area is quiet.

'The calm before the storm.' replied the HQ radio operator.

I wonder what he meant by that. Cpl Souter's voice comes over the radio.

'Alpha Four to Alpha One, men with weapons to our right, over.'

I stop the patrol and check the area with my bino's - I can't see anyone - but that doesn't mean that Souter hasn't.

'Alpha Two take Alpha Four and check the area, over.'

'Alpha Two - wilco, out.'

I stand the rest of the vehicles to. After about 20 minutes, the two vehicles return.

'There are plenty of footprints, but no bodies Sir.' Taylor informs me.

'I'll tell HQ when we get back, mount up and let's get out of here.'

We arrive back in camp covered in yellow dust.

'Leave the ammo and stores on the vehicles and get cleaned up. I'll arrange some scoff for you in the cookhouse.'

I inform HQ of the facts. We have now completed one very safe patrol. I walk back to the tent with CSM Taylor.

'Not a bad bunch of lads are they? Keen to get stuck in.'

'Souter is pretty keen Sir, he definitely saw something, and there were loads of footprints around the area where he said he saw those men.'

'Yes, he should do well in the Army, how long has he been in?'

'I think about 6 years; he has just been promoted to Corporal.'

We arrive back at our tent. I must write to Jane tonight and let her know how I am.

'Would you like a drink Sir?' said CSM Taylor producing a bottle of whiskey.

'Is the Pope a Catholic?' I reply.

Together we sink half the bottle. Taylor is okay, he is my kind of man.

'What's your first name?' I ask him.

'Tim.' he replied.

'Mines Dave, I don't mind you using my first name Tim when we are on our own, forget rank in here, okay.'

'Fine, by me, Dave.'

'It's my turn for a bottle tomorrow, that is, if we get the time to drink it.'

I write to Jane and explain to her what is going on and who I have met since being out in Aden. God forsaken place this is. I finish my letter and turn in, I'm too tired to go and get any food.

'I'm off to the Mess tent, you want me to bring you anything back Dave?' Tim asked.

'No thanks Tim, I'm going to get some sleep, thanks anyway.'

Over the following weeks we carry out many patrols, mostly pretty boring yet extremely dangerous.

One morning I'm woken sharply by one of the Guard.

'You are wanted in the Ops tent Sir.'

'Bloody hell, what time is it?'

'0400hrs Sir.' the Guard replied.

I get dressed and make my way to the Ops Tent.

'You wanted to see me Sir?' I ask the 2IC.

'Ah David, just the man, in half an hour, I want you and your boys to start a patrol of this area, (pointing to an area on the map) we believe there is a large concentration of rebels there. I want you to check it out, but don't go further than here; (pointing to the map) otherwise you will be in trouble from the Rebels encamped here.' (Again pointing to the map)

'How long are we to be out for Sir?'

'I want you to complete the patrol by 1300hrs as I have a further task for your boys this evening, any further questions?'

'No Sir.'

'Right on your way then, you should aim to be on the road by 0515hrs at the latest.'

Bloody hell! I'm glad I went to bed early last night. I head back to the tent and wake Tim Taylor.

'What's up Dave?'

'Get the boys woken up Tim we have pulled a short straw; we are heading for the hills. Forget about washing and shaving get all equipment stowed in the vehicles, and ready to roll by 0515hrs.'

'Fucking Heck.' Said Tim rushing out of the tent doing up his trousers.

After a while Tim returns and we both gather our kit and load it on our vehicles.

'Sergeant Major, you take two vehicles with you and I'll take the other three with me. Check radios with HQ and then Radio Silence. Once we get out of camp, stop at the 3 mile marker and I'll brief the men.'

'Will do Sir.' Taylor replies.

They all seem keen to get on with the job. I have the most irregular bunch of men you could lay your hands on. None of them fully know each other, yet they are so in tune it is as if they have served together for years. I'm quite proud of them.

At the 3 mile marker I brief the men on the task we have to carry out. I show them on the map the area we will be covering and what to look out for.

'We are not to go further than here; (pointing to the area on the map which the 2IC had shown me) we should be back in camp by 1300hrs at the latest as we have a further task to complete this evening, any questions?'

We remount the vehicles and move along the road to Thurmier. After going about 11 miles, CSM Taylor stops his vehicle. I drive up alongside him.

'What's up?' I ask him.

He points to some dust coming towards us. It looks like a load of vehicles.

'Dismount lads, and be prepared for action.' I shout at them.

They all dismount and take up firing positions around their vehicles. Suddenly the radio crackles into life.

'Hold your fire we are friendly forces, password is CREAM CRACKER.'

'Stand down lads, they are ours.' Shouts CSM Taylor.

'Watch out for bandits.' Shouts a driver as they hurry by.

'Who in the name of hell are they?' Asked my driver.

'SAS I expect.'

'Christ, they out here as well.' Said my driver.

'I think everyone including the kitchen sink is out here.' I reply.

I wouldn't mind joining the SAS, I bet it is a lot more fun than what I am doing now. We remount the vehicles and over the next 6 hours thoroughly check the area and find nothing.

'Right, back to Camp, lads.'

About 2 miles from the Camp, my Land rover suddenly lifts into the air. There is a very loud bang and I feel extreme pain in my legs. I am propelled through the air and that is the last I know of anything.

After I don't know how long, I regain consciousness, and see CSM Taylor hovering over me. He puts his hand on my shoulder.

'Don't get up Sir, you passed out for a time; you are okay, just a bit of concussion that's all.'

'I can't feel my legs Tim, are they mangled?'

'No, I think they are numbed with the force of the vehicle floor coming up, it looks as if you ran over a hidden mine, just lie still, the medics are coming.'

'Any of the lads hurt?'

'No, thank goodness. We were lucky though the vehicle wasn't. It must have been one of those Russian Landmines.'

The medics from the Camp arrive and as my vehicle is totally knackered, I'm taken away in an ambulance to the Field Hospital.

At the hospital I'm seen by a doctor who has only just come out to Aden.

'Your legs are okay but you are going to feel a lot of pain in them over the next few months Lieutenant; I'll give you an injection to ease it for the time being.'

'My legs are still there then?'

'Oh Yes, the force of the vehicle floor coming up constricted the veins and stopped the blood flow, I'm afraid you may have problems in the future, but we shall see.'

'Thanks Doc.'

I'm glad no one else was hurt, I have been in Aden for 32 days and now I'm injured, what the hell next. The pain is really bad and the doctor gives me another jab in both legs.

On the 2nd day in the hospital, the pain eases and I try to walk. The pain returns, but I persevere. I am determined to walk again. After 7 days, I am able to walk around unaided. The doctor gives me a spray to use on my legs.

'That should ease the pain for you.'

I hope he is right; the pain in them is awful at times.

As I can't walk properly at the moment I am stuck in Camp whilst the rest of the guys carry out tasks around the area. Tim Taylor is in charge whilst I am incapacitated. He is a good man and the guys like him.

The CO calls for me and I attend his tent.

'I'm afraid I will have to send you home Dave, I have spoken to the Doc and he thinks that you should be sent back to the UK for treatment on your legs, so get your kit packed. A plane is leaving at 2000hrs. Thank you for the assistance you have given me since being here and I am sorry if this little episode upsets your posting to Malaya, good luck.'

The CO shakes my hand and I go back to the tent to pack. What a stroke of luck, I'll be back in England for the weekend, Jane here I come.

The men are out in the desert till 2200hrs so I will not see them again. I write a note to Tim and leave it on his bed. I hope he looks me up when he can.

On the way to the airfield, I remember the tasks we did in the Radfan, God what a place that was. I'm glad I'm leaving Aden, I can see this place exploding and I certainly don't want to be around when it does. I've been told that I will get the General Service Medal with the clasp Radfan, my first British Medal. I will miss the lads; I hope I meet up with them again sometime.

I board the Andover and after refuelling twice arrive at Brize Norton.

I am met by a Rifleman from the Kings Royal Rifle Corps.

'Are you Lt Stubbs?' he asks.

'I am he.' I reply.

'I'm to take you to the Rifle Depot Sir.'

'You haven't come here in a Land Rover have you?'

'No Sir, a Staff Car.'

'Bloody Hell, a comfortable ride.'

'I don't understand Sir.'

'No matter, lead the way Macduff.'

'My name is Baines Sir, not Macduff.'

'Well Rfn Baines, let's get the hell out of here and lead me to my comfortable carriage.'

He takes my suitcase and holdall and using the crutches they gave me in Aden, I hobble to the car.

Staff car treatment and treated like a King at last, but how long, will this last, I wonder.

We arrive at the Rifle Depot in time for breakfast.

'Drop me at the Officers Mess will you.'

'Certainly, Sir.'

At 0900hrs, Baines re-appears.

'I have to take you to the Orderly Room, Sir.'

'Thank you Baines that will save me a walk.'

'I have been told that I have to drive you everywhere you want to go Sir.'

'Now that is what I call service, thank you.'

I'm taken to the Orderly Room and see the Adjutant.

'Well, Well, Well! You have only just left us and you are back again, what's the matter, didn't you like the 1st Battalion? I'm only joking David. It was unfortunate that you happened to arrive at the Airport when the signal went out to ship everyone to Aden. I hope it wasn't too ghastly. By the way, how are your pins now?'

'I still get a lot of pain, but I'm coping. Am I still going to Malaya?'

'No, you are swapping postings with John West, you take over his platoon in "D" Company, 2nd Battalion KRRC and he will be going out to Malaya. In fact, he should be on the plane now.'

Damn! I was hoping to see him in Colchester before I went to my Battalion. I bet he loves me.

I'm sent on leave for a few days before joining the Battalion. It will be nice to see Jane again, I have missed her.

Baines drives me to the station and I board the train for Fareham. I will surprise Jane by just turning up at her house instead of ringing her.

My mum and dad are pleased to see me and I explain the reasons for not going to Malaya. I tell them John has gone in my place.

'Stone the Crows Son, Tina West isn't going to be very pleased with you.'

'I know dad, but it isn't my fault, I didn't want to get blown up, I was looking forward to going to Malaya.'

I change into civvies and hobble down to Jane's house. I knock the door and her dad opens it. He is about to shout Jane and I stop him.

'I want to surprise her.'

'Come in lad, she is upstairs.'

I follow him into the lounge and sit by the TV and read the paper. After about 10 minutes, Jane comes into the lounge.

'Oh sorry dad, I didn't know you had company.'

I still keep the paper in front of me.

'Shall I make you some tea dad?'

'Please love and a cup for my friend here.'

Jane goes into the kitchen and soon returns with a tray and cups. She passes me a cup and saucer and I put the paper down.

I never get the cup of tea as she drops it onto the floor.

'You are supposed to be in Aden. I saw you off. Anyway, I have a bone to pick with you. I have only received one letter, what are you doing home?' She retorts.

'Aren't you glad to see me?'

She leaps at me and smothers me in kisses.

'Oh darling, I have missed you.'

'I have missed you as well, Ouch! Mind my legs. I have had a sort of accident with them.'

I tell her about the land rover blowing up and being posted to Colchester instead of Malaya and John taking my place.

'Maureen isn't going to be very pleased about this, is she?' said Jane.

'I have to deal with John's mother first. She expected him to be in England for quite some time, and this is something even I don't relish.'

I stay at Jane's talking till well into the early hours and then return home. My mother is waiting up for me.

'Are you going to see John's mother today Dave?'

'I think so mum, after all, he has taken my place in Malaya and she will need an explanation.'

I retire to bed and sleep the sleep of the dead.

After breakfast I go to see Tina West.

'Hello David, nice to see you, why are you limping?'

'Hello Tina, I had an accident, my land rover was blown up and I injured my legs. The veins contracted and they have given me a lot of pain ever since. I have to go to hospital every other day to see if something can be done for me. The doctors say that short of taking the veins out, there isn't much that can be done. They have given me a pretty good spray to use and it helps a bit.'

'I understand John has taken your job in Malaya?' Tina said making a pot of tea.

'Yes they shipped him out as I was returning to Winchester; I didn't even get to see him. I asked the Adjutant if I could see him before he went, but was told that he had already gone. I'm sorry he had to go.'

'It's not your fault Dave, I was hoping that he would be staying in England a bit longer, but not to worry, I'm sure he will enjoy himself.'

I didn't have the heart to tell her that there was a war going on out there.

Having spent a few hours with Tina I then return home. My brother is home on leave.

'Well, hello Sir, I trust all is well with you.' My brother said.

'Cobblers, and stop calling me Sir, I'm your brother, not your CO.'

We both laugh and go off to the town together.

'How's your legs Dave?' He asked.

'Not bad mate, they give me gip now and then, I wish I was still in Aden, I miss the excitement.'

'You are better out of it, that place is going to go off with a bang, you mark my words.'

I meet up with Jane in the evening and we go to the cinema. The film isn't much and we slowly walk to the town and spend an hour in the Mocambo Cafe.

'What are you going to do now Dave? When have you got to report to Colchester?'

'I've got to return on Tuesday, so we have got some time together.'

We slowly walk home and I kiss her goodnight at the door.

'Do you want to come in darling? Mum and dad will be in bed and I want you to make love to me.'

'As much as I would very much like to make love to you, I think we should wait until we are married, I know I'm old fashioned, but that is the way I am.'

'Oh you spoil sport, get off home before I pull the trousers of you.'

I kiss her goodnight and walk up the street to my house.

As much as I love Jane, I don't want to have intercourse with her, so do I really love her. Any other person would have jumped at the chance to get her into bed. I am totally fucked. We spend every waking hour together but Tuesday finally comes.

I say goodbye and board the train for London and onwards to Colchester. At Colchester I ask the Station Master where Roman Way Barracks is.

'It's a long walk, you will have to take a taxi Sir; it is quite a way out of town.'

Outside the station is a Taxi Rank where I ask a driver to take me to Roman Way Barracks. Once there I report to the Orderly Room.

'Welcome to the 2nd Battalion Kings Royal Rifle Corps, you will be taking over 16 Platoon; our other man had to replace someone in Malaya.' The adjutant said.

'Yes I know that man was me.' I reply.

'Cpl Woods, take Lt Stubbs to "D" Company Lines.'

'Very good Sir, follow me Sir, it is just over there.'

I follow Woods to "D" Company and he introduces me to Major Radford.

'Welcome to "D" Company Stubbs, you have a fine Platoon, the men are very experienced and the Platoon Sgt and the Corporals are first class, learn from them.'

'Very good, Sir.'

'Come with me and I will show you where they are.'

We go to the Platoon lines and find the Platoon Sgt giving lessons. As we enter the room, he calls the Platoon to attention.

'Sgt Johnston, this is Lt Stubbs, your new Platoon Commander.'

'Welcome to 16 Platoon Sir.'

'Thank you Sgt I'm sure we will get along fine.'

I tell the men that I will be seeing each one in turn so that I can get to know them.

'Fall the men out for a break Sgt Johnston, I want you to take Lt Stubbs around the Battalion and show him all the places of interest, be back in my office by 1400hrs the both of you, any questions Stubbs?'

'None, at the moment, Sir.' I reply.

Sgt Johnston shows me the different Company Lines.

'Each Company has its own Stores and Armoury, these buildings are our Company Stores and that one (pointing to a small brick type shed) is our Armoury.'

'What weapons do we have in there?' I ask him.

'There are about 100 Self Loading Rifles (SLRs), 25 Sterling Sub Machine Guns (SMGs), 25 Bren Guns, 5 Pistols, a few Rocket Launchers, 2 inch Mortars, and Flare Pistols, the Bren's are shortly to be replaced with the General Purpose Machine Gun (GPMG) which we understand fires about 1000 rounds a minute. I think we should make our way back to the OCs office Sir.'

We return to Major Radford's office and I bang on the door.

'Come in!'

We enter his office and salute. Inside are more people who I don't know.

'Find a seat both of you, what I have to tell you all is at the moment for your ears only. You are not to discuss what I am about to tell you with anyone, is that clear?'

Everyone in the room nods in agreement.

'I have to inform you that the Battalion is now on Spearhead and "D" Company is Spearhead Company. That means if anything happens in the world and the British Army is required, we are the first to go. Any questions?'

'How does that affect the long weekend that is coming up Sir?' One of the sergeants asks.

'Everyone is to fill in a form with their contact address and hand it into the Company Clerk before they proceed on weekend leave. Inform each member of your Platoons that if they fail to return to Camp, they will be treated as deserters and not absentees. So make sure you get your entire Platoon back.'

A few more questions are asked and we are told to leave.

'Lt Stubbs, stay behind please.'

I wonder what he wants me for.

'I have been going over your record since joining the Green Jackets, it is quite impressive, you did extremely well at Mons and your grades were excellent. I also see that you have a commendation from the Brigade Commander for saving a fellow Rifleman's life, well done. I believe the person was none other than Lt West who has replaced you in Malaya.'

'That's correct Sir, he had acute appendicitis, and anyone would have done it given the same circumstances.'

'Quite so, the true spirit of the Green Jackets, I want you to get fully conversant with the men of 16 Platoon, your Platoon will be the first to go if we are called out, don't let me down, I expect great things from you.'

'Yes Sir.'

I return to the Platoon and instruct Sgt Johnston to send each man in turn to my office so that I can get acquainted with them.

'I'll see the Corporals first and you last, who is the first one?'

'Cpl Tyne Sir, He's a very good NCO and has been selected to attend the Sergeant's Course in the summer.'

'Well, let's have him in then.'

Cpl Tyne enters my office and salutes.

'Sit down Cpl Tyne, as you know I am interviewing the entire platoon so that I can get to know you, please tell me something about yourself?'

'Well Sir, I'm 26 years old and have a wife and baby girl, I've been in the Army for 6 years and have served in Libya and Germany. I have been selected to attend the Sergeants Course in June this year.'

'Is your family in quarters?'

'Yes Sir, I live in Leathy Grove, just opposite the Army Nick, the quarter is quite nice except for the big bell over the front door, which rings every now and again.'

'Big bell.'

'Yes Sir, every time a prisoner escaped, the bloody bell rings, they put them in all the quarters in Leathy Grove because they were once occupied by the Military Provost Staff Corp who staff the prison.'

'I see. Can't the bells be removed?'

'I don't think so Sir, it would cost too much and you know what the government is like at spending money.'

'Yes, I suppose you are right, but let me know if this bell annoys you and I will definitely get something done about it, in fact, I will ring the Ministry of Works and see if they can disable the bell. Are you the only one living in ex Provost Staff Corp quarters?'

'Sgt Johnston and Cpl Dicks live a few doors down from me Sir.'

'Have you any questions to ask me Cpl?'

'No Sir, except welcome to the Platoon Sir.'

'Thank you Cpl Tyne, I'm sure we will make a great team, can you send in Cpl Dicks please.'

Cpl Tyne salutes and leaves the office. He seems a capable man and he should do well on the Sgts Course. A knock at the door and Cpl Dicks enters and salutes.

'Hello Cpl Dicks, please sit down and tell me a bit about yourself.'

'Well Sir, I've been in the Army for 10 years and have spent most of it on detached duties in Germany. I'm married and have 3 kids, 2 girls and a boy. I live in married quarters opposite the Nick. I have been in 16 Platoon for nearly 2 years and have attended the Platoon Sergeants Course and I'm just waiting to be posted as a Platoon Sergeant to "A" Company, I don't really want to leave "D" Company, but they won't let me stay here on promotion Sir.'

'It would seem that I will be needing, 2 new Cpls, is there anyone in the Platoon worth promoting?'

'Only LCpl Jones, Sir.'

'What's he like as a soldier?'

'Very good Sir, he received a GOC's commendation in Germany for stopping some people from breaking into a station armoury.'

'Did he now, what does Sgt Johnston think of him'

'Hard to say Sir, Sarn't Johnston keeps thing very close to his chest.'

I ask Dicks some more questions and he then leaves the office. I interview the rest of the Platoon and it would seem that I have got a great bunch of lads. Sgt Johnston enters my office and I ask him a lot of questions about himself and what he has done since being with the Company. He seems a very able Sergeant and I like him, he is my kind of guy, we should get on very well together. It would seem that Major Radford was correct when he told me that I had a great Platoon. I think I am going to like the 2nd Battalion.

Over the next few days I get everything sorted out about the Platoon and even get the Ministry of Public Buildings and Works to get the bells disconnected in the married quarters. That in its self was no mean feat. They are real buggers to deal with. I think of Jane and look forward to the weekend. I miss her in a funny sort of way. Perhaps I am in love at last.

I receive word from the OC that the Company is to muster in the Gymnasium with the rest of the Battalion. I wonder what is up.

The Colonel tells the whole Regiment that it is now on Spearhead and explains what it would entail. "D" Company are Spearhead Company for a month and 16 Platoon is Spearhead Platoon. All our equipment must be packed and ready at all times. All men must book in and out at the Guardroom and leave where they can be contacted at all times. Weekend leave may have to be curtailed. Bloody Hell! I hope they don't stop this weekend.

'Well! Sgt Johnston, what trouble spots have we got in this wide world of ours?'

'To be perfectly honest Sir, I don't know.'

'Well, if there are any, let's hope they don't explode this weekend.'

'I'll agree with that Sir.'

We return to the Company Lines and I collect the packing lists from the Company Clerk. All kit on the list must be packed in the equipment stated. There is nothing to it really; it is no different than when we pack for exercises. I give each Corporal a list and tell them that I will carry out a Platoon inspection in a couple of hours. Any man who requires kit must report to the Company Colour Sergeant immediately to get the items missing replaced.

A few hours go by and I return to the Platoon lines and carry out an inspection of each man's kit. Thank goodness for really switched on NCOs, no one has anything missing.

'Sgt Johnston, I want all Platoon weapons bundled and labelled and stored in the Company Armoury in the boxes provided. Make sure that all the weapons are cleaned first.'

'I've already got that sorted Sir; the men will clean them this afternoon.'

'Well done Sarn't, I knew I could rely on you, right, let's get busy, the sooner we get all this sorted, the sooner we can relax. By the way, I will be buying in the All Ranks NAAFI tonight for anyone who wants to join me for a drink.'

I return to my room in the Mess and pack my kit, Christ! Some of this kit has never been used. After dinner, I go to the All Ranks NAAFI. The whole Platoon is there.

'This is going to be an expensive evening; I didn't think you would all turn up, what are you all having?'

Just before closing, a bugle is sounded.

'Does anyone know that Bugle Call.' I asked.

'Company Lines Muster, Sir.' The barman informs me.

We all leave the NAAFI, slightly worse for drink and parade outside "D" Company Office. The OC and the Company Sergeant Major are waiting. I ask the OC what is wrong.

'I'm glad you didn't go out tonight David, because I have just received instructions. We have been ordered to British Guiana to quell some riots.

Get your platoon together and parade ready to move in one hour, coaches will be arriving to take you your Platoon to RAF Lynham. The rest of the Company will be following in a few hours' time. All the instructions are in this pack, read it on the coach. Good luck, see you in BG.'

Bloody Hell! Bang goes my weekend.

I return to the Mess and write a quick note to my parents and Jane and hand the letters to the Mess Sgt.

'Post these for me please.'

'Certainly, Sir, Good luck.'

I make my way back to the Company Lines with my kit. The Platoon is already there waiting.

'Well Sarn't, it looks like we will get first crack at whatever is happening over there. It's a bloody long way; top end of South American isn't it'

'That's correct Sir, just by Devils Island, the old French Prison where Papillion was incarcerated before he escaped. They make Demerara Sugar and Rum in Guiana.'

'Real knowledgeable bloke is our Sergeant.' Said Cpl Tyne.

'How long do you think we will be there Sir?' asked Childs.

'To be perfectly honest, I haven't a clue, has anyone been on Spearhead before?'

'Not that I know of Sir, perhaps the pack will tell you more.' Sergeant Johnston replies.

The coaches arrive and we load our kit on and take our seats.

'Sit in the front with me Sarn't Johnston, so that we can go through this pack, I believe in keeping everyone informed of what is going on at all times.'

'Very good, Sir.'

'I also have a policy that first names are used when we are on our own, so Jim, let's get at this pack. You take the maps and see what is on them whilst I read up the paperwork.'

We will be billeted just outside Georgetown on a sugar plantation; each platoon has been allocated an area to patrol. Apparently the country has a mixed population comprising of Indians and Negroes and it is these two factions that are causing all the trouble. We are to commandeer vehicles from anyone who has them and to issue notices to individuals that the Army will return the vehicles in good working order. We have to get enough vehicles so that each Company when it arrives will have vehicles for their respective Platoons. Sounds like a ruddy big order to me. Permission for this has come from the Governor of British Guiana, Sir Ralph Grey, a New Zealander, who didn't really have any staff.

After reading the pack, I hand it to Jim.

'Here, see what you make of it, it makes lousy reading.'

'The maps make a lot of sense too.' He replied.

'I'll brief the guys as we go along, that way they will know just as much as we do'

Just as we arrive at RAF Lynham, I finish the briefing.

'Any questions about what I have told you?'

There are murmurs but no questions.

'Okay, we are going out there to do a job of work, let's not let the Regiment down.'

The coach pulls up at the Air Terminal and we all get out and go inside. I report to the movement's desk and I am informed that we will be flying out in 40 minutes. Christ! We are certainly moving on this one. I go back to the Platoon and tell them.

'Do you think this is going to be dangerous Sir?' A spotty faced Rifleman asks.

'No, a piece of cake, you see if I'm not right.' I tell him.

We board the plane and make ourselves comfortable. First stop will be Gander in Newfoundland, 2nd stop will be Bermuda, and then on to Atkinson Field in British Guiana. The flight altogether will take about 24 hours. I hope the food is good. Because, I'm bloody starving.

CHAPTER EIGHT

Our arrival in British Guiana is greeted by the Second in Command of the Coldstream Guards.

'Welcome to the most humid place on earth. At the moment, you are billeted on the edge of the airstrip, follow me and I will show you to your new accommodation.'

Having lived in a variety of wooden huts and tents in my short time on this earth, and seeing a long line of tents, nothing shocks me about service accommodation.

We are taken to this line of tents in an old beaten up flatbed lorry belching smoke.

'Who lives in those brick buildings over there?' I ask, pointing to some building on the road.

'Oh, they belong to the Yanks. There is an Air Mapping Unit out here, not many of them, but they do have some great accommodation.'

'Do you mean to tell me that my Battalion will be living under canvas for the whole time we are here?'

'No, of course not, you will be moving into the barracks behind those brick buildings as soon as we move out. As one of your Companies arrives, one of ours goes. These are the Officers Tents, chuck your case on a bed and I'll show you around. Do you want any food for your men? If so I'll get the Cook Sgt to rustle something up.'

'Thank you Sir, that would be most appreciated.'

'Follow me then.'

We trudge to some large tents, which have been deemed the Cook House. I find a Sergeant and about 6 Privates.

'Can you cook something for the troops who have just arrived Sgt Fry.' asked the Guards 2IC.

'Eggs, Bean's and Chips already on the go Sir.' Fry replied.

'Good man.'

I find Jim and tell him about the meal and to keep the Platoon together till I return.

'Where are you going Sir?' Jim asked.

'Their 2IC is going to show me around, when I come back, I'll take you around, okay, see you in a little while.'

We walk off across the road and past the American accommodation and come to a brick built barracks.

'This will be your barracks when we move out. It belongs to some Sugar Planter named Bolton. I have only seen him once since we arrived 6 months ago.'

'If we didn't use this barracks, who would be billeted here?'

'I've no idea, some South American outfit I suppose.'

He shows me around the barracks and insists on taking me to the Mess for a drink. I need one, the sweat is pouring off of me.

'Is it usually this humid?' I ask him.

'Afraid so old man, the humidity is extremely high, and what with the 90 degrees of heat, not the best place in the world. Everything seems to grow to a big size out here. Wait till you encounter the mosquitoes, they have hob nailed boots on.'

I don't think I am going to like this tour.

After a very convivial time in the Mess, I make my way back to the Platoon.

'Well lads, we are billeted here till the Battalion arrives then we will move to a brick built barracks over there, (pointing in the direction of the buildings by the road.) It doesn't look much different than a barracks back home. Don't ask me who had it before the Guards because I don't know, anyway, make yourselves as comfortable as you can for the time being. If you are going into the town, by the way it's called Georgetown; I want you to go in pairs. No-one is to go out alone, is that clear.'

'Yes Sir'. They all replied.

I leave the Platoon to get sorted out and return to the Mess. I go through the folder that the Guards 2IC had given me. Bloody Hell! These people are at each other's throat all the time; I can see the Battalion will have its work cut out. As for the vehicles, the Guards have already got most of them, so there shouldn't be any problems. I hope!!!!

I return to the Platoon lines.

'Right Jim, I'll show you around. The 2IC has given me a folder that I want you to read. It sets out the jobs we have to complete before the arrival of the Battalion.'

I take Jim on the tour of the area that the 2IC had given me.

'Well, that's it mate, I'll leave you to brief the men. No need for an early start, 0900hrs will be early enough, see you in the morning, Goodnight Jim.'

As I am at a loose end, I go over to the Americans and introduce myself.

'Welcome to BG, I'm First Lieutenant Hank Martin; I'm the Commanding Officer of this bunch of reprobates. We heard you guys had just flown in, come and have a drink with us. You may find it not quite British, because no one uses any rank here, what do I call you Lieutenant?'

'My name is Dave.'

'Okay Dave, this is Pat, Johnnie, Fat Arse, his real name is Stuart, Jody, Phil, Mark, and the drunk in the corner is Harry, the rest of the guys are either shagging down town in one of the seedy brothels, or they are on duty. We do quite a lot of night work here. The government wants us to re-map the whole of the country and as they pay great wages, we oblige.'

'How many men do you have?'

'You are not going to believe this, but that is classified, off the record, I have 25 men under me, mainly photographers and a few ground crew, who work with the pilots. If you are not doing anything tomorrow afternoon, I'll show you round.'

'I'd like that, thanks.'

I spend an hour or two with them and then get up to go.

'Cheers for the drink, sorry I can't stay longer, but I have to catch up on some files that have been left for me concerning the Battalion coming out, see you tomorrow.'

I return to the Officers Mess tent, what a bloody place. Still we will soon be in the barracks, once the Guards have moved out. I go through the files and make some notes ready for the morning. I should write to Jane but I'm too tired, I crawl into bed, and soon fall asleep. I'm woken by a soldier carrying a tray.

'Good morning Sir, I've brought you some tea, breakfast will be in 30 minutes, the 2IC is in the Mess now Sir.'

'Thanks, put the tea on the table please and tell the 2IC that I will be with him shortly.'

'Roger, Sir.'

Breakfast isn't too bad for field conditions.

'Well David, I trust you slept okay, you have a plane arriving at 1300hrs. The one that should have arrived at 1000hrs has had to be cancelled owing to a battery burning through the plane deck. Someone loaded it on upside down.'

Over the next few days the Battalion arrives in BG and we move into the barracks vacated by the Guards. I'm glad, I never did like tents.

During the months that follow, my platoon carries out patrols of the East Coast Demerara District and helps stop the Indians and the Africans from killing each other. It is a hard job as frequently the Indians would report that the Africans had burnt down some houses and when we investigated, we found that the reverse was the norm. We have to be armed at all times as the population seemed to carry cutlasses everywhere they go. And as these cutlasses are extremely sharp, we can't take any chances.

The Company gets a choice area and I'm billeted in the house of one of the Sugar Cane Managers. The house is on stilts beside a small river which isn't very deep. Right opposite, is the club house where there is a bar? Every night I wade across the river which is only 14 feet wide and 1 foot deep and go to the bar. This is the life.

One morning, I take the platoon out for a patrol along the river. As we come to a small bridge, I find a guy fishing off of it.

'Hi! What fish are in the river?' I ask him.

'Pee-rye.' he replies.

'What's a Pee-rye?'

'Wait a moment man, and I'll catch one.'

A few minutes go by, when suddenly; the man is pulling on his rod.

'I told you man, I would get one, and my, he's a big bastard.'

I go over to the guy and he shows me a fish about 8 inches long with the biggest set of choppers I have ever seen.

'That's a bloody Piranha Fish!' I exclaim.

'Sure is man, we call them Pee-rye.'

You can guess I now use the bridge to cross the river even though it is half a mile up and half a mile back to the clubhouse. Had I not come across this guy, I'd never have known about these Piranhas. Yuk!!!!

The country starts to have elections and things seem to get a bit quieter. We don't get as many incidents to go to, and the Police are taking over more and more. There is the odd dead body found against a tree with its throat cut.

The Battalion starts to do some training as our time is coming to an end. The exercises in the Savannah Region of the country are quite an eye opener. The sand gets everywhere and even the water when sterilized, tastes bloody horribly.

A few of the Battalion visit Kaieteur Falls on the River Pataro, and some carried out expeditions into the Amazon Jungle and visit virtually extinct tribes of Amerindians.

In view of the terrain, the NCOs Cadres are held and many Riflemen are promoted. I visited the Demerara Sugar Factory. I'm not sure even now if the colour of the sugar is due to un-refinement or the colour of the Demerara River. I also visited the Duggar Rum Plant, which was quite rewarding in a liquid sort of way.

In the 6 months that I have been here, I have been billeted in Police Stations, on Sugar Plantations and a variety of Schools. Whilst in the jungle, I meet a guy in the SAS called Don, who with a few other chaps were carrying out jungle training. So all in all, the six months has pretty well flown by.

Our tour has finally come to an end. I won't be sorry to say goodbye to the place. Everything here seems to grow to an extremely large size. The spiders are huge and the small black ones with a red hour glass on their undersides (Black Widows) are very poisonous. The snakes all want to eat you, especially the Anacondas. We drove over one that must have been 20 feet long if it was an inch. The mozzies, have hob nail boots on and do Kama Kazi attacks on you when you least expect them. The country is far too humid and bloody hot. Clothing soon develops mildew and rots away. It's a bastard place this.

I receive a message from our Second in Command that the President of the United States has just been assassinated by a gunman whilst in a motorcade in Dallas, Texas, and as I got on with the Mapping Wing, could I go over to tell them, just in case they did not know about it. Now this is a task I'm not relishing. As luck would have it, they were listening to the radio as well, so already knew. They thanked me for my concern.

Will I be glad, to leave this country. It is too big and the population will always be at each other's throats. Roll on England and the rain. Mind you, when it rains here, it really, really comes down. You can't see across the road.

We hold a party in one of the bars just outside the town and on the way there, we knock down a guy riding his donkey. The driver, a local, didn't even stop the bus. Life is cheap here. I go to the local Police Station to report the accident but no-one is interested in me making a statement, so left again.

After more patrols and training our 6 months tour finally comes to an end. And I am glad to be leaving South America, and not before time to. British Guiana is not for me.

CHAPTER NINE

At last the Battalion arrives back in the UK, but to the worst weather for many years. Owing to problems at Heathrow, we are diverted to Prestwick in Scotland. A train is waiting to take us back to London and onward to Colchester. I need this like a hole in the head. It is extremely cold as we are all dressed in light clothing which is only good for hot climates. The journey to London is horrendous, the train is cold and I have to stand up all the way. Why they couldn't lay on a Military Train I will never know.

We arrive in London, knackered. Coaches are waiting to take us to Colchester. At least we will be able to sit down this time. The battalion has been given 7 days leave, so the sooner we can unpack the Company kit the better. Once that's done we can be off on leave. On the way to Colchester, I ask the men if they want to work straight through so that they can get off on leave quicker. They all say "yes." This is just the job as I too will be able to see Jane sooner.

The last six months have gone pretty quickly but must admit I'm pleased to be back in the UK. I didn't much like the humid heat of British Guiana. I wish the driver would turn the heat up, it's bloody freezing.

The coach finally arrives at Colchester and we immediately start unloading the trucks that have the Company kit on. Thank goodness they came earlier in the day. It shouldn't take long to get all the stuff back into the Company Stores.

'Make sure all the weapons are cleaned and stowed away Cpl Tyne.'

'All in hand, Sir.' He replied. It's great having really efficient NCOs.

It is 0300hrs and we have completed the unloading and stowing.

'If you want to draw bedding and get your heads down, I'll get the Block opened up.' I tell the Platoon.

'If it's all the same with you Sir, we want to get back to the Station ready for the first train out.' Said Rifleman Jackson.

'Is everyone in agreement with this?' I ask them.

They all reply "yes."

'Very well then, I'll get the three tonner to take you all to the Station, have a great leave, you have all earned it, see you in a week's time.'

Now to get my head down. I go off to the Officers Mess and climb into bed, boy! Am I whacked?

I wake at 1000hrs and ask the Mess Steward if he could arrange some scoff for me.

'No problem Sir, I'll get one of the batmen to bring something along to your room.'

'Good man.' I tell him and proceed to pack my case.

After a smashing breakfast, all thanks to the Mess Steward, who certainly excelled himself, I ring for a taxi to take me to the station. I'm looking forward to seeing Jane and my parents. I hope they like the souvenirs I've brought back. I'm sure my mother will love the shrunken head I picked up when I went down the Amazon.

I arrive back in Gosport late in the afternoon.

'Welcome home Son.' My mother said hugging me.

'Steady on mum, what's for tea?'

'Trust you to think only of your stomach.' She says laughing.

Boy oh Boy! It's good to be home.

'Are you seeing Jane tonight?' Asked my mother, switching on the TV.

'Yes, I can't wait to see her again, in fact, I think I will go and surprise her, see you all later.'

I arrive at Jane's house and bang the door. Jane's father opens it.

'Good gracious me, hey mother, It's Dave, he's home.'

'Is Jane in?' I ask him.

'What am I doing, come in lad, don't stand on the doorstep, Jane is in bed with flu, go on up, her bedrooms the one on the left as you reach the top of the stairs.'

Now this wouldn't have happened with Kathryn's mother, she wouldn't have let me anywhere near Kathy's bedroom.

I go up the stairs and bang on Jane's door.

'Come in.' she says feebly.

I enter and she looks at me.

'Dave, oh, it's lovely to see you.'

Jane jumps up from the bed. She hasn't anything on.

'Oh! I have missed you.'

I kiss her and pull her away.

'Do you realise that you are naked Jane?'

I can't take my eyes off her. She has a lovely body. Her breasts are small and pert. The triangle of pubic hair is blonde.

'I'm sorry Dave I have missed you so much.'

I push her back down onto the bed and pull the covers over her.

'A few more minutes and I don't think I would have been able to stop myself making love to you.' I tell her.

She pushes the covers down to reveal her naked body.

'Jane cover yourself up, your dad might come in.'

'What is the matter, don't you like me?'

'Of course I do Jane, but I don't need to have sex with you. I'm not like the rest. And I'm not queer either. When the time is right I will make love to you, believe me.'

'Don't leave it too long Dave, I want you to make love to me, I want you inside me.'

'Why Jane, what is this obsession with sex? Why do we have to make love, isn't me loving you enough?'

'No it isn't, I need you in me. I will know then that you are mine.'

'Jane, I am already yours. It's enough that John and Maureen are at it all the time like rabbits. We don't have to be like them.'

'Dave, all my friends are doing it, so why can't we. I can get some of my dad's durex; I know where he keeps them.'

Shit! This is getting out of hand. I don't know how long I will be able to keep my hands off her.

'Cover yourself Jane, we can talk about it later, you just don't understand do you'.

I leave her and go down stairs. Jane starts to cry. Damn this, I know it sounds like rejection, but the time is not right and I am not going against my feelings just so that she can say to her friends that she has done it as well.

I knock on the door to the lounge.

'Come in son, is Jane getting up then?'

'I think so she said she is feeling much better.'

'That's only because you are here son, she has been waiting for this day.'

Don't I know it?

Jane re-appears, her eyes are red.

'You don't look too good love do you think you should be up?' Her mother asked.

'It's alright mum; I'll take some aspirin that should lower my temperature.'

I don't think aspirin will do the job, not for what she has been crying for.

'Take me out Dave?'

'If you want, but don't you think you should stay in?'

'I want you to take me out please, so can we go.'

'Okay, but wrap up warm, I don't want you going down with pneumonia.'

'How very considerate of you.'

'Now, now Jane, Dave is only looking out for your health, there is no need to get up tight.' said her dad.

We walk off along San Diego Road towards the Ferry.

'What's wrong Jane?'

'It's you Dave, what have I got to do to get you to make love to me, we have been going out together for some time now and you haven't once put your hand up my skirt or touched my breasts, don't you like what you have seen?'

'Jane, you have got a lovely body and if that is what you want, I will do it.' I tell her.

'I don't want you to do it just because I have told you to, I want you to do it because YOU want to.' She replied.

Bloody hell! This is really getting heavy.

'Jane, please understand, It's not that I don't want to, in my heart I believe we should wait to have sex and it will happen at the right time, just because I have been away from you, we don't have to show our feelings in a sexual way.'

She starts to cry. I pull her to me.

'Don't cry darling, I can't help the way I am.'

'Dave, you are the first boy who has never made a sexual pass at me.'

'That is because I respect you Jane; let's not argue over it, it will happen when the time is right, you see if I'm not right.'

We walk to the Ferry and catch the bus back.

'I really think you should be in bed darling, this flu isn't doing you much good.'

'You could come and keep me warm I would get over it then.'

'Don't start that again, I thought we had sorted that out?'

'You might think we have, but it won't be sorted out till I have you in bed.' She shouts.

I walk her to the door of her house and kiss her goodnight.

'Aren't you coming in?' She asked.

'No, not tonight, I'm whacked and I need some sleep.'

'Will I see you tomorrow then?'

'Of course you will, I'll be round about 7pm.'

She looks at me sheepishly, but says nothing.

On the way back to my house, I keep thinking about what she has said. Do I really know this girl, has she been in the sack with every Tom, Dick or Harry or is it that she really is in love with me, I just can't make up my mind. Sex to me is something you do when you are married, not just for the fun of it. These strong principles were bred in me by my parents, and anyway, I'm just not that experienced, and I would only make a cock up of it, and then where would I be. She would probably tell her friends that I was hopeless in bed, so Jane - you have shit it.

I have a lousy night's sleep; I keep thinking that my girlfriend is a nymphomaniac. I've got a lot to learn about sex, I must be the most naive Officer in the British Army when it comes to it.

Having spent most of the day visiting old mates at their places of work and I even went back to the school I use to go to. They were certainly surprised that I had made something of myself.

During dinner, I think closely about what Jane had said.

'What's wrong son? You seem far away.' Said my mother.

'It's nothing much mum, just something I was thinking about.'

'Bloody heck, if that is what you look like when thinking, I'll not bother.' My younger brother replies.

'You wouldn't know how to think.' I tell him.

I meet up with Jane in the evening and I take her to a restaurant. During dinner I say to her, 'How do you fancy getting engaged.'

She drops her fork and looks straight at me and says, 'Stop pissing about and eat your dinner.'

'I'm not pissing about as you call it, I'm deadly serious.'

'You mean it, don't you?'

'Of course I do.'

'Bloody Hell!'

'Well, what's your answer?'

'What's brought this on?'

'Just answer the question, will you get engaged to me or not?'

'Can I have a drink?'

'Jane, be serious, how do you feel about getting engaged?'

'Does this mean we can go to bed and make love all night?'

'No it fucking doesn't.'

'But engaged couples are allowed to go to bed and make love, it's part of the engagement rules.'

'That doesn't apply, to this fucking couple.'

'Now, now David dear, no need to swear, of course I want to get engaged - you have made me very happy darling.'

'At last an answer.'

I slip the ring onto her finger, thank goodness it fits.

'How did you know my ring size?'

'I asked your mum.'

'You devious wonderful bastard.'

'Now who is swearing?'

'Does my mother know about this?'

'No Jane she doesn't, I asked her what your ring size was and told her I was thinking of buying you a small ring for your birthday.'

'Who knows about this then?'

'No one except you and me.'

'Dave, are you really sure about this?'

'If I wasn't, would I have brought you a one and sixpence ring?' I say laughing.

'Oh Dave, I'm so happy.'

I lean over the table and kiss her. As I pull away she whispers, 'Let's go to bed.'

'The only bed you will be getting into young lady is your own, alone, behave yourself, people are looking at us.'

'So what, I'm the happiest girl in the whole world, sod them.'

'Jane, stop swearing and finish your meal.'

'Let's go home and tell my mum and dad, I'm sure they will be pleased, they like you ever so much.'

'Okay, but eat your dinner first.'

We leave the Restaurant and return to Jane's house and tell her parents.

'Congratulations, we are very pleased for both of you, this calls for a celebration. Get that Sherry out of the cupboard mother, we said we would keep it for a special occasion, and I think this is it.' said her dad.

The Sherry arrives and her mother pours each of us a glass.

'To you both.' said her parents.

I take a sip of the Sherry. Bloody heck! It's disgusting.

'Holy Cow!' Said her father, 'this stuff is awful, don't drink it troops, mother put the kettle on.'

I stay at Jane's till the early hours and then make my way home. This will be the second engagement I've had. I hope this one lasts. I tell my mum and dad, they seem pleased, though I suspect my mum isn't.

It is my 4th day of leave and I'm getting bored. I wish I was still in Africa with Colonel Mike. It was dangerous, but fun. I miss the guys and the excitement. I wonder how John is getting on in Malaya, I haven't heard from him since he joined the 1st Battalion, I wish he would write and let me know how he is.

The days go by and Jane still tries to get me into bed. If it carries on, I know we will end up in the sack, who could resist a girl like her. I know she isn't a virgin as she told me on our 3rd date. That worries me a bit as I won't be the first one to make love to her. I still can't understand why I got engaged to her, I need my head read.

The final day of my leave arrives and I begin to pack my case to return to Colchester.

'Hey Son! There is a big thick letter for you, from Malaya.' Shouts my mother.

I rush down the stairs and she gives me the letter.

"Hi Dave,

Arrived here safely, the place is crawling with terrorists; we made a landing at Muara with 42 Commando, 1/2nd Ghurkhas and the Queens Own Highlanders. 1RGJ was taken in by a naval ship. Funny really, the ship was only allowed to take 125 soldiers and kit. Dave, we had 689 men plus vehicles and stores on it. The Captain of the ship at one stage said that we had better sail before we sink. I can tell you it was pretty hairy at times. Our main task was to capture the oilfields from the terrorists. Would you believe it, we were welcomed on Miri beach by a Major giving us a speech. What a prat. We are up against an 8000 strong force of the North Kalimantan Nation Army (TNKU for short) someone called Yassin Affandi is in charge of them. They launched an attack on the Sultan and tried to take him hostage, but didn't succeed. They captured the Seria Oilfield but not for long. The Ghurkhas swept through Brunei town suffering heavy casualties but retook the Oilfields. So you can see I'm having fun. I wish you were here instead of being in England; I miss your company mate. Let's hope we will meet up again real soon. Hope all is well in the UK and your parents are still in good health. I had a letter from my mum; she said you had been round to see her.

Keep in touch mate. How are you and Jane progressing? Have you got to the bed stage yet? Haven't had any letters from Maureen, even though she said she would write, but, you know how women are. Well must go now as we are due to carry out a 10 day patrol. Look after yourself mate, and don't do anything I wouldn't, that leaves you a wide scope. Write soon.

Your old pal,

John.

PS. The women out here in the jungle have got really big knockers."

I put the letter back into the envelope, shit, he's better off than me, at least he is seeing some action, all I've done is carry out IS (Internal Security) duties in a God forsaken country. What I would give to be in Malaya now. I wonder if I can wangle a posting there. I'll have a chat to the Adjutant when I get back to Colchester.

Jane comes round and accompanies me to the station.

'When will you be home again darling?' She asks.

'I've no idea, it may be the weekend, but I'm not really sure. We are still on Spearhead so we will have to play it by ear, Oh! By the way, I had a letter from John; he is enjoying himself in Malaya. Apparently he is up to his arse in muck and bullets, lucky sod.'

'That's not lucky Dave, it is dangerous, and how do you think Maureen feels about him out there.'

'It's what we joined up to do, fight for Queen and Country, anyway he will look after himself, he will have to, because I'm not there to look after him. I wish I was there with him.'

'You don't mean that Dave, do you? It would mean we would be apart.'

'Jane, I know this will sound terrible and please don't take it the wrong way, but I would give anything to be out there with John, he's having a great time. It may be dangerous, but that is what we both joined up for, action and adventure. This is the first time we have not done anything together since we met up at Brockhurst Infants School at the age of five.'

'I'm sorry Dave, it's just, I thought us being together was more important.'

'Of course we being together is important. But I am in the bloody Army and my job for want of a better description is, killing people, and that is what John is doing, the lucky sod.'

Jane starts to cry, it is obvious that I have upset her, she will have to understand that I want lots of adventures before I decide to settle down, and if that means being apart, and so be it.

'If you want us to be apart, why did you get engaged to me?' She said, tears falling down her cheeks.

Oh fuck this! There is nothing worse than a girl crying, especially one who doesn't realise true friendship.

'Jane, the train will be going in a few minutes, come on give me a kiss and tell me you love me.'

My hand brushes against her right breast as I pull her to me.

'Oh! That's nice.' She replies.

'A mistake.' I tell her.

'If I didn't know you better, I'd have thought that you wanted to hold one, you can if you want.'

The train guards whistle blows. Thank Christ for that. I kiss her goodbye and the train starts to pull out of the station.

'Bye darling write as soon as you can, I love you.' She shouts.

I blow her a kiss and then make my way to a seat. I have really got to think about our relationship. Was getting engaged the right thing to do. I am now beginning to think it wasn't. I settle down in my seat and re-read John's letter. Gosh! I wish I was out there, the lucky bastard.

I arrive back in barracks just in time for dinner.

'How was your leave David?' The CO asks.

'Fine, thank you Sir, I got engaged.'

'So congratulations are in order, I hope you both will be very happy, will we be meeting the young lady?'

'Certainly Sir, I will be bringing her to the Summer Ball.'

'Good, I look forward to meeting her.'

The CO is a funny guy; he has never married and relies on his batman for everything.

The weeks go by and we are informed that we will be going to Libya for desert training but should be back in time for the Summer Ball. I see Jane about 2 weekends in 5. She doesn't like it, but can do nothing about it. I'm looking forward to Libya; the country has an old king called Idris who insists that the British use his Country for Desert Training. It is rich in oil since the Yanks found it for him. It should be great fun.

On the few weekends I have off, I try to get Jane to understand that the Army is my life and that she should be prepared to accept that we will be apart for weeks on end. This is something she just cannot accept and I can't make her see reason.

'If you loved me, you would chuck the Army.'

She said one evening. I couldn't believe my ears.

'What made you say that Jane?'

'You are never at home with me and we don't go anywhere anymore.'

'It's not my fault, the Army is my job and I must go where they send me, in fact, I have applied for Special Forces.'

'And what are they when they are at home?'

'I can't tell you, all I will say is, if I am accepted, I could be away from you for long periods of time and I won't be able to tell you ever, where I have been or will be going. So darling, you had better get used to the fact that I am away quite a lot.'

'You can't be serious about this Dave, it will wreck everything, surely you realise that?'

'Why should it Jane, I'm now going to put the ball in your court, if you love me, you will accept it.'

'Oh! How could you be so heartless?'

'Jane, what you have got to realise is that the Army has the first hold on me and you have the second, you will be no different than all the rest of the Army wives and girlfriends who have experienced their husbands and boyfriends going away for long periods of time.'

'I just don't know Dave; I'll have to give this some serious thought. Perhaps we shouldn't have got engaged, I just don't know anymore.' She replied.

'Well! That has buggered up this weekend good and proper, do you want to go down the pub for a drink?'

'I suppose so.' She replies.

We spend a couple of hours in the Kings Head, she doesn't speak much. I can see she is deep in thought about what I have said. She has to get it in her head that things are changing and I want to change with them.

I take her home and we sit in the lounge with her mum and dad.

'What's the matter with you Jane?' asked her father.

'Leave me alone dad.'

'Strewth! What's got into her Dave?'

'I think it is something I said to her this evening and she didn't like it.'

'What was that then son?'

'I told her that I was applying for Special Forces.'

'What the SAS?'

Jane looks up at me.

'You've applied to join THEM, are you mad, they go to every cock up in the world, Maureen's nephew is in that lot and he is never home, you really can't be serious about this Dave?'

'Yes, I am.'

'I just don't believe what I am hearing Dave, we will never see each other if you join them.'

'I think you are over reacting Jane, of course we will be able to see each other. It isn't THAT bad.'

Jane storms out of the room.

'I've never seen her in this state before.' said her father.

'She won't accept that I'm in the Army and they have the first and last say when it comes to me being at home with her, can you talk to her for me and try to make her see sense.' I ask her father.

'I'll try son, but she is a stubborn little girl when the mood takes her.'

Don't I know it?

Jane refuses to come back down, so I say goodnight to her parents and make my way back home. This has been the worst weekend I've had, I won't be sorry to get back to barracks.

Jane doesn't see me off from the station. I presume she is still mad at me for what I said. Perhaps she is finishing with me. How I wish I was in Malaya with John, I bet he isn't having the trouble I am.

We get notice that we will be off to Libya at the weekend for Desert Training with the Hussars. I'm looking forward to this very much I hope it isn't like Guiana.

Jane hasn't contacted me and I don't intend ringing her. I haven't done anything wrong. She will either finish or she will get in touch when she has calmed down.

Friday comes and I'm getting all my kit ready for the move at 0600hrs when I'm summons by the Mess Steward.

'There's a phone call for you Sir.'

It is Jane.

'I'm sorry for the upset I've caused you Dave, my dad has had a talk with me and I can see that you were right all the time, please forgive me; I don't want us to break up.'

'Are you sure you still want to go out with me, you must realise that the Army comes first at the moment, even though I love you.'

'Yes, I understand now, we must speak when you come back off of the exercise, I love you darling.'

'I must go Jane as I have to finish packing, see you when I return, love you.'

Returning to my room, I complete my packing. Jane's dad must have given her a right talking to for her to phone me. I'll write her a letter when I get to Libya.

0600hrs and the Company are mustering at the Company Lines.

'Everything in order Sgt Johnston.'

'Sure is Sir, no absentee's and all the Platoon kit is loaded, ready to go.'

'Well done, right, let's get under way, get the men boarded on the coach marked with the Red "16," we should he at RAF Lynham in a couple of hours, all being well.'

The flight out to Libya is quite boring, the food is good, as food in containers goes and the cabin staff are excellent. We land at El Adem and get into trucks to take us out into the desert. Why they call this desert, I will never know. It is just dried reddish yellow mud and plenty of rocks. After a couple of hours or so, we arrive at the camp. I don't believe the sight I am seeing, rows of bloody tents. Certainly not my idea of fun, that's for sure.

We are shown the Company Lines and each tent accommodates 4 men. The Officers tents are situated around the camp and I am shown to a very small looking tent. This is home for the next few weeks, worst luck. What I would give for a nice soft bed, these camp beds don't look very comfortable. I am proved wrong, they are excellent.

The OC has called for a Company briefing at 1900hrs, to tell us what we will be doing on the exercise. We will be operating with the Hussars at one stage and then they will be acting as the enemy in another part of the exercise.

The Battalion will learn quite a bit from the experience. This so called desert is nothing like they said in the magazine I was reading on the aircraft. Damn! It is starting to rain. The OC completed the briefing and we all return to our tents. The rain is coming down very heavy now. I wonder how long it will last, let's hope my tent is waterproof.

The rain lasted for 3 hours and all around us is large pools of water. In fact one pool is quite deep and could be rented out as a swimming pool. The so called sand turns to mud and it is pretty heavy going to get about.

Dinner is a grand affair all of us eat in a very large tent. A few six foot tables have been put to one side for us Officers. We all have to get our own grub from the other side of the tent and are supposed to jump the queue. I don't believe in this, each man is entitled to get his meal without some interloper jumping in front of him.

I queue up with the rest of the men. I don't think the OC likes this. It would seem that I am the only Officer who is in line. I'm sure I have gained the respect of the Platoon for this. I have always believed that my men come first. I don't intend to change now.

Over the next few days we carry out live firing exercises and play out many different roles for an Infantry Battalion. I have enjoyed the experience immensely. I even wrote to Jane and have received a letter back from her. She seems pretty down because I am away from her. She will learn.

The final days of the exercises come to an end. Our kit is totally ruined, dust and mud is everywhere. When it rains, it certainly comes down. It is just as if someone has chucked a bucket of water over you. The exercises have gone extremely well and we are given a day off to see the sights in the town of Tobruk. I visit the War Cemeteries of the English and Germans.

The German one is very sombre; it has a large Black Marble wall with all the names of the German dead carved in white with their Regiments alongside. The place is immaculately kept. The British Cemetery has rows of White Stones with each man's name and Regiment on each one. Again they are kept immaculate. It is an honour to be able to see these places, the men laid to rest in the graves fought hard and long, heroes every one of them.

I have done something that possibly some of the widows and mothers haven't done, seen where their loved ones are buried. They can rest assured that the places are well kept.

Returning to the tented camp, we pass a point which has a stone cairn with "KNIGHTSBRIDGE" inscribed on it. This is where a fierce battle was won over the Germans. It would seem that there are quite a few things like this dotted around the area where different battles were fought. If I was in the scrap business, I would be worth a fortune, what with the rusting tanks about the place. In places we have to be careful as there are still old minefields, though most have shifted with the moving sands and are not where they should be, as I found out the next morning.

I had been plagued with stones under my camp bed for days, and decided to get rid of them. I threw out about six and now have a hollow under the camp bed. In the morning, outside the tent I find a nice neat pile of World War 2 hand grenades all rusty with pins intact. Our tented camp is in the middle of an Ammo Dump, left over from the last war. It certainly shouldn't be here, according to the map it should have been 800 yards to the west. A very dangerous country is this Libya.

The Exercises are a great success, everyone in the Battalion has learnt something, and this is also the first time that we have been able to work with tanks in the desert. It was strange map reading by the stars, but never the less it was fun and I enjoyed it. One guy nearly got his Platoon lost. He had taken a compass reading on a camel, which as you would expect, moved off. Everyone laughed at this, but a good lesson was learnt, make sure the point you use is permanent and dead.

I received another letter from John. He is really enjoying himself in Malaya; he has put in for Special Forces Selection, and should know whether he has got it by now, as his letter is 2 weeks old. I hope he is on the same course as me, as I am on the Winter Selection Course.

The Battalion returns to the UK and is given a few days off. We are still on Spearhead Duties though. I must have the best Platoon in the Battalion, they all rally together to help each other and there seems to be no malice towards each member. I can't think of a time when any member of the Platoon had a disagreement. They all seem to discuss the problems and sort them out themselves. The last time I had a Platoon like this was when I was in Africa as a Mercenary. What I wouldn't give to have those guys in the Army with me. I must write to Colonel Mike, his last letter wasn't very encouraging.

I miss the train to Portsmouth and wait for the last one of the night. I hope it gets into Portsmouth in time for the last ferry, otherwise I will have to get a taxi all the way round the hill and that will be quite expensive.

At last my train arrives and I board and find a seat that I can lay out on. There don't seem to be many people on this train, so it should be okay to get my head down for an hour. Even if I over sleep it won't make any difference, as the train stops the night at Portsmouth Harbour.

The train arrives at Portsmouth just in time for me to get the midnight ferry. Thank goodness for that, I must admit I wasn't looking forward to another long journey. I find a taxi and 10 minutes later I am entering my home. It's lucky my parents are always late in going to bed. Otherwise I would have had to wake them up.

'Welcome home Son,' Said my dad, 'How did your exercises in Libya go?'

'Not bad at all dad, we learnt a hell of a lot.'

'Would you like a cup of tea son?' My mother asks.

'Now that's a good idea, I haven't had a decent cup of char since leaving home.'

We talk right into the small hours and I give them the gifts I bought for them in Libya. I give my dad the smallest lighter in the world and my mother some wall mats and chair back covers. Everyone brings back mats from Libya.

'When have you got to go back son?' My mother asks.

'I'm here till Tuesday morning mum.'

I leave them and go off to bed. I sleep the sleep of the dead.

I wake at 11am and my mother asks if I want breakfast.

'Not really mum, I'll just have a bowl of flakes.'

'Are you seeing Jane today son?'

'Yes, I've got something to sort out with her; she has been acting rather strange.'

'She came round the other day and didn't seem as if she was with us, if you know what I mean.'

'Yes mum, I do know. She has been acting very strange for over a month now. I think I know what is wrong, I've applied for Special Forces Selection and it will mean that we won't see each other very often.'

'You have applied for what!'

'Special Forces Selection, I can't tell you any more than that mum.'

'Is that the SAS son?'

'Yes mum, but please, no more questions.'

'Whatever is your dad going to say about this I wonder?'

'Dad can't be told Mum. Just think of it as joining the Royal Marines.'

'Royal Marines be buggered! Your uncle Harry was in that outfit during the war, he spent more time living with the enemy than with his own side. He won the Military Medal for some action or other, be careful son, that's all I ask.'

'Don't you worry on that score, careful is my middle name.'

'Is that how you got that medal in the Congo son?'

'That was different mum; I've changed a lot since then.'

I leave the house and make my way to the town. It hasn't changed any and I don't see anyone I know, so I return home.

'Are you going to see Jane?' asked my mother.

'I suppose so, I've got a lot of things to talk over with her, and she should be home now.'

I arrive at Jane's house but no one is in. Strange, she is usually in by now. I wonder if she is at Maureen's. As she only lives round the corner I make my way there.

'Have you seen Jane?'

Before she can speak, I notice that she is pregnant.

'Is that John's?' I ask.

'I haven't seen Jane, she is working late at the shop, they are stocktaking, and no, it isn't John's.'

'Oh Shit! He is, going to be surprised.'

'I have finished with him; I sent him a letter the other day, telling him that I did not want to go out with him anymore. Please don't tell him, he wouldn't understand.'

'No, I bet he wouldn't, what was it, a one night stand, or don't you know.'

'It wasn't like that. I knew the bloke before I became really serious with John. He came round one night when you both were away and one thing led to another. I regret what happened, and because of it, I have finished with John. It's for the best. I don't want to hurt him. Please believe me.'

'It doesn't make any difference whether I believe you or not, it is John you should be talking to.'

'I know, but I just can't.'

'I have to go, I'll see you.'

I walk off to the paper shop and just as I arrive I see Jane talking to some guy.

'I'll see you later.' I hear her say as I walk up.

'Who's this then?' I ask her.

'Oh! Hello Dave! This is Phil; he has just started working at the shop.'

'Hello.' Said Phil.

'Yeah!' I reply.

Phil walks off and I ask Jane how long he has been working at the shop.

'He's been there about 3 weeks, I think.' She replied.

We walk back to her house.

'Where are your mum and dad? They weren't in when I called earlier.'

'They have gone to my Grans for a few days.'

'Jane, did you know Maureen is pregnant and it's not John's kid?'

'Yes she told me a few weeks ago.'

'And you didn't tell me?'

'She told me not to; she wanted to tell John first.'

'She won't tell him, she's too scared.'

'Yes, I know I have just spoken to her.' Said Jane.

We arrive at her house and she asks me in.

'Jane, I don't think I should come in, especially as your parents are not home, I don't want the neighbours talking about you.'

'That's very considerate of you.'

'Don't get sarky, you know how I feel.'

'I'm sorry Dave, things are getting me down.'

'How about going out for a meal, I'll pick you up in an hour.'

'Okay.' She replies.

I walk off home and get changed. We have got to talk things out.

'What's up son? You seem deep in thought.'

'Jane, mum.'

'I thought things were not going well for you two, just remember this son, if you don't have love, don't stay together.'

'I don't feel the same towards Jane as I did towards Kathryn. Things are just not right anymore. We seem to be drifting apart and I don't know how to stop it. I've tried talking to her, but she seems to be firm in the belief that we should always be together. And that just isn't possible with me being in the Army. I can't get her to see that the Army must come first, Oh! I just don't know.'

Returning to Jane's house we go to a restaurant in the town. The food is excellent, but the conversation is crap.

'Do you want to end our relationship Jane?'

'No.'

'Then you must understand that the Army comes first, and I will be with you every minute of the day when I am home.'

'I'll try, but it won't be easy.'

We talk some more but I don't think Jane is listening.

The meal is finished in silence and then we take a taxi to her house.

'Are you coming in Dave?'

'No, I better not; you know what the neighbours are like round here.'

'Stuff the neighbours, come on in and I'll make a cup of coffee.'

'Only, if you don't start your antics again.'

'I can't make any promises.' She said laughing.

This is the first time that I have seen her laugh for ages. I leave the house in the early hours and make my way home. For once she hasn't made a pass or said anything suggestive, now I know something is up.

After breakfast, I take a trip into town to the Mocambo coffee bar.

'Well, Well, Well! Fancy meeting you here. How are you Dave? It's a long time since I last saw you, how you been keeping?'

'Nice to see you again Roger, I'm okay, still in the Army, you still in the Hampshire's?'

'Yes, I'm on 2 weeks Leave, I understand from Gordon that you are an Officer, I suppose I have to salute you now.'

'You can forget that crap; we are still mates and always will be.'

We spend a couple of hours drinking numerous coffees and getting up to date with all the gossip.

'Does John know about Maureen?'

'I don't think so, and I'm not going to tell him either. She will have to do that, this is something I'm not getting involved in. Have you got a girlfriend?'

'Sure have, we hope to get married in about a year's time, how are you getting on with Jane? She is a funny girl. I never thought I would see the day, you going out with her. Whatever happened to you and Kathy?'

'It's a long story and you only have 2 weeks Leave. Let's say we really drifted apart, did you know her mother is a dragon, or is it a witch.'

We both laugh. I look at my watch.

'It's been nice seeing you again Roger; let's hope we see more of each other in the near future. Keep in touch, you know where I live. You can contact me there or at the Regiment.'

'Will do mate, see you.'

Sunday comes and I make my way back to Colchester, what a bloody awful weekend, these are becoming too damn frequent. During Monday morning the CO asks to see me. I knock his door and enter.

'You wanted to see me Colonel?' I asked.

'Ah! Dave, come in and sit down. The Adjutant has a movement order for you to go to SAS Hereford on Friday. I know it is a bit quick, but they are holding an extra Selection Course and obviously need the men for some operation or other. Now don't let the Regiment down, we are relying on you to set a good example.'

'No worries on that score Sir; I hope Lt West is on the same course, it would be nice to see him again, especially as I took his place in "D" Company.'

'If I find out anything before you go, I'll get a message to you, good luck Dave, and I hope it is what you want.'

'Thank you Sir.'

I salute and leave his office. At last I can get some excitement, it is pretty boring being a soldier in barracks, I prefer the active service life, but at the moment, there doesn't seem to be any for a Rifle Platoon Officer.

On returning to the platoon lines I bump into Sgt Johnston.

'Well mate, it looks as if you will be getting a new platoon commander. I've just been informed that my SAS Selection has come through. I leave on Friday.'

'That's great news, I mean, for your course, not losing you as the OC. The platoon will miss you without doubt, they have never been as proficient as they have since you took over, in fact, and I don't think they will be very happy when I tell them you are leaving. Are we having a farewell piss up before you go?'

'You bet we will, ask the entire platoon to be in the NAFFI tonight.'

'Will do Dave, see you tonight then.'

I will certainly miss the men. They have performed extremely well as a platoon. I reckon they would have made a great mercenary force, and I would have been proud to have led them.

I return to the mess for dinner. Just as I sit down, the Mess Steward informs me I am wanted on the telephone. It is Jane.

'Are you coming home this weekend?'

'I'm afraid I won't be able to. I have to go on a course and I don't know at the moment when I will be back, I'll write and let you know as soon as I can. I will miss you.'

'And I'll miss you too darling, but as you say, it can't be helped. Come home soon. Mum and dad are visiting my Aunt Mary this weekend, and they have asked me to go with them. I hope you are not away for too long Dave, I miss you heaps.'

'As soon as I get sorted out, I'll phone you, okay.'

She hangs up and I return to my dinner. I quickly gulp everything down so that I can get over to the NAFFI.

On arrival in the NAFFI, I'm cheered by the platoon.

'It is our turn to buy you a drink, what are you having Sir?'

'I'll have a whiskey and ginger please.'

'Coming right up Sir.'

We sink a few and suddenly Sgt Johnston makes a speech.

'On behalf of all in the platoon, I would like to say thanks for being our platoon commander, and we would like you to accept this small gift of our appreciation for being the best we have ever had.'

He hands me a regimental plaque which is inscribed:

To 2Lt David STUBBS,
OC 16 Platoon, D Company 2 RGJ
From all the Platoon,
"Good luck for the future."

'Thanks guys, I really appreciate receiving this, we have had some great times together, and one day we will all meet again I'm sure, I hope you give your new platoon commander the same loyalty that you all have given me. I will miss you, thank you very much for the plaque, this is something that I will treasure always, thank you.'

Sometime during the evening, I must have returned to the mess, though I can't remember getting there.

Morning arrives and I slowly make my way to breakfast.

'Had a good night Dave?' Asks Simon Richards, running down the corridor.

'Platoon party.' I tell him.

'Hair of the dog, dear boy, that will sort you out.' He shouts closing his door.

Where in the name of hell am I going to get a whiskey at this time in the morning? I try and eat breakfast, but it doesn't seem to go down. What did they put in my drink? I'm sure I didn't drink that much.

I go to the platoon lines and as I enter my office, I am met by Cpl Sykes.

'Great night Sir, pity you left early, we were just getting into the swing of things, and you missed all the fun.'

'What in the name of hell was I drinking? I can't remember a damned thing about last night.'

'Well, you were mixing it a bit Sir.'

'I must have been mixing it a lot, I reckon.'

'The platoon, are out in the woods doing section advances Sir, are you going out to them? If so I'll come with you.'

'Yes, I think that's a good idea, it will help clear my head a bit, let's go.'

The trip to Cooks Mount is in total silence, bloody heck, does my head hurt. The platoon has split up into sections, and is doing advance to contact exercises against each other. I stay with them for an hour or so and then return to barracks. Thank goodness the bar is open in the Mess. I need a very large whiskey and ginger.

Friday comes and I say goodbye to the platoon and make my way to Hereford. On the train I strike up a conversation with a passenger.

'Are you going far?' I ask.

'Hereford.' He replies.

'So am I.'

'What luck, we can travel together, my names Terry Grant, I'm in the Ox and Bucks Light Infantry. I've just finished a couple of weeks leave.'

'Dave Stubbs, Kings Royal Rifle Corps, and unfortunately, I didn't get any leave. My posting order was rather swift to say the least.'

Thank goodness I've got someone to chat to; I honestly thought the journey was going to be boring.

'Do you know a John West?' I ask.

'I sure do. In fact, I am meeting him at Liverpool Station. Why, do you know him?'

'Well, you could say that. We have been friends for years, we joined up together. He took my posting to Malaya when I got blown up in Aden.'

'Hang on a moment you must be the guy he keeps on about. I know so much about you, I could have known you for years.'

'I hope it is all good.'

We chat all the way to Liverpool Street. Waiting at the station is a tanned, very tall, guy.

'Hey, lanky, how's, the air up there?' I shout.

'Fucking Hell! What are you doing here? I thought you were going in September. This has made my day, am I glad to see you Dave.'

He nearly shakes my hand off.

'Hello up there it is me down here speaking.' Terry said butting in.

'Sorry Terry, It's just that I haven't seen Dave for ages, glad to see you mate. Come on, let's find a bar and have a drink, we have some serious talking to do.'

The three of us go into the station bar and John orders drinks.

'Still gin and tonic Dave?'

'Nope, whiskey and ginger now.'

'Wow, whiskey for you Terry?'

'Sure is.'

John brings the drinks to the table.

'To us three, let's hope we survive - cheers.'

For the next hour or so, John and I are deep in conversation and leave poor Terry out in the cold.

'You will have to excuse us Terry, but we have got a lot to catch up on.'

'No problem, you carry on, I'll sit and listen, another drink guys'

'How are your legs now Dave? Are they still giving you pain?'

'Now and again mate, if I stay on them for any length of time they hurt like hell, but otherwise they are coming along fine.'

We carry on talking for hours and hours and are slowly getting pissed.

'Don't you think we should make a move to the next station guys?' Terry said in a slurred sort of way.

'Yeah! I suppose we had better, otherwise we will be late getting to Hereford.' I reply also in a slurred sort of way.

After many trips to the wrong station we finally arrive at the right one, and only just manage to get the train. If we had missed this one we would have been declared absent without leave, that's for sure.

'I think I'm going to get my head down for a few minutes.' John said keeling over in his seat.

'I think I'll do the same.' said Terry, also keeling over.

'Well one of us had better stay awake to make sure we arrive at the correct place, and I suppose that someone is me.' I said looking at two loudly snoring drunks.

Boy! It is great being with John again. I have missed the antics we use to get up to. This guy Terry doesn't seem a bad sort either. Let's hope we all get through the Selection. I wonder what it will be like, I've been told we won't be having an easy time, but then, I didn't expect to, especially as we are hoping to join the best fighting unit in the world.

At last the train arrives and as we get out, we fall into a heap on the platform. Not really a heap, but near as. I look up and see an oldish sort of chap coming towards us. I don't like the way he is looking at us.

'Are you who I think you are?' he asked or rather shouted.

'I think we are they.' Terry said trying to gather his cases together.

'Bloody stroll on, as if we haven't got enough pillocks to mother, come on, get your stuff and follow me, what have you been drinking, meth's?'

We follow the guy out of the station. 'That's the way you should be going.'

He leaves us to it and walks back to his kiosk, hands in the air. Now do we get a taxi or do we walk. In our condition, I think we will walk. After all, it can't be that far. Or can it? Anyway the walk will sober us all up. I hope.

CHAPTER TEN

"WE ARE THE PILGRIMS MASTER; WE SHALL GO ALWAYS A LITTLE FURTHER: IT MAY BE BEYOND THAT LAST BLUE MOUNTAIN BARR'D WITH SNOW. ACROSS THAT ANGRY OR THAT GLIMMERING SEA."

(J E FLECKER)

The trip to Bradbury Lines (Now named Sterling Lines after David Sterling, the founder of the SAS) didn't take too long. We did go down some wrong streets at first, but soon found Billingham Lane. Fancy them putting a barracks in the middle of a housing estate. They do say if you can't find the barracks, then there is no point in joining. I suppose they are right.

After showing our movement orders to the Sergeant on the gate, we go into a wooden building for documentation.

'You men are to lose your rank for the duration of the Selection,' Said an oldish guy who is a Major, 'If you pass, which I doubt, you will be reinstated with your present ranks, but as from now you will only use your surnames, NO RANK, is that clear?'

'Yes Sir.' We reply.

'Sergeant Major, show these three to their accommodation and then get them kitted out for Selection, briefing by the CO is at 2000hrs, right off you go, and, Good Luck you will need it.'

So this old guy is a CSM, he must know his stuff.

'What's your name then?' asked Terry.

'James White, BUT you can call me SIR, okay.'

'Sorry I spoke, SIR.' Terry said flippantly.

'Right, follow me - Officers - I shit em!'

We are taken to a wooden spider and shown our hut.

'This is your basha for the length of time that you will be with us. Some of you will pass Selection, some of you won't. It is up to you gentlemen, put your heart and soul into Selection and you will win, otherwise it is Platform 4 at the station.'

'What's Platform 4 Sir?' John asked.

'RTU,' replied the CSM.

'Oh!'

We collect our kit from the stores and put it away in the small lockers provided by each bed.

'I don't think this is going to be easy, do you Dave?'

'I reckon you are right mate, this could be the hardest thing we have done.'

2000hrs - We report to Training Wing. There are about 120 of us. A tall guy starts to speak.

'My name is Colonel Bennett and I am the Commanding Officer. It is nice to see you all. Some of you will be here tomorrow night and some of you won't. This is no reflection on you, and you should not think that it is. Selection is hard, it has to be. If you fail you can come back for another try, but if you fail that go, that is it. Remember, it is not a blemish on your character; the pass rate is very small into the SAS. Give it your best shot, you may think once you are in that is it. Well it isn't. It is hard to get the beige beret and even harder to keep it. Remember our Motto "Who Dares, Wins," good luck to you all.'

'He didn't give much away, did he, in fact, I now know as much as I did when I arrived.' Terry said.

'I think that goes for us all mate.' John said.

The briefing lasted all of 15 minutes.

A soldier approaches us. We haven't a clue what rank he is as he doesn't wear any.

'Each of you is to fill your Bergen with the kit on this list. Collect the numbered bricks from the Quartermasters stores and be outside your hut at 0400hrs tomorrow.'

This is a weird outfit; no one wears any rank, at least no one I have seen so far.

We pack the kit and bricks, it is bloody heavy, and then get our heads down. After about 5 minutes, two soldiers dressed in Para smocks come into the hut.

'Welcome to Selection gentlemen, my name is Sergeant Major Swann and this is Staff Sergeant Flynn, we are your instructors for this stage of the course. In the morning we are going on a small hike just to get the cobwebs out of your system, any questions?'

'How far are we going Sir?' Asked someone at the other end of the hut.

'Now that, is on a need to know basis, you will know when you arrive at the end, goodnight gentlemen.' Said SSgt Flynn.

0400hrs - We climb on the truck and move off out of the camp.

'Bloody roll on, we needn't have packed all this bloody kit, no-one has checked it off.' Said a voice from the front of the truck.

After what seemed like hours we arrive and dismount.

'Bring your Bergen's over here for weighing.' Shouts SSgt Flynn.

Everyone has the correct weight except 3 men.

'You three, get back on the truck.' Said CSM Swann pointing to the 3 guys whose Bergen's were under weight. We never saw them again.

'Right, you lot, form two ranks, ready - quick march.'

The march along the road isn't too bad, but we suddenly turn off into a field and start up a ruddy steep hill.

'Shit!'

CSM Swann starts to laugh.

'Come on get it together, left right, left right, keep the pace going.'

God knows how many miles we have gone, uphill and downhill, uphill and downhill. In the distance we see a truck waiting.

'Double march.'

Having run down the hill we fall in a heap beside the truck.

'Well done lads, you only just made it with 26 seconds to go. That was a small speed march. Learn from it, the next one will be longer and harder, get on the truck.'

As we are returning to camp, I notice that blood is seeping through my shirt. I must have burst some blisters. I'm not alone most of the guys have burst blisters as well.

We dismount the truck and Swann shouts, 'Weapon training in one hour, be at hut 22, and don't be late.'

As if we would, there is no fear of that happening; no one wants to be RTU'd.

We clean the many blisters that have broken on our backs and feet and apply Jensom Violet. At this rate we will run out of the stuff pretty quickly.

'Christ! Will we ache in the morning.' said a small wiry guy named Joe.

'Tell me about it.' said Terry.

Hut 22 is the weapons hut, and we arrive dressed in clean kit.

'We'll soon get that dirty.' Said a very heavily built guy holding an Ingram machine gun.

'Right lads, my name is Stocker and I am the weapons instructor for this course. You will now learn about the many weapons that are used around the world. So make sure you pay attention, there is a lot to take in.'

The lesson goes on for hours and suddenly we break off for grub. The first meal of the day except for breakfast that is. I'm starving; all this training is making me hungry. It reminds me of the time we were in the Congo, when we had to jam in all that training, at least the AK47 didn't come hard.

After dinner we return to our hut and get our kit ready for the next day. Just as we are about to turn in, CSM Swann enters the hut.

'Today's march was an easy one you have to complete the next one in 3 hours and 30 minutes. You must pass this march before you can go onto the next stage of training. I warn you now; this is going to be the hardest march you will ever have to complete. Fail and you are out; remember the blisters you got today, well, tomorrows will be worse. If any of you want to pull out, now is the time to do it.'

No one answered. Now, this is a new strategy, trying to demoralise the troops, crafty bastard. What will they think of next?

Morning comes far too quickly. As we get dressed I turn my socks inside out.

'Why you doing that Dave?' John asked.

'Well, the seams will be on the outside and that will stop them rubbing against my toes causing blisters.'

'What a bloody good idea, I'm going to do the same.' said John.

'Me too.' Said Terry.

We stick field dressings to the areas of our backs that are constantly rubbed by our Bergen's. That should make it feel better. Once all the kit is packed, we parade outside the hut.

'Right lads, on the truck.' Shouts CSM Swann.

The drive takes an hour to complete. Where the hell we are, I've no idea. Swann weighs our Bergen's, webbing and even the rifles just in case we have taken the working parts out to make them lighter. Everyone has 461bs. This time we don't lose anyone to the dreaded Platform 4.

'This march must be done in the time allotted; failure will result in you being RTU'd, Oh! By the way, there are some ruddy big hills on this march, steeper than yesterday, ready - form 2 ranks - quick march.'

The two guys in front set off at a cracking pace. It isn't too bad at the moment, but when we make for the hills, we will know it. We have been walking for over 2 hours and are totally knackered. The pace is killing, every part of my body aches, including my feet. In front of us are the biggest fucking hills we have ever seen.

'Oh my god!' Said Stan, 'These are going to kill us.'

'I think that bloody big one is Pen-y-Fan.' I say to no one in particular.

We keep going and as we round a left hand bend we see a truck.

'That's our truck.' Said someone in the middle.

No orders are given for us to halt, so we carry on straight past the truck. After what I thought was about a mile past the truck (it was in fact 2 miles) we see another truck.

'Keep going guys, it's not ours.' Said Stan.

As we march past the truck, Swann shouts, 'HAAAALT.'

We all bump into each other as we are taken completely by surprise.

'Well done lads, you have completed the march in 3 hours and 17 minutes, that was a fast pace, drop your kit and have a drink from your water bottles.'

Boy! Does it taste good? I didn't know water could taste so nice.

'Come over here.' said Swann, 'I want to debrief you on the march. First of all, take a look at yourselves. You are totally knackered. That is because you never paced yourselves, you went off like a bull at a gate. You could never have carried out a fire fight at the end of the march. Learn from this mistake, second, did any of you notice the two men with guns at the first truck we came to? NO, of course you didn't. You were too busy marching. Remember, observation at all times. If this was a real battle situation, you would all have been killed.'

Damn, there is more to this than I realised. No wonder the SAS is the best unit in the world.

'Okay, onto the truck and let's get back to the Lines.'

Back in our hut we clean up and dress the blisters we have got. Thank goodness there are no blisters on my toes. The inside out socks worked a treat.

SSgt Flynn enters the hut. 'Get your kit ready as for the march; we are going out into the countryside for map reading. This exercise will finish sometime tomorrow morning.'

'It's never ending is it, on the go all the time.' said Joe.

Back outside the hut we are split into teams of four. Each team has an instructor, and we are given a map and compass each. My team consists of Terry, John and Stan. Our instructors name is Stacey; he has just come back from a tour of duty in Oman.

'Right, pay attention, I'm going to teach you how to map read the SAS way and how to find your way at night using the stars. Right get your kit and let's go.'

We load our kit into a land rover and make our way out into the countryside.

'Okay, follow me.'

We walk for about 2 miles and come to a plateau.

'Get your kit off and gather round. As you can see, we have hills to our front and right side. By looking at the map and the contour lines, we can turn it so that the map lines up with the hills in front of us and the hills to the right. Now how are we going to find north? We know the sun rises in the east and sets in the west, but, it depends which Hemisphere you are in, the sun at 12 o'clock midday will be due south in the Northern Hemisphere and due north in the Southern Hemisphere. How do we know, which Hemisphere we are in? Shadows move clockwise in the north and anti-clockwise in the south. Stick your daggers in the ground. Now note the shadow it makes. In about a quarter of an hour, note where the shadow is. By joining the two shadows at the tops, you will get east and west. Dissect at right angles to this line and you will get north and south. Remember, the first shadow will indicate west.'

We are taught how to use a clock face to find north, it is found to be not very accurate. Once we have mastered the way to find our position using different methods, we are shown how to make a compass from items that we have in our Bergen's.

'Right, gather up your kit, we are off to another position.'

Off we go up a hill and along through to a valley. After about an hour we stop on some flat ground which has some trees surrounding it.

'Take your kit off and gather round.'

I wonder what we are going to learn here. We leave our Bergen's in a line but take our rifles with us.

'Well done, you are learning, never leave your rifle, always have it with you, no matter what you are doing, right let's get on. I'm now going to teach you how to find north by plants and trees. Take a look at this tree stump, you will see that it has rings and that the rings get wider here, (pointing to the stump) the rings are wider spaced towards the equator which is south. So this side, (again pointing to the stump) is north. Plants grow towards the sun and are more prolific south in the Northern hemisphere and north in the Southern hemisphere. How do we find out which hemisphere we are in? - you at the end.'

'By looking at the shadows, which are clockwise in the north and anti, clockwise in the South.' answered Terry.

'Well done.'

We look at different plants that will tell us which direction we are travelling. This is extremely interesting. Even the trees can tell us, from lichen on the trunks.

'Okay lads, we will break off for a bite to eat, use one of the ration packs from your Bergen's and make yourselves a meal.'

I pull out a pack and proceed to open it. It is full of small packets not tins like I'm used to.

'Before you ask, these are Dehydrated Ration Packs. You have only to boil the water and place a packet in it, for instant food.' said our instructor.

I open a packet that says "Steak and Kidney Block" it smells horrible. At least we still have the little hexamine cookers. I unfold one and get my mess tins (which take up far too much room) from my Bergen and boil up some water. After about 10 minutes the water is bubbling and I place the block in. I give it a stir and low and behold instant Steak and Kidney pudding. I take a mouthful and spit it out.

'What the fuck is this shit, it's horrible.'

'Get used to it because these are the meals you will be having on the course.' The instructor said.

'Jesus H Christ! This makes my mother a Cordon Bleu cook and she definitely can't cook. This stuff is real shit.' Terry said.

'I'll give you guys some real advice, buy up as many Mars bars as you can get, they are far better than those Dehydrated Meals, which need about 8 pints of water to cook.'

Night is coming in fast and the stars are coming out.

'Okay lads, now that it is getting dark we can carry on with the training. You have learnt how to move about using the map and other items that are about, now I will teach you how to find north by using the moon and the stars. Let's start with the moon, we know it circles the earth every 28 days, and in that time it changes shape, this is called waxing and waning. The moon reflects light from the sun, we are only interested when the moon is rising, if it rises before midnight then the side of the moon that is visible will be west, after midnight then the side that can be seen will be east. So you should be able to find your way at night. Just remember, it won't be dead accurate, but near enough to get you out of problems. Any questions so far.'

None were forthcoming.

'Okay then, let's see what we can get with the stars, and I don't mean the horoscope type. First of all, let's look at the types we have in the sky. They will change depending on which hemisphere you will be operating in. We have up there, the Plough, known as the pan and handle. Then Cassiopeia, that's the "W" shaped set, and at the bottom you can see a cluster called Orion. If you look between the Plough and the W, you will see a very bright star. That's the Pole Star. If you look at the bottom of the Plough, you will see two stars. They point to the Pole Star. The stars always stay in relation to one another. Their passage over the horizon begins 4 minutes earlier each night that works out at about 2 hours over a month in the northern hemisphere. The stars are visible throughout the night providing they are not covered by clouds, and revolve round the Pole Star. Stick these into the ground (passing us two poles, one bigger than the other) now line up any of the stars. From the movement of the star you can see what direction you are facing. If the star rises, you are facing east, if it falls, you are facing west, if it goes to the right, you are facing south and if it goes to the left, you are facing north. These directions are not one hundred per cent accurate, but again, enough to get you out of trouble. If you are in the Southern hemisphere, all this will have to be reversed, any questions.'

None were forthcoming.

'Okay then, we will practise some direction finding just to see if you have assimilated all that I have taught you so far. Pick up your Bergen's and let's get going.'

After about an hour, we halt.

'Not bad at all lads, get some grub out of your Bergen's and get your breakfast going. You have a Map Reading exercise starting at 0300hrs. You will pick up different items found at the grid references you will be given. Make sure you memorise them, they won't be given to you twice. I suggest that each member in the team memorises one of the grid references.'

Breakfast consists of hard tack biscuits and tea. Jesus! Are they hard? We have had no sleep and now we are marching over god knows how many hills, this is becoming extremely knackering. So called breakfast over, we are given maps of the area. Each one of us memorises a grid reference. We are not allowed to write anything down in case the enemy finds it. Even the map must be folded on its original creases, so nothing is given away.

John is given the job as team leader for the exercise. The exercise has to be completed in 5 hours.

'Bloody Hell! Do you see how far we have got to go in that time? What have we got to find.' Terry asked.

Stan hasn't said anything for ages.

'You all right Stan?' John asked.

'Totally buggered mate, I don't think I will finish this Selection, I'm so tired, I could sleep for a week, and me feet are tired as well. I've never walked so far in my life. I can't think what made me apply for the SAS. I need certifying.'

'I think we all do mate, but don't give up now; they are definitely trying to demoralise us, hoping we will give up. So don't mate, we will see it through, you see if I'm not right.'

The first hill we go up is a bastard, straight up for about 600 feet. At the top is a Trig Point where we should find the first item.

Suddenly the hill levels out, and what is in front of us, another fucking hill, only this one does have the Trig Point on it.

We pick up the first item which is a penknife and proceed along a track which in places is pretty muddy. After about an hour we are only a quarter of the distance we have to travel. I don't think we are going to make it, and if we don't, It's hello 2RGJ, goodbye SAS. The ground starts to drop sharply and we start to run down the hill. At the next grid reference we find another item, 2 yards of string. Further along we find a poncho, then another, then another and then another. Who thought up these items, I wonder if they will be needed later on.

Three hours have now passed and we are still 10 miles from our objective. We are going up a very steep hill which is bloody hard going especially with the amount of kit we are carrying. Once at the top we see below us a sodding wide river.

'Shit.' said John aloud.

'How in the name of mother fuckers are we going to get over that? We can't go round, we haven't the time.' said Terry.

We make our way to the river's edge. In a tin is an envelope.

'What's it say?' I ask.

'We have to swim across using the items we have found.'

'Let's see what we have got.' said Terry.

We take the items found out of our Bergen's.

'Okay, we have a penknife, 2 metres of string, 4 ponchos, any ideas?' John asked.

'I reckon we have got to put all our kit in the ponchos and tie the ends up so that they will float. I think we have to use them as floats to get across the river.'

'Well done Dave, I think you are right, let's get to it, time is getting on.'

We cover our kit with a poncho each and tie the ends up.

'I'll go first. Bloody hell! It's fffucking fffreezing.'

I'm now out into the middle of the river and turn round and shout to them, 'Hurry up and get in, it works.'

They launch themselves into the river and start swimming across. I reach the bank and pull myself up. I must get out of these wet clothes quickly or else hyperthermia will set in. I have just changed and stowed the wet kit into my Bergen when they arrive on the bank.

'Get out of those wet things quickly,' I tell them, 'we've got a ruddy long way to go and we better get cracking.'

The pace speeds up. In front of us is an enormously high hill. The going is really tough now especially after swimming a freezing cold river. After 20 minutes we reach the top of the hill. On the other side we see a guy waiting for us; down the hill we go and run up to him just in case he has any messages for us.

'Congratulations, you are the first home.'

'You mean we have finished.' Stan said.

'You certainly have, and with 14 minutes to spare, here, have a drink.' He says passing Stan a water bottle. Stan takes a swig.

'Stones the crows, Rum!' passing the water bottle to me. I take a hefty swig.

'Smashing stuff.'

'You don't like Rum Dave.' John said.

'I bloody well do now.' I say in return.

'My turn,' said Terry, 'Rum isn't my tipple, but let the horse see the water. Ah, nectar!'

By the time John gets the water bottle there is hardly any left.

'Thanks a bunch mates.' He says indignantly.

As we wait by the road, ten more men turn up.

'You lot had better start running,' the soldier shouts at them, 'You have exactly 26 seconds left.'

Ten knackered men race towards us just in the nick of time.

'There now, aren't you glad that's over? Park your bums, a truck will be here in a few minutes.'

Once on the truck, we head back to Bradbury Lines.

'You know what Dave, I'm sure we didn't do 10 miles from the river crossing to when we stopped.' Terry said.

'I think you're right, they seem to be using demoralizing tactics on us.'

'Do you think they'll do that again Dave?'

'More than likely, they are bloody devious bunch, and I wouldn't put anything past them.'

Are they trying to wear us down, I just don't know.

We arrive back at the Lines and remove our kit from the truck.

'Clean your weapons and be in hut 22 in 45 minutes time.' Said a soldier who appeared from nowhere.

'Sodding hell, don't we get any sleep on this course?' Stan said

'Don't let them hear you Stan; they might think you don't want to carry on with the course.' Terry said.

'Fuck them, I just don't care anymore.'

We report to Hut 22 where we carry out 2 hours of weapon training. I'm beginning to learn every weapon we are presented with. I didn't know there were so many weapons around the world. The armoury here must be very extensive.

After training we return to our hut.

'I suppose I had better write to the girlfriend.' Terry said getting his writing kit out.

Bloody heck, I haven't thought of Jane since I've been here. I should write to her and let her know how I'm getting on. No, I'll give it a miss for now.

'Coming over to the Club John?'

'Why not, I could do with a drink, you guys coming?'

'I'm with you.' Stan said.

'I must write this letter, see you later.' Terry said.

We go to a wooden hut called the Paludrin Club (named after a little pill to stop malaria) and have a few drinks. The place is full of men in civvies. I wonder if they have completed Selection. Unfortunately, the golden rule is "mind your own business." After a while we return to our hut. Terry is fast asleep.

'I think I'll do the same, we have to get up early in the morning.' Stan says climbing into bed. He is absolutely right; we need all the sleep we can get.

0400hrs - Jesus Christ! It's not getting any easier. We have to parade outside the hut in 20 minutes dressed in combat kit and full equipment, and in the same teams as yesterday.

We move out of the Lines in a tatty Bedford truck and head for the hills. After an hour, the lorry stops.

'All out.' shouts a soldier in the same clothing as us.

'Get your kit on and follow me.'

We collect our kit and move out after the soldier. An hour later we halt.

'Gather round lads and I'll tell you what you are going to do today.'

It's another compass march over the Brecon Beacons, with obstacles in the way.

'This march is against the clock.'

'Excuse me, but I noticed that there was a clock on the square back in the Lines. What are all the names on it for?' I asked.

'That clock has the names of all members of the SAS who never made it back from an operation. Your aim, once in the Regiment, is to beat the clock, that is, DON'T GET YOUR FUCKING NAME ON IT. Does that answer your question?'

'Bloody Hell! They keep a tally of who gets killed.' Stan said under his breath.

We move off on a compass bearing and end up at a river which is pretty damn wide.

'Well, how are you going to cross this then?' A soldier asked.

I move towards the river and survey it.

'I think we should strip off and wade it, that way we will keep our clothing dry.' I tell him.

'Well, do it then.' He replies.

We all strip and put our kit in our Bergen's, and wade across the river. Bloody hell, it is cold, my dick nearly disappears. The water turns us blue and our teeth begin to chatter. After a few minutes we arrive at the other side of the river. Getting dressed is pretty difficult as we are shaking with cold.

'Sodding Heck! I hope we don't have to do that too many times.' Stan said trying to warm himself.

'Where's that soldier?' Terry asked.

I look round and I'm just about to speak when the soldier comes over the hill in front of us.

'How did you get across without getting wet?' I ask him.

'You get wet, I don't, you learn, I teach. You would have seen the bridge, if you had looked at your maps properly. But then, you couldn't use it anyway.' He replied.

'Right let's get on, we have a long way to go yet.'

We carry on walking up and down various hills until we come to some flat ground.

'See that stick in the ground 50 yards in front of you, I want you to crawl from here to it, do not get up. Is that understood?'

We start crawling and suddenly we are in water. Shit!

'Keep down you lot.' The soldier shouts.

As we crawl through the water we come across dead sheep and other unmentionable things. The water is level with our mouths. Christ all mighty! I hope I don't drink any of this stuff. I dread to think what I might catch. We finally make the stick, which has a sheep's skull attached to it. Evil bastards.

'Get changed into some dry kit and let's get on.' Said the soldier.

'How much more of this have we got to take I wonder.' said John panting a bit.

There is a burst of laughter from the soldier. Dry kit is disappearing fast.

We have been walking for about 2 hours and the hills are getting steeper.

'That gentlemen, is Pen-y-Fan. I want you to go up and down it by three different routes. I will be waiting for you at the top, get moving.'

This is the highest bloody hill in Brecon, 2906 feet above sea level. I'm not looking forward to this, one little bit.

'He's got to be joking, surely he don't want us to climb that?'

'I'm afraid he does, so let's get at it, the sooner we get it over with, the better.' I tell them.

This part of Selection is called the Fan Dance.

After God knows how long, we have all climbed this bloody hill three times. We are totally knackered.

'Well! What are you waiting for, get over to the wagon, we have other things to do, MOVE IT.' The soldier said.

After a small drive and a long walk, we arrive at a small hut deep inside the Brecon Beacons.

'You will now be taught how to live off the land, so take notice of what you will be shown.'

A very tall man appears as if by magic, he looks quite old, but I'm sure he isn't.

'Hello lads, my names Sid, I'm your survival instructor, all around you are things to eat, it is recognising them that is the secret. I intend to show you how to live off the land without going hungry. Take notice of what I tell you and make notes of the different things you are shown. Your life could depend on what you are going to be taught.'

The big guy produces a frog. 'This is edible, but, don't eat the skin, it is poisonous. Don't eat toads, they are, poisonous. Toads are bigger than frogs. Make sure you skin your frog before you cook it. They are good eating; ask the French, they have been eating them for years. In fact, France is the only country that has a disabled Frog Association, because of all the legless frogs out there. Only joking.'

We are shown various insects and grubs that are high in protein that can be safely eaten. This includes worms after putting them in water to get the muck out of them.

'One secret you should know. DO NOT eat any grubs or worms that are eating off of dung heaps or carrion or under leaves, they could be poisonous. Also any that are brightly coloured, leave well alone.'

He then went onto roots and leaves and how to identify which types can be safely eaten. I didn't know you could eat a Puffball. I thought they were Toadstools. It is surprising what you can eat when you know where to look. I was quite fascinated with the way that you can tell whether water is safe to drink using ear wax. I'll stick to sterilizing tablets. They are safer.

The lectures go on for hours and are very interesting. It is surprising what there is to eat all around you.

'Okay lads, you are now going to spend the next few days out in the wilds of Brecon with no food or water. Each one of you will keep your maps and compasses as you will need them. You are to be totally on your own. You are to meet up at the reference points given by your instructor by 0900hrs Friday. You will leave this position at 10 minute intervals on the bearings that will be given to you, good luck.'

It's now my turn.

'Okay Stubbs, Grid Reference 055197.'

I repeat the grid reference.

'Show me on the map.'

I point to the right grid.

'On your way.'

There is a large hill in my way which will make the going tough. According to the instructions I have been given I have to make 14 miles before I can stop. I am heading for the Talybont Reservoir. That is my RV in a few days' time. Shit! The easy way to it, is only about 8 miles.

The route I've got is over the worst terrain I have ever seen. Brecon certainly is a bastard of a place. I've never been up so many hills, and fucking big ones at that. I hole up at the edge of some trees. I cache my Bergen. I must remember to keep my weapon with me at all times. You never know who is watching.

This outfit is very devious. Well! What shall I have for dinner? Christ knows, I've got to find it first. I look around the area and find some Puffballs. As I am circling around the trees, a bird flies off screeching. It is a Lapwing. I nearly tread on the nest which has eggs in it. I take 3 and leave one behind.

(Note: It is now illegal to disturb nesting birds or take their eggs.)

I'm not going to get fat on this. After a further search, I find some nettles to make tea. What I need now is water.

Further out on the hill, I find a little trickle of water coming down from some rocks. What did the instructor say, collect water near the source. I climb up and put my water bottle to the trickle. After 10 minutes I have a full bottle. I make my way down to where I cached my Bergen, and make a small fire using a flint and some sheep wool.

I cut up the Puffballs and break open the eggs and fry the lot together. What a concoction. It tastes pretty good though, but then, anything will taste good if you are hungry. The nettle tea is quite refreshing, and I eat the leaves as cabbage. I must now make a basha. I look for two trees that are close together and make a hammock out of my blanket and tie a line over the hammock and drape my poncho over it like a tent. At least I will be dry if it rains and I am off of the ground. I clean up and climb into it and try to sleep. I must make the most of any sleep I can get, because I am sure I have bigger hills to go over.

Having cat napped throughout the night I'm wide wake at 0400hrs. It is misty as hell. I find dew all over the poncho. I tap it and let the water run into a mess tin. At least this will be fresh. Well, as fresh as can be. Only thing is, there isn't much of it, just a few mouthfuls. I take the twigs out and gulp it down. It tastes okay. Water is called the silent killer, for obvious reasons. I go to where I filled my water bottle, and fill it up for the next phase. 2 pills should make it safe.

Having packed up my makeshift tent I prepare to move off. I have to make about 10 miles before I can stop. I check the map and find that I have got a small incline about 600 yards away before it drops down into a valley. I also notice on the map that I have got some bloody big hills in my way.

I've been walking for about 4 hours and I am near to the 10 mile point. I think I have got a couple of miles to go before I come to the marker.

The last few miles have really taxed me; I must be losing energy as I haven't had anything to eat. I look around and find some mushrooms. I break them in pieces and chew them. They don't taste too bad. I check and find that I have still got a little water left which I swill my mouth with. Sod this lark; I'd rather have my meals ready than have to find them.

I remember what the soldier told us, stock up on Mars bars. What I wouldn't give for a few of them now. I finally reach the marker. I have taken 40 minutes longer than I should have. How in the name of Hell am I going to make that time up?

At the marker there is a letter pinned to it. I have to dig in and be prepared to be attacked. They have got to be joking. Who would want to attack me, I'm in the middle of nowhere, surrounded on all sides by fucking big hills. BANG! BANG! BANG! Dirt is kicked up in front of me. Fuck me! Who's using live ammo? No-one told me this was going to happen. I run and make for a mound of rocks 25 yards to my right. I jump over the rocks and get behind them. I undo my Bergen and push it in front of me. I can't see anyone, what are they doing using live ammo, gulping in great mouthfuls of air. Sod this for a game of soldiers. Nothing more happens and I wait behind the rocks for what seemed like hours, but was in fact, only 10 minutes.

Getting up, I move off towards the side of a large hill. I start to dig in. The ground is pretty soft and it doesn't take me long to dig down about three feet. All of a sudden the trench starts to fill up with water. Stuff this! I'm not getting into that. I look around and find some rocks which I put on top of the earth that I have dug up. This should be good enough. I hope!

All the digging has made me thirsty. Checking the trench I find that it is nearly overflowing with water. I fill up my water bottles and also the mess tins. I chuck in a few Sterilizing pills and wait for them to work. Boy! Am I fucking knackered.

I haven't thought anything about food and from the lie of the land, there doesn't seem to be much about. It looks as if I will be dining on water alone tonight. I wonder how the rest of the guys are getting on.

It has been very quiet for about half an hour, so I put my Bergen on and start walking over the hill. I'm not leaving anything behind in the camp area, except the 2 mess tins filled with water which I hide under a rock. After going about 600 yards, I find a partridge which I club to death with my rifle. Real food at last.

I return to my camp and find that someone has thrown a dead sheep into my water pit. The bastards, I didn't even see them. Well, that's the water undrinkable; thank goodness I filled my two water bottles up and the mess tins. I check under the rocks and find that the mess tins are filled with mud. The bastards. Well! At least the mud is going to come in useful. I cover the partridge with it and begin to gather materials for making a fire. I hollow out the ground and make a fire in it. I place the cocooned partridge on top of the fire. I haven't a clue how long to cook it for. Whilst it is cooking, I add some bits of wood to the fire; I don't want it going out.

I check the map and see that I have got about 20 miles to go before 0900hrs tomorrow. The worst bit is that it is over the highest hills. I don't think I have got a flat bit till the end.

Why, Oh, why! Did I want to join a mad outfit like this? I need my head read. 4 hours have gone by and I check the mud caked partridge. I pull the mud off and the feathers come away as well. The flesh looks cooked and I taste it. Oh! What lovely grub. I pull the rest of the mud off and pull the partridge apart.

BANG! BANG! BANG!

Bullets whistle over my head. Shit! They are firing at me. I grab my weapon and my Bergen and run from my position, to around the side of the hill. Sod this.

'Don't try getting back to your camp, you won't make it.' Someone shouts.

'Bollocks.' I reply and make off across the side of the hill. I was enjoying that partridge.

I swig some water and start the long trek up the hills. It is no use going back they will have eaten my lovely partridge, the rotten fuckers. The walk is a killer, I've had no food except the water and I'm beginning to feel the cold. What did that instructor say, if you start to get cold put some warm clothes on? I dig into my Bergen and fish out a heavy jumper and put it on over my combats. If I get hot it will be easier to take off this way. It doesn't look as if I will be getting any sleep tonight.

I follow the compass bearing and as the night settles in, I make a note of the surrounding area. I have some pretty big hills to cover. I must make as much distance as I can before it gets totally dark. I find some shelter beside some rocks, and dig out a hollow. This will have to do for now. I cover myself with my poncho and try to get some sleep. It is not easy and I keep waking up. Sod those bastards; I could do with that partridge now.

I must have had some sleep, but wake just as the light starts to come through. I pack up my kit and swig some water and start up the hill. Christ! I'm shattered. My back aches, my legs ache and I'm bloody hungry. I swig some more water. I must keep going. I wonder how the other guys are getting on. I reach the top of the hill just as the sun starts to rise. Shit! I'm too far to the South. I check the compass; I need to make for the left hand hill. I start to run and fall to the ground. Fuck this, I've had it, I'll never make it now.

It is 0630hrs. I'm never going to make it. I slowly walk up the hill and as I reach the top, I see the reservoir. How far is it I wonder? It can't be more than five miles. I start to run down the hill towards the RV. As I hit the track, a vehicle pulls up alongside me. Christ knows where it came from.

'Hop in lad and I'll take you to the reservoir, you look absolutely shattered.' The driver said.

'No thanks sport, I'll get there under my own steam, thanks anyway.'

'Come on Dave, get in.'

I look at the driver and sitting in the rear of the vehicle is Stan.

'Get out of there Stan, it's a setup, this bastard will take you straight to the station.'

The vehicle keeps up with me as I am running.

'Come on Dave, this guy is all right, I watched him from a hill getting his sheep together, he's not in the mob.' Stan shouts from the vehicle.

'Like hell he isn't, fuck off sport, I'll do it on my own, so piss off.'

With that, the vehicle shoots off and leaves me running on my own.

'You stupid bastard Stan.' I shout.

I stop running and drink some water. Am I hot? I take off the jumper and put it in my Bergen. I am just putting it on my back when another vehicle arrives.

'Get in the back soldier; you have completed your exercise.' Said the driver who was dressed in combat gear.

'Like hell I have,' I tell him.

As the vehicle slowly drives past me, I see Terry sitting in the back. I know there is something wrong and start running along the track.

'Where do you think you are going?' The soldier asked.

'Bollocks, I don't need your help.'

The vehicle stops and I keep running. After about a mile, I see another vehicle parked by the side of the reservoir. Oh! No, not another one.

'Well done lad, you have 20 minutes to spare, get yourself something to eat from the wagon, there is tea and sandwiches in the back.'

'No thanks, I'll get something at the RV.' I tell the soldier.

'If you look at your map, you will see you ARE at the RV.'

I'm still not convinced so don't take my Bergen off.

'You are at the RV, so get your kit off and get some scran.' said the soldier.

At this, John comes from behind the wagon.

'Hi ya Dave, have a brew?'

'So this really is the RV then John?'

'Sure is mate, have you seen Stan and Terry?'

I'm just about to answer when someone puts a black sack over my head and my arms are tied behind my back.

'What the fucks going on?' I shout through the sack.

'Shut up arsehole.' Someone screams at me.

'You all right John?'

Whack. I'm knocked to the ground. Shit! Someone wants to play rough. My feet are tied together and I'm bundled into some kind of vehicle. I hope John is okay.

After driving for what seemed like hours, I'm pulled out of the vehicle and taken into what I think is a building. I'm thrown to the floor and left.

'Are you with me John?' I shout.

'Yes mate; I'm here, any idea what they are up to?'

'I haven't a clue; they seem to want to play rough though.'

I manage to lift part of the hood by working it up with my mouth. We seem to be in some sort of barn. At this point someone comes in and whispers in my ear.

'Remember, tell them nothing about the flaming sword, they must not be told anything about it, do you understand?'

'I don't know anything about it anyway.' I tell the person.

(The SAS beret badge is actually a flaming sword designed by Bob Tait in the desert during the 2nd World War; it isn't a winged dagger as everyone says it is)

There is a commotion outside and the person disappears. What have they got for us now I wonder?

After what seemed like hours, some people enter the barn and pull me to my feet. The hood is pulled off and all I can see is 4 men dressed in suits with hoods over their heads. I'm pushed into a chair and tied to it.

'What is your name?' One of the men asks.

'I cannot answer that.' I reply.

Whack. I'm knocked to the ground, blood coming from a cut inside my mouth. Fuck this.

'I'll ask you again, what is your name?'

'I cannot answer that.' I again reply.

This gets me a whack in the ribs. Shit! That hurt. The chair digs into my arms. I'm pulled up and water is thrown at my face. The questions go on with more thumps and more kicks.

I finally give them my right name.

'Now why didn't you give us that in the first place, it would have saved you a lot of pain. Now give me your rank and number?'

'Lieutenant, my number is 424923.'

'You are lying. You are not an officer, you are only a private. You have only said you are an officer hoping to get better treatment. Well you won't, we don't like officers.'

I'm knocked off of the chair and onto the floor. Bloody hell, they are really going to town.

'You have some information we want, what do you know about the "Flaming Sword"?'

'I can't answer that.' I reply.

KICK, KICK, KICK! Shit, this hurts; I must be black and blue.

I'm pulled up and knocked down many times and the questions go on and on. I don't know how long they have been beating me but suddenly it stops. I am all alone in the barn.

'Are you there John?' I whisper.

No answer. They must have taken him away while I was being interrogated.

Two men come into the barn and I'm pulled to my feet. My arms are untied and I am marched out of the barn. It is dark. A hood is placed over my head, my arms are retied and I'm thrown into a vehicle. The ride is pretty awful and I'm thrown about. I try counting the seconds, but find it difficult as I'm bounced about a lot.

The vehicle finally stops and I am pulled out of it and my arms are untied. The hood is removed and I see my Bergen. A map is thrust into my hand.

'Are you alright?'

'I think so.' I reply.

'You are to be at grid 553673 by 0900hrs. Repeat the grid and show me on the map.'

I repeat the grid and quickly look for it on the map he has given me and point it out.

'Good, now on your way.'

Looking at my watch. If it is correct, I have 12 hours to get there. I've lost a day somewhere. I haven't a clue where I am, so I check the surrounding area and just make out large features. I then orientate the map. I ache all over, and find I can only just lift my Bergen.

'Fuck this for a game of soldiers.' I shout out aloud.

Now what was I taught about map reading at night, Oh yes, the moon, it is facing me so that must be West. I dive into my Bergen and find my pencil torch. From what I can remember of where I was before being hijacked, I should be due east.

I find a farm on the map, is this where the bastards had taken me? I can't find any other buildings, so that must be the place. I reckon that I must have been in the truck for at least 15 minutes, so I should be pretty near it. I hazard a guess and start walking due north, at least I think I'm going due north.

The Bergen is giving me shit. My body aches like hell. I'm still not use to the dark yet; it takes about 35 minutes for your eyes to get use to the dark. I'll keep to the middle of the road away from the trees, that way I will be able to see better.

I come across a road sign and check it on the map. Bloody hell! I'm going in the wrong direction. I get my compass out of my Bergen and check the bearing. I'm going in the right direction. I check the sign and find that it has been pulled up. The rotten bastards have turned the sign round. Thank goodness I checked the compass bearing.

After walking for about an hour, I stop and sip some water. I must remember to stop every 45 minutes to save my energy. I have a bloody long way to go. I'm hungry, tired and ache all over. I hope John is okay, I wonder what happened to him.

I start to move off and as I reach a small bridge over the road, I see the lights of a vehicle coming towards me. I dive for cover and wait for the vehicle to pass. As it reaches the bridge it stops, two men get out.

'Well, he should be along this stretch of the road, if he is as good as they say he is. Get the night scope out and see if you can see him?'

'We'll pick him up don't worry.'

They scan the road with the night scope and then get back into the vehicle and drive off. Boy! That was close.

I walk for another 45 minutes and sit down by the side of the road. A figure comes at me from a field. I lay flat on the ground hoping he doesn't see me. The figure trips over a small fence.

'Fuck it!' It shouts.

I know that voice.

'Hey Soldier!' I shout.

The figure leaps back over the fence and hits the ground.

'It's all right, it's me John.'

'That you Dave? Fucking Hell! Am I glad to see a friendly face?'

John tells me how he got on with the interrogation exercise. He seemed to have had it rougher than me.

'What in the name of stewed balls was the "Flaming Sword" mate?'

'I think it was the SAS Badge, everyone says it is a Winged Dagger when in fact it is a Flaming Sword, it was designed by a Sergeant Bob Tait in the 2nd World War, as the cap badge for the SAS.'

After a short rest we move off along the road. I check my watch and it is 2330hrs.

'I think we should start making our way across country, we could save some time that way.' John says pointing to some open ground.

'I think you could be right mate, let's go.' I reply.

We move off to the left and start walking up a small hill. As we reach the top, some torches light up to our right. We both hit the ground together.

'Who are they, mate?' John asked.

'I don't know, keep quiet.'

Six men pass in front of us, three of them are carrying rifles.

'I think they are poachers John.' I whisper.

We wait for them to go by and then get up and move off.

'I wonder what they were poaching.' John asked.

'No idea mate and I don't particularly care, we've got enough troubles without adding to them, come on, let's move it.'

It is just like old times, the two of us together. After about an hour we stop for a breather.

'Have you written to Jane, Dave?'

'Christ! I forgot all about her, no, I haven't, I suppose I should really, after all, she is my girlfriend, I think.'

'Why do you say that Dave?'

'I don't know, I think there might be something going on with a chap she works with, I'm not sure, but something is nagging me.'

We shoulder our Bergen's and move off. We have gone about 6 miles over the hills and suddenly come to a large stream.

'I am not taking off any clothing to swim that, let's find a way round it.' said John very despondently

'I'm with you mate. At this stage of the walk, I don't relish the idea of swimming in the dark, come on, and let's move up stream.'

'Which way is up?'

'Well, the stream is flowing that way, so up must be this way.'

The walk up stream is pretty hard going as the ground is bloody boggy.

'Hold up mate, I'm whacked, it must have been all that kicking I got back in the barn.' John said sinking to the ground.

'You all right John?' I ask walking back to him.

'Need my second wind mate, I must be getting old.'

I rummage in my Bergen and find a Mars bar.

'Here, have a bite of this, it will give you energy.'

'You are a little darling, where did you get that from?'

'I was keeping it for emergencies, and this sounds like an emergency, go on take a bite.'

'Thanks mate, a life saver.'

'Morning will be here shortly, let's see how much further we have got to go.'

I check the map and it looks as if we have a further 3 miles to the rendezvous point.

'I'm pretty sure we will make it in good time John, we have only got about 3 miles to go.'

'Thank goodness for that, I feel as if I have been walking for days.'

Once again we move off, the Bergen's are getting heavy on our shoulders. It is probably due to the fact that we are hungry and tired, because mine should be lighter, we ate the Mars bar.

As we get to the crest of a hill, we hear voices.

'Get down.' I whisper.

We crawl to the top and see a vehicle, two men are cooking something.

'That's the RV, I'm sure of it.'

'Who fucking cares, let's get down there, I've had enough.' said John getting up from the ground.

We walk up to the vehicle.

'Well, Well, Well, if it isn't our 2 wanabees. Where you been lads? Couldn't you get here? Get those Bergen's off and get some of this scan down you, the Sergeant Major will be here in a while.' One of the men said holding a mess tin.

I scoff the food; I don't think it touched the sides of my throat. Just as we are washing the mess tins, another vehicle turns up and the Sergeant Major gets out.

'Congratulations you two, I have had good reports about you, once you have finished here you are to return to the Lines. You are not required until 0400hrs tomorrow, so get some sleep, you deserve it.'

A day off, what bliss, or is another of their rotten tricks. We climb into the vehicle and return to Bradbury Lines. Having handed in our weapons we make our way to our basha. I don't remember anything after that, as I sleep the sleep of the dead.

I'm woken sometime in the afternoon by an explosion. 'What the fuck was that?'

'Explosives.' Someone replies.

There is no way I can get back to sleep now. I collect my washing kit and go for a shower. The water feels great. John comes into the shower room.

'What woke you up?' he asked.

'A bloody big bang, that's what.'

'Yeah, me too.'

I write to Jane and leave it in the box to be posted. She will be surprised getting a letter after so long. Letters are the last thing on my mind at the moment, I need to pass this Selection, and the adventure it offers is far too great to miss.

We spend the early part of the evening in the Paludrin Club catching up on what has been happening over the last few days.

'Anyone know what happened to Terry and Stan?'

'RTU'd.' Clive said sitting down at our table.

'That's a bummer; I thought they would make it.'

'I don't think Stan really wanted to, he left his address in the hall, just in case anyone wanted to contact him.'

'Not many of us left are there?'

We leave the Club and walk round the Lines. I stop opposite a large monument. This is the famous Clock. There are a few names on it. All are dead, they failed to beat it. It is every SAS Troopers dream, to beat this clock. I don't want my name on it. I shudder and we move off.

As we are walking back to our billet, we are stopped by the picket on patrol.

'Have you got any means of identity on you?' He asked.

We show him our ID Cards, which he scrutinises very thoroughly.

'Thank you gentlemen, goodnight.'

'Goodnight mate.' We say together.

Well at least they have a guard here at night, I'd hate for anything to happen to us.

0400hrs and we are told to get ready with full equipment.

'What now I wonder.' John said pulling his boots on.

We fall in outside our hut.

'This morning, you are going to be shown the art of pistol shooting, get aboard the truck.' said a soldier in cammy kit.

I wonder what rank this one is.

The vehicle drives out of the Lines and heads towards Abergavenny. I hope it isn't the Fan, I hate that bloody hill. After about 30 minutes we arrive at an Army Training Camp just off of the A465.

'All off.' shouts the driver, who then drives off.

'Not another walk.' John said looking miserable.

'Follow me lads.' A soldier said coming from the guard room. We pick up our Bergen's and follow the soldier into the camp.

The soldier produces a hand gun.

'This lads, is the .45 High Power Semi-Automatic Pistol, it will be your standard hand gun. I am going to teach you how to get a group so tight, you will think you have only one bullet on the target.'

He hands each of us a pistol.

'The magazine holds 13 rounds of .45 jacketed, this is how it strips down.'

He proceeded to slide of the magazine base plate and pull out the spring.

'Always loosen off the spring if you are not using the weapon for some time, that way the magazine won't jam up. Now let's look at the weapon. It is easy to strip down.'

He pulled back the slide and then pulled out a pin on the side, and slid off the barrel assembly.

'There is no need to strip it down any further than this; everything is now easy to clean.'

I find this bit very easy as I have used the weapon before. He hands each of us a large box containing ammunition. There must be 1000 rounds, in each box.

'This is the only Regiment in the British Army where you can shoot as much ammunition as you like, no-one will stop you. Right, fill up these magazines with 10 rounds.' He said, handing us 5 mags each.

Once the mags are filled we walk off to the range.

'What I am going to teach you now is the double tap. Because in the SAS, we use this technique to make sure the person we are firing at, is killed first time. One shot to the chest and one in the head, just below the nose. It also stops who ever want to make a martyr of the person from allowing people to see the body in its coffin. They don't like showing bodies with their heads blown off. Right, let's see what you are like at hitting a target using this method of shooting.'

Everyone seems to get on with it quite well, and we get great scores. Even I am getting pretty proficient at it. I can hit the target exactly where I want, I like the .45 immensely.

Shooting carries on for most of the morning until another soldier appears, who tells us that we are now off to the "Killing House."

'The object of the exercise is to learn how to evaluate a situation and kill the right person instead of the good guy. Each one of you will be given a different scenario, that way; you will not be able to tell each other what is happening inside the House.'

This is the most horrendous experience I have ever had. We have to shoot at targets which are dotted around the room and miss the guys sitting at a table.

Once we have entered the room we start firing at the targets. All I hope is that I miss the chaps and hit the right things. Surely this shouldn't be allowed, it's bloody dangerous for the guys sitting at the table.

(This is later changed owing to a member of the SAS being killed)

The technique is practised over and over until it is 100% correct. There can be no room for errors. Lives may depend on it.

Six hours have gone by and we finally get it right, I'm exhausted, but very pleased with myself. There is briefing after briefing concerning the "Killing House" procedures. I'm now really happy with the technique, it certainly works.

The weeks go by and we come finally to the last part of the Selection. We have been through hell and out of the 120 odd men on the Selection

Course, there are only 8 left. The psychological effect that it has had on us is tremendous. I knew the training would be hard but it was harder than I ever imagined. Whether I pass or not, at least I tried, and I gave it my best shot. I know everyone else feels the same way.

I write to Jane and tell her that I may be home the weekend all being well. At the moment, it wouldn't worry me if we had finished, I have been far too occupied with the course to worry about girlfriends. John has the same outlook, the course comes first.

Morning arrives and each of us is given an exercise to complete in a given time. The completion of these exercises will decide whether we will be accepted in the SAS. God! I hate Brecon.

(**Authors note: None of the Selection process mentioned so far is completely true; it is only fair not to detail the real Selection as, whoever applies to join the SAS, would know what to expect.**)

Continuation training is now carried out in a place far away, in the jungle. This has to be completed before we gain the coveted "Beige Beret with Winged Sword Badge."

After many months, the Selection comes to an end. I and John have passed.

There is no ceremony just the CO handing those who passed a Beret with badge.

'Just remember, it is harder to keep than get.' he tells us.

We are now badged members of the SAS, the finest Regiment in the world, second to none. Our training will continue so that we can carry out specific tasks. I have also got my rank back, but now with the rank of Captain. The weekend is ours till 0900hrs on Monday. Gosport here I come.........!

CHAPTER ELEVEN

It's nice to be home again after being away for so long. I intend, to find out for sure, if Jane is two timing me with someone else. How, I'm going to do this, I haven't worked out yet.

I spend the day sorting out my kit ready for any eventuality that may crop up.

'What are you doing son?' asked my mother.

'I've got to get this stuff sorted mum, just in case.'

'Are you going off somewhere then?' She asked.

'Not at the moment, I have still a course to complete before I can actually sod off under my own steam.'

'I see.' she replied.

'You do know mum that you can't tell anyone about what I am doing or what Regiment I'm in, don't you.'

'Well, I didn't, but I do now, is anyone allowed to know what you are up to?'

'I'm afraid not mum.'

I go round to Jane's. She has gone out with Maureen. I leave a message with her mother telling her I am home for a few days.

John comes round and we go to the pub.

'I'm glad that bloody course is finished Dave, I was beginning to think it would never end. I wonder where we will be sent, I hope it is somewhere sunny.'

'You and me both mate, still we have a few days off before we have to worry about that, what are you going to do?'

'Not a lot if I had my way, but mum wants me to do some gardening for her, she is getting a bit old to dig the ground. I said I would, so I will probably be digging all weekend. What about you?'

'I'm trying to sort out this problem with Jane, so I will probably spend all weekend with her.'

We sink a few more pints and then head off to our respective homes.

'Let me know how you get on Dave, won't you.' John shouts as he walked off.

I go back to Jane's house. She has just got in.

'Hello Dave, nice to see you.' she said flinging her arms round my neck.

'Have you missed me then?' I asked.

'Well sort of - of course I've missed you - you silly nit.'

'Let's go for a walk.'

Jane puts her coat on, and we walk off towards the Ferry.

'Why didn't you write to me every day Dave?'

'Honestly Jane, I didn't have a minutes peace, we were on the go all the time, it was bloody hard going at times, and, getting very little sleep. When we did get time off, we spend it sleeping.'

'I see, but surely you could have found time to telephone me?'

'I tried on quite a few occasions, but no one answered.'

'Oh!'

'What do you mean, Oh?'

'Nothing, really.'

'Were you out with someone else then?'

'I did go out with Phil from work a few times, but there is nothing in it, believe me, we went to the pictures a few time that's all.'

'And you expect me to believe that you were not doing anything, what do you take me for, a bloody idiot. Jane, you shouldn't be going out with another bloke, you're engaged to me, what do you think you are playing at?'

'Honestly Dave, nothing has been going on, trust me.'

'I'm sorry Jane, but I don't think I can. What will happen if I get a six months posting. Will you be at home waiting for me, or out with this Phil. I'm sorry Jane, but I can't take that chance. I think we should end it now, before one of us gets hurt, namely me.'

'Don't say that Dave, I love you as much now as I have ever done. There is nothing going on between me and Phil, I'm telling you the truth.'

'Then why am I getting this feeling that something is going on. If you can go out with someone when I'm only away for 12 weeks, what is it going to be like if I'm away for a year. I'm sorry Jane, but I think we should call it a day.'

'Dave, you have been under a lot of pressure, you have said so yourself. Please think about it before you make any decision you might regret. I have not been getting up to anything with Phil. Believe me, I haven't. I don't want to break off our engagement, I love you.'

'Then why have you been going out to the pictures with him?'

'I just went because I wanted someone else to talk to instead of mum and dad. I only went for the company.'

'And you mean to tell me that he never once kissed you, what do you take me for, someone who has come down the river on a soggy pasty, come off it Jane. Remember the time I met you and him outside the shop, you didn't know what to do, so don't make me out to be a bigger prat than I already am.'

The walk back to her house is in silence. She knows I don't believe her. At her gate I say goodnight and start to walk off.

'Will I see you again?'

'I don't know Jane.'

'Please Dave, don't end it. It won't happen again, I promise.' She shouts.

'It shouldn't have happened this time Jane.'

I leave her looking stunned and walk off home.

'Please Dave, don't go like this, we have to talk.'

Ignoring her I continue walking home. I hear her crying but don't look back. What I have got to decide now is, do I completely finish with her or give her another chance. And, if I do give her another chance, can I trust her. Bloody Hell! I don't need this agro. Women!!!

I can't sleep and get up and go for a walk. The streets are very quiet. I walk past Jane's house. The light is on in her bedroom. A policeman rides past on his bike and suddenly stops. He dismounts and walks back towards me.

'Anything the matter, Sir?' He asks.

'Sorry Constable, I was miles away, no, there isn't anything wrong, I couldn't sleep so fancied a walk.'

'Do you live nearby then Sir?'

'Actually, I live up the road there, No 61. This is my fiancées house, we had a row. My name is Stubbs; I'm a Captain in the Army.'

'Fair enough Sir, we have to check you know.'

'Yes, of course Constable, I appreciate you are only doing your job. I think I will go home now, good morning Constable.'

'Good morning Sir. I hope everything turns out okay.'

'Thank you Constable, I hope it does too.'

I return home and make some coffee. I want to sleep but can't. I'd like to bash her head in, but I won't. I must decide soon. I can't leave her not knowing what is going to happen between us.

I'm dozing in the chair, when suddenly I'm woken by banging on the front door. I look at my watch. It is 6am. Am I being called back to Camp? I open the door and find Jane standing there.

'We have to talk Dave. I've been up all night worrying about us.'

We talk for nearly 3 hours. My mother comes down and finds us sitting in the dining room.

'Hello Jane, what brings you here at this time in the morning?'

'Good morning Mrs Stubbs, I had to talk to Dave about something very important and it couldn't wait, I hope you don't mind me being here?'

'Do you want some breakfast Jane?'

'No thank you but a cup of tea would be nice.'

We still haven't really sorted anything out. I have decided to give her another chance, though I doubt if I will ever trust her fully again.

'I promise Dave, nothing like this will ever happen again, I promise.'

'That's all I ask Jane, let us put it behind us now, are you sure you don't want any breakfast?'

Jane goes back home and I change and go to see John.

'What have you decided to do about Jane then mate?' He asked.

'I'm going to give her another chance, but if she does anything like this again, that's it as far as I'm concerned.'

'Good on you mate, I'm sure she was just lonely, look at me.'

'Bollocks, you big lanky streak of piss.'

The day is spent between Portsmouth and the Dive Cafe.

'Has anyone said anything about what we will be doing when we go back to camp Dave?'

'Only that we will have to do another course which lasts about a month, that's all.'

'I read a paper on the Adjutants desk at HQ, that there is a war going on in the Oman, do you think we will get out there?'

'Who knows, anything is better than soldiering in England.'

'Yeah, you are right about that.'

I spend the evening with Jane, she seems a changed girl. She is trying hard to please me and I let her carry on. It is nice to be pampered.

The weekend finally comes to an end and we make our way back to Hereford. I wonder what they will have in store for us.

It's nice to be back in camp, away from the moans and groans. Over the next month, we fly off to Malaya to carry out jungle training. We also carry out training at Abbey Dore, near Pontrillas, for specific tasks within the Regiment like Close Protection, driving, lock breaking, explosive entries etc. etc.

I am enjoying every minute of being in 22 SAS, the job is so varied, and you don't get a chance to be bored. There is always something going on, if it isn't the Killing House where we expend 1000's of rounds it is something else. I'm glad I passed the Selection.

I am busy learning how to make some explosives out of certain household items when I am summons to the CO's office.

'Come in Dave, I have a job for you. How would you like to go back to Aden?'

'I'd like that very much Sir, when do I leave?'

'2200hrs tonight, get over to the Ops Room for a briefing this is a 4 man job.'

I meet John on the way to the Ops Room.

'Guess what mate, I have a job in Aden. I'm just off for a briefing.'

'I'm off to Malaya again, something about Terrorists in the jungle.' he replied.

'When do you go to Malaya John?'

'Friday, why?'

'I'm off to Aden tonight, it must be pretty important.'

'Bloody Hell! That soon, good luck mate and stay away from land mines, you know what happened last time you were in Aden. See you later.'

I attend the briefing. I'm to take 3 men from "D" Squadron with me. This is great, I get to pick the men I need and not have them shoved on me by some arsehole who doesn't know what he is doing.

We are to recce an area north of Dhala for a Battalion that will be arriving in a few days' time. It doesn't sound too bad except that the area we will be going to is the same area of hills where I had my accident. That place is full of mines especially around the roads. Still, I expect they will have cleared them all by now, I hope!!!

I pack my kit and say goodbye to John and the rest of the gang.

See you when I see you.' I say to them as I get into the waiting vehicle.

'Okay driver let's get to Brize Norton, I have a VIP plane to catch.'

We all laugh and start swapping jokes. By the time we get to Brize, I can't remember any of them. I never was one to remember jokes. The plane is waiting as it usually is for the SAS. One is always on standby for us thanks to the Special Forces Squadron of the RAF.

The flight takes off as soon as we get aboard and we try and make ourselves comfortable in the string seats of the Beverley. The noise is terrible and I put on my ear defenders. Mack has put his radio on to drown out the noise of the engines. He hasn't succeeded. I don't like the Beverley, though it is great to parachute from and it can take off in about 200 yards and stop nearly on a sixpence. It's the noise that you have to contend with, but you get used to it, after a time.

We have a way to go. We will be stopping once more before we actually land in Aden. My bum is getting sore and I make up a cushion of some curtains and put it across the string seat.

'That's better.' I say out loud.

Mack looks up from his book.

'I see you have sussed it at last Boss; I was wondering when you would do it.'

'Well, you could have told me, you ginger headed git.'

'And spoil the fun.' Tommy said.

'Bastards.' I shout at them.

From behind a curtain comes Ken.

'They could have emptied the shitter before we got on, it is nearly full, all I hope is, we don't get any turbulence; there is nothing worse than a plane full of shit!'

We all laugh at what he has said. He looks at us as if we are all mad, come to think of it, we probably are.

The plane lands in Bahrain where we get more food and drink and a bit of rest from the din of the engines. This is the last refuel before Aden. We should arrive at Khormaksar sometime in the early hours of the morning, all being well.

We are not allowed out of the airport lounge owing to it being a stopover point only.

'Christ! This place is the pits, not even allowed to walk outside. God! It is hot in here.' said Ken kicking a chair.

'Don't worry, we will soon be in Aden, and then you can kick as much as you like mate.' Mack said.

We get back onto the Beverley and make ourselves as comfortable as possible. As soon as it is in the air, sleep comes quite quickly, even with the drone of the engines.

At last we arrive in Aden. Our equipment is unloaded and we are met by an officer in the Royal Marines.

'Jolly nice to see you blokes, I hope you enjoy your stay with us.'

'This isn't a fucking picnic mate.' Mack says.

'Quiet Mack.' I say to him.

We are taken to the Marines Camp and billeted in tents away from the rest of the people there.

'Look, we are on our own again.' Cries Mack.

This is just what we want. We then go for a briefing on the situation. Our job is to do a recce at first light. We return to our tents and get our heads down for some zeds, (sleep)

At about 0450hrs we are woken by an explosion. Thinking we are being attacked we grab our weapons and make for the bunker outside the tent. As we rush outside, a sentry stops us and we are informed that a burner had exploded in the cookhouse.

'Thank Christ for that.' said Ken trying to put on his trousers, 'I thought I was going to have to shoot with me knickers on and me trousers round me ankles.'

'Well that's sleep done away with, let's go and see if we can get a brew from what is left of the bloody cookhouse.' Mack said, throwing his weapon, over his shoulder.

The cookhouse is in a bit of a mess. One guy is covered from head to toe in what looks like porridge. There is a whacking big hole in the roof of the tent. Probably, where the cooker went through. We ask a Sgt if he needs any help.

'If you can get me some new burners, I'd be much obliged, these bastards have just about had it, seriously though, thanks for the offer, but we can manage.'

Mack finds a tea urn and we have a big mug of near cold tea.

'Well! It wets the whistle doesn't it?'

'Prat.' Ken said aiming a boot at him.

We drink our tea and then head back to our tent.

'In another 2 hours we will have to get up, God help any more interruptions.' I shout out aloud.

'QUIET YOU SOD.' Someone shouts, from a nearby tent.

'BOLLOCKS!' We all shout in unison.

For some unknown reason, we are not woken with the rest of the unit. I wake at about 0900hrs and get up for a pee. The camp looks deserted. I go back into the tent and wake the guys.

'Come on you lot, up and at them, we have got work to do.'

After a very hurried breakfast we load the vehicle that has been assigned to us.

'Make sure there is plenty of ammo Mack, I know the place we are going to, it is full of bastards who don't like us.'

'Will do Boss, Ken have you checked the radios yet?'

'All done and we have plenty of batteries.'

'And have we plenty of water as well.' I ask them.

'We sure have Boss.' said Tommy humping some jerry cans onto the vehicle.

I am pretty apprehensive about getting into a vehicle, especially here in Aden. I remember the pain in my legs from the last time I was here.

'How do you know so much about this dump Boss?' asked Mack.

'I was here with a detachment of men in the same camp, only a different Marine Unit occupied it then. I got blown up in a land rover, on the same road that we will be using today.'

'Shit! I hope they have cleared the place then, I would hate for it to happen again.' Tommy said, jumping into the driving seat.

'You and me both mate.' I say to him as I get into the passenger seat.

Our journey out of the camp and into the area we have to recce is non-eventful. We see a few people milling around a water well, but that is all. The trip so far is very quiet. Is this the lull before the storm, I wonder?

As we approach a steep climb we see coming towards us some vehicles.

'Ours or there's?' Mack asked.

'I can't make them out, pull over to the side behind that rock.'

We drive behind the rock, weapons ready.

'If the bastards aren't ours, let them have it.' I said cocking my weapon.

The vehicles are about 200 yards from us when they stop. A man stands up and looks through a pair of binoculars at us. He waves. It is a Marine detachment, thank goodness.

The vehicles move towards us and the guy with the bino's gets out.

'Good morning, nice day for a drive.'

'He's fucking mental.' Ken said, putting his finger to his head.

'Quiet you prat.' Mack said.

I get out of our vehicle and shake his hand.

'The names Dave Stubbs, I'm the manager of this motley crew.'

'You must be the sneaky beakies, heard you had arrived, my name's Arthur Meadows, I'm in charge of 2 Platoon here. We are just completing a night patrol, are you going far?'

'Sorry mate can't tell you that, we have to go, probably see you around the camp.' I tell him getting back into my vehicle.

We leave him standing beside his vehicle and head off in the direction he had come.

'Lots of people out here Dave, It's getting a bit crowded.' Mack said.

(In the SAS, Officers are called Boss or their Christian names are used as a sign of respect.)

Tommy puts the vehicle into 4 wheeled drive and we head out over the desert. After about an hour we arrive at our destination.

'What have we got to do now? Pick our noses.' said Ken jumping out of the vehicle.

'Observations, dear boy.' said Mack laughing.

At this point a spurt of dust erupts in front of the vehicle and a second later we hear a bang.

'Fucking Hell! Someone is firing at us.' Tommy shouts diving behind the vehicle.

We take up positions, ready to return fire.

'See anyone?' asked Mack.

'Can't see anyone.' I say, looking through the bino's.

We keep in position for 15 minutes, nothing is seen or heard.

'Could have been a fluke, I suppose.'

'Fluke my arse, someone was definitely shooting at us.'

'God help them if I catch up with them.' said Ken checking the safety catch on his weapon.

We are about to move off when a boy pulling a donkey appears like magic. He is carrying a very long rifle. He stops in front of us.

'I am sorry, my gun went off trying to get this unhelpful beast to let me sit on It.' he said pulling at the reins.

'So it was you then?'

The boy then explained that he is on his way home and decided to try and ride the donkey who really didn't want anyone on its back, and the gun accidentally went off.

'Are you the soldiers from the base?' The boy asked.

'You speak very good English, where did you learn it?' asked Ken.

'At my school, we are all taught to speak English, it is our second language. I must go; I have to be back home before night fall, goodbye.'

The boy pulls the donkey along and walks off down the track.

'Something's not right here Boss, I think there is more to that kid than meets the eye.' said Mack.

Before I can answer, a mortar bomb explodes in a great cloud of dirt and metal.

'Let's get out of here, everyone into the vehicle.' I shout leaping into it.

They all dive into the Land rover and we speed off out of range.

'That little bastard had set us up, I wish I could get my hands on him.' said Tommy putting his foot hard down on the gas.

After about a mile or so we stop. We have come to a large gully. We alight from the vehicle and walk to the edge.

'Well, Well, Well, Look what we have here isn't that a rebel camp down there?' asked Ken.

'It sure is, get the map so we can mark it, I'm sure we can call an air strike on this.' said Mack looking through his bino's.

'Check the co-ordinates and radio them back to base, for an air strike, we will give this lot a pasting.' I said with glee.

Twenty minutes go by and we make out that there are about 35 people in the camp. This is a large gathering for such a small camp. Crackling is heard on the radio.

'This is Foxtrot 29, I will be in the area in figures 4, make smoke so that I can see you, Over.'

'Chuck a green smoke grenade in 3 minutes Ken, the pilot should see that, I hope.'

The roar of a jet is heard and Ken throws a grenade behind us. Just as it starts to emit smoke we see coming towards us the jet at a very low level.

'The enemy is in the gully in front of us, do your stuff.' said Mack into the microphone.

The aircraft passes over us and 2 canisters are detached and hurtle towards the camp. There is a mighty big bang and balls of flame reach up into the sky.

'Bull's eye.' Mack shouts, into the mike.

'All in a day's work.' Replied the pilot, 'If you want any more just ring, good luck.'

We don't bother to go down into the gully. We remount the vehicle and continue on our way.

'Some bloody recce this turned out to be, we have been shot at, mortared and now we wipe out a camp, is this supposed to happen Boss?' asked Tommy.

'Nah! Just a bad start, to a lovely day.' I reply.

Everyone laughed. The rest of the day is non-eventful. We see no one and lay up behind a large outcrop of rocks.

'Make a brew Tommy?' said Ken picking up a shovel and moving off a few yards. 'Shit time.'

We return to base via a different route. I'm called to the "O" Group in the HQ tent.

'Well, Mr Stubbs, looking at the reports I have received, you have been in action already, well done, 35 rebels killed, very well done.' said the CO.

After the briefing I go back to my tent.

'Have we got anything to do now Boss? Only I promised my girlfriend that I would drop her line if I could.'

'There isn't anything that I know of Ken, see you in the morning.'

I suppose I should really write to Jane, but I can't be bothered. I collect some more maps from the Intelligence Section and the Password for the next day. Who thought up "Rupert Bear?" Oh well! It takes all sorts to make a world.

A lovely night's sleep. I wake and go for a shower as this might be the last one I get for a few days. We are going on a 5 day patrol of the Radfan. This is a God forsaken piece of territory which contained the Qotaibi tribe. These are a tribe of rebels who can endure anything, and if wounded, will crawl away to die somewhere rather than surrender or be captured.

We are to patrol to within 10 miles of the border with Yemen. Should be a piece of cake - I hope.

There are many attacks on the Dhala road, and one of our jobs is to find out which tribesmen are carrying them out. This is going to be no mean feat. Everyone out here who isn't British is trying to kill us, and anyone trying to stop the warring factions from killing each other is definitely in the firing line.

Our vehicles are kitted out with everything including the kitchen sink; they have to be in this bug ridden place.

The patrol starts and we make our way out of camp. On reaching a wadi called Wadi Reba we dismount, and we leave the vehicles and travel on foot and position ourselves about 200 yards from a camp.

The camp is patrolled by armed tribesmen. A man sees us as he is attending his goats and a fire fight ensues. I call up an air strike, and the Hunter aircraft strafes the camp. The hunter leaves the area and we make our way back to our vehicle. Unfortunately, we now suffer a couple of minor casualties. Mack gets bit by a snake and Tommy hits his head on the .5 machine gun in the back of the vehicle.

Not a very good start. I will be glad when I leave this bloody country.

After many small fire fights and having collected a great deal of intelligence for the "Green Slime," (Intelligence Corps) we return to base. I need a shower urgently, all of us are starting to pong a bit, and, a nice cold drink wouldn't go amiss.

Aden and the Radfan, I am pretty sure, will erupt into a full scale war if we are not careful. The country is absolutely unbearable. Heat and flies and the constant firing, is beginning to take a toll on the troops. There isn't much sleep available.

Whilst we are here, it is patrol and more patrols and not a lot of time to do anything else. The inhabitants definitely do not like us, that's for sure.

The gang have now been in Aden for 6 months and we are informed that we will be succeeded by some members of "A" Squadron. This is good news. I can't wait to get back to Blighty.

0600hrs - I am informed that we are required to do a job in the Crater District. This is a definite hell hole and we will be up against the urban guerrilla. Very nasty indeed. Still that's what I joined for, excitement. I must be mad. They call this patrol "Keenee Meenee."

I've received several letters from Jane. They make life slightly bearable. She seems to have accepted the fact that I will be away from her for long periods. At least, I think she has accepted it. I can't wait to see her again, and that won't be long as "A" Squadron arrive tomorrow.

Having handed over duties to Johnnie Moore, we start packing in earnest. We are booked on the next plane out. I hope it isn't a Beverley there is nothing worse than a Beverley.

'Do we get any time off when we get back Boss?' Asked Ken.

'I think we have got a couple of day's mate, that's all, but I'll go and check with the head honcho.'

I nip off to the HQ tent and see the pen pusher.

'Here's your Movement Orders Sir.'

The pen pusher says handing me some papers. I quickly glance at them and see that we have got 3 days off. How kind of the Kremlin. England, here we come!

CHAPTER TWELVE

Why is it that every time I return to England, it is pouring with rain? We are met at the airport by a driver who takes us to Bradbury Lines, where we carry out a debrief.

'Well, you certainly seemed to enjoy yourself Dave, what did you think of the place?' asked the Ops Officer.

'Do you want lies or the truth, if you want lies, the place was smashing, the truth is, it was the most awful place I have ever been to.'

'I think we will be over there for a lot longer, I am sending more of "D" Squadron out there.'

'Stone the crows, I hope we don't lose anymore guys, (A Captain and a Trooper were beheaded and their heads stuck on poles) the place is the pits.'

Once the debrief is over, I get transport to the station. I'm looking forward to seeing Jane again, and my parents. It is still raining, good old English weather. Makes a change from the heat of Aden. People at the station are looking at me. It must be the tan. Mind you, everyone in Hereford knows that anyone with a tan probably comes from Bradbury Lines.

The journey to Gosport is long and tiring and I don't speak to a living soul. What is wrong with the English, are they afraid to talk to each other. Anywhere else in the world and people, who have never met before, talk as if they have known each other for years. But the English, Boy! Are we reserved?

The train arrives at Portsmouth Harbour station and I make my way to the ferry. I bump into a guy who turns out to be an old buddy from my school days.

'Stone me, if it isn't Dave Stubbs, how you keeping mate? I haven't seen you for ages.'

'Hello Max, nice to see you again, Christ! How long has it been?'

'Too long, fancy a drink or something? There is a pub I use not far from the ferry.'

The ferry arrives at Gosport and we make our way to the pub Max frequents.

'What are you having?' I ask him.

'This is my shout.' He replies.

'I'll have a whiskey and ginger please Max.'

'Coming up mate.'

Max brings the drinks to a table I am sitting at.

'Well Dave, what are you doing these days? The last time I saw you, you were on your way to Africa for some job or other.'

'Not much, I work for a government outfit, mainly abroad, the job isn't too bad, I get a little excitement now and again. You still with the Gas Company?'

'Yes, I'm afraid so, there isn't much work around at the moment. Do you know, I've been fitting central heating in for people all this week because there isn't much to do?'

'Is the money good, that's the thing?'

'Well, I could do with a bit more, but I get by, how about you?'

'Not too bad, but, like you, I could do with a lot more. Getting it is the problem.'

'Yeah! I know what you mean; I have to work all the hours God sends to get a decent wage each week.'

'You should have my hourly rate, it's extremely low, I can tell you.'

We talk over old times and sink a few drinks. I look at my watch.

'Bloody Heck! I better get going, and I've a girlfriend to see. We will have to do this again Max the next time I'm in Gosport, see you soon.'

'Take care Dave, nice having a chat about old times, see you.'

I grab a taxi from the nearby rank and soon arrive home.

'Hello son,' my dad says as I open the door, 'You have just missed Jane. She came round early this evening, if you hurry, you might catch up with her. Does she know you are coming home?'

'I don't think so, I can't remember if I told her or not.'

Leaving my case in the hallway, I make my way to Jane's house. I catch up with her just as she is opening her front door.

'Hoy Blondie!' I shout at her.

She turns round and her mouth drops open. 'Sod me! If it isn't my boyfriend, why didn't you let me know you were coming home?'

'I thought I did, the letter must have got lost in the post.' I lied.

She walks back towards me and I kiss her.

'You bastard, Dave Stubbs,' she says breaking loose from the kiss, 'Why am I the last to know you are coming home.'

'I'm sorry Jane, I only left Aden at 0100hrs this morning, so I couldn't let you know, anyway, I thought I would surprise you, aren't you glad to see me?'

'Of course I'm glad to see you, come here and give me a big kiss, you swine you.'

We go into the house and her dad greets me.

'Why hello Dave, nice to have you back, stone the crows, you have got a lovely tan, been anywhere nice?'

'If you can call Aden nice, then I have.'

'Well I never, so that is where you have been, not a nice place by all accounts, I read about that place in the paper. I don't think the locals like the British out there.'

'Of course they do, they only shoot at us when they get bored.'

I begin to laugh but see that Jane does not like it one little bit. Although I make like of the Aden situation, it really is quite dangerous for the guys out there.

It's nice to be home and out of it for a few days, but I suspect that I will soon be back in the thick of things shortly. I could even find myself back in Aden, God forbid. The lid is going to blow off of that place real soon, and I don't want to be there when it does.

I take Jane for a walk and tell her that I am home for 3 days.

'Are you sure?' She asked.

'Well, you know what the Army is like Jane, nothing is certain.'

'Tell me about it.' she sneered.

'Let's make the most of the time I have and not argue, how would you like to go to London for the day tomorrow?'

'Oh Dave, that would be lovely, what time will you be round?'

'Just after breakfast, so be ready.'

I take Jane home and kiss her goodnight.

'Aren't you coming in darling?' She asked.

'No sweetheart, I'm a bit whacked and I need some sleep. We want to get the early train to London, so goodnight, sleep tight mind the bed bugs don't bite.'

Do I, need my pit. All this travelling is doing me in.

The trip to London is ruddy expensive, but Jane enjoys it. We visit the Planetarium and Madam Tusaudes and the Imperial War Museum. I would have like to have stayed there longer, but Jane said it reminded her of the Army too much. I doubt if she will ever get use to me being in the Army, and I'm not going to try to explain things to her any more, she will just have to lump it.

We return to Gosport late in the evening.

'I'm starving; let's stop of for some scran.'

'What in the dickens is scran?' she asked.

'Food you numb nut, its Army slang.'

'Oh! My mum will cook us something when we get home, if I ask her.'

'We can't ask your mum to cook for us after we have been out all day, it wouldn't be fair. Anyway there is a Restaurant over there, come on.'

We enter the Toad Hole Restaurant and order a meal. It is bloody disgusting. The food is shit. I can see why there aren't many people inside, if this is the standard of cooking. It reminded me of the time we were at Yockster. We won't be coming here again in a hurry. I pay the bill and don't leave a tip and we head off home.

'That must have been the worst meal I have ever had in a Restaurant.'

'Oh, I don't know, you want to taste my mum's cooking.' Jane said laughing.

As we approach her house, I ask her what she would like to do tomorrow.

'Stay in bed with you.' She replied.

'No chance.' I reply.

'Oh well, I'll just have to take the cucumber to bed with me.'

'Take the WHAT to bed?'

Jane bursts out laughing, 'You should see your face Dave, it is a picture.'

'Behave yourself, you scarlet women you.'

'That's about all I do these days, behave myself.' She replied.

As Jane is about to open the door, her mother comes out with some milk bottles.

'Did you have a nice day you two?'

'Smashing mum, but Dave is just going home, he says he's whacked.'

'I'll see you just after breakfast, I think we will go to the Isle of Wight, how's that grab you?'

'That would be nice darling.'

I kiss her and go off home.

I'm making a cup of tea and my dad asks how long I will be home.

'Only 3 day's dad.'

'Blimey, that isn't long.'

'It was all they would give me.'

'Does Jane know?'

'Yes, I told her tonight, she wasn't very pleased.'

'I bet she wasn't'

I spend a few moments watching the television, then go to bed. I'd better get some shut eye; I've got to get up early, if we are going to the Isle of Wight.

Morning arrives and I look out of my window, it is chucking it down with rain. Shit! That's the Isle of Wight trip out the window. I get dressed and go round to Jane's.

As I walk up the garden path, I meet Jane's mum.

'Hello Dave, not very nice is it.'

'I think the weather has put paid to our trip to the Island, it won't be very nice in this weather will it. Now what will we do?'

'Don't let the rain stop you, it might not be raining on the Island. I'm off to the shops; go on in, I'll see you later.'

I go into the house as Jane comes down the stairs. Her father is at work.

'Hello darling, I'm just getting changed. Are we still going to the Isle of Wight?'

'Jane, it's chucking it down with rain, so perhaps we should postpone the trip to the Island, what do you think?'

'It's probably not raining over there and anyway, I want to top up my tan, look I'm quite white.'

She undoes her housecoat and pulls it open. She isn't wearing anything under it.

'See how white I am?'

Her breasts are small and erect and the triangle between her legs is blonde.

'Do your housecoat up, you brazen hussy.'

'Spoilsport.'

She pulls the coat together and walks back up the stairs.

'Jane?'

'Yes darling.'

'You have got lovely breasts.'

She pokes her tongue out and goes into her bedroom. She shouts down, 'Is that all I have got that is nice, what about my furry thing?'

'Get dressed.' I shout back.

We get the ferry from Portsmouth to Ryde on the Isle of Wight. It takes three quarters of an hour to arrive at Ryde. A small train is waiting to take us to the end of the pier. It costs 1 penny (½p).

I find a car hire garage in a back street and rent a car for the day. It costs £2 and 10 shillings (£2.50p) for the day inclusive of insurance.

(Try getting that today)

I take Jane to virtually every place on the Island. The view from the headland overlooking the Needles is spectacular. If only we had all round sunshine, we would have the best tourist industry in the world. There is more to see in Great Britain than anywhere in the world.

Having seen just about everything, we return the car to the garage, and go the pier to get the boat to Portsmouth.

'Oh Dave, it has been a lovely day, thank you.'

Jane puts her arms round my neck and starts kissing me. Everyone on the pier is watching.

'It's okay, He's my lover, my husband is at sea.' She shouts to a couple nearby.

'Jane, stop that, you are embarrassing me.'

'But why. I want everyone to know, I love you.' She says out loud for all to hear.

The boat arrives to take us back to Portsmouth. Thank goodness for that. We have dinner in a small restaurant on the Hard.

'It's been a lovely day Dave, I don't want it to end.' says Jane over her coffee.

After the meal, we have to run to get the last ferry to Gosport. We disembark and as we walk up the ramp I see a taxi waiting.

'Let's walk home, we don't need a taxi.' Jane says grabbing hold of my arm.

'You go back tomorrow darling, don't you?'

'I'm afraid so, it has been a smashing few days though.'

We arrive at her gate and I kiss her goodnight, and make my way home.

My mum and dad are watching the TV. I sit down with them. This is the most TV I have watched for months.

'Something troubling you son?' My mother asked.

'Sorry mum, I was miles away, no, there isn't anything troubling me, why?'

'You looked distance that was all.'

'I was just wondering what my next job will be.'

'Nothing dangerous, I hope, then again, being in your outfit, everything is dangerous, just be careful son that is all I ask.'

'What outfit have you joined now Son.' Asked my dad.

'Recce platoon dad.'

'Oh! I see son, a platoon within your regiment eh.'

'That's right dad, but don't worry, careful is my middle name mum.'

'Is that how you got that medal in the Congo - being careful.'

'I've changed since then mum, believe me?'

'Have you heard from John lately Dave?'

'To tell you the truth, no I haven't, I'll go and see his mum tomorrow before I go back, she may have heard from him.'

I wake early and go and see Tina West.

'Hello David, it is nice to see you, would you like a cup of tea?'

'Please Tina. Have you heard from John?'

'I had a letter about 3 weeks ago, he is in a place called Sabah, do you know it?'

'Never heard of the place, but I bet he is enjoying himself.'

I spend an hour with Tina and then make my way to Jane's.

'Can I see you off today Dave?' Jane asked.

'Only if you behave yourself.' I tell her, 'And no shouting at the passengers.'

'As if I would.' She replied with a glint in her eye.

Leaving Jane's, I head for the town to get some things that I will need. As time is getting on, I have lunch in a right grotty cafe. The food is great, cheap and plenty of it. No wonder the place is packed.

After lunch, I return home to finish packing. As I am about to open the gate, a car drives off. My mother opens the front door.

'That was for you Dave, they gave me this.' she said handing me a letter.

Opening the envelope I read the note inside. "RETURN IMMEDIATELY - URGENT." That was all it said, no indication of who had sent it, but I knew.

I go to the telephone box up the street and dial a special number in Hereford, and speak to the Ops Officer.

'Ah Dave, how long will it take you to get back?'

'I'm not sure, there is a train at 1520hrs from Portsmouth Harbour station, and I could get that one.'

'Right, get it and I'll have someone meet you at Hereford, you are off to Malaya.'

'Bloody Heck!' I reply.

The phone goes dead.

(Pagers are now used to contact personnel)

I return home and start to finish my packing.

'I've got to get the 1520 mum; it doesn't leave me much time does it.'

'Can you tell me where you are going son?' She asked.

'Afraid not mum, but it should be fun, I hope.'

'Just be careful, that's all I ask.'

Jane arrives and I say goodbye to my mother. The journey to the station is in silence. Finally as we reach the station, Jane says, 'You have been called back to camp haven't you?'

'Yes Jane I have, but it isn't anything to worry about.'

'Where are you going?'

'I can't tell you sweetheart.'

'How long will you be away for?'

'I really don't know, as soon as I find out, I'll write you.'

'That's what you said last time.'

The train is waiting at the platform. I board it and pull down the door window.

'Be careful darling, and don't do anything silly, promise me?' Jane says, tears starting to fill her eyes.

'Don't worry on that score, I'm no hero.'

'That's not what that Citation says from the Congo.'

'Careful is my middle name, trust me.'

I wish people wouldn't go on about that bloody medal.

The guard blows his whistle and the train starts to move.

'I love you.' She shouts, tears streaming down her cheeks.

I keep waving until the train goes round a bend and she is out of sight.

Having made my way to a seat I try to strike up a conversation with the guy opposite me. It is hard going, so I give it up as a bad job. The journey to London is in total silence. The journey from Paddington to Hereford is just as silent.

I'm met at Hereford by Keith who tells me the whole Squadron is off to Malaya.

'I'm glad it isn't bloody Aden again.'

'You and I both boss.' Keith replies.

The journey to the Lines only takes a few minutes; traffic is next to nothing at this time of day. I show my ID card to the Policeman at the gate and make my way to the Ops room.

'What's up then?' I ask the Ops Officer.

'Welcome back Dave, get your kit together, your Squadron is off to Malaya tomorrow. You are going to help out an Infantry battalion in 1 Division in Borneo, but first you will be doing some jungle training at the Jungle Warfare School at Kota Tinggi. Best get over to the stores and get your kit; briefing will be in an hour.'

'Shit! I better get a move on.'

As I leave the office the Adjutant informs be that my rank to Captain has been made substantive. The lowest officer rank in the Regiment is Captain. This should help my career.

(Note: In the early 70's the Government decided that any officer who had been with the SAS would not have to go to the Staff College to gain promotion to Major and above)

At the stores, I collect my OG's (Olive Greens) and the rest of the kit that will be required in the jungle. Once everyone is kitted out and our equipment stowed on the truck, I head for the Blue Room for the briefing.

The trip to Brize Norton is full of laughter. Guys are cracking jokes and seem very happy to be getting out of England. We board an RAF plane for a 19 hour journey to Singapore with a stop off for fuel in Colombo.

We land in Singapore and trucks are waiting at the airport to take us to the Jungle Warfare School which is across the causeway. As we arrive at Kota Tinggi I notice that there are a few other units being trained there. Our accommodation is away from them and we make ourselves as comfortable as we possibly can under the circumstances. I am told that training will begin at 0600hrs. Whatever happened to "getting acclimatized first?"

The Squadron receive information that a couple of guys have been killed in Borneo. The Troops want to go there without training so that they can settle the score. I doubt if we would last very long without the special training we will be doing here at the Jungle Warfare School.

0600hrs and we trudge off into the jungle with the training staff. After about an hour, I have my first encounter with Atap. It is a very large green plant with extremely long leaves which have bloody thorns on them. Some of the leaves are 20 feet long and they are a bastard to get through. The thorns catch on everything. It is bloody hard going and not to mention, noisy.

All I hope is that there isn't any Atap in Borneo; it is too horrible for words. The rivers here are totally black and stinking. In the water are little worms called leeches that turn to vampires and suck the blood out of you. At 1500hrs daily the heavens open up and down comes heavy rain. We have arrived in the monsoon season, worst luck.

When it rains here, it really rains. You can't see more than 10 feet. The jungle is crawling with things that either want to eat you or bite you. You have to be very careful if you cut yourself, as cuts soon fester and turn pussy. Because we won't be able to wash, sores develop on the skin very quickly. I hate the jungle.

The troops that have been here before us have said that the Malayan jungle is the worst in the world. I believe them. Hygiene is virtually non-existent as we cannot wash in the jungle due to the enemy being able to smell soap a mile off. I have yet to meet anyone who loved the jungle. Especially that fucking Atap.

According to the instructor, we should never go short of water in the jungle as the vines hold water. Some of them are poisonous so we have to identify the correct one. It soon becomes second nature. The vines are called Rattan. Flies are everywhere and ants abound in huge numbers. And the little buggers bite.

It is easy making a basha in the jungle. You have to get off of the ground otherwise you get eaten alive. You make an "A" frame, and bob's your uncle, easy. I'm glad I bought that thin nylon sheet. It makes a great rain cover and is a lot lighter than the military poncho. Because it is so humid, we have what is called wet and dry kit. The dry kit we wear at night whilst in bed and the wet kit during the day. It is really freezing in the morning putting it on, but we get used to it.

(If you think living in the jungle is good fun, it isn't. I don't even go camping for a holiday)

Thank Christ we don't parachute into the jungle now. It was stopped after a guy in the Regiment broke his back coming down through the trees. There is nothing worse than coming down a 100 foot strap, after parachuting and ploughing through the tree tops. Especially as the strap has a bloody big wheel by your balls, not my cup of tea.

I find a great use for the mozzie repellent, if you put it on the tops of your jungle boots; it stops the leeches climbing up. The stuff is no good for stopping the mozzies from biting you, they love it. I wish I had some B6 tablets or marmite, mozzies don't like yeast.

The training finally comes to an end and we board an LSL called Sir Galahad and float away to Borneo.

After a few days at sea we dock at Kuching. 1st Division in Sarawak is expecting a large contingent of Indonesian Commandos to attack the forward bases and we have been chosen to supplement the infantry in the border region.

Our basha is above a girls bar in Kuching. The only problem being is that the girls bar, is in fact a brothel. The Squadron Commander doesn't like this one little bit and we move into a hotel. This doesn't last long either as the bills start to mount up. Our final basha is a bungalow that is owned by a Chinese family who have rented us the place. They in turn have built a better place with the rent money.

The District Officer appraised us of what is happening in his area. His intelligence is first class. We will be patrolling along the border ridge. We are not to go over the border at any cost. Says who - Who Dares Wins and all that.

Over the next few weeks, my Troop patrol along the border. We meet up with our first Dyaks. They are a very primitive race of Indians, but we need them on our side, as they can tell us much about what is going on in their areas. The system is called Hearts and Minds, and it works, as the information we are getting is first class.

The Dyaks are very friendly and quite childish. They laugh at the least thing. The girls are bare chested and have large breasts and giggle all the time. Our medic does a wonderful job dishing out medicine for minor ailments. Most of the men have large tattoos on their body. Something to do with their religion.

Some of my guys have tattoos done on their hands, but it looks far too painful to me. The women use a bamboo cane comb and dip it in some kind of ink and hammer a design onto the skin. Not for me.

I learn a few words of Dyak which might come in use at some stage. "Ada Biek," (pronounced Adaa Bike) which means "How are you?" to which the reply is "Biek," (Bike) which literally means "Okay, thanks."

The patrols go on and on and we have not seen the enemy yet. One day as we are patrolling along the ridge between Sarawak and Kalimantan we come across a small patrol of Indos (Indonesian Soldiers). A fire fight ensues and 2 Indos are killed. The bodies are searched for information that might help the spooks (Intelligence Corps) back in Kuching. A few maps are found, but nothing else. We return to our base along a quite well used track. For some reason we stop dead. In front of us are some disturbed leaves. Using my foot, I slowly push away the leaves. There is a large pit and at the bottom is some very sharp sticks called "Panji sticks." These sticks are covered in what looks like shit. Falling into this pit would certainly do extreme damage to the body. i.e. killing it.

On another patrol we find posters pinned to trees, saying "Winged soldiers beware." Paul pulls one down, looks at it and screws it up into a ball and kicks it into the jungle.

'What prats, don't they know their paper can't kill, but our bullets can?'

Paul always did have a way with words. At last we are given the green light to go over the border.

CHAPTER THIRTEEN

My Troop is to carry out a 10 day patrol near the border and lay an ambush in an area known as Alpha 10. We are now going to take the so called "Confrontation" to the enemy.

'At bloody long last.' Spike said.

Everyone is eager to get going. There is supposed to be a large contingent of Indonesian Special Forces in a camp there.

How special these forces are, will remain to be seen. So far, I wouldn't give them house room. I have to place an ambush that is to be in position for 4 days on a track leading into the camp. I won't know how easy it will be till we get there. Spike is raring to go.

'It's about time we had a crack at these prats Boss, all this hearts and minds, although it does a good job, just isn't for me.'

Having collected enough Claymores (Shaped mines) and ammunition for the trip, the Troop sets off. We are choppered into about 6000yds from our objective.

'Now I suppose we have to hoof it.' Keith said getting to grips with his Bergen.

'Once we are near to the area we are putting in the ambush, we will cache our Bergen's and use only our belt kit.' I tell them.

The patrol through the jungle is bloody hard going. We can't use our gollocks (Jungle machetes) in case we are heard. After about 8 hours, we finally come to the place for the ambush.

'Remember SOP's, (Standard Operating Procedures) if it gets bad, we shoot and scoot, you all know what to do, let's get to it.'

Everyone goes about the tasks that have been allocated. The Claymores and the Dingbat mines have been put out as have the sensors for the Seismic Detector. That will make it easier for us at night.

'Okay lads; adopt hard lying routine, no smoking or fires for the next 4 days.'

Each man gets into his position and cams up. Nothing happens for the first 2 days, and everyone is getting restless. Not only are we being eaten alive by everything that walks or flies, having a crap in a plastic bag is not my idea of fun either.

0800hrs on the 3rd day and all hell is breaking loose in the jungle. There is something moving towards us making one hell of a din. Everyone is stood to with weapons at the ready. My heart is going at a right old pace, when all of a sudden, an Orang-Utan comes towards us swinging through the trees. It is oblivious to us and swings on its way. I wonder if they are friendly.

At least we didn't take it for an Indo. I remember the old tale about the people of Hartlepool. How they hanged a monkey, because they thought it was a French Sailor. I must admit that appeals to my sense of humour. Mind you, how anyone could mistake a monkey for a Frenchman, I will never know. On the other hand, there isn't much difference really.

The Seismic Detector starts to ping. I believe we have company. 2 Indos are walking along the track and are about to enter our ambush position. They don't seem worried and are chatting away to each other. I don't really want to show ourselves for just 2 of them. The problem is soon sorted out. Spike and Keith leap from their dugout and using their Fairburn Sykes Stilettos, kill them quietly. The bodies are removed from the track and all marks in the ground erased.

A search of the bodies reveals only personal items. One of the Indos has some pictures of his wife and kids. His wife will never know what happened to her husband. I hope she gets compensation, which is more than our war widows get. The sooner they get rid of Sukarno the better.

(Sukarno later puts a bounty on the head of each British soldier)

A further day goes by and I break the ambush up. 2 Indos killed isn't a bad bag though I would have like to have killed a few more.

The camp is shelled by some mortars as we are leaving the position. These must have come from the Infantry Regiment that is up the track a ways. We move closer to the camp and watch the fun. One Indo is killed just as he is about to fill his plate with rice. A mortar bomb lands smack in the middle of the pot.

It is becoming harder and harder to entice the Indos from their bases. They know what will happen to them if they leave the safety of their camps.

The camp is wiped out and we leave the position and head back to the border. We have just been given another assignment on the radio.

'Gets better and better.' said Tomo digging his Bergen out of the Ulu (Jungle).

The trek back to the border is uneventful. I think the Indos have had enough for the time being. They lost a big chunk of their army today.

The Troop teams up with 3 Royal Green Jackets for the operation. We are going to take out an Indo camp. As we are moving towards the camp, a sharp sentry opens up with a .5 machine gun. Lucky for us, he is shooting in the wrong direction.

We move away from the camp as it will be useless trying to attack, it now. The element of surprise has gone. Fuck his hide. From the camp, mortar bombs start raining down on us. All hell breaks loose and we start running towards the river and a safe place to hide.

Just as we are about to cross the river, two New Zealand SAS lads are having a chat.

'Hey Joe, carry me across the river mate?'

'What the fuck for - can't you wade across like the rest of us?'

'Come off it mate, I've only just changed me socks, they will get wet.' He replies.

'Okay mate, jump on and let's get out of here.'

Both guys are probably carrying about 80lbs of kit each. That's friendship for you.

Just as they are about half way across, a mortar bomb land really close to them.

'Fuck this for a game of soldiers.' said the guy carrying the Maori, who promptly lets his passenger fall into the water.

'Thanks mate.'

At this point, 2 mortar bombs land extremely close to them, and they both quickly cross the river and run into the jungle. The mortars are raining fast and furious now.

Having waded the river, we meet up with one of the companies of 3RGJ.

'Mind if we tag along with you tonight?' I ask a Major.

'Sure, nice to have you aboard.' he replied handing me a hip flask of whiskey.

'Right cock up this time.' Said Keith taking the flask from me and having a hefty swig. He hands the Major back his flask who then turns it upside down - empty. If looks could kill...!

We basha up for the night. No fires are to be lit. Further down the line are the two New Zealanders. One is smoking a pipe and the other is brewing some tea on a hexamine stove. So much for orders. My Troop joins them and we smoke ourselves silly. The tea tastes good as well.

The operation ends and the Troop are choppered back to our base. We are given a few days R & R in Kuching.

I have received information that "B" Squadron is relieving us in a month's time, which is excellent news. I've had enough of the bloody jungle.

After our stint of R & R, we return to the base and pack for another operation over the border. We are going back to the camp we had to get away from. This time it will be different. I can feel it in my water.

The Troop is to carry out a recce of the surrounding area for an Infantry Regiment to attack the camp. I hope we can get in on the fighting.

To get to the camp we have to wade through stinking swamps and hack our way through very thick jungle, plus cross a few pretty awful rivers. I remembered what the Kiwi had said and have packed a few more pairs of socks.

We have been out for 4 days and I start to feel extremely ill. My limbs are aching and I'm spewing up every 10 minutes or so. My head really hurts and I can't focus properly. I can't concentrate on anything and suddenly collapse. Kevin rushes over to me.

'I think you have got the dreaded Leptospirosis Boss, you need a Casevac immediately.'

I'm far too weak to say anything. Spike gets on the radio and calls for a chopper to take me out. This disease is caught through wading in rivers that rats have pissed in, then it's, bob's your uncle.

I leave Spike in charge and I'm flown to Kuching Hospital where I spend the next few weeks. I am told that Leptospirosis is a killer and I was lucky to be alive. My sincere thanks to Kevin for diagnosing my condition correctly and saving my life.

(Kevin is later killed in a motor accident in Hereford)

After spending some considerable time on convalescing, I'm told that I am being sent back to England. My tour in Borneo is over, for the time being. I say goodbye to the lads and board the boat for Singapore. At last peace and tranquillity. No more stinking swamps and bloody jungle.

Back in Hereford I report to the SMO who informs me that I'm not fit to carry out anything at the moment.

'But I feel fine.' I tell him.

'My tests prove otherwise Captain, you are grounded until I say you are fit, is that clear?'

Leaving the MI Room I feel thoroughly dejected. What the hell am I going to do now!

I walk over to the Training Wing and ask if they need any help with any part of the Selection that is taking place. I become an RV monitor, (i.e. I take the names of the lads as they pass through a given location, and give them the grid Reference of their next location.) Perhaps I can train a bit as I carry out this very arduous duty.

Morning comes and I climb aboard a truck taking some of the men out to the Storey Arms. A well-known drop off point. The place has been used for years. The group I'm with is doing the "Fan Dance," that is, hiking it across Pen-y-Fan and a few other unmentionable hills to the Talybont Reservoir and back a few times, all within a time limit set by the Trg Wing.

The Brecon Beacons are not the nicest of places when you are humping 50 odd pounds of kit on your back and a bloody 7.62 rifle with no sling. It is an even worse place in winter. These guys are lucky it is still summer. I'm sure the Regiment could find a better way of holding Selection. The costs involved of transporting men 40 odd miles and the time taken surely is counterproductive. If they operated the Selection process from one of the Camps nearby, I'm sure it would be more beneficial and the fact that the travelling time would be less, more could be done on the training side. Perhaps they will one day, who knows.

(They now do that)

I have decided to take a Bergen with full weight and climb Pen-y-Fan with the group. Each man has his kit weighed and then given a specific grid reference to go to. They start in small groups up the hill towards Pen-y-Fan. By the time I reach the top, I'm totally knackered. Sweat is pouring off of me in buckets. I feel absolutely buggered. I can't breathe properly and I'm shaking as if I'm frozen. Perhaps I've over done it. I sit down by the Cairn and pull out a water bottle and pour it over my head.

At this point in time, one of the instructors is coming along the track that runs along the top of the Fan. He sees me sitting down and starts to run towards me.

'Bloody hell Dave! What's the matter, you look all in?'

'I think I have overdone it a bit Pete.'

'You didn't come up here with a Bergen did you?'

'I thought I'd try and get a bit of training in whilst helping out.'

'How much weight have you got in that Bergen? Let's have a look.'

Pete opens my Bergen and finds the rocks in it.

'Fucking hell mate, there must be at least 40 pounds of stone in here, what do you think you are doing?'

Pete pulls out all the stone and leaves it in a pile by the cairn.

'Bloody fool, come on mate, let's get you back down the hill and back to Hereford.'

He shoulders my Bergen and we walk back down the hill to the Storey Arms and a waiting Land rover.

(Pete later dies of stomach cancer)

An hour later, I'm in the SMO's office. He is absolutely livid.

'I told you not to do anything, didn't I, yet you disregard all that I said to you. Captain Stubbs, you are on medical leave with effect this minute, leave Hereford and go home. Report back for duty in 3 weeks' time, AND don't go training when you are home either, that's an ORDER, now sod off.'

I think I have upset him.

I ache all over and feel like shit. Perhaps the SMO is right; in fact I know he's right. I return to the mess and pack my case. As one of the lads is going into town, I cadge a lift with him to the station. The dreaded Platform 4. Only I'm still in and not being RTU'd. At least not yet. (Platform 4 is to London)

On arriving home, I go straight to bed. The travelling has taken it out of me. Fuck this Lepto crap. I hope there aren't any lasting effects from it. God! I ache.

My mother contacts Jane and she comes round to see me.

'Oh Dave, are you alright?' she asks.

'Yes, of course, I've just overdone it a bit that's all. I went training when I shouldn't have done, my own fault really, I'll be okay in a few days.'

After an hour or so she leaves and I don't see her again for a few days. I want to get as much rest as I can and she certainly would make matters worse, that's for sure.

I've been in bed for 4 days and start to feel a lot better. I get up and watch the TV.

'Do you want Jane to come and see you Dave?' My mother asked.

'God forbid mum, no, not yet.'

'I thought things were okay with you two now?'

'They are mum, but I want some time by myself.'

'Okay son if you say so.'

'I do mum, I really do.'

Although I love Jane, or I think I do, I am sure my feelings for her are waning. I don't seem to want to be with her as much as I use to. This could possibly be the illness I'm getting over, or is it!

Jane arrives one evening and asks to see me. We go into the front room to be alone.

'Why haven't you let me see you Dave, what is the matter?'

'Nothing really Jane. I just wanted to be by myself.'

'Dave, you have changed since coming home.'

'I don't think so, what has changed about me?'

'I can't put my finger on it, but something is very wrong.'

'You are imagining it.'

'No I'm not, there is definitely something up.'

'Well, I don't know what it is then.'

My mother knocks the door and asks if we would like a cup of tea.

'No thanks mum.' I reply.

'When do you go back to see the doctor Dave?' Jane asked.

'In a couple of weeks' time and with a bit of luck, he will give me the okay to start training again, I'm getting pretty bored.'

'Well thank you very much; I didn't know I was that boring.'

'Come off it Jane, stop finding things for an argument, you know I didn't mean you.'

'I wonder.' she replied.

I can see she is angry - why?

'Jane, if you have only come round for an argument, sod off, I don't need it.'

'If that's how you feel, I'm going - goodbye.'

She opens the door and storms out of the house.

'What was that all about?' asked my mother closing the front door.

'Christ only knows, I think she came round to pick a fight and I wouldn't bite, so she left.'

Over the next few days, I don't see anything of Jane. She makes no attempt to contact me. I suppose she is still angry. Still that's her affair.

I feel much better and decide to have a trip into town. As I am leaving Woolworths, I see going into a shop opposite, Jane with a guy. They are holding hands. It is that guy Phil from her shop. No wonder the bitch picked that argument. Well that's it this time. She is two timing me. We are definitely finished. Why did I give her another chance? The fucking bitch.

I'm fuming and catch the bus home. My mother can see that I'm angry.

'What is the matter son?' She asked.

'You are not going to believe this, but I have just seen Jane arm in arm with that prat she works with.'

'Oh, in that case I can now tell you what I saw the other day.'

'What is that then mum?'

'I saw Jane with a bloke in town, they were kissing and cuddling on the bus, she didn't see me though.'

'I should have guessed what a bloody fool I've been.'

One thing is for sure, if I meet up with Jane now, I'm going to do something I will regret. I walk to the paper shop and bump into Kathy.

'Hello Dave, nice to see you again, what's been happening in your life lately?' She asked.

'Kathy, if you have a year to spare I'll tell you.'

'That sounds interesting.'

'I've just seen Jane with another guy down the town.'

'Well, that shouldn't worry you any, you've finished with her.'

'I beg your pardon!'

'You have, finished with her - haven't you? - because she has been going out with Phil for ages, I assumed it was all over between you.'

'Not until now.'

'Oh Dave - I'm so sorry.'

'Not half as sorry as she will be.'

'I really am sorry Dave, you don't deserve this. I may not be going out with you, but I still care about you.'

'Thanks Kathy, it is appreciated. Are you seeing anyone?'

'Just someone now and again, nothing really serious - why?'

'No reason, as long as you are happy, I'm happy.'

'Don't tell me you want to try again?'

'Darling, if I knew it would work, I'd jump at the chance, but you know and I know it wouldn't.'

'I suppose you are right.'

'Look Kathryn, I'm not good company at the moment....'

Kathy puts her finger on my lips and says, 'I'm here if you want to talk.'

I pull her finger away and kiss it.

'Thanks I may take you up on your offer.'

'Anytime Dave - see you.'

'Bye Kathryn and thanks.'

Why, oh, why couldn't we have made a go of it? Sod it; I'll see what the bitch has to say. I walk to Jane's house and ring the doorbell. No-one is in. She must still be down the town.

The more I think about Jane "two timing" me, the more angry I get. There is no point talking to her in this state of mind. I might hurt her. Twice she has done this to me; she won't do it a third time.

At home I write Jane a letter and tell her it is all over between us and the reason why and that I never want to see her again. Writing the letter is the best way, because, if I see her I am sure I will smack her one. I post the letter and don't even get a reply. That proves she wanted to end it as well. Even if she did reply, it wouldn't make any difference. It is all over between us.

A week goes by and my mother sees Jane at the shops. Jane gives her the engagement ring to give to me. I tell my mother to sell it and use the money for her Bingo; I want no reminders of her.

I start packing ready to go back to Hereford. Going through my photo album, I notice that I haven't one photo of Jane in it, nor can I remember ever taking a photo of her. This must be an omen of some sort. (To this day, I have never seen her again, even in the street) With my leave over, I return to Hereford to see the Medical Officer.

'Well, I trust you did as I told you,' said the SMO, taking my blood pressure.

'I didn't do anything whatsoever for the whole three weeks, except get rid of my girlfriend.'

'Good - and anyway, girlfriends get in the way of things, you are better off without them. Okay, how do you feel in yourself?'

'I feel great, raring to go, no pains anywhere, and I feel just great.'

He checks me over and says, 'Okay, I'll pass you fit for duty then.'

I leave the MI Room and go to see the Squadron Commander, Major Johnston.

'Hi boss, anything for me?' I ask him.

'Well blow me down; you are back at last, everything okay, health wise?'

'Sure is boss, I've been given the green light by the SMO.'

'Good because I have a small task for you. But first, get yourself fit again by tagging on the end of a few hill walks with the current Selection; I'll see you again on Friday.'

At last I'm back in the fold. I go to the stores and see Pete.

'Give us some kit mate, I want to go hill walking again.'

'Nice to see you back Dave; I knew about the SMO putting you on sick leave, I hope you are all well now.'

'Yep, back to the grind Pete, I'm as fit as a fiddle and glad to be back. Its murder sitting at home doing nothing.'

I spend the next few days walking up and down the hills of Brecon getting fitter by the hour. There don't seem to be any lasting effects from the Lepto crap. At least not now anyway.

Friday arrives and I go to see the Squadron Commander.

'Fit and raring to go boss.' I tell him.

'Good, because you are off to the Trucial Oman Scouts tomorrow.'

'Bloody Hell!' I exclaim.

'Probably,' replies the Boss.

'Get your kit packed you are on the 1130hrs flight from Brize Norton, have a good trip.'

He hands me an envelope which will contain everything I will need to know about the assignment.

My life with the Regiment has so far been bloody hectic, and it would seem, will continue to be so for the immediate future. I am really glad that I have finished with Jane; she was beginning to complicate matters. My posting, if you could call it that should be quite interesting as the country is at war with its neighbours.

Having packed my kit, I decided to have a run round the camp. As I am approaching Training Wing I see coming towards me a tall skinny figure.

'Hey you tall git, what are you doing here?' I shout at the figure.

'Fuck my boots - Dave - I thought you were in Borneo?'

'Nah! I got that Lepto crap and they shipped me home. Touch and go so they say. How are you doing, mate?' I say to John shaking his hand.

'Fine mate, did you know Maureen had a kid?'

'I knew she was pregnant, so she's had it then?'

'The bastard isn't mine; the cow had been playing around.'

'I know how you feel, Jane was doing the same.'

'Christ mate, we don't half pick em, don't we.'

'We sure do sport, come on let's go for a drink?'

'I won't say no to that.' John replies.

We walk back to the mess and I change into some civvies, and we walk to the pub outside the camp. I order some drinks and we park ourselves in a corner.

'I'm leaving the Regiment.' said John nonchalantly.

'You are doing WHAT!' I replied shocked.

'Yep, I was on my way to HQ when you stopped me, I've had enough, our time is nearly up and I want to do something else with my life.'

'But I thought you liked the Army?'

'Not anymore, I've had it.'

'Is this anything to do with Maureen?'

'I suppose so in a way, but that isn't the real reason.'

'Well, then?'

'I'm sick of being away all the time, I'm missing out on too many things.'

'Have you thought about what you will do if you leave the Army?'

'Not at the moment, I'm sure something will turn up.'

'John, I'm off to Oman tomorrow, can we talk about this when I get back?'

'Not this time Dave, I've made up my mind and nothing is going to change it. What do you mean you are off to Oman?'

'I've just been given a job to do; I leave in a few hours' time.'

'Write to me at home once you get out there, I don't want to lose touch.' John said solemnly.

'Don't worry mate you can't get rid of me that easily.'

'Did you know my mum has been pretty ill lately? That is another reason why I must leave the Regiment.'

'Yes, I did know, I went and saw her a few times when I was home last.'

I am absolutely dumbfounded. There has got to be more to this than John is saying. He loves the Army and especially the Regiment. The Oman trip has come at the wrong time I think.

Last Orders are called and we return to the Lines.

'John, think about what you are doing, and don't make any rash decisions. Look after yourself mate and keep your head down, I'll see you when I get back.'

John shakes my hand and walks off. There is something bloody well wrong here, but what it is, I have no idea.

Transport picks me up from the mess and takes me to Brize Norton for the flight to Oman. There will be a couple of stops on the way. Pity, because it will only give me more time to ponder over what John is planning to do.

The airport staff at Brize is pretty efficient and I am given pretty near

VIP treatment. Coffee and stickies (cakes) are in good supply, whilst waiting in the lounge. At last I can board.

I wonder what it will be like in Oman. The flight is quite boring, but the RAF staff are really good, they pampered to my every whim, which is quite nice really, as it has never happened to me before on a flight.

At last the plane lands in Oman and I'm greeted by an officer dressed in sandy coloured kit.

'You must be Dave Stubbs? Welcome to Oman.' he said holding out his hand.

I shake his outstretched hand and we walk towards the airport lounge.

'My name is Richard Lang, fancy a drink before we drive off into the sun?' he asked.

'Is the Pope a Catholic, lead the way mate.'

He orders two glasses of orange squash (what else) and brings them to the table I'm sitting at. And I thought I was going to get a drink.

'It's bloody hot here, what's the temperature?'

'I think it is 102 at the moment. It gets worse I'm afraid, what with the dust and all.'

'Sodding hell! What have I got myself into?'

'You are relieving me actually once I have handed over to you.'

'What's it like here?'

'Well, I could say it is a marvellous place, but you wouldn't believe me. The population, adult wise, are just like children really. Nothing seems to worry them, though further up country it is a different story. Some of the villages have been bombed every day and the casualties are pretty heavy. If you like sun and sand, and the occasional bomb, this is the place to be.'

'Well, at least no-one said it would be easy out here. When do you go back to the UK?'

'Wednesday, so I think we had better start on our way, we have a long way to go.'

Outside the airport lounge is an Austin Gypsy, but nothing like I have ever seen before. This one has leather seats and air conditioning. On the doors are badges of the Trucial Oman Scouts. The journey is in silence. Whether it is because of the driver, I just don't know. After what seemed like hours we drive into a camp.

'This is the Frontier Regiment. I have to drop off some letters to the CO, I won't be long.' Richard said getting out of the vehicle.

Ten minutes go by and Richard reappears. As he gets into the vehicle, two jets fly over very low.

'Who the fuck are they?' I asked.

'They belong to the Sultan's Air force; they are just up the road a ways. They do flying patrols over the mountain area and report back any rebel activity.'

'Oh.' I reply.

We again move off out into the desert. The sand is pink coloured and nothing like Brighton beach. After a further 20 minutes we arrive at the barracks.

'Blimey, this is a grand place, are we billeted here?'

'We sure are come on I'll show you to your room.'

Inside the Officers Mess, which is very deceiving from the outside, I'm shown to my room.

'I'll come and pick you up in an hour, that will give you time to unpack and have a shower.'

'Thanks mate.'

I unpack my suitcase and put everything away. I haven't a clue what to wear, so after my shower I put on a pair of sand coloured slacks and my desert boots. Not knowing who I might meet, I put on a plain white shirt. I don't think my multi coloured one will go down very well here.

There is a knock on the door and a small soldier enters.

'I am your servant Sir, is there anything you would like me to do?'

Stone the crows, I'm not use to this, I'm use to fending for myself.

'Could you get the clothes I arrived in cleaned?' I asked him.

'Of course Sir.'

'What's your name?'

'I think Sir, it will be unpronounceable, but everyone calls me Jaffa.'

'Then Jaffa it is.'

This is a novel experience, having a servant to look after me. I'll have to make the most of the occasion, as it can't last. I say to myself. Richard arrives and then shows me around the barracks. He introduces me to the other British Officers who are not out on operations in the desert. We then go off to see the Commanding Officer.

'Welcome to the Oman, I trust you had a pleasant trip.' said the CO shaking my hand.

'Not bad at all Sir, the service was excellent.'

'Well, as far as your job out here is concerned, it will be to train the Sultans Army to defend this country. I want you to learn everything you can from Richard; he has a vast knowledge of how things work out here. I even ask for his advice at times. Richard has been out here for over two years as he has probably told you.'

The CO then went on to tell me what the situation was in the Oman and how the Trucial Oman Scouts operated, and in what areas.

'You will get briefings from the Intelligence Officer, Captain Andrew Gent before each operation to keep you abreast of the situation at the time.'

'So this war out here isn't going to plan then Colonel?'

'I wouldn't say that as such, we are making inroads, the rebels are not getting their own way, well at least, not all the time.'

This statement made me start to think what I had gotten myself into.

The CO then explained the vehicles and equipment we had at our disposal, which I must admit was quite extensive. Money was no object and we could indent for anything we wished. It reminded me of my Mercenary days when Cyril said we could order anything we wanted.

As the sand is pink, so are the Operational Vehicles. Richard it would seem is very anxious to leave the Oman as he had been in situ for over two years. He told me about the fierce battles that were fought in and around the hills. Even the SAS had a bash in the late 50's at Jabal Akhdar gaining quite a few decorations. (The SAS would be involved again in Oman in the Battle for Mirbat where 8 SAS soldiers and an officer held off many hundreds of rebels with the loss of 2 men killed, and one seriously wounded. The officer would later die on a training exercise in the Brecon Beacons.)

I don't like the idea of my job out here being only training and not being involved in full scale battles. Though, if I get really bored, I'll try and get out with one of the seasoned units.

The days go by and I learn a bit about the old Sultan, Sa'id bin Taimer, the 13th Hereditary Monarch of Oman. He never leaves his palace in Salalah and conducts the running of his country by telephone through intermediates.

He is feared by his people and very few defy him. There are no schools for the children, and anyone who wants to learn anything must become an exile and move away from the country. There is no hospital for the population in Dhofar. Salalah is ringed with barbed wire to keep food in and arms out. There are very few foreign goods, and the population is forbidden to wear anything western. Anyone who steps out of line is badly beaten, and their villages burned. Rebels are hung in the square for all to see.

I have really come to a wonderful place, especially as I am here in the monsoon season. Thank goodness it should finish around September, which is only a few months away. It does leave the place nice and green in places though, as I found out when being taken around by Richard.

As we are driving through a valley I point out some weird looking shrubs to him.

'They won't give much cover if there just happens to be a battle going on, will they?'

'Ah, now they are special shrubs, they are the Boswellia Shrubs for making Frankincense Resin. They boil it up a couple of time and throw it away but on the third boiling they keep the liquid and make the resin.'

'You have definitely been out here far too long Richard.'

'I know and I'll be glad to leave.'

The tour around the area lasted for 3 days. I have seen quite a bit of the country and I don't like it. The sooner I'm away from here the better.

We are sitting outside the mess one evening talking about things in general when there is five explosions one after another just outside the perimeter fence.

'What the hell is that?' I ask.

'I think the tribesmen are playing again, we had better take cover.' said the Adjutant.

Someone shouts, "Incoming."

'What incoming?' I asked.

BOOM!

'Fuck! - That incoming.'

I dive for cover and the place is surrounded by the Sultans soldiers.

'Where's the armoury?' I ask one of them.

'Don't worry Sir, everything is under control, the persons who have done this deed have been caught and will be executed immediately.'

'What!' I shout.

At this Richard grabs my sleeve.

'Don't get involved Dave, leave it to them, it is their country, we are only guests.'

'Fair enough, but this is some weird country.'

Later in the evening the CO arrives and he's appraised of what had happened.

'I thought the little buggers might start something, so I had the Frontier Force standing by.'

'Well you could have told us Sir?'

'Sorry chaps, but it would seem we have got a spy in our midst, so I couldn't say anything, still no-one was hurt.'

After the excitement, we all go to bed. I definitely do not like this place. I think the trouble is that I am use to being active. It doesn't look as if I will be here.

I can't understand why HQ has sent me here, the job is only training and an ordinary infantry officer could do that. And anyway, my commission is up soon and I would have thought that HQ would have given me something on the training side at Hereford. I'm sure that would be better than this.

Richard leaves for the UK and I take over his office. All the training schedules have been made out for the next 4weeks by Richard, which helps me no end. I have now got even less to do. I grab a driver and we do a recce of an area I want to do an exercise in. Well, I've got to do something.

I'm absolutely bored; I can now understand why Richard wanted to get away from here. I really must sort myself out and get motivated.

The CO calls me to his office.

'Dave, I want you to liaise with the SAS unit that is coming out next week, I believe we may have some trouble in the not too distant future.'

'An SAS unit, who is it Sir, do you know what squadron?'

'I think it is "B" Squadron, do you know anyone in it then?'

'I sure do Sir, it will be like old times, what makes you think that we are in for it Sir?'

'Intelligence has gotten hold of some plans, don't ask me how they got them, I don't know, but suffice it to say, we could have a battle shortly.'

'Now you're talking my kind of language Sir.'

I can't wait to see the guys again, anything is better than this. The Regiment must be coming out to do some training.

The days go by and all I do is check that the training is going to plan. I have brilliant staff, all British. So there are no language problems. My Arabic is pretty dismal to say the least. I have learnt just enough to get by on, but should have learnt more, especially as 99% of the soldiers don't speak English.

At last the Squadron arrives, complete with their vehicles. They are on operations in the Dhofar area again, but combining it with some desert training.

Talking to Fred one day I see him using some glue to stick some equipment together.

'Here stick this under the seat for good luck.' I say handing him a silver 50 fil coin.

'Do you think we will need it?' He asked taking the coin and covering it with glue.

'Anything is a help mate.'

(Authors note: This coin was found still attached under the driver's seat of a Pinkie by a Military Vehicles enthusiast, after he bought the vehicle at a Donnington scrap yard.)

The Squadron leaves and I get a call from the Adjutant that my posting has been cut short and that I will be returning to England in 2 days' time. Now this is the best news I have heard since being told that a Squadron was coming out.

I ask the Adjutant why the posting is being cut short.

'Man power reductions, the TOS (Trucial Oman Scouts) has decided that it can do without a Training Officer and combine the task with another job.'

Who am I to argue, I totally agree with him.

As there isn't anything to buy in Oman, I don't go into the town. I pack my case ready for the off.

The flight back, again by RAF is very nice indeed. Good food and I'm well looked after. Goodbye Oman. Well, that was the shortest posting or job I have ever had. 1 month long from start to finish.

Arriving back at Hereford, I speak to the Sqn Commander, Major Johnston.

'Morning Boss, anything for me?' I ask.

'Hello Dave, welcome back, sorry the job didn't last as long as it should have, but these things happen now and then.'

'Not to worry Boss, I didn't like the place much, and the job wasn't me anyway. I had a chat with "B" Squadron that came out; they seemed to be looking forward to the training out there.'

'Yes, they are out there for 4 months and could be rotated with further Squadrons.'

'Bloody hell, poor sods.'

'Your time with us is nearly up isn't Dave?'

'Yes pretty near I think Boss.'

'Get over to HQ and find out exactly when you will be leaving us, and in the meantime take the day off.'

'Thanks, I could do with some time to myself.'

'Right off you go, be back at 0900hrs tomorrow.'

I walk to HQ Block but call in to see Pete in the stores.

'Hi ya, you old bastard, how's thing treating you?'

'Fuck my boots, Dave Stubbs, what are you doing back here, I thought you were in the Oman?'

'I was, but I was made redundant, they cancelled the posting.'

'Blimey that was a short trip, where you off to now?'

'HQ, I want to find out when I finish with the Regiment.'

'Oh.'

Pete never asked what I would be doing next, it is an unwritten law that you don't ask these sorts of questions in the Regiment.

I only wish I could stay on with the Regiment, but my commission is up soon and I will be out of a job. Still, I had fun while it lasted. The Chief Clerk informs me that I have only one month left with the Regiment and a further month left in the Army. Shit! 2 months and I'm out of a job. The worst part is that I won't be able to get a second tour as I'm on a Short Service Commission. Damn! Damn! Damn!

The rest of the day is spent getting my kit together ready for any drama that might happen. I brood all the time about leaving the Regiment. Shit! I've got to snap out of this. I collect a pistol and some ammunition and head for the "Killing House" and take it out on some targets with the resident CRW Troop. It stops me moping as all my attention must be paid to the training in hand.

0900hrs and I attend the Squadron Commanders office. The room is sparse; there are no pictures on the walls only the blue curtains covering every wall. Beneath these curtains are maps on all the operations the Squadron is involved with around the world. The maps are all secret.

'How do you fancy going to Training Wing for your last month with the Regiment?' The Sqn Commander asked.

'I'd like that very much Boss.'

'Good get over there now and get at it, a new Selection starts in two days' time.'

Now this is where I should have been instead of going to the Oman.

I'm looking forward to being on the Directing Staff. In Training Wing, I meet up with an old friend. We talk about old times over a brew.

'Shame you couldn't have come to us earlier Dave.'

'I couldn't agree more Lofty.'

The next Selection will be starting in 2 days, so I spend the time hiking around the Brecon Beacons and looking for the RV's. The trip from Storey to the Talybont Reservoir brings back memories. That bloody mountain Pen-y-Fan, how I hate it.

The new Selection aren't going to like it much either, the weather is starting to change, and not for the better.

There are 200 men from a variety of Regiments on this Selection course. I reckon by the end of the first day we will have lost at least 36 of them. Some will just give up and the others will fail for a number of reasons.

Many who attend Selection are not motivated enough and have not done the required amount of pre-training to pass the course. The first test is a speed march just to blow the cobwebs away. This is where we will lose the first men.

No-one can knock a man for failing the course, he had to be pretty special to get this far and there is no reflection on his character for failing. I can remember one guy who argued with me about getting to an RV after the time allowed and then demanding to do it again. He became instant Platform 4 material.

Another guy who will remain nameless failed to get out of bed because he wanted a lay in as he was up late the previous evening. Again Platform 4 material.

During the long dash, an officer argued that I had given him the wrong grid reference. He didn't like it when I told him to get on the vehicle. Why have a go at me, I'm already in the Regiment he was trying to join.

The wastage continues until there are only 15 men left to go on Continuation Training. And some of these will fail. I have even known a complete Selection to fail. Those that are left after Continuation Training, which consists of parachute, jungle and weapon training, will be "badged" into the Regiment.

Unfortunately I will not know who has passed as my time has finally come to an end with the Regiment.

I report to the Commanding Officer to say goodbye. The CO presents me with a Regimental plaque and a certificate of service and then shakes my hand.

'You have done well whilst with us Dave, I will be sorry to lose you, I wish you luck for the future. Come back and visit anytime, you will always be welcome.'

I leave his office and pack my kit. I have been given 2 weeks leave before going to the Rifle Depot at Winchester for demob.

I arrive at Platform 4. RTU has finally come for me after nearly 2 years with the Regiment. I will certainly miss the life that's for sure. How can I go back to ordinary soldiering after this? The train to Paddington arrives and I board and find a seat near the window. I look out and silently say "Goodbye" to the Regiment and Hereford.

CHAPTER FOURTEEN

I arrive in Gosport late in the afternoon. I have no girlfriend and 2 weeks leave. I haven't a clue if John is home as he hasn't got in contact. Things don't look good. I stop off at the pub on the ferry and as I am about to order a drink, Max turns up.

'Hello Dave, nice to see you again, how are you keeping mate? It's been ages since I last saw you.'

'Hello Max, fancy a drink, sit down and I'll bring it over.'

'Thanks Dave, I'll have a pint of mild.'

I get the drinks and take them to the table. We talk over all the troubles of the world and more. After a few pints, I start to feel light headed.

'I think I will call it a night Max, perhaps we can do it again in the near future.'

'I look forward to it Dave, see you soon.'

A taxi is at the rank and I fall into it.

'Take me to 61, Cherry Road; if I fall asleep wake me up when we get there.'

The journey only takes a few minutes and we soon arrive at my house. I pay the driver and lug my kit up the path. Opening the door, my parents are surprised to see me.

'We thought you were away son.' My dad said.

'I was, but the job was cut short and they returned me home. I've been on the Directing Staff for the last month helping out. I have two weeks leave, before going to the Rifle Depot at Winchester, to get demobbed.'

My dad goes out to the garden.

'What are you going to do then son?' My mother asked.

'I haven't a clue mum, though I was toying with the idea of re-joining up again.'

'Don't you think you have had enough excitement for one life time son?'

'Not yet mum, though I don't know how I will cope if I join up as an ordinary soldier after being with the SAS. But I'm willing to give it a go, if they will have me.'

'Is John still in?'

'No, he left weeks ago; I'll go round and see him tomorrow, that is, if he is still around.'

'I haven't seen Tina West for ages.' said my mother.

'I understand from John, that she hasn't been at all well of late.'

'That will explain it then.'

I'm bushed and head for my bed. My head hits the pillow and sleep comes quick and easy.

Whilst having breakfast next morning, I ponder over everything I have done over the last 7 years or so. When at school, everyone said that schooldays were the best days of your life. What a load of bollocks. Now are the best days of your life.

If I had my life over again, would I have done anything differently? I don't think I would have joined the Merchant Navy, knowing what I know now. I don't think I would have gotten involved with girls as early, and I would have definitely stayed longer in Africa and the Regiment. Other than that, I wouldn't have changed a thing. So far I have had a pretty adventurous life and have enjoyed every minute.

My mother comes into the lounge.

'What's up son? You look miles away.'

'Sorry mum, I was just thinking about all I have done over the past few years.'

'You have got nothing to reproach yourself for son.'

'I know mum, even with Kathryn, it wasn't to be, and as for Jane, well! - rebound I suppose.'

'What happened with you and Kathryn was meant to happen, your Mrs Right is out there waiting for you, mark my words. And as for that other little trollop, the less said the better.'

After breakfast I head off to John's house.

'Well, Well, Well, nice to see you Dave, are you out yet?'

'I'm on 2 weeks leave and then have to report to Winchester for demob, though I'm toying with the idea of re-joining.'

'You have got to be fucking nuts to re-join the Army mate; surely there is something better to do?'

'Well if there is mate, it hasn't shown its ugly head yet.'

We sit chatting for hours.

'Do you remember the time we had to give that talk to the DS and we were ripped to shreds by them.' said John.

'I sure do, but I think it made us better officers because we could take criticism from the lower ranks and in doing so, found a better solution to the problem.'

John becomes serious.

'Do you miss it Dave?'

'You bet your sweet life I do, there will never be anything like the Regiment, and everything will seem quite dull after it.'

'I know how you feel, but life goes on and I'm joining a force in Angola.'

'You are doing what?'

'I've decided to join an outfit in Angola; they need men with my experience, so I should make Lt Colonel at least.'

'John, you have got to be joking, after all the talk you gave me about having enough of the fighting, what do you want to be a Mercenary again for?'

'Don't ask me to explain it, all I know is, I want to be one again.'

'It's not me that is nuts mate, it is you, fuck me, you have got to be raving bonkers.'

'I know.'

No matter what I say, John is adamant that he wants to become a Mercenary again. I can't persuade him to do anything else. He is determined to go to Angola.

'Why don't you come with me Dave?'

'Piss off, I've been a Mercenary, it won't be the same as when we were in the Congo, you see if I'm not right.'

'I wish you would come with me mate, this will be a great adventure, I know it will.'

'Sorry John, but this is one you go on alone.'

John starts to laugh.

'Come on mate stop being so serious, I'll buy you a drink in the Whitehorse tonight, and we can celebrate you leaving the Army and me being a Merc again, how's that?'

'Okay, you win, how is your mum John? My mother hasn't seen her for ages and was wondering if there was anything wrong.'

'She is alright now, she had some tests a couple of weeks ago and it would seem her heart is a bit dickey, so she has been taking it easy.'

'I'm glad, she always was a one for rushing about, and perhaps this will slow her down.'

'I hope so mate, she did say that she was going round to see your mum, I can't think why she didn't.'

'Give her my love and I'll see you tonight.'

'Will do mate, see you later.'

I go off home and spend the rest of the day getting my kit sorted for handing in. Christ knows what I'm going to do if I can't get back in the Army.

The evening at the pub is a great success. I win all the prizes in the raffle, to the annoyance of the regulars. Tough shit, they could have bought the same amount of tickets.

John is still adamant about Angola and I stop trying to change his mind. He's a big boy now and can stand on his own two feet.

'Just be careful mate, that's all I ask.'

'Don't you worry about that mate, I'm not as daft as you, remember those nuns you rescued, only a crackpot like you would have done that, and I'm certainly not in your league, you keep the medals.'

'I'm glad to hear it, but seriously John, be careful out there, I've heard some pretty bad things about that place.'

'Don't you worry about me; you worry about what you will be doing in a week's time when you haven't got a job mate.'

'Thanks for reminding me, who needs enemies when they have you for a friend.'

We leave the pub and stagger home. This is the first time in nearly two years that I have been able to enjoy myself without someone telling me to return to camp.

The next morning I have the biggest headache I have had for ages. I bet John feels the same or worse, he had more drink than I did. I had better go round and see him.

I have 4 cups of coffee and umpteen Alka Seltzers but it doesn't do any good. I should have drunk loads of water when I got home. That is the only way of stopping the body from dehydrating and causing the hangover. What a prat I've been.

John isn't answering the door, and as I am about to leave, Tina opens the door.

'Hello Dave, nice to see you.'

'Hello Tina I've come round to see if John is all right after our little party last night.'

'John isn't here; he left for Angola an hour ago. He left you this letter.'

Tina hands me the letter and I open it and read:

Dear Dave,

Sorry I didn't tell you the truth. I have already signed up to go to Angola and I will be on my way by the time you read this. I didn't want you trying to persuade me not to go. I'm only sorry you are not coming with me. I hope you get back into the Army and enjoy yourself. Don't worry about me I'll be okay. I don't intend winning any medals, I'll leave that up to you mate. You are better at it than me. Keep an eye on the old lady for me and don't do anything I wouldn't do, that leaves you a wide scope. I'll keep in touch when I can. Don't forget me. See you.

Your old mate,

John

PS: Thanks for the great evening.

I hand Tina the letter to read. She reads it and passes it back to me.

'I will miss him Dave.'

'Me too Tina, it is like having your arm cut off, you have had it around for so long, when it goes you miss it.'

'I know how you feel.' She replies.

I hope he gets on okay out there, and don't do anything stupid. The reports I have received on that place don't bear thinking about. I tell Tina that I will drop by and see her before I go back to Winchester.

Now what! My best friend has buggered off to pastures new and I'm stuck with nothing to do. Christ I'm a poet and didn't know it. Back home I lounge about the house, totally bored.

The days go by and my leave will soon be over. I haven't seen Kathy or Jane whilst I have been home. Not that I want to see Jane, I think I could quite easily murder her if I saw her again. As for Kathryn, I just don't know.

My leave is over and I report to the Depot at Bushfield Camp which is on the outskirts of Winchester. Nothing has changed; it is still a hutted camp though I did hear that it would shortly be moving to Peninsula Barracks in the town. Probably a good thing, but not so for the taxi drivers, as the recruits will be able to walk back to camp when they are drunk.

The Adjutant calls me into his office and I sign all the forms required for my discharge from the Army.

'You did bloody well with the SAS Dave; I understand congratulations are in order?'

'I beg your pardon?' I reply.

'You have been recommended for the Military Cross for your actions in Borneo, and I understand that it has been approved by the powers that be.'

'Well bugger my boots; I didn't know anything about it.'

'What are you going to do now you have finished with the Army?'

'I haven't a bloody clue, got any suggestion?'

'Something will turn up, you'll see.'

'I hope so.'

I leave the Depot and make my way to the station for the train to Fareham. I'm now officially out of a job. On the train home I ponder over what I should do about it. I could re-join the Army, but how I will get round the fact that I have already been in, I don't know yet. Whatever happens, I can't be out of a job and sponge of my parents.

At home I watch the TV for the first time in ages knowing that no-one will be coming to get me to go somewhere in the world. I can totally relax. I fucking hate the feeling, this isn't me, and I need action.

Whilst watching a documentary, it suddenly hits me what the Adjutant said in his office. I had totally forgotten about it in the rush to leave the Depot.

'Guess what folks, I've been told that I will be getting the Military Cross for Borneo.'

'Good God! Dave, how did you win that?'

'Don't ask me, all I can think of is that it must have been for those ambushes, or something like that, I really don't know.'

'And you said you wouldn't do anything dangerous.'

'To be honest mum, I don't think I have.'

'You go to see the Queen for that son, don't you?'

'I think so dad, this is the first time anything like this has happened to me in the British Army. I suppose someone will inform me of what will be happening and where I will have to go.'

'Stone the crows, the MC, hey! That's about 3rd down from the VC isn't it?'

'Don't ask me dad, I haven't got a clue.'

'To get that medal son, were you in the SAS?'

'Yes dad I was.'

'That was kept pretty secret.'

'Sorry dad but no-one could be told I was in it'

'What do you intend doing with your life now Dave?' asked my mother.

'I'm going to re-join the Army as a private.'

'You are going to do what!'

'Re-join.'

'Haven't you had enough for one life time?'

'It is only just beginning, I've got to be accepted first, and then we shall see.'

'The mind boggles, you have just left army and now you want to get back in, you have certainly lost some screws somewhere son.' Said my dad getting up from his chair, 'who wants a cupper?'

'Not for me dad, I'm off to bed, see you both in the morning, goodnight.'

After breakfast, I decide to go to the Recruiting Office in Portsmouth and see if I can sign on again. I won't tell the Sergeant about my previous Army service unless he asks.

The Staff in the office have changed since I was last in it. I take the test and pass with flying colours.

'You can join just about any regiment you like with these marks.' The Sergeant tells me.

'I want to join the Rifle Brigade; I understand it is part of the Green Jackets Brigade?'

'Well you have certainly picked a fine regiment, one of the best in the British Army. They are at present in Felixstowe, and are due an overseas posting.'

'Great, when can I take the medical?'

'How about this afternoon, I'm sure the Medical Officer can be contacted. He's at Aldershot till 1400hrs, come back about 1500hrs and we will see. How's that suit you?'

'Fine, I'll look forward to seeing you this afternoon then.'

I leave the Recruiting Office and walk round the town to pass the time away. So far so good, no-one has cottoned on that I have been in the Army before. Let's hope I can keep it that way.

1500hrs and I'm waiting in the Recruiting Office, the Medical Officer should be here shortly. I don't think I will have any problems with the medical, though I will have to lie a bit about what ailments I have had. At last, he turns up and I'm ushered into a small surgery.

'Strip to the waist and sit on the couch please,' said the doctor, 'Have you had any serious illness?'

'No.' I reply tongue in cheek.

He wraps a rubber bandage round my upper arm and takes my blood pressure.

'Well that's normal. Do you do any fitness training?'

'I usually go walking in the hills and the occasional run, why?'

'Nothing in particular, you look very fit.'

'I try to keep myself in trim.'

The medical lasts for about half an hour and the doctor informs the Recruiting Sergeant that I am fit for service in the Army.

'Well, all that remains is for you to be sworn in and be issued with a rail warrant for Winchester. Welcome to the Army.' The recruiting sergeant said.

'Thanks, when do I have to report to Winchester?'

'Monday morning at 1000hrs.'

I leave the office with a day's pay and the warrant for a train to Winchester from Fareham. This is going to put the cat among the pigeons, especially when I report for documentation; the Adjutant is going to go bananas.

As I haven't anything to do this evening, I go and see my sister. She is living with a guy in a Prefab, which should have been pulled down at the end of the war, but the council kept them up to put families in, as there was a shortage of Council accommodation in the area.

I'm walking to my sister's place when I bump into Kathy pushing a pram.

'Don't get any ideas, this isn't mine.' She says pointing her finger at me.

'I wasn't thinking anything honest.'

'How are you keeping Dave, everything okay?'

'Well, I left the Army last week and re-joined this week, daft aren't I.'

'Goodness gracious me, what in the world did you want to join up again for?'

'I didn't want to be unemployed and I really liked the Army life.'

'Have you got a girlfriend yet?'

'Nope, not at the moment, I'm free and easy, why?'

'Oh nothing, what are you doing tonight? Fancy a drink in the Queens Head?'

'That sounds a good idea, I am at a bit of a loss as to what to do in the evenings, and I could meet you in the pub at 8pm?'

'Fine, I'll be there.'

My sister isn't in and I return home. I hope Kathy don't think that we will be getting back together, because it would never work.

8pm and I'm standing at the bar. Kathryn arrives looking absolutely stunning.

'Bloody hell girl! You look great.' I tell her.

'Why thank you Sir.'

'What would you like to drink?'

'I'll have a glass of white wine please.'

'Coming right up, find a seat somewhere and I'll bring the drinks over.'

Kathy finds a table by a window and I carry the drinks over to it.

'If I knew you were going to dress up, I'd have put something decent on Kathryn.'

'You look okay as you are.'

I put her drink down on the table and she picks it up.

'Cheers.' she says taking a great gulp.

Bugger me; she sure can sink the booze.

'Cheers.' I reply.

She never drank like that when we were going out together.

'Do you want another?' I ask her.

'Sorry Dave, I'm a bit nervous that's all.'

'Why?'

'Well this is the first time since we split up that we have been together on our own.'

'I see, well, let's get smashed because I'm just as nervous as you.'

Throughout the evening we have got on like a house on fire, no arguing or snide remarks. It is just like it was when we first started dating. How I wish we could be like this all the time.

'I think I had better go home.' said Kathy slurring her speech.

'I'll walk with you or should I say stagger with you.'

'Can we get arrested for being drunk in charge of shoes?' She asked laughing.

We reach her house after about 20 minutes. No mother shouting for her to come in. That's novel.

'I've had a great time Dave, thanks.'

'The pleasure is all mine, I…'

She places a finger on my lips.

'Don't say anymore leave it as it is.' She says kissing me on the cheek.

I start to walk off.

'Dave.'

I turn round and face her.

'Thanks again.'

I blow her a kiss and she walks down her garden path to her front door. If only we could have made a go of it, Oh well.........!

CHAPTER FIFTEEN

Monday arrives and I make my way to the Rifle Depot at Winchester. On entering the camp gates, I go up to a Sergeant holding a clip board.

'I'm Rifleman David Stubbs reporting for training, Sergeant.'

He looks at the board.

'Good man, go wait in the guardroom with the other recruits.' he says pointing to a door.

Once in the building, I see 20 men of differing sizes. Some are fat, some pimply and some like racing snakes. They all have one thing in common, they don't speak. I remember the pimple faced lad when I first joined up who had all the questions but no answers. It looks as if they have all lost their tongues.

Twenty minutes go by when the Sergeant returns.

'Right you lot, outside on the road forming 2 ranks.'

We leave the warmth of the guardroom and parade on the road.

'I'm now going to take you to the Orderly Room for documentation, after which you will be introduced to your platoon NCOs, let's move off in a military fashion, no slouching.'

After a few minutes we arrive at the Orderly Room. What a shambles, just like last time, a right cock up. No-one knows how to march, except me.

Whilst waiting outside, an office door opens in front of us. Out of it comes the Depot Adjutant. He looks straight at me.

'What the fuck are you doing here Dave, with this motley bunch.' he says coming towards me.

'Hello Sir, I've joined up again.'

'You've done what? But you can't, it's against the law, I think.'

'Well I have and here I am.'

'Come into my office, I want to sort this out before it gets any further.'

We enter his office and he tells me to sit down.

'What's going on Dave? You have only just left us as an officer with the MC for fucks sake; you can't be serious about re-joining.'

'But I am, there isn't anything for me to do as a civvy, and I thought the best thing was for me to join up again. I miss the life, even though it has only been a few weeks.'

'Bloody Hell!' What's the CO going to say about this, sit there I'm going to have a word with him?'

After 10 minutes or so, Simon returns with the CO, Lt Colonel Richards.

'What are you playing at Dave, do you honestly think I'm going to allow you to re-join the Army as a Rifleman after what you have being doing, you have got to be joking.'

'Sir, I've passed all the tests and I'm fit, and I'm here, I don't think I have broken any rules.'

'Did you tell the Recruiting Staff you had already served in the Army?'

'They didn't ask, so I didn't tell them.'

The CO rattles on about everything that I have done and that there was no way he would have me at the Depot.

'What is the point of you doing any training, you know more than the rest of us put together. You are definitely not staying at the Depot. You will be posted to a Battalion as soon as it can be arranged and in the meantime, I will post you to the 4th Battalion at Sun Street, good luck David. I have never heard of this before. Just out of curiosity, how long have you joined up for this time?'

'Nine years Colonel, I want to get back to the SAS if I can.'

'Bloody amazing, I wish all our soldiers had your attitude.'

The CO shakes my hand and leaves me with Simon. I'm sure deep down he approves of what I have done. Though he will never admit it. Lt Colonel Richards is one hell of a soldier; he won the DSO and then got a bar to it. Not many have done that.

'Well Dave, it looks as if you have been posted before you have had a chance to get use to the place again. You must see the CO is right, there is no way we could have you here. Christ you know more than the Training Staff, and I don't think it would look too good if a Rifleman turned up on parade wearing the Military Cross, do you?'

'They haven't given it to me yet, so I really can't answer that, can I.'

We prattle on about the good times for over an hour and then I leave and make my way home. I have been given home leave until I report to Sun Street in the near future. Boy! Have I put the cat among the pigeons this time?

The train journey back to Fareham is pretty boring, and I speak to no-one. We are a very conservative race of people, and I can't understand why.

As I arrive at our front gate, my dad pulls up on his bike from work.

'Stone the crow's son! What are you doing here; I thought you would be tucked up at the Depot by now.'

'It's a long story dad, but I will tell you over a cup of tea, because I'm parched.'

My few days at home don't amount to much. I spend most of my time drinking coffee in the Mocambo Cafe in the town. The only person I speak to is the Cafe owner. None of my mates are home; they are either at work or away in the forces.

Finally, my movement orders arrive posting me to the 4th Battalion in London. I am to be there my 1400hrs. I say goodbye to my mum and make my way to the station to get the train to Liverpool Street.

The journey is bloody boring as usual, no-one talks. The passengers are either reading books or papers, some upside down. They ignore everyone in sight, what a miserable race of people we are. I hear moaning from the seat behind me. The guy is obviously touching his girl up.

4 RGJ is easy to find and only a stone's throw from the station. I report to the Orderly Room and tell them I am the new man.

'Ha! Ha! The new lad has arrived.' Said the Orderly Room Sergeant, 'You are on CO's orders at 1430hrs.'

'Yes, I know Sarge, any idea what I'm supposed to be doing?'

'Stores, I think, why?'

Fuck! - I don't what to be a store man; I want to get out in the field with a Rifle Platoon.

1430hrs arrives and I'm marched in to see the CO.

'Welcome to the 4th battalion Stubbs, I hope you will enjoy your stay with us, I see from your file that you held a short service commission and spent time with the SAS. Well I can't have you here as a Rifleman, especially as you have got the MC. You are promoted to Corporal and will work with CSgt Hines. If you have any problems let me know soonest, okay that is all, you may go.'

I spend 30 minutes telling the RSM how I got the MC with the SAS and about my commission. He seems impressed, especially as I have re-joined.

'You will be the first Corporal I have ever heard of with the MC, that's for sure.' He said showing me to CSgt Hines office.

'Your new man Fred, look after him, He's quite special.'

'Do what Sir?' Said Hines as the RSM walked off.

'I think he's having you on Colour, believe me I'm not special in any sense of the imagination.'

'So you are my new store man, what's your handle?'

'Dave Stubbs, Colour.'

'When the Rupert's aren't about; you can call me Fred okay.'

'When did you leave the Regiments Fred?'

'Now how did you know I was in the Regiment?'

'You said Rupert's; ordinary squaddies wouldn't have used that phrase.'

'Given myself away haven't I.'

'Sure have Fred, how long have you been away?'

'I was with the Regiment till the end of '61; I took a bullet in the leg in Malaya.'

'I've just left them, my time was up and I got demobbed. There wasn't anything I wanted to do as a civvy, so I re-join.'

'You have got to be some fruitcake to do that mate, once out, you should have stayed out.'

'I missed the life too much and anyway, who would employ a trained killer, I know I wouldn't.'

We talk and talk as we have lots in common.

'Where do I bunk down Fred?'

'In that room over there, but tonight, you are coming home with me, we have lots to talk about, and we can do that over a few beers.'

'I don't want to put you out Fred, what will your wife say, bringing someone home without telling her?'

'Julia is okay, she likes me bringing mates home, and it gives her a chance to show off her culinary skills.'

'Fair enough mate.'

Throughout the rest of the afternoon, Fred shows me all the equipment that is on charge to the 4th battalion.

'This stuff here is for our eyes only. If a guy needs kit which he has lost and will have to pay for, we issue it from here for a small price.'

'Bloody Heck! We earn money as well.'

'You wouldn't chuckle, I'm on my run down and I'm going to need all the money I can get. Just remember Dave, the head shed are not to know about this stuff.'

'I've gone blind Fred.'

'Right, let's have a brew.'

Although I don't want to be a store man, this posting could be quite profitable.

The afternoon comes to an end. I have learnt quite a bit about the company stores, Fred is a good instructor. I think I may get to like this posting after all. Fred seems a decent sort, especially as he has invited me to his house for the evening.

I put my suitcase in the room and then we go off to Fred's quarter. I'm introduced to Julia, who I find comes from Gosport.

'I lived in Elson Road for years; I met Fred when he was on a course at St Georges Barracks.'

'What a small world, I lived in Cherry Road; in fact I still do when I am in Gosport. My parents still live there.'

'Don't you have a girlfriend to share your life Dave?'

'Not any more, I was engaged to a girl who ended up going out with someone else when I was away, she didn't like the Army or me being in it.'

Julia cooks a smashing meal and we sit around drinking and talking about the Regiment.

'So you have got the MC Dave, how did you win that?'

'Everyone keeps telling me that I have got it, I haven't seen the citation or anything yet.'

'Don't worry mate, it will come soon enough, and when it does, It's off to the jolly ole palace to meet the Queen and those blasted corgi dogs.'

The evening goes by quite quickly and it is 2am when Fred says, 'I think we had better turn in, your rooms down the hall on the left Dave.'

'I don't want to put you out mate; I'll get a taxi back to Sun Street.'

'Oh no you don't, you will sleep here and that is the end to the matter.' Julia said, getting up from her chair.

As I'm walking down the passage, Fred says, 'you're not bad for an ex officer, I like you and so does Julia.'

'Thanks mate, that means a lot to me, goodnight, see you in the morning.'

Entering the room; I find it is decorated as a baby's room. I wonder if they are trying for a child.

I undress and my head hits the pillow. Zappo! Zeds are pouring out.

BANG! BANG! BANG!

I wake with a start.

'Come on - Wakey, Wakey - It's time to rise.' Fred says from the other side of the door.

'Breakfast in 10 minutes.'

'Cheers mate, be out in a tick.' I shout back.

I climb out of bed and make my way to the bathroom. What the hell was I drinking last night? My mouth is all furred up.

Having washed and dressed, I return to the lounge. Julia is just putting my breakfast down on the table.

'Did you sleep okay Dave?'

'Like a log, thanks Julia, and thanks for putting me up.'

'Anytime, in fact, I've asked Fred to bring you home tonight.'

'That's very kind of you Julia, but you don't want me around, surely you two want to be on your own?'

'Don't argue with her Dave, you will lose.'

After breakfast we make our way to the 4th Battalion. The Battalion is going on an exercise at the weekend, but we are rear party.

'Your Julia is a smashing girl Fred; you have got one in a million there.'

'I know mate, you must have noticed the decoration in the room you are using, we have been trying for a baby for over a year now, but nothing seems to be happening, I just don't know what to do mate, I reckon there must be something wrong with me.'

'My sister was the same Fred, then all of a sudden, bingo, don't lose hope mate, it will happen when the time is right, you'll see.'

'I hope so, because I think it is getting Julia down.'

The rest of the day is spent in sorting out my documentation and allowances and getting the Battalion ready for the exercise that will be on at the weekend. Thank goodness I'm not on it, I don't like Stamford PTA.

Work finished we make our way to Fred's.

'Hang about Fred; I want to get some flowers for Julia.'

'Now that's a nice thought, good on you mate.'

'It's the least I can do for her; she's a bloody good cook, that's for sure.'

'I told you she was.'

We stop off at a small florists and I buy the biggest bunch of flowers they have.

'Christ Dave, there's enough there to deck out the palace.'

'The best, for the best Fred.'

Over the next few weeks, I spend a lot of time round at Fred and Julia's.

'How would you like to take in a show tonight?'

'Oh I would love to Dave, I've always wanted to see, Guys and Dolls.'

'Then see it, you shall.' I say to her producing 3 tickets from my pocket.

'How did you know I wanted to see it?'

'Fred told me.'

'Oh you devious bugger you.'

'Don't mention it, actually Julia, It's to say thank you for all you have done for me since being posted to the 4th Battalion.'

'Oh Dave, think nothing of it, Fred and I have loved having you stay with us. We think of you as part of the family now.'

The show is great, though we have to look through bino's to see the stage. Julia loves it and is bubbling over all the way home.

We sink a few beers and Fred finally asks me why I left the Regiment.

'It wasn't my idea to leave, my time was up. I was on a Short Service Commission, and it had come to an end and I couldn't extend.'

'How, did you get the MC?'

'Don't ask me, Fred, I knew nothing about it until the Adjutant told me at the Depot when I was getting discharged. I expect it was for the operation we were on when we got zapped and I led the patrol out. It was pretty hairy, but I don't think it warranted the Military Cross. Though quite a few gongs were given out on that operation I recall.'

'Well you certainly have led a pretty hectic life so far, Dave.' Fred remarks.

I then tell Fred about the time I was a mercenary in the Congo.

'They gave me a gong for an operation I was on there, but I can't wear it, at least not without the Queen's permission.'

'Bloody hell mate!' Fred remarks, 'You have definitely got to have been one serious nutter.'

'I'll go along with that, as I sure as hell, scared the living daylights out of my mum and dad. Mind you, it wasn't all my doing. I have a mate called John who got me into most of the things I have done.'

'Is he still in the army?'

'Good heavens no, he was, in the Regiment, but left and became a mercenary again, in Angola.'

'Fucking Hell! That place is dangerous they are having one hell of a battle out there. I read a bit about it in yesterday's paper.'

Shit, I hope John is okay.

We finally sink all the beer, and turn in for what is left of the night. As I am about to close my bedroom door, Fred asks what I will be doing in the morning.

'I was thinking of going to see my parents in Gosport, but I haven't really decided.'

'Fancy bombing around London, we could call in at the Special Forces Club for a few jars.'

'That will do me mate, I'm game.'

The Special Forces Club was founded by my doctor's father, Colonel Smith when he was with the OSS in the 2nd World War.

The weekend goes by like an express train and is over before we know it. Julia has looked after me splendidly.

'Thanks for a great weekend you two.'

'Don't mention it, it's our pleasure Dave, and you have been great company for Fred. He doesn't see many people nowadays.'

Julia is a lovely person and all I hope is they have the baby they both want badly.

I receive a letter telling me to attend Buckingham Palace for the presentation of the Military Cross by the Queen. Civilian clothes are to be worn. I can't understand why I'm not wearing uniform, is it because I won the gong in the SAS, perhaps that's why. It would have caused a stir if I had had to wear uniform. I'm only a corporal now, not an officer. I wonder how the army would have played that.

I show Fred the letter.

'So that is your citation. Well you deserve it mate, from all accounts you did a first rate job. Well done.'

We now know why I have been awarded the MC. What I did as far as I'm concerned didn't warrant a medal. I was only doing my job as leader of the group.

The day finally comes and I head for Buck House with my mum. I'm quite nervous; I've only seen the Queen from a distance. There are several people getting different Honours and Awards etc. We are all ushered into a room and informed what will be taking place. I'm the first to be presented to the Queen. Each person has to go towards Her Majesty and bow.

We remain in the room until the major domo calls our names. My name is called and I walk smartly towards the Queen. I stop in front of her and bow. The major domo reads out my citation:

"Captain Stubbs displayed coolness and a disregard for his own safety worthy of the highest praise. His actions and skill in withdrawing his patrol after their successful ambush through enemy country were of a very high order and his determination in completing his mission was far beyond the call of duty."

The Queen steps forward and pins the Cross on my lapel.

'Thank you very much Captain Stubbs for all you have done for the country under very trying conditions. It is with great pleasure that I bestow on you the Military Cross.'

'Thank you Ma'am.'

Her Majesty asks me lots of questions which I answer.

'You are a very brave man, thank you Captain Stubbs.'

This is my queue to bow and return to my place in front of her. My mum is all smiles. Once everyone has seen the Queen, we go into a room for refreshments. They are a bit tight with the sandwiches, little triangles with the crusts cut off. After a few hours, we are all shown the way out. I suppose, another pain in the arse day for Her Majesty, is over.

On the train back to Portsmouth, my mother asks to see the Cross. I hand her the brown leather box which she opens.

'Oh Dave, what a lovely thing.'

'It is the best looking decoration the army has mum, though I don't think I deserve it.'

'Is it silver Dave?'

'Yes, I think it is.'

I close the box and put it into the inside pocket of my suit. Well! That's two decorations and two medals and a few bars so far, there is still time to get a few more to add to the collection. On arriving home, my brother asks to see the decoration, but I can't find it anywhere. It looks as if I have either lost it or it has been stolen on the train. Someone must have seen me put it in my inside pocket. I am furious, I've just had it presented and now it's gone. Damn, now what do I do. I'm really pissed off.

'Don't worry son, I'm sure you will be able to get a duplicate.'

'I hope so mum. But it won't be the same.'

I inform the Police of the theft, but they don't hold out much help. Unless it is sold to a shop, the chances are, the culprit will never be found.

I'm at a loose end and buy a fishing rod and some equipment and go to fish the moat at Fort Brockhurst. Well, it passes a few hours away.

After about an hour, two small boys arrive and are watching me from the top bank.

'Have you caught anything mister?' one of the boys asked.

'Not a ruddy thing, why, do you want to have ago?'

'Can we.' they both cry.

'Here it's all yours, I never was much good at fishing, enjoy yourselves.'

I hand over the rod and tackle and start to climb the bank.

'Don't you want this gear mister?'

'Nope, it's all yours, bye.'

I leave the kids fighting over who is going to fish first. Well, at least it has made someone's day. Five pounds worth of kit has made two kids very happy. Now what do I do.

Having decided that fishing is not my scene, I go round to see my sister who lives in a prefab. Prefabs were put up by the local council to house people after the war. They should have only been up for ten years but somehow stayed up longer.

(The regulations on the use of asbestos, would mean, these building would never have been built in today's society.)

I spend a few hours with her talking about things in general. She is moving to a place in Romsey shortly, which will be a lot better, especially as she is pregnant.

I've spent the week doing absolutely sod all. What a leave. None of my mates are at home and John is away, I'm totally bored.

At last my leave comes to an end and I make my way back to London. The journey isn't too bad. I strike up a conversation with a guy who is going to Davies Street. (Kings Royal Rifle Corp TA) I think this is the second time in my life that I have actually had a conversation on a British train, other than with John.

I arrive at Sun Street and go to see Fred.

'Had a good leave Dave, come on then, let me see your gong.'

'I wish I could show you mate, but I haven't got it. I lost it on the train. I remember putting it into my inside pocket of my jacket and, wait a minute, I remember now, just as I was getting off of the train someone bumped into me. It must have been then, when it got nicked. The rest of my leave was totally bloody boring mate, absolutely fuck all to do.'

'I wish I had leaves like that; not losing your medal mate, but Julia gets me doing all sorts when I'm on leave, never a moment's peace. Don't get married Dave.'

'I'll bear that in mind Fred, What's on this week?'

'Not a lot, "A" Company are off to Northumberland this weekend, that's about it.'

Over the following months we go out into the field on small exercises and the like, but nothing that taxes the brain or stamina. I spend most of my time either at Fred's or just lazing in my room. I have the occasional night in the bar or go to the pictures. Life is becoming pretty boring.

After spending a great weekend with Julia and Fred, on returning to the office I'm handed a large buff envelope.

'What's this then?' I ask the orderly room clerk.

'Posting orders.' he replied.

Opening the envelope, I find that I'm posted to the Ministry of Defence.

'What the bloody hell do I want to go there for; whose idea of a joke is this?' I shout at no-one in particular.

I show the orders to Fred.

'Well, we both knew this posting wasn't permanent, and anyway, the MOD isn't far away, you can still come over to stay at weekends.'

'I suppose you are right Fred, though what the hell I'm going to do at the MOD, God only knows.'

'Okay, tonight we'll have a piss up to celebrate.'

'Celebrate what, for fucks sake?'

'You're posting to the MOD mate.'

'You're off your rocker Fred.'

'Anything for a piss up mate.'

The rest of the day flies by for some unknown reason and we head for Fred's house.

'Guess what Julia; Dave has got a posting to the MOD.'

'Oh, I'm sorry to hear that Dave, still it is only down the road, so you can still come and visit.'

'That's what I told him.' Fred said, laying the table.

After a lovely meal we head for the nearest pub, The Green Dragon. At closing time we stagger back home slightly the worst for wear.

'I've enjoyed tonight, thanks for looking after me since I've been here especially you Julia, I've really had a great time and I'm going to miss you both.'

'Shut up you Pillock, we've enjoyed having you, what are you trying to do, make us cry?'

'No, really, thanks guys.'

Having rolled into bed the room starts to spin. Bloody hell - I'll have to leave the beer alone. I keep opening and closing my eyes, but it doesn't make any difference, the room still keeps spinning. Jesus H Christ, do I feel sick. I make my way to the bathroom. Fred is coming out.

'You feel how I do?'

'No worse.' I tell him rushing into the bathroom. Up come the carrots.

I return to my bed and lay dying. I must have fallen asleep as the next thing I hear is banging on the door. Christ, is it morning all ready. I get up and wash and then go down to the lounge.

'That will teach you both not to get blotto in future,' said Julia, 'Do you want breakfast?'

'Err, no thanks, I'll give it a miss.'

'What about you Fred?'

'Coffee, just coffee, thanks, sweetheart.' He replied.

'What the hell did we drink last night?'

'Everything and anything, I think.'

'That will teach you two buggers; I bet you don't do that again in a hurry.' Julia said laughing.

'Bitch.' Fred replies.

My posting with the 4th battalion comes to an end and I report to the Duty Officer at the Ministry of Defence. I hand him my movement order and he tells me to go to the canteen.

'Any idea, why I've been posted here Sir'

'I can't tell you at this moment in time, but all will be revealed shortly. Go and have a cup of tea and I'll send for you when the time comes.'

I follow his instructions and make my way to the canteen. Bloody odd place this, and pretty secretive. I wonder what I will be doing.

An hour goes by when I'm asked to go back to the Duty Officer. About time to, I was beginning to wonder if they had forgotten me. I'm introduced to a Major called Croxley. He is apparently, the army's Chief Tactician and a very highly thought of officer.

'You Stubbs, because of your service record and qualifications, are to be employed as a bodyguard to Major Croxley. You will be armed and will only answer to me. We have reason to believe that there may be an attempt of the Major's life. You will stop that attempt. You will stay in a house near

Major Croxley's house. Familiarise yourself with the surrounding area and report to me anything that you feel is wrong. Major Croxley will brief you on the day to day tasks. Don't let me down. I'll leave you both to get acquainted. Remember what I said, don't let me down.'

Croxley tells me that he has a wife and two boys and a nanny living with him. He is attending a course at the Staff College, in Latimer, for 6 months, and in that time he would like me to look after his family when not needed by him. He asks me lots of questions about what I have done in the army and the SAS. He concluded that I am the right man for the job and will feel safe with me around.

I ask him when he wants me to start.

'Now of course.' He replied.

'Then I had better get that gun.'

I go and find the Duty Officer and ask him where I pick the firearm up from.

'I've arranged for you to collect it from the Duke of York's Barracks, I think an old haunt of yours, they know you are coming.'

And so another job starts. This should beat being a store man. I hope. I return to Croxley and tell him I am just off to collect a weapon. Before I go, I ask him why he needed a bodyguard, after all, he was in the Regular Army and there were plenty of soldiers about.

He replied, 'Since working with the Ministry of Defence, I have on occasions, upset certain people. These people do not like me nor do they like what I do. It has come to the notice of the Chief of Staff or should I say, it has come to the notice of the Army that certain factions will try to either harm or kill me. That is where you come in. Your time with the SAS means that you know how to look after yourself as well as others. You are young and to be perfectly honest, you do not look like a soldier, so will not be obtrusive. That is why you got the job.'

'Can you tell me who these people are Sir?'

'You will have to ask the Duty Officer those questions as; I am just like you, in the dark.'

It seems that Croxley is not giving anything away, why, I ask myself. I'm to accompany Croxley to the house he is renting in Wendover. I'm also to take all the kit that I will require with me, as my accommodation, is only 2 houses down from his. I will be staying in a house that already has 3 other men sharing it. They are from a little known outfit in the Intelligence Corp.

I leave Croxley at the MOD and go off to collect my weapon. It is one of the new 9mm Browning's that have just been issued to the army. Now this beats the old .45 and .38's that I am use to.

'Do I get a chance to zero this in mate?' I ask the armourer.

'I think you just point it and pull the trigger brother. It will do the rest. As you can see the sights are not moveable, they are fixed.'

'What about ammo?'

'You get that from him in there.' he said pointing to the stores.

I check with the Staff Sergeant about testing the weapon. He states that there are no ranges near, so will have to take pot luck. Fucking help he is. I've got a weapon that I don't know much about and no chance of testing it for accuracy. This is becoming farcical.

Having collected the weapon and ammo, I return to the MOD and collect Croxley. This is the first time that I have ever been armed with a weapon in a shoulder holster. It feels really strange. Still I had better get used to it. I would like some practise though, and I tell Croxley this.

'Don't worry, there is a range close by that you can use, it's run by MI6, they have a small network in the area.'

'How do you know that?'

'You will be attending many meetings with me, and some of the people you will meet are from MI6 and MI5. I think that is enough info for the moment.'

The drive to Wendover is quite enjoyable. Croxley tells me about his family, who own half of bloody Cornwall, Prince Charles owns the other half. Croxley's father is a Knight, a title that Croxley will inherit if the old man dies. He will also inherit the family mansion "Fleetwell" just outside Truro.

(Croxley became a Lord but later dies of natural causes at the age of 71)

On arrival at the house Croxley has rented, I help him unload his kit and take it inside. The family are already there, as they followed the removal van to Wendover. I'm introduced to his wife Mary, Daphne the nanny and Josh his youngest son. The oldest, Phillip, is at present at a boarding school and will be home at the end of the week. Now that Croxley is unpacked, I am shown the house I will be using whilst on assignment. The house is only two down from his and is occupied by three other army personnel who are in the Intelligence Corp. They are not at home, so must work in London I would suppose.

I make myself at home and then return to Croxley.

'What is the SP for tomorrow Sir?' I ask him.

'You can take me to work and then come back here until I require you to pick me up. If Mary is going out, I want you to go with her. You know the score and what is required.'

'What time do you want me here in the morning?'

'I have to be at the Staff College at 0800hrs, let's say about 0715hrs that should give us ample time to get there.'

'Right, I'll see you in the morning.'

Back at the house, I find that the three guys have returned from wherever they have been. I introduce myself and they in turn tell me who they are. One is called Brian and the other two Sam and Ginger. They work for an intelligence gathering detachment which will be based in Northern Ireland in the near future. (This is now call 14 Int or The Det for short) I tell them that I am on an armed assignment protecting a major who lives two doors down.

'Oh you mean Croxley, you lucky sod, I hear he is quite generous, but, quite a few people would love to have him removed.' Sam replied.

'Did you know I was coming here then?'

'Well, we knew an ex Special Forces guy was going to be his bodyguard, and that he would be staying in the house with us.' Brian said.

'Then let's hope we all get on well together.'

I check with Croxley and tell him I will be back to check the area out. All four of us then go into Wendover for a drink, which is only 600yds away. It is a very, very, small place. Not many shops and definitely nowhere to go except the local pubs. The nearest big town is Aylesbury and that isn't exactly big. After sinking a few pints we return to the house and the guys turn in. I go and check Croxley's house grounds out.

0700hrs and I knock on Croxley's door. The nanny opens it.

'Morning nanny everything okay.'

'Hello Dave, you are bright and early, the major is having his breakfast, would you like a cup of tea?'

'That would be nice nanny; I'll just have a check round and look at the car before I come in.'

Everything is secure and there are no problems with the car. Nanny has poured me a cup of tea in the kitchen. Josh is having his breakfast on a small table in a room just off the kitchen. I think this is the room that nanny will be using when she has the kids at home. After a few minutes, Croxley comes into the kitchen.

'How did you find your accommodation?' He asked.

'It's okay, though I would like to be nearer than two houses away.'

'I was talking to Mary about that and she said the same thing. Let's see how it goes for the time being and if we have to move you into the house we will. Right, I think we had better be going.'

The journey to the Staff College is along winding lanes, with just enough room for a car to pass. As we approach the College I notice a graveyard at the entrance.

'Blimey, I bet there are some old timers in that.'

Croxley just smiles. He drives to the entrance of the Officers Mess and hands the car over to me.

'Pick me up at 1800hrs, if I need you before then, I'll ring home.'

'Fair enough.' I reply getting into the driving seat.

'Are you sure you will be okay?'

'Yes, no problems here, I'm not using my correct name, so no-one will know me.'

'Are you sure.'

'I'll be fine, off you go.'

Boy! This Hillman Hunter Estate is some car. Leather seats and lots of gadgets. I bet this car cost a bomb to buy. But then again, he can afford it.

The journey back to the house is nice and quiet. I pull into the drive and park outside the garage. The car will have to be put in at night from now on. I knock the door and tell Mary that I'm going to have a look round and should be gone about an hour.

The house is situated in a lane that is only wide enough for a car and a half, and comes to a dead end at the western end of it. There is though, a public footpath at this end. Trees align the southern side about 600 yards from the back of the house, and an open farm field to the north.

I can't see the farm house as the field rises up for about 500 yards. There is only one way into the lane from the main road. Anyone coming up this lane would be seen. The rear of the house has a very large lawned garden which drops down towards a barbed wire fence some 200yds from the house. This fence separates the garden from adjoining properties which also have very large lawned gardens.

Only one of the 5 houses faces the main road. Although anyone could get onto the property if they put their minds to it, the chances of this happening without being seen are very slim. At the moment, there did not seem to be any point in making it harder.

I return to the house and tell Mary what I have found. She seems to like the idea of being body guarded.

'Graham will be pleased to know that he doesn't have to spend hundreds of pounds on extra security, thanks to you, may I call you Dave?'

'Of course, what do you want me to do now?'

'I have to go into Princes Risborough and see about a school there for Phillip, will you accompany me?'

'That's what I am here for, the Boss said I was to go everywhere with you except the toilet and the bathroom.'

'And, the bedroom?'

'No comment.'

Mary starts to laugh, 'Come on, and let's see this school.'

At the school, which is a boy's private school, I am introduced to the headmaster. He is informed that the only people that can pick Phillip up, are me, or Mary, no-one else, not even the nanny or the major. The headmaster wants to know why. I tell him that it is a security matter and the less he knows the better. He doesn't like this, but has to accept it. The school costs £600 a term. Bloody Expensive.

I accompany Mary into Aylesbury to do some shopping. The town isn't very big compared to Portsmouth or London, but it does have a good range of shops.

We return to Wendover and Mary asks if I would like a cup of coffee. Nanny comes in from the garden with Josh.

'Are you going to be my friend?' He asks.

'Of course I will, and I will be Phillips friend as well when he comes home.'

I don't want to alarm the lad, even if he is, only four. I tell nanny that if she is going out with the boys at any time, I must be informed, without fail. She nods agreement.

Over the next few weeks things start to happen. I catch a man in the back garden with a shotgun. He is a local poacher and the police have been after him for months. His excuses are pretty feeble and I believe he was trying to steal. The police also agree with me.

One night as I am walking the lane, I see two men coming towards me. I hide in some bushes and wait for them to pass me by.

'You sure this is a short cut Sid.' One of them said.

'Perhaps not mate; I think we had better go back.' the other replies.

They turn round and make their way back down the lane. Now, is this a genuine mistake, or are they checking the area out, I wonder. I make a note of their descriptions and return to the house and inform Croxley.

'What do you think Dave?' he asks.

'They could be genuine, but surely, if they lived in this area, they would know the dead ends, and which are short cuts.'

'I agree. You are to move into the house immediately, get all your kit now.'

Croxley seems to be on edge. I collect my kit and return to the house. My room overlooks the lane and the eastern side of the garden. It is quite comfortable and I'm made extremely welcome.

'Please do not sit in your room every night; you are most welcome to use the drawing room with us, nanny that goes for you as well.'

'Thanks Boss, but my job is keeping the shit at bay, sorry Mary, I didn't see you there.'

'Don't mind me Dave; I'm only glad you are here.'

I then carry on, 'Most of my time will be outside till after midnight. I do not want to be caught out, especially now that Phillip will be at home.'

'Thank you, the MOD certainly knew who to pick for this job, that's for sure.'

Yes, ME! I say to myself.

Now that I am billeted in the house, things become a lot easier. I don't have to cook my meals for one thing. I spend more time with the two boys as well as carrying out tasks for Croxley and Mary. The job is pretty boring though it did have a few minor incidents during the weeks that follow. But nothing too serious.

One evening I have to accompany Croxley to the Staff College where he is giving a presentation called "Vostok." Once he is settled in, I go over to the College Club.

As I am having a quiet drink, two girls come into the club. The one with dark hair and wearing glasses looks gorgeous.

'Hello.' I say to her. 'Fancy a game of darts.'

She looks as me but doesn't say anything.

The girl, who came in with her, speaks to her in a foreign language.

The gorgeous girl replies, 'Si.'

'Yes.'

The other girl tells me.

'If I win, we go on a date, ok.' I say to her, through her friend.

'Nessuna possibilitá, non vincerá.' Gorgeous replies

'No chance, you won't win.' Her friend interprets.

'My name's Dave, what's yours?'

Her friend relays what I have said.

'Mi chiamo Anna.'

'Pardon!' I reply.

'Her name is Ann, mine is Maria and we are Italian.'

Throughout the game, I keep fiddling the scores. She is a really stunning girl. I find out that she is a Captain and a Contessa to boot; in the Italian Army and is attached to the Staff College as a lecturer in Ciphers and Codes. I can't tell her what I am doing, though she does ask through Maria her friend. Maria is also a Captain in the Italian Army and is Anna's interpreter as Anna does not speak English.

At the end of the game I tell her that I have won and ask her for a date.

'Cosa ti fa pensare che voglio uscire con te.' Anna replies in Italian.

'What did she say?' I ask Maria.

Maria replies: 'What makes you think I want to go out with you?'

'I won the bet.' I tell her.

I walk her and her friend back to their mess. I kiss Anna on the cheek, and say goodnight.

'You will fall in love with me and we will get married.' I tell Anna.

Maria translates what I have said.

'Non a caso' She replies in Italian.

I don't know what she has said.

'What did she say?'

'No chance' said Maria.

'Wait and see.' I tell her.

Maria translates and they both go into the mess laughing.

I collect Croxley from the Mess and we return to Wendover.

'How did your presentation go?' I ask him.

'Well, let us say, it was interesting.'

He then asks me what I did whilst waiting for him.

'I met a very nice girl and we had a game of darts, but she doesn't speak English except through an interpreter. I want to ask her out on a date in the near future with a bit of luck. But I don't speak her language.'

'What is her name and where does she work'

'Her name is Anna; she is a Captain in the Italian Army and is the Cipher and Codes lecturer at the Staff College.'

'Well, at least one of us has had a good night.'

The rest of the journey is in silence.

Over the next few weeks, I see a lot of Anna. We go everywhere together with Maria her interpreter as she still does not speak English. I know that this is the girl for me. I have never felt what I feel for Anna, with anyone. Through her interpreter I find out that she feels the same about me. She will be mine in the end. I will bet money on it.

One weekend I go with her to Italy to meet her parents. Thank goodness her interpreter, Maria, comes with us. They live in one hell of a size villa in Castlemare di Stabia. They are really down to earth but I don't know how they feel about me, especially as they speak no English. Through Maria, I find out her mother does ask Anna how long she has known me, and Anna says that she has known me for some time.

We have a great weekend but then have to return to the Staff College.

Croxley informs me that when he leaves the College at the end of his course he will be taking up a job as Second in Command of a Rifle Battalion, and would I like to go with him. I tell him that I will have to think about it as I wanted Anna to marry me.

'Oh.' He replies.

That night I ring Anna and ask her to marry me. I know Maria is listening in and translating what I had said.

After a few minutes, she replies, 'Si.'

I'm over the moon; I'm going to marry the girl of my dreams.

Croxley informs me that he is on a Staff Exercise all over the weekend, so I am not needed.

The weekend comes and I take Anna to see my parents. Maria stays at the Staff College. To converse, we draw pictures in a small notebook plus use a phrase book.

I want to show her off to everyone. I tell my mother that we will be getting married in a few weeks' time.

'What's the rush son, she's not pregnant is she.'

'Good heaven no mum, It's just that I have a chance of a great posting and I want Anna to come with me.'

I'm not sure she believes me, but I know she likes Anna.

The weekend over, and the notebook is nearly full, we return to the Staff College, but miss the last train and have to get one that stops short of our destination.

'Che cosa intendiamo fare adesso?' Anna asks in Italian.

I draw in the notebook 2 people walking and say very slowly,

'We'll walk, it isn't very far and we should be back by midnight.' I say to her pointing to different phrases in my phrase book.

The walk is longer than I thought and we get into the College in the very early hours of the morning, totally knackered. Because of it, Anna sleeps in and misses a lecture period on ciphers.

The weeks go by and Anna still can't speak English and six weeks to the day virtually, we get married. The only words of English she knows are the ones she had been practising. "Yes" and "I Do."

As we get married in a Register Office our marriage is not recognised by the Catholic Church. This will cause us problems later in our married life.

Our honeymoon, if you could call it that, is at a Caravan Park at Walton-on-Naze. Nothing is open and the nearest town is Clacton-on-Sea. We spend the first night at the cinema as it is chucking it down with rain. The next day we have had enough and fly to Italy to Anna's parent's villa. What a honeymoon. Still, we did enjoy ourselves if you know what I mean.

After a week, I leave Anna at her mums and return to duty. I'm informed that as I am now married, I could not continue with the job I was doing. This I think is rather unfair, but the army is the army and their word is law.

I stay with Croxley until he is settled in Felixstowe and another guy takes over. I join the same Battalion and just after Christmas, I'm on my way to Malaya again. And who have they attached me to - 22 SAS Regiment. At last I will have some adventure. I can't tell Anna or any of my family what I am doing.

The Boss of the Squadron I'm joining is Johnnie Watt. He's a great guy and I'm looking forward to meeting him again.

The trip to Malaya is boring, but the anticipation of what is happening in the area we are going to in Borneo, gets the adrenalin flowing.

On arrival in Malaya, we again go to the Jungle Warfare School where we carry out up to date training in the art of Jungle Warfare.

Malaya must have the worst jungle in the world. Whilst we are out in the jungle, an aircraft flies over us and a load of soldiers exit it by parachute. We haven't been told that we are having an enemy on the training.

As we make our way towards the area they have dropped into, we are informed by radio that a large force of Indonesian Commandos have parachuted into the area. I presume these guys are they.

We change magazines to live rounds and just as we reach a small clearing, 50 soldiers are looking at us. They immediately raise their hands in surrender. The silly prats had forgotten to jump with their weapons. All are taken back to the Warfare School.

So ended, the Battle of the Malay Peninsula. (We even get a bar to our medals for this.)

Once we have completed the Warfare Course, we head off for Borneo on the LSL Sir Tristram.

(This LSL is later destroyed in the Falkland Islands War)

There are plenty of patrols and I love every minute of it. Two very good scraps with the Indos resulted in quite a few kills. Boy! How I wish I could stay with the Regiment when this little lot is over. All my mail has to be written as if I am with my battalion. Each letter is posted every couple of days, so that no-one will know what I'm up to. I really hate this as I have never kept a secret from Anna, well not too many anyway.

The highlight of this tour must be Kerangan. A bloody big hill, which you can only get up by being choppered in. A great laugh that turned out to be, I slid down a rope, let go, and find I'm still 40 feet from the deck. Having crashed through the trees with all my kit on, it's a wonder I wasn't killed or seriously injured. I wave to the guys not to come down until the rope is longer. Spike being Spike thinks he is John Wayne and slides down the rope as the chopper starts to reduce his height. And you have guessed it, Spike lands on his face. PRAT!

Once everyone is on the top of Karangan, the chopper leaves us. The basha's go up and would you believe it, we have land crabs. How they got up here I've no idea, but they have.

Over the next few days, we carry out long range observation on a couple of Indo Commando camps. They even send out a mortar party to try and shift us, but the stupid bastards can't get at us and their mortar bombs go harmlessly over the top of us and explode in the jungle.

It rains cats and dogs every day and I'm beginning to know how the navy feels when at sea. Bloody wet! I receive a radio message in code one night and after deciphering it, find that I have a baby girl and her name is Karen. What a fucking place to be told you are a dad.

If Anna knew what we were getting up to, she would have a heart attack. She now speaks perfect English, after going on an English Language Course at Beaconsfield. I have to be careful what I say as she understands everything, in fact, she speaks English better than me.

The operation comes to an end and the chopper comes and takes us off. I won't miss the place. I'm looking forward to a nice shower and a shave. Anna would hate the way I look at the moment.

The months go by and I return back to the 3rd Battalion just in time to return to England. I receive a photo of Anna and the baby. I write my first real letter to Anna, and tell her that I am looking forward to seeing them both.

Weeks go by and finally I arrive back in England. We are a family and we spend lots of time together until we get a posting to Germany. The barracks we are going to is at a place called Iserlohn which used to be inhabited by the Nazis during the war. Nice place but the people didn't like us. After a few months we ended up in a place called Celle. This is a lovely place and I get on great with the Housemaster of the block of flats we are living in. Anything wrong with the place and Richard fixes it immediately. We try for another baby and after a miscarriage we finally get Caroline.

The next few years are enjoyed travelling all over Germany with Anna and the two girls. Finally we get another posting. This time, away from the battalion. I'm posted to the recruiting office at the Depot in Winchester.

It is here that I learn how the Brigade spends money on recruiting. My budget is £500,000 a year to spend on literature and the like. My job is to look after the Display Teams who are near permanently on the road visiting different shows and schools throughout the year.

I'm at my desk typing a letter, when the door opens and a guy dressed in a suit comes in.

'Are you David Stubbs?' He asks.

'I am he.' I reply.

I would like to talk to you about working for us.'

'Who are us?' I reply.

'Um, the Secret Intelligence Service.'

'Do you mean MI6?' I ask.

'Err, Yes.'

'Bloody hell, what do you want me for? I'm no-one important.'

He talks for an hour on the service and what he would like me to do.

'Will you join us?'

'I'm not sure; I'll have to discuss it with my wife after all. It will affect her.'

'I'm afraid no-one must know about you working for us, and that includes your wife and family.'

'Stone the crows, you mean spying.'

'In a way, I must have your answer now.'

'I remember a mate of mine having the same conversation with someone in Germany, his name was Ronnie Colston, do you know him?' I asked.

'No, I don't know him, now are you going to join us?'

'Yes, I think so; after all, this job isn't exactly adventurous is it.'

'Well done, you will enjoy the experience, I can assure you. I will leave you now don't worry if you don't hear from us you will be contacted for training in due course. Welcome to the Firm.'

'But I am still in the Army, doesn't that matter?'

'No it won't, don't worry.'

As he leaves my office, he turns and says, 'Do not mention my visit to anyone.'

'Just out of curiosity, how did you get in?'

'I told the guardroom I was your brother.'

He then left. What in the name of Hell, have I got myself into?

Now that is another story................!

PART TWO

CHAPTER SEVENTEEN

What a day! Bored out of my tiny mind! There isn't much going on as the team is away in Budchester on a KAPE (Keep the Army in the Public Eye) tour, and being in charge, I'm stuck here to carry the can if anything goes wrong. The phone rings, it is Rfn Smith, my photographer; he is in the darkroom playing at being a photographer.

'Have you got those photographs back from the COI (Central Office of Information) yet Sir?'

'Not yet mate; I'll give them a bell and find out what has happened to them.'

'Just my luck, I was hoping to get them on the posters so I can finish early, Shit! Shit! Shit!'

Smudge isn't too bright but his hearts in the right place. They gave him the job as Recruiting Team Photographer because his CO (Commanding Officer) wouldn't put him in a Rifle platoon as he was quite dangerous with a rifle, i.e. he points it in the wrong direction. Just as I put the phone down, the office door opens and in walks a guy in a grey pinstriped suit.

'Hello Dave, how are you keeping?'

I rack my brain, the face looks familiar but I can't place it, then suddenly I remember.

'Simon isn't it?'

'Ah! You remembered it's been a long time since I last saw you, must be nearly a year.'

'Doesn't time fly when you are having fun?' I reply sarcastically.

Simon works for the SIS (Secret Intelligence Service) better known as MI6.

'What do you know about al Qa'eda?' he asks.

'Some sort of breakfast food is it.' I reply.

'Very droll, we have reason to believe that it is a terrorist group, operating in Asia. Our agent in Pakistan picked up some intelligence a couple of weeks ago, but no-one is saying what it or they are.'

'Well, I can assure you, I have never heard of al Qa'eda. Are you sure it is to do with terrorism?' (In Arabic, al Qa'eda means "the Base")

Who, or whatever this outfit is, it has certainly made MI6 jumpy. Simon carries on with his story.

'We know a man called Osama bin Laden is involved with it or may even be the head of it, but we don't have a clue what he looks like.'

'Well, Well, would you believe it, I met bin Laden once in Afghanistan, he is quite tall, about 6 foot, got a scraggy beard and is pretty skinny, I believe he is a multi-millionaire so would have money to fund a terrorist cell. Fanatical fighter by all accounts, he hates yanks though, not a guy I would trust.'

'Do you have any photographs of him?' Simon asked enthusiastically.

'Nope, not that I can think of, I seem to remember he didn't like his photo being taken.'

Simon changes the subject and hands me a large brown envelope.

'We want you to do a job for us, everything you need to know is in that envelope, once you have read it, destroy the contents, is that clear? Do not show it to anyone and that includes your wife, do you understand?'

'Perfectly.' I reply.

'Good, then I will be off; you will be debriefed when the job is completed, bye for now.'

With that he opens the office door and leaves.

Bloody hell! That was short and sweet, what the hell have I got myself into now? I can't even blame John; I don't know where he is. I must ring his mum sometime and find out, I'm sure she will know.

I'm just about to lock the office door when Smith turns up.

'Sir, all right if I bugger off, I can't complete those posters as I haven't got the photos!'

'Yeah! Push off, there isn't anything else outstanding, so go and enjoy yourself with your wife.'

'Some hope, you ain't seen my wife.' He replies walking off down the passage laughing.

I lock the door and open the envelope. Inside is a folder with **"SECRET"** stamped in red on the front. I open the folder and see a 6 by 8 colour photograph of a man. I turn it over; on the back are the man's details. The photo is pinned to 12 sheets of A4 paper. I start to read, line for line. Blimey, this little twat McWilliams is a PIRA Commander (Provisional Irish Republican Army) and has he done some things in his short life.

He has six murders to his name, two of the murders being soldiers, two bombings and a couple of bank jobs. He's also involved with gun running, and drug pushing. I am beginning to hate the man already. I detest drug dealers. They spoil the lives of everyone they come into contact with. And, as for killing soldiers, the less said the better. Killing soldiers in peace time is not on. They are in Northern Ireland acting as Police trying to bring some resemblance of normality to the provinces and, as such, have their hands tied.

The IRA and PIRA are causing more problems with their stupid ideas than you can shake a stick at. I have yet to fathom out how a man's funeral can bring out two or three thousand people none of whom knew the dead person. Talk about being brain washed. Some say that the troubles are over religion, others over a free united Ireland. Personally, they should pull the troops out, and napalm the country from top to bottom and give the place to the Russians as a submarine base.

The IRA and its counterparts are just hired thugs and contract killers who should be exterminated, as the Daleks say. Now let's get back to Mr McWilliams. This prat deserves a bullet. He lives on the outskirts of Galley gay. He has to be terminated before the 31st March. Why the 31st? Also in the envelope is a map, tickets for the train to Liverpool and for the boat from Liverpool to Belfast, and 60 pounds in ten pound notes. I have to pick up my equipment from a Johnnie Cole at 39 Infantry Brigade HQ in Lisburn to do the job. Christ! I hope they are not involved. Many a truer word spoken in jest!!!

I re-read the papers about 6 times, to make sure I know everything I need to know. I commit everything to memory and then put the papers one by one into the waste paper bin and set them alight.

I hope no-one sees the smoke otherwise the fire piquet will be up here. I mash the ashes into tiny pieces, unlock the door and go to the gents toilets and empty the bin into a pan and flush the chain. That's that lot gone for ever. I lock the office up and go home to plan when I will go to Northern Ireland. I'm quite lucky with my job, I can go anywhere in the country and no-one will bat an eyelid. That's what you can do when you are recruiting for your regiment.

My weekend is split between taking the children out and parachuting which I love. I did have a friend once who on operations, would say, "Why do we have to jump out of a perfectly serviceable aircraft." He was so scared to jump; I had to push him out. I must admit, I did admire his guts; he was absolutely shit scared but still jumped when he had to. Looking back on it, I suppose if you look at it logically, he was right. The mind boggles!!

Sunday night whilst watching the TV, totally exhausted from playing with the kids, I try to work out when I am going to go to Northern Ireland.

I will have to give the boss man, some excuse, like I have been invited to see how the other Regiments carry out their recruiting procedures. He's daft enough to believe it. I hope! I cannot understand why I have been recruited to the Firm or Box as it is sometimes known, though a friend of mine a few years ago was asked to join a weird outfit but never said who or what it was. He left the forces and I never heard of him again. I wonder if he joined the same outfit.

It is strange that after all this time the Firm suddenly comes and gives you something to do. I thought I would never hear from them again as it had been so long. In fact, I have never given them a thought. Although the man deserves to die, I don't know how I will feel when I do this job. It is nothing less than murder really. I mean we are not at war or anything, and what backup do I get from the Firm especially if things go wrong. How do I contact them, do I use the number on the back of the photograph. Not a very good way of running a department, or is it. They can deny all knowledge that I worked for them. The crafty bastards, I don't like the sound of this.

My head is spinning and I go into the kitchen to make a cup of coffee.

'You okay Dave?' my wife asks.

'Yes, I'm alright, I have some things I have to sort out before I go back to work. I might be away for a few days next week though, I want to go round some of the recruiting offices to see if they are up to date with our new posters and photos.'

What an excuse, but it's the best I could think up.

I hate lying to my wife, but the Firm said no-one was to know what I do for them and they specifically mentioned not informing my wife. I'm new to this game and I don't like it much. It would seem that this outfit wants someone to kill for them, and they take no risks whatsoever apart from giving you the information needed to do the job.

They can deny any knowledge that you ever worked for them; they could even have me killed by another operator for all I know. I wish John was around, I miss that old bastard, I wonder what he is up to, something to do with a woman that's for sure. He was always a buck rabbit. I only wish I had his flair for girls. The last time I heard from him he was joining a mercenary outfit somewhere in Angola. I must go and see his mum, I'm sure she will know exactly where he is and what he is up to.

CHAPTER EIGHTEEN

The boss, Major Alan Long, has agreed to my request to visit the Recruiting Offices in Liverpool and Nottingham. I knew he would. He is not really the type to be in charge of Recruiting. He certainly doesn't know much about the job, because he leaves everything to me. He was put into the job because he was passed over for promotion. Well, they had to put him somewhere and recruiting was the place.

My plan is to leave for Northern Ireland on Wednesday night. I'm going to get the 2300hrs night crossing from Liverpool which should get me into Belfast at about 0730hrs on Thursday morning. At the moment how I get to 39 Brigade is any ones guess. Do taxis go there or do I hire a car. I haven't worked that out yet.

I ring the number given to me and inform the operator that I will be catching the 2300hrs ferry from Liverpool to Belfast on Wednesday the 18th. The operator replies, 'I will pass the message on, thank you.' The phone then goes dead. That's them told. Happy lot, I don't think.

Wednesday arrives and I pack my gear for the trip. I tell my wife Anna that I will be gone for a few days and should be back by Saturday all being well. My train is the 0930hrs to London. I kiss Anna goodbye and make my way to Wantree station. The train leaves on time but is 10 minutes late arriving in London and I have to rush across town to get the train from Euston. I arrive with minutes to spare. I run to the barrier holding out my ticket.

'You've just made it Sir.' cried the ticket collector, 'Another minute and the gate would have been shut.'

I find a seat in a compartment of the 3rd carriage and put my case in the overhead rack.

'Going far?' asks a guy sitting opposite smoking a pipe.

Damn! It's a smoking carriage.

'I'm going over to Belfast on business.' I reply.

'Better you than me, I was over there a few weeks ago visiting a sick relative, nearly got blown up, terrible place, what business are you in then?'

Now I don't need people asking me a lot of questions especially at this stage of the game.

'I work for an insurance company, we have an office there, one of our managers requires some help with a claim and as I'm the expert in the type of claim under dispute, I've been detailed to go.'

I open my paper hoping he will take the hint that I don't want to talk. A whistle blows and the train shudders back and forth then starts to move out of the station.

'Well, I hope things turn out okay, I think I will go and get a cuppa, there is a buffet car on this train, fancy one?'

'No thanks, I've just had one at the station.'

He gets up and leaves. Thank Christ for that, I hope he stays in the buffet car all the way because I could do with some peace and quiet. I begin to sweat. It is probably something to do with nerves. I remove my jacket to cool down and begin to read my paper.

I must have dozed for an hour or so because the guy who asked me if I wanted a cuppa is shaking me.

'I think this is your stop?'

I look out of the window and find the train has arrived at Lime Street station.

'Thank you.' I reply getting up and putting on my jacket. I then pull my suitcase down from the rack and start to leave the train.

'Enjoy your trip.'

I mumble something in reply and leave the train. My first port of call is the "left luggage" office to leave my suitcase in. It's a long time before the ship sails and I don't want to be lugging a suitcase around when it is not necessary.

Liverpool is in the throes of being modernised. There are quite a few houses around the docks area being pulled down and modern ones being built. I find a café near the Adelphi Hotel and have a bite to eat. Afterwards, I have a look around China Town. The entrance to China Town has an ornate gateway which is pretty impressive. There must be thousands of Chinese living in Liverpool.

I while away the hours by looking into different shops and stalls. The place is a hive of activity. You can buy virtually anything in the market area.

I have tea in a Chinese café and then return to the station to collect my suitcase. The boat doesn't sail until 2300hrs so I've still got a long wait. Just round the corner from the station is a pub. I'll spend a few hours watching the TV in the lounge.

The publican is a very friendly guy.

'Are you going or coming from a trip?' He asks, pointing to my suitcase.

'I'm going over to our Belfast office to investigate a complicated insurance claim, it could take a few days or possibly a few weeks, I just don't know at present.' I tell him.

We continue talking between bouts of him serving customers drinks. He tells me he was once in the army and when he retired, bought into the pub with his mate. They have been running it for about seven years.

'What regiment were you in?' I ask him.

'The 2nd Green Jackets, the Kings Royal Rifle Corps.' He replies.

Blimey, that's a turn up for the books I say to myself. The hours fly by. I look at my watch; it is coming up to 2145hrs and I ask the landlord if he could call me a taxi. He nods his head and dials a number.

'Have one for the road.' He says giving me a gin and tonic. 'It's on the house.'

I thank him and just as I finish it, the taxi arrives. I shake his hand and thank him for his help.

'I hope I see you again.' He replies waving his hand.

In the taxi I tell the driver to take me to the Terminal for the overnight ferry to Belfast. We arrive and I find a large queue of people waiting to board. After ten minutes waiting, we finally start to embark and I make my way to a seat.

This is going to be a long night. I stow my suitcase under the seat and just as I am about to close my eyes when a voice says, 'Are these seats taken?'

I look up and see a very ugly girl.

'No, be my guest.' I tell her.

With that she starts to plonks herself down and shouts to someone further down the boat.

'Jan, up here, I've got us some seats.' Another ugly girl comes hurrying along carrying a baby.

'Thank God for that, I thought we would have to sit at that table all night, here look after Jamie for me while I go for a pee.'

With that, she dumps the baby in the girl's arms and scurries off. Both girls have Belfast accents.

After what seems like hours, the girl returns to her seat and takes hold of the baby. From their dress and the way they act I would say they come from a very run down council estate. The child stinks of piss, in fact the girls don't smell too good either. To think, I've got to suffer these three all night. At last, the boat starts to leave the dock and I try to get some sleep.

The seat is pretty upright and very uncomfortable as there isn't much leg room.

A few minutes go by when the kid starts to cry. Bloody hell! I don't need this. His crying has started another couple of babies off a few rows down. This is all I need. The mothers try to pacify their charges and after a few minutes, silence rains. Thank Christ for that; I hope it stays that way. But I know deep down it won't.

Throughout the night I manage to get a few minutes sleep. That is, between bouts of babies crying and mothers shouting. The stink from the girls is terrible, I wonder when they last had a wash, and in fact I wonder when the baby last had a wash. The smell now incorporates the smell of shit. I can't wait to get off this boat. The smell seems to permeate everything. All I hope is that they are not on the return trip. That would just about put the cat amongst the pigeons.

My watch says 0715hrs; people are milling around, putting on their coats and collecting their belongings and seem to be making for the exits, so we must have arrived. I retrieve my case from under the seat and gradually make my way to the queue to disembark. I've still got the smell of baby crap in my nostrils. How the hell people can travel like that, I'll never know. I finally leave the boat and make my way to the arrivals lounge. Once inside, I see a man holding a square of white paper with the name **"STUBBS"** on it.

'I'm Stubbs.' I tell him.

The man then informs me that he has been sent to take me to HQ 39 Brigade.

'Thank Christ for that, I was beginning to wonder how I was going to get there'

The journey is through some pretty hairy areas, you can see all around the pictures of the IRA, UDA and PIRA on the houses and the burnt out vehicles littering the side streets. I cannot understand why they get so worked up, it certainly isn't religion. It is just plain and simple murder that is committed by these factions.

Northern Ireland may be British, but it would be better if the government just handed it over, and let them get on with it. Let them kill each other and leave the rest of us alone. In fact, I still can't understand why we were not allowed to arrest and inter all the commanders we knew of in 1969. It would have saved us a lot of problems and the IRA wouldn't be as strong as they are today. The government has a lot to answer for, they caused the problem in the first place and now they can't get away from it. Because of this, Ireland has become one big "hands on" training ground for the military.

We finally arrive at the main gate to 39 Brigade. The driver shows his pass and the military policeman then asks me to get out and follow him into the guardroom. My case is taken from me and opened. A search of the inside is made. I am asked to empty my pockets and a search wand is passed over me.

'He's clear.'

'Blimey, you're thorough.' I say as I put the items back into my pockets.

'You can't be too careful, this is, Northern Ireland or haven't you realised that yet.' Says a chap in a blue pin striped suit. I look at him dumbfounded.

'Please come with me Mr Stubbs, there is someone who wants to meet you.'

We leave the guardroom and walk down the road and enter a small brick building. It is some sort of office and the place is in darkness. Pinstripe switches on a light. There are pulled blinds at all the windows.

'Please sit down Mr Stubbs; I'll be back in a few minutes.'

Pinstripe leaves the room and I'm left looking at bare walls. I notice in one corner a large grey aluminium case about 4 feet long. It holds my glance for a few seconds when pinstripe arrives back with another person.

'Hello Dave, how are you doing?' I look at the person who has just spoken, my brain works overtime.

'Fuck my boots, Ronnie Colston, what are you doing here? I thought I was supposed to meet a Johnnie Coles.'

'That's me, I work for SIS, and it has been a long time since we last met. We have a lot to talk about, would you like a drink or something?'

'I could do with a shave and a shower, I had the most awful family sitting next to me on the boat over, I'm sure I stink of shit.'

'No problem, let's go and see what we can do for you, I've got you a nice room in the mess, Oh, by the way, can you bring that case with you.' He said pointing to the ally case in the corner.

I pick up the case which feels quite heavy and follow Ronnie out of the room.

'The mess is just up here a ways, here let me carry your suitcase.'

I hand Ronnie my case and I follow him along the road. After a few minutes we come to a fairly large building.

'Here we are, the officer's mess, your room is just along the corridor, follow me.'

Ronnie shows me into a small ground floor bed-sit and pulls the curtains.

'Don't want anyone looking in, switch the light on.'

I find the light switch and click it on. He picks up the telephone by the bed and dials a number.

'Could you send coffee and sandwiches for two, to room 23 as soon as possible please and put them on my bill, Colonel Colston, thank you.'

Stone the crows, I didn't know Ronnie was a Colonel.

'Dave, why don't you get that shower while we are waiting?'

I rummage in my suitcase for my washing kit and undress. This is the life, en suite bathroom.

Having shaved and showered I now feel refreshed from the journey, I am about to ask Ronnie some questions when there is a knock at the door. Ronnie opens the door and a steward is standing there holding a tray of coffee and sandwiches.

'Thank you I'll take that.' Ronnie says taking the tray from the steward and closing the door.

'Right let's get down to business.'

'Fire away.' I reply pouring the coffee and taking a bite out of a sandwich.

'You have read the file that Simon gave you; do you think you can pull it off?'

'I'm not very happy with "Deniable Operations," what guarantees have I got that I won't be jailed for killing this guy?'

'You are working for us now that should be guarantee enough.'

'How much time have I got to check the place out?'

'Someone will show you the house where McWilliams lives. How you do the job and get out is up to you, believe me Dave, you are the best man for this job. We would not have asked you to join us if we thought you couldn't do the jobs we want you to do.'

'How the fuck did you get into this Ronnie, did they pressure you or something?'

'When I was in the Green Jackets I was summoned to the CO's office, there a guy put lots of questions to me and then asked me, if I would like to join the SIS, just as you were asked. I decided that as I wasn't getting anywhere in the mob, it might be just the thing I was looking for, no-one made me join, it was my decision, I haven't regretted it, after all, would I have made Lieutenant Colonel in the Green Jackets, I think not.'

'Have I got any choice in this?' I ask.

'Do you want lies or the truth?'

'Truth'

'No you haven't got a choice.'

'Oh well, I thought I'd ask, no harm done.'

'Right, let's get on, bring the ally case over.'

I pick the case up and put it on the bed, there is a digital lock on the side.

'The number is 1098.'

'How appropriate, the number of a stores requisite.'

I key in the number and the case opens. I lift the lid and find nestling in thick soft foam rubber an Accuracy International AW 7.62mm Suppress barrelled Sniper Rifle complete with a Hensoldt 10-60x 72 telescope.

'Good God!' I say out loud, 'This is some beast.'

I take it out and look it over. The frame work is all aluminium, but still feels heavy. I undo the bipod and put the rifle on the floor. The rifle is based on the British Army L96A1 Sniper Rifle designed by Malcombe Cooper; an excellent target shooter (now deceased).

The scope is one of the best I have seen; it has great magnification at 300 yards. This rifle will take the pip out of the ace of spades at 600 yards easily. The magazine should hold 12 rounds of 7.62 but this one only holds 3.

I can't wait to fire this rifle but it will need to be zeroed first as it will fire low due to the very long silencer. The ammunition will be less powerful to.

'When do I get to zero this beast Ronnie?'

I again look inside the box and find 25 rounds of green spot 7.62mm ammunition lined up neatly in their own respective holes and 25 rounds of 7.62 ceramic head ammunition. (This ammo shatters on impact so there is no ricochet) The ammunition must be sub-sonic specially designed for this rifle. Normal green spot ammo has a full metal jacket of about 168 grains and about 175 grains of powder for accuracy. God knows what these rounds have. They certainly won't be as powerful that's for sure.

Also in the case is a military 15x56 Night Scope and a Welrod Silenced 7.65mm Pistol with 2 magazines, and 25 rounds of 7.65mm ammo.

The Welrod is a brilliant weapon, very accurate at up to 50 feet and extremely silent. Even close up you won't hear it. I used one once in the SAS to great effect.

'Tomorrow I want you to take the rifle to the ranges to get it zeroed in. No-one will see you I have made sure that there will not be any other person on the range except a friend of yours, Pete Dickson'

'Is Pete involved with this job?'

'Partially, he will be around for your protection and to drive you about.'

We finish off the coffee and sandwiches and I put the rifle and pistol back into the case and lock it.

'This case will be available to you whenever you require it.' Ronnie said taking the case off the bed and putting in a cupboard.

'Shouldn't that be put into the armoury?'

'You must be joking; the bastards would be prising the hinges off to see what was inside. No, it's safer here. Come on I want to show you round before Pete turns up for your recce.'

We leave my room and just as we are leaving the mess Pete turns up.

'When they said I was to look after a very important person, they didn't say it was you, you old sod, how are you?

I grab Pete's hand and shake it.

'Nice to see you as well, you are just as bald as ever; have you ever thought of wearing a wig?'

We both laugh and hug each other.

'Boy, am I glad to see someone else I know, you coming with us or waiting here?'

'I'll wait mate, I can see Ronnie wants to talk to you on your own.'

Pete is a mate from when I was with the SAS; we went on quite a few jobs together and drank a few jars as well. Pete leaves us and we go off down the road towards some porta cabins.

'Your mates are in them together with 14 Int. They do lots of undercover work over here.'

'Yes, I know, I came over once in the early years of the troubles for a month or so, nothing has changed then?'

We continue down the road to some buildings that house the Intelligence Corp. We enter a room, not un- familiar to offices I have seen before.

'Sit down Dave, while I look for the file.'

Inside the room is a long table covered in green baize and 12 upright chairs. There are filing cabinets along one wall. Above the filing cabinets the walls are covered in red curtains, just like my old bosses room at Hereford, only they were blue. Ronnie is looking through a cabinet and suddenly pulls out a file.

'This is it.' He says walking back to the table.

'You have the rest of today and part of tomorrow to recce the area, Pete will take you in an undercover car to the drop off point.'

'So I have got plenty of time then.'

'I want you to read this file and digest every bit of it especially the photo of the man you are going to terminate. This man as you know is a Commander in the Provisional IRA and has been a thorn in our side for months.'

'Why haven't the Security Forces taken him out?'

'The security forces have tried on numerous occasions, but he seems to get away each time. He is well known to the people in the area and as such, he is hidden by them if he needs to lie low. He is, for want of a better word, their mascot. He is staying with a family who are staunch Republican supporters. It isn't going to be easy; he has many disguises and will never venture out on his own.'

'Really! What's he scared of'?'

'He is guarded day and night by at least 4 men that we know of who are heavily armed. This man must be terminated by early Friday evening at the latest as you must be back on the mainland by Saturday afternoon. Read the file and I'll be back in a few minutes.'

Bugger me, it's Thursday now, I've got to zero the weapons and do a recce of this prats area, it doesn't leave me much time.

I read the file; it is the same as the one I read and destroyed in Winchester only with a bit more detail. Chummy is a right little bastard, he has quite a few kills to his credit and 2 are soldiers. The security forces are here for their benefit, not to be killed. It seems that soldiers are fair game to this man, well, with a bit of luck, I'll change all that.

The man lives on a Republican estate just outside Galleygay. If I remember correctly, the troubles started there in 1969. I know the area very well, I was undercover with the Regiment in '69 and Galleygay was the place to be at the time. I remember lifting a guy who had a stiff leg which turned out to be a 1914/18 bayonet stuck down his trousers. A particularly nasty little scrote he was.

As I close the file, Ronnie comes back in.

'Well what do you think?'

'A right nasty little wanker, who will get his comeuppance very shortly, I didn't like the bit where he killed the 2 soldiers, that's not on in my book, let's get on with it.'

We leave the room in silence and make our way back to the mess.

Just as we enter the mess, a vehicle turns up. It is a bit battered and the driver looks familiar. The driver gets out and hands Ronnie the keys.

'Stone me,' the driver says, 'What the fuck are you doing back here?'

'Nice to see you as well Colin, sorry can't tell you mate.'

Colin was another of my team in the Regiment and I haven't seen him for well over a couple of years.

'Wait till I tell the lads I've seen you, you owe quite a few of them a drink from the last fiasco we were on, come on Ronnie what's he up to?'

'Sorry Colin, but it's a bit hush hush at the moment.'

'Fair enough, you don't mind me telling the lads that he is here though, do you?'

'They probably already know, Pete has seen him already.' Ronnie replies.

Colin starts to laugh and walks off back the way he had driven waving his hand in the air. Christ, how many more of the buggers are here, this could get really outrageous, in the drinking stakes that is. Ronnie uses the hall telephone. A few minutes later, Pete turns up.

'Take him to Port Lake Road Pete and show him the area.'

'Does Pete know what I am here for?' I ask Ronnie quietly.

'Yes he does, but he is the only one, no-one else knows. Pete is your backup if things go wrong, and they might, especially in the area you are going to, just be careful and don't stand out like a sore thumb.'

Pete and I climb into the beaten up car and make our way to the gate. The barrier lifts and we are waved through, no-one checks us. I did see the guy write down something on a pad though. Our journey is in silence.

The minutes tick by as we proceed down the M1 to junction 9 and turn off onto the A3. We are soon on the outskirts of Galleygay. Pete stops in a lay-by and checks that we have not been followed. He hands me a small radio.

'It's on frequency, only use it in dire emergency, the bastards have scanners and are always listening, keep it in your pocket switched off. You had better take this as well, the mags full.' He says handing me a 9mm pistol.

'Thanks mate.'

'About 300 yards up there on the left is Port Lake Road, the house you want is number 12, and it is on the right 6 houses down as you enter the road. The houses either side have dogs, be careful, I'll wait here with the bonnet up, that way people going by will think I have got something wrong with the engine. Now off you go and get the recce over with.'

I get out and put the pistol in my waist band at the back. I look out of place; I haven't had time to change my appearance to any degree. This is going to be some recce. I make my way along the road and turn into Port Lake road. I can see it is a very small road. It is tree lined on one side. The gardens at the front are very small with little wooden fences about a foot high. Each garden has a dustbin by the gate. They must empty the bins from the front.

Just as I get to number 12, the door opens and a dog runs out.

'Come here you little fucker.' A man shouts as he comes out of the front door carrying a bag of rubbish.

I can't believe my eyes, the man is McWilliams. This is too good to miss. I pull the 9mm pistol from the back of my waistband and aim it straight at him from about 10 feet. He looks at me and there is a shock of horror in his eyes.

'What the……!'

Bang, Bang.

I fire off 2 rounds in quick succession. One round hits him in the face and the other in the centre of his chest. McWilliams falls to the ground and I immediately turn round and run as fast as I can back the way I came.

As I turn the corner I see Pete closing the bonnet of the car and jump in. He has obviously heard the shots. The vehicle speeds towards me and as it is level, the passenger door opens. I dive in and we speed off up the road.

'What the fuck went wrong?' He cries trying to keep the car straight.

'An opportunity came up that couldn't be missed.' I tell him, 'the bastard came out to empty a bag of rubbish just as I got to the house. No-one else was about, so I took the chance and shot him, one in the face and one in the chest. It was an opportunity too good to miss.'

'Let's get out of here.'

As we turn onto the main drag back to Lisburn, 2 police cars and 4 land rovers full of troops shoot past us.

'Now I wonder where they are going.' Pete said slowing the vehicle down to the correct speed.

'Must be dinner time I suppose.' We both laugh out loud.

I begin to get the shakes as the reality of the incident kicks in. All I hope is that no-one saw me, I'm sure no-one did, but you can't be sure.

By the time we enter Brigade HQ, my hands stop shaking. The soldier on the barrier stops us, checks the vehicle registration and us and then waves us through. They have obviously done this many times, but you can't be too complacent, who knows, someone else could be in the vehicle. Pete stops the car outside the mess.

'Keep the radio and pistol with you Dave, you never know when they might come in useful, come over to the porta cabins tonight and meet your old buddies.'

'Okay mate, I'll be over after I've had some scran, see you later.'

Returning to my room I lay on the bed. Jesus am I knackered, I haven't stopped since I got here. Bloody hell! What a start to the day. The phone rings and Ronnie is on the line.

'Well how did the recce go?'

'McWilliams is dead.' I tell him.

'I'm coming right over.'

With that the phone goes dead. I suppose this is going to be a big bollocking.

Ronnie enters my room and asks for an appraisal.

'We got to the road and as I was walking down it, who should come out, but McWilliams, he was alone except for a dog which ran out in front of him, it was too good a chance to miss, so I took him out, I don't think anyone saw me either. It was just a stroke of luck.'

'Jesus! I'm impressed, everything about you seems to be justified as I knew it would be, the reports on you certainly bear out your actions.'

'I am a great believer of, if you can do it straight away, then do it, saves time later.'

'I'm glad you have joined us Dave, the jobs that you will be given, will save this god forsaken country from being overrun by terrorists, we need more people like you, but and I mean but, we can only afford one and that one, is you.'

'Christ, I'm going to be unique then.' (This is something I will later regret)

'I'll have to report this to London immediately. The car will have to be scrapped so it can't be used again, bloody heck; I didn't expect to change the cars this soon.' Ronnie says as he starts to leave.

The grin on his face says it all, I'm glad I've made someone happy. The reality of it is, I am numb inside. I have just committed murder for the government.

CHAPTER NINETEEN

The Department now has me over a barrel and I am committed to them. It does look as if they will be able to manipulate me any way they see fit. Any job no matter what it is, they will be there in the wings, ready to make me do it. What the hell have I got myself into?

I take another shower and whilst the warm water washes over me, ponder over the last few hours. After my shower, I lie on my bed and doze off.

Some hours later, I'm woken by noise coming from the corridor. It is some officers coming back from an op or something. I get up and dress. Just as I am leaving, the telephone rings. I answer it, it is Ronnie.

'Before you go to dinner I want to talk to you concerning another job. Meet me in the mess bar.'

Now what did I say, another job which I won't be able to refuse. I put the pistol and radio in my bedside cabinet and leave the room.

On the way to the bar, I think to myself, I suppose I should go and see the lads and have a drink with them, but they will have to wait until I have seen Ronnie and had something to eat, I'm starving.

The bar is packed with officers from 39 Brigade and visiting regiments who are on the streets of the surrounding towns. I wonder what poor sap is on duty in the control room. I bet it is some 2nd Lieutenant wet behind the ears that, if anything happens, will carry the can. Poor sod. I don't envy him.

After about 10 minutes, Ronnie enters the bar.

'What will you have Dave?'

'Gin and Tonic, please Ronnie.'

He gets the drinks and ushers me over to a table away from the rest of the rabble.

'How do you feel now?' He asks.

'Numb is the only way I can describe it.'

'Don't worry; you did the country a great service. Now, I have another job for you, my team are getting the file together as we speak. This one will take a bit longer to do. Are you religious?'

'No, I don't believe in that crap, do you?'

'You can't afford religion in our job, your code name from now on is "God".'

'What's that, the difference between life and death?' I say sarcastically.

'You could say that.' He replies.

A steward comes over to the table.

'There is a telephone call for you Sir.'

Ronnie thanks the steward and gets up. 'I won't be long.'

With that he goes off towards the bar. I sit watching the other mess members and down my drink.

'You're new here, aren't you? Haven't seen you in the mess before, my names Arthur Dennis, I'm the G2 Ops, what's your name then?' A rather oldish major asks.

'Captain Dave Stubbs, I'm just visiting the Brigade for a couple of days to see how the other half live.'

'Well I hope you enjoy your visit, do come over to HQ and have a chat and a cuppa, catch you later then.' With that he left. Friendly people, I say to myself.

Ronnie returns. 'Well, you can forget that job, it's off. The person concerned has just been killed in a road accident, now that saves us a job.'

Thank heavens for that, I didn't really want to do another killing just yet.

'What a shame, just when I was getting my hand in.' I say with a smirk.

'You are a sarcastic bastard.' Replied Ronnie laughing, 'Piss off and get some scran and then get drunk with your mates, and don't forget you have to be on the range early.'

Ronnie leaves and I make my way to the dining room where I have a wonderful dinner. After coffee I make my way over to the porta cabins. Just as I enter, a very large guy pushes passed me.

'Steady on mate.' I say as he kicks the door open.

'Fuck off.' He replies.

'Fuck you too sunshine.' I say in retaliation.

'Hi ya mate.' Says Pete as I enter the bar area.

'Who the hell was that prat who just left?' I ask.

'You've met Garth then, don't take any notice of him, he's just been told he is going back home.'

'And he's anti because of that?'

'Well not only that, he was also told he has been RTU'd.' (Returned to Unit)

'Oh, I see, no wonder he's in a bad mood, what's he done?'

'He told the RSM (Regimental Sergeant Major) to go fuck himself.'

'That's not a sack able offence; we use to do that all the time when we were on ops.'

'Yes, but he also asked him if he wanted some porno pictures of his missus.'

'Oh dear.'

'Let's get pissed before the mob returns, your round I think Dave?'

I make my way to the bar and get waylaid by a further 3 guys I know. After paying for their drinks, I return to Pete.

'Sod this mate, it's getting bloody expensive here, who else am I going to bump into?'

'Have you met Blue yet?'

'Christ is he here to? There must be the whole of 16 Troop here.'

'Not quite but near enough, here, it's my round.' Said Pete.

We sink quite a few, before all and sundry turn up.

'Well look whose here, about time you bought a drink.' Blue said grabbing my hand.

'Trust you to turn up for free drinks, you old bastard, how you doing?'

'Pretty damn good mate, what are you up to out here?'

'Secret squirrel stuff.' I tell him tapping the side of my nose.

The drinks flow fast and furious and everyone is getting slightly the worst for wear. I must try and keep a clear head; I have to be on the range in the morning. Just as I am about to get another round in, a siren goes off.

'What the fuck is that?' I ask.

'That's to tell us someone has burnt the bloody dinner.'

The mind boggles!!!

As the evening progresses, I begin to get very light headed.

'I think I'll call it a day guys, I've got to be on the range early.'

Everyone tries to get me to stay but they don't succeed and I stagger back to the officer's mess and crash out on my bed and sleep the sleep of the dead.

'Wake up Sir!' Someone says shaking me, 'Your breakfast has been arranged for 0800hrs Sir.'

I look at my watch. Through the blue haze I see that the luminous hands say 0700hrs.

'Thanks mate.' I say not knowing who had woken me or which or what day it is.

I get a quick shower and shave and go to the dining room. After I have my breakfast, Ronnie comes into the mess.

'Christ you look like something the cats dragged in, good night was it?'

'I don't know, I can't remember.'

'Never mind I've only come to make sure you get to the range to zero your weapon in, Pete will be here shortly. He will be bringing the ammo with him. I will arrange a seat on tonight's boat for you to get back to the mainland. Make sure you do a good job on the rifle. You should be back by 1500hrs; I'll see you then, enjoy yourself.' Ronnie then leaves the mess. After about 10 minutes, Pete arrives, and we drive off to a firing range. No one is about and we unload the weapons box.

'Right let's see what you can do with this monster.'

Targets are put at 100, 200, 300, and 500 yards. The ammunition is green spot 168 grains. The stock is bolted to a vice which has been anchored in the ground. This is to make sure there is no shaking. I move the rifle by using the dials on the vice. I then turn the rifle onto the 100 yard target. The cross wires are dead centre of the target.

Boof!

Through the telescope I can see the shot has hit the target 4 inches to the left of the centre and 2 inches high. I turn the sight dials a couple of clicks and fire again.

Boof!

The shot is central but still an inch above the centre. I turn the dial another click.

Boof!

The round has struck dead centre. I carry on until I have sighted all the distances to dead centre. I then take the rifle out of the vice and manually sight the 200 yard target.

Boof!

The round hits dead centre. Great! I've now zeroed the rifle. This is one hell of a weapon.

Pete hands me the ceramic ammo.

'Try these rounds with the ceramic heads; they say they will stop ricochets, but will still go through a body. You can use them up to 300 yards. They don't have the same grains as the green spot, so will shoot lower, make a note of the settings you have now that the rifle is zeroed with jacketed. Then make a note of the settings for the ceramic ammo.'

I load a round into the chamber and aim at the centre of 100 yard target.

Boof!

The round hits the centre about 1 inch low. I turn down the elevation 2 clicks and reload a round.

Boof!

This time it is dead centre. I then aim at the 200 and 300yards targets.

Boof!

The rounds all hits dead centre. I finish of the rest of the ceramic rounds just to make sure, all go into the centre of the target. That's it, all zeroed. I make a note of the settings on a piece of paper and put it in the lid of the weapon container. We use up the rest of the jacketed ammo, and then I clean the rifle, and pack it away.

I have never been pushed so hard. The few days that I have been in Northern Ireland have been non-stop. I feel totally drained.

'Well mate, its back to the mess for you, I'll take care of the rifle.'

'Thanks Pete, your help has been much appreciated. I have really enjoyed your company.'

'Piss off you pillock, what are mates for?'

We drive back to 39 Brigade HQ and Pete drops me off at the mess. Back in my room, I have a shower and then pack my case. I leave out my blazer and slacks for travelling home.

Someone taps on the door. I open it and Ronnie hands me an envelope.

'Your tickets for the journey, the boat goes at 1900hrs, Pete will drive you to the ferry.'

He shakes my hand and leaves. As he walks down the corridor he turns and says, 'Thanks Dave.'

Thanks for what, I say to myself, I am now totally beholding to the Firm.

I ring the mess sergeant and ask for a sandwich and coffee to be brought to my room. As I am eating my sandwich the phone rings.

'I'll be with you in 10 minutes.'

'Okay mate I'll be ready.' I tell him.

Pete arrives and I throw my case into the car and nearly hit Blue sitting in the rear seat.

'What the hell!' I say out loud,

'Thought I would ride shot gun.' He replies.

'I could have caved your head in, dumb nut.' I tell him.

'Do him the world of good if you had.' replied Pete.

We leave the safety of 39 Infantry Brigade and drive off in the direction of Belfast to catch the ferry to Liverpool. Five minutes into the journey, Pete starts up a conversation.

'It's been great seeing you again Dave; we really haven't had much chance to talk, have we? What have you been up to since we last met?'

'Would you believe running a Recruiting Office in Wantree.'

'Bloody hell!' replied Blue, 'That must be as exciting as watching paint dry.'

'No! Watching paint dry is more entertaining.' I tell him.

'How did you get involved with the Firm then Dave?' Pete asked.

I proceed to tell him how I had a visit from a member of the Firm asking me to join them.

'I was dubious at first as I wasn't really sure what to make of them, I knew about them, everyone does, but joining them was a different kettle of fish, I never heard a thing from them for nearly a year then they turn up one day and give me this job, the rest you know.'

'They have got you by the short and curlies now Dave, that's for sure.' Pete replies.

'Don't I know it, did you know I use to serve with Ronnie in 3 RGJ.'

'I didn't know that.' Pete replied.

'Yep, he had the same type of recruitment; he was just coming up for demob when they offered him a job.'

'You must be the first member of the Regiment to be asked to join them, because I haven't heard of anyone else being asked, have you Pete?' Remarked Blue.

'No I don't think so, Dave you must be the first.'

We drive in silence for a mile or so when Pete says,

'Do you remember the time we were on that Operation in Borneo to take out those Indonesian Commandos and that cook came at us with that fucking great machine gun.'

'I sure do, I kept telling you to kill him and all he did was keep coming, I remember saying you were missing when in fact he had more lead in him than on a church roof when he dropped, it was the weight of the gun that made him come on.'

'Those were the days mate.'

We all laugh.

Blue pipes up,

'Do you remember the time I got my head down amongst the Av-Gas drums and they received a direct hit?'

'Of course I remember, there was a hundred feet of flame and you came running out with your clothes smouldering shouting "fuck me, it was hot in there," and I thought you had copped it.'

'What about the time we were in that ambush position and that grenade landed by your arm and you said, "It's been nice meeting you" as you pointed to the grenade, and all it did was fizz. We were really lucky that day mate.' Pete said.

'We trained hard and fought easy, things were different in those days.' Blue said.

'Yes, but the best one was when we were in that ambush position and you decided to take up bird watching, and because of it, the Indos walked straight by. Those were the days.'

We carry on talking and thinking back to the days long gone. I think they were the good old days.

As we turn into the port, I say to Blue, 'How's old Sid these days?'

'He was retired from the Regiment about 5 months ago, got a bullet in the lung in Columbia.'

'Christ! I didn't know that, why didn't anyone contact me?'

'No-one knew where you were, the feelers went out, but was blocked at every angle, so we couldn't contact you.'

'I bet the Firm blocked you.' I reply.

'Well we ended up here before any of the boys could check it all out.'

'I'll go and see him when I get back, does he still live in that cottage on the Brecon road?'

'Sure does, he uses it as an office now, does freelance work showing people how to protect their houses, for a fee of course.'

'Always out to make a buck is our Sid, do you remember the time he parachuted out of that jet into my shell scrape during that fire fight because the NAAFI (Navy, Army and Air Force Institutes) had run out of fags. I told him I had stopped smoking and with that got up and started running to another position when that Colonel in the Scots mob saw him running towards the enemy, got his men up and they all charged and the enemy surrendered. The silly prat was recommended for bravery and got the bloody DCM (Distinguished Conduct Medal) and for what, trying to get a fag. If only that Colonel knew, Sid didn't even have a gun.'

'That was our Sid.' Replied Blue.

'Well mate! We are here, don't leave it too long before we get together again.' Said Pete.

'I second that.' Said Blue.

'Sod off you pair of useless articles; of course we will meet up again.' I tell them.

I retrieve my suitcase from the back seat.

'Now piss off you two, I don't like goodbyes.'

The car drives off and I make my way to the departure lounge.

At the desk I show my ticket and wait in the queue to board. I hope I don't have to sit next to another bloody grubby bunch like I did on the way over. It was great seeing the guys again, shame I couldn't stay longer.

I hope Pete keeps out of trouble, though I doubt it, trouble is his middle name, that's how he got the DCM and bar and four mentioned in despatches. A real trouble maker is our Pete and Blue is no different, three mentioned in despatches and the MM (Military Medal).

The boat journey is very relaxing, virtually empty and definitely no unmarried mothers with screaming kids thank goodness. I stretch out on three seats, luxury.

The whole trip has been go-go-go from start to finish. I now know what happened to Ronnie and why he left the Green Jackets. It's a strange old world we live in.

On arrival home, I'm greeted by Anna and the kids. I kiss Anna and cuddle the girls.

'I have really missed you, what's for dinner, I'm starving.'

After we have eaten and washed up, I settle down on the couch with Anna and before I know it, I'm out for the count. It has been a hell of a few days.

CHAPTER TWENTY

Nearly a year has gone by and my time in the Army is up. I won't say I will miss it because I enjoyed what I did, and have made many friends along the way who will be friends for life. What more can I say.

The quarter is packed up and we move to a house in Languard. The house is pretty grand with a lovely big garden, but it has one hell of a big hedge all around it. This hedge is about 8 feet high and about 5 foot in width.

Over the next few weeks we sort the house out and plant out the garden with all sorts of vegetables.

One day whilst planting out some lettuce my neighbour shouts, 'Shame these hedges are so big, we could chat if they were lower.'

I tell him that I'll cut a gap so we can chat. After about 20 minutes, I have cut a gap out of the hedge 4 feet wide and I can now see my neighbour.

He introduces himself as Bob Wyatt an ex RSM in the Royal Marines. I tell him who I am.

'Do you know, if this hedge was gone we would have one hell of a big garden.'

'I suppose you are right mate but it will take forever to take this hedge out, I hate the thing because I have to bloody cut it.'

I get called in for lunch and leave Bob looking at the hedge.

I tell Anna that I have met our neighbour and that he seems a very likeable chap when all of a sudden there is an almighty whoosh and I see 60 feet of flame in the garden.

'Holy cow we've been nuked.' I tell Anna, and with that, run outside to where Bob is standing by the blackened stumps of the vanished hedge rubbing his hands.

'There, that got rid of it.' He tells me.

'Fuck me mate what did you do?'

'I sprayed it with petrol and bobs your uncle - we'll be able to dig the stumps out easily, shouldn't take more than a few hours labour.' He tells me.

We spend all afternoon digging out the stumps.

'What did I tell you, we have got a lot more ground?'

I must admit he is right.

Over the coming weeks we plant out the extra bit of garden with different vegetables so that we can help ourselves from either garden.

My other neighbour has also got a bigger garden since removing the hedge. He comes out and introduces himself.

'Hope you are settling in okay, my names Henry, can I get in on the action?' He asks. Henry works for a bakery in the town called Johnston's. (This bakery no longer exists)

I start a job in Woodcote about 20 miles away. Not my scene really but it will help to keep the wolves from the door.

As I am about to clock off, I'm stopped by a guy in a leather jacket.

'Are you Dave Stubbs?' he asks.

'Who wants to know?' I ask in return.

He shows me an ID card, a type I have seen before.

'I need to talk to you alone.' He replies.

He is from the Firm and his name is Jason Coombes.

'Every time I see one of you people something happens.' I tell him.

We go to my car; a blue mini cooper parked in the road outside my works, and get in.

'We have a job for you. You will need to be billeted at Fort Duncan. Do you know where it is?'

'Yes.' I reply.

'You will go to Fort Duncan on the 29th of September. Just show this letter to the Security Guard at the end of the bridge; he will direct you to the relevant personnel. I know you live in Languard and you could get home every night, but you will be carrying out things at night so it has to be residential, do you understand?'

'Anna isn't going to like this one bit.' I tell him.

'I'm afraid it cannot be helped. Tell her you are visiting some workshop up country for a few weeks.'

'How long will I be there?' I ask him.

'You will be told later.' He then tells me that he is now my controller and hands me a large envelope.

'All you need to know is in that envelope.'

He gets out of the car and then walks off. Talkative bastard.........!

I drive off home getting stuck in massive traffic jams on the B27 to Sumpton. As I live on the peninsula of Languard, the traffic is horrendous since they built the fly over at Sumpton. Languard will never be able to stop the long tail back of traffic entering and leaving the town, no matter how many investigations they will probably hold in the years to come.

Having spent an hour in traffic jams, I finally arrive home exhausted. Before going into the house I open the envelope and read what is inside. The course starts in a week's time. That will give me time to think of a good excuse, though the one Jason told me sounded just about right. I think I will use that. I put the envelope in by bag and go into the house.

The children are arguing over who should get a cuddle first. I grab them both and we all go into the lounge and sit on the sofa. I'm then told what they have got up to at school.

The weekend comes and we take the kids out for the day. When we arrive back home, I tell Anna that I will be away on Monday the 29th visiting a company up north and that I won't be home for about a week or so. She isn't pleased.'

'We were going home to see my mum that weekend.' She says walking out of the lounge.

'I know sweetheart, but it can't be helped, we can go when I come back, I'm sure your mum won't mind.'

I look at my watch it is 6 o'clock. 'Come on let's take the kids for a drive.'

We drive off to Hamber sea wall and walk along it. Quite a few people are sea fishing. About 50 yards out on the sea a guy is pulling in his catch. As he pulls the fish into his boat, it turns out to be a big conger eel. It takes a chunk out the gunwale just where his foot would have been a few seconds earlier and he leaps into the water and tows the boat with his rod, to the safety of the sea wall. The hook is still in the eel's mouth. He climbs up the slope of the wall.

'Look at the size of this bugger; he'll make ruddy fine eating.' He says laughing.

Better him than me.

Fort Duncan is at the end of the sea wall. I can see that it is fenced in with a 10 foot high wire fence with razor wire on the top. There are cameras situated at different point around the place. I bet they cover every inch with no gaps.

As we walk round to the golf course I see the entrance to the fort is over a little bridge. Standing at the entrance is a guy wearing the uniform of the MOD Police. I didn't know there was a contingent of Mod Plods at the fort. (I later find out that there isn't)

As I am looking at the fort, a helicopter flies into the fort. I can't see who is in it as it flies down into the court yard. We turn around and walk back to the car parked at the sea wall; three cars of people pass us and enter the fort over the bridge. They must be on a course.

It is getting late and we return home. The children are shattered and take off to bed.

Fort Duncan is a weird place. The stories that I have heard about the place take some believing. If they only knew, it was used by the Firm for courses. One of the courses they conduct there is on surveillance. They use the streets of Brandon town centre sometimes. Even the SAS use the place, hence the helicopters. The firing range is used virtually every day, as the red flags are always flying. Security there is extremely high, that's for sure.

I am slowly coming to terms with being an operator with the SIS (Secret Intelligence Service) takes some getting used to. The envelope didn't say what job I would be doing. It can't be anything else but killing people, I wouldn't think it would be on explosives, I know all about them, even to making explosives out of house hold materials. It can't be on concealment either; I had the best training in the world on that. Could it be medical? No, I can already do an appendectomy with a pen knife in an emergency. I even know how to shit in a black plastic bag. Done that many times. I just don't know what it could be. But, I will soon find out.

Whilst Anna is putting the girls to bed, I re-read the letters in the envelope. They give nothing away. There is a lot of stuff on the security of the fort and who I have to report to on entry and that everything to do with the place is subject to the Official Secrets Acts. There is no mention of what I will be doing.

Perhaps I am reading too much into this. I put the envelope and its contents onto the fire just as Anna shouts that one of my daughters wants a story read. Never dull moments in my house hold. At times the kids run me ragged, but I enjoy it. My wife and children are my life. Heaven help any person who tries to do them harm. I am paid to kill, but if I found that anyone had tried to harm them, I would kill that person or persons for free and to hell with the consequences.

Now that the girls have settled down, Anna and I settle down to watch TV.

'Dave?'

'Yes darling.'

'Are you up to something?'

'Now what would I be up to, I have finished with the Army, I'm now a happy family man.'

'I found a letter in your bag, it says you are to go to Fort Duncan, we went past that place tonight with the girls, are you keeping something from me?'

'Ah! You really shouldn't have read that darling, but as you have, what I am about to tell you is extremely secret. I work for the government in a position you do not want to know about. They have sent me to Fort Duncan to do a job, what it is, I do not know. I have no idea why. That is the truth.'

'Is it dangerous for you?' She asks.

'Possibly.' I tell her.

'But you said you had finished with all that, and I believed you. Do I have to go through all the worry again?'

'I honestly don't know darling, I really don't.'

Anna doesn't speak to me and gets up and leaves the lounge. There is no point in continuing the presence that I was going on a visit as she now knows the truth. And to top it all she isn't speaking to me now.

Anna returns to the lounge.

'You said that you would now be at home as you had finished with the army, you said we would be able to spend more time with each other, it looks as if that has now gone out the window.'

'Darling what I am about to tell you is very highly classified and must never be discussed with anyone except me. I have already carried out a job for the government. I went over to Northern Ireland just before I left the army; remember when I told you I was going to visit some recruiting offices. That was when it was.

I hated every minute of not telling you. I hate keeping things from you but they wanted it that way, I'm sorry, I know I should have told you, but I had no choice in the matter.'

'So nothing has changed from when you were in the army then?'

'Not really.' I tell her.

The rest of the evening is total shit.

Monday arrives and I drive over to the Fort. I am stopped at the end of the bridge by a guy in uniform wearing a MOD Police hat. He certainly isn't a copper.

'Good morning Sir, can I help you?' He asks.

I show him my letter which he reads. He checks my name against a list.

'Through the archway and park your vehicle, then go into the office on the left.' He says pointing into the Fort.

I drive through the arch and park up near some cars already parked and follow someone who had just parked his car.

At the reception desk I am interrogated by a person sitting at a desk. I say interrogated, because that is what it felt like.

'Your room is at the top of the courtyard, take your bag to your room which is number 12 and then go to the mess room which is on the left of the courtyard, you will be briefed there. Enjoy your stay with us.'

What a cheerful bugger!

I follow the directions and end up at room 12. No bathroom, just a bed and sparse furniture which included a desk. For studying I suppose. After a few minutes there is a knock at the door. I open it and find a tall guy standing there.

'Hi! I'm Richard, I'm next door.'

'Dave.'

We shake hands and he says, 'You going to the meeting?'

'Yes, I can unpack later, you fit? Let's go.'

We make our way to the mess room, which is a glorified canteen. There are 24 people in the room.

After a few minutes 4 guys wearing suits arrive and sit down behind some desks. The chairs have been laid out in rows in front of the desks.

'Please sit down gentlemen.' One of them tells us.

We all sit down and are then told what is expected from us whilst we are on the course. The candidates are then paired off all except me.

The guy with the moustache then says, 'Please introduce yourselves and then tell the other members of the course a bit about yourselves.'

After 17 candidates have spoken, I get up to introduce myself.

'Mr. Stubbs please sit down, this does not involve you.'

I sit back down and everyone in the front rows turn around and look at me. I feel like a fish out of water.

The rest of the course continues introducing themselves. They are then told what the course is about.

'This does not apply to you Mr. Stubbs.' Again everyone in the front rows turn to look at me. After an hour the talk comes to an end and everyone is dismissed.

As we are leaving one of the suited guys says, 'Stay behind Mr. Stubbs.'

'I'll see you later Dave.' Says Richard as he leaves.

'That's if I'm still here mate.' I reply.

When everyone has left, I'm told to sit with them at the desks.

'Mr. Stubbs you have been assigned to course 34A for documentation only. You are here to carry out a job for us using the Fort as a base.'

One of the guys leaves the room but returns a few minutes later with an aluminum case that looks very familiar.

'You know what is in this case don't you?'

'Yes.' I tell him.

He hands me a bulky envelope.

'When you have read the contents, seal them in the enclosed envelope and hand them to the reception officer. Do not discuss the contents with anyone on the course or for that matter anyone not on the course, you may go Mr. Stubbs.'

I take the envelope and the case back to my room.

I lock my door and open the envelope and remove the contents. There are 4 sheets of A4 paper, a photo of a girl, some press cuttings and a plastic tube which contained a syringe of blue liquid. On the tube in big red letters are the words,

'HIGHLY DANGEROUS – POISONOUS – DEATH IN 12 SECONDS'

The papers are on a girl called Mary Martin. She is aged 25 years. Single. Dark haired in Rastafarian fashion. Metal adornments to her face. Height 5 feet 3 inches. He address is 23 Grand Avenue, Languard. She is unemployed and claiming benefits. She is also a Heroin user. Associates with known members of an illegal faction called Agent Orange. Lives with another member of the faction named Jonah Drake, a known thief and heroin user. They want her killed before the demonstration at Greenham Common on the 21st of October.

Agent Orange are a fanatical group of people who will go to great lengths to disrupt the way of life of any industry that is associated with the testing of products on animals. They will stop at nothing; they have been known to kill laboratory personnel on several occasions, including a director of a company in Cambridge.

Martin is at present number one on the departments list of undesirables. I have to contact 0811506749 when the serial is completed. They will arrange the disposal of the body.

I look at the photo of Martin, she looks gaunt and she certainly looks a junkie. She also looks older than her 25 years. Probably due to the drugs she uses. I go back over the papers and cuttings Martin has been under constant observation since she joined Agent Orange two years ago. She is responsible for the destruction of five sites used for testing and was involved in the deaths of three directors of laboratories around the country. She is planning to break into the bunkers holding cruise missiles at Greenham Common Air Base used by the USAF (United States Air Force).

I keep reading the papers over and over until I remember everything. I then seal the papers less the tube containing the syringe in the envelope supplied, and take it to the reception officer, who then puts it in the safe. 'Thank you.' is all that is said.

I then return to my room and unpack my bag. Not a lot of room in the cupboards. Very sparse. (Accommodation has since improved.)

The evening is spent with Richard who comes from a little village called Hawes in the Yorkshire Dales. Hawes is a lovely quaint place. It has an old rope making company there and Wensleydale cheese is also made there. His parents are sheep farmers.

He volunteered to become a spy by answering an advert in the Telegraph paper. Probably seen too many James Bond films. The bar at Duncan is not cheap but we have a very convivial time before turning in. Their course starts in earnest at 0600hrs; I can do what I like.

The next morning I am at a loose end for a few hours and I ask the reception officer if I can attend any of the lectures that are going on.

'Why do you want to?' He asked.

'Well I might learn something that could be of use to me in the future.'

'Very well, go to room 30B they are just starting a lecture on the destruction of material.'

I rush along to the room just as the lecturer arrives.

'You staying for this lecture Mr. Stubbs?'

Bloody hell everyone seems to know me.

'If you don't mind, I would like to stay.'

The lecturer tells us how to read and destroy papers that have been burnt. The ashes are sprayed with a solution that stops them crumbling, so then you can read what is written. We try it out on some burnt papers. Very ingenious.

At the end of the lecture I go back to my room and look at the kit that has been dropped off. The kit consists of a camera, binoculars and a small tape recording machine made by Sony. Neat little thing.

I collect my car and drive out the gate. The Police type guy stops me and hands me a pass to show on entry.

'It will save you going through the search procedure, keep it hidden from prying eyes when outside the Fort.'

I drive off into Languard and look for the address of Martin. It is in an awful part of Languard renown for trouble makers and junkies. Walking around this area would certainly draw attention. I will need to change my clothes if I am going to frequent this place.

Having recce'd the place; I drive to a café in the High Street for a drink and a bacon buttie.

As I enter the café I see Martin sitting at a table talking to a very ugly little git. Bloody hell! First day on the job and I have found the subject.

I buy a coffee and a bacon sandwich and proceed towards her and the little git she is talking to. When I am a foot away I slip and the coffee goes all over her table. I grab her chair to stop from falling to the ground.

'Bloody heck!' I say as I pull myself up.

'Sorry about that, I must have slipped on something on the floor.'

The owner comes over.

'Sorry mate, I'll get you another cup and a sandwich. I can't get the staff to clean up properly.'

I apologize to Martin and tell her I will pay for the cleaning of her jacket which is splashed with coffee.

'Don't worry about it, there's no harm done, it's an old one. It wasn't your fault.'

'Let me buy you a drink, it's only right that I should compensate you if you won't let me get your coat cleaned.'

'If you insist, you can buy me a cup of tea and a cake.'

'No problem.' I tell her, 'Does your mate want anything?'

'No, I'm just leaving.'

With that he gets up and walks out the door.

'Is it something I said?'

She laughs and I order her tea and cake and then sit opposite her.

'My name is Alan, what's yours?'

'Mary.'

'Pleased to meet you Mary even if it is due to an accident.'

We chat away as if we have known each other for years. Her tea and cake arrives and she gulps them both down as if she hadn't eaten for a week.

'Steady on girl, you will get indigestion.'

'Sorry, but I haven't eaten for a few days, bit strapped for cash at the moment.'

'You mean to tell me that you don't have any money for food.'

'My giro won't come till next Wednesday. I've had some big bills to pay.'

'Here let me get you some lunch, to compensate you for chucking coffee over your coat, what would you like?'

'No it is alright, I will manage, and anyway, you have only just met me, why should you buy me food?'

'Sorry if I have become presumptuous, but I'm that kind of guy, someone did the same for me when I was on the streets not knowing where my next meal was coming from. This guy just handed me £50 and told me to have a slap up meal on him as he had just won the pools, I have always remembered that, so that is why, I want to help you.'

'That is very kind of you, I don't get many offers like this, get me some eggs and chips and beans, sausages and plenty of bread, I'm pretty hungry.'

'No problem.' I tell her and go up to the counter to order it.

This is one way of getting close to her, Christ! She stinks, and is very bloody ugly. Just think of queen and country. I tell myself.

On returning to my seat, I notice she is rubbing her arm.

'What's wrong?' I ask her.

'Oh, it's nothing; just a bit sore that's all.'

'Here let me have a look, I was a bit of a medic once.'

I roll up her sleeve and notice little blue pin marks around her arm vein, but don't say anything.

'I'll give it a rub for you perhaps you have got a trapped nerve.'

I start rubbing her wrist and arm and she says, 'You know I use drugs don't you.'

'Not my place to tell people what to do with their life. If it makes you feel good, fair enough, I used drugs when I was on the streets, ended up in clink on many occasions. Got caught doing the wrong things so many times I decided to call it a day and get clean.'

'I can't, I've tried but always go back to them, and, I'm just not strong enough.' She replies.

Her food arrives and she starts to eat it ravenously.

'Bloody hell girl, slow down, you'll give me indigestion.'

As she is eating, now a bit slower, I tell her that I am going to a demo at Greenham Common on the 21st.

'Well would you believe it, I am organizing that demonstration; you can come with me and Jonah.'

'Who's Jonah?' I ask her.

'He is the guy I was talking to when you came in. He sometimes gets me my "H" (Heroin), we sort of shack up together, we don't sleep together, though we tried it once but he couldn't get a hard on, the drugs see to that.'

'I know how he feels, done that and wrote the book.'

We both laugh.

She then informs me that she planted an explosive device at the Windsor Pop festival in February.

'No-one was killed, but it certainly scared the shit out of the authorities.' She says laughing.

Christ! Is she a calculated bitch? I then ask her if she is still active.

'Too right mate, it is about time this government took notice of the people, our country is in Shit Street, the politicians don't care, all they want to do is look after themselves, back handers are bloody rife in this government and it is about time it changed.'

'Steady on girl, it is me you are talking to not the politicians, come down off your soap box.'

'Sorry, but it gets to me and action has to be taken. We are going to try and get into a silo which has cruise missiles in it; the government will take notice then.'

'Blimey! How are you going to do that, the place is guarded by Yank soldiers isn't it?'

'Don't worry, we will get in, we have a contact on the inside.'

Jesus! I wonder if the Firm knows this, I will have to contact them soonest.

Martin finishes her meal.

'Do you know anything about Agent Orange?' She asks.

'That's the stuff the yanks used to kill trees in Vietnam wasn't it?'

'They kill, but not trees, how would you like to join them?'

'Mary! You shouldn't ask me things like that, you don't know me, and I could be in the police or something.'

'You aren't in the police Alan, anyone who talks like you isn't in the authorities, so what do you say?'

'That's a big step to take at this stage, let me think about it for a few days.'

'Come round to the house, this is my address.'

She writes her address which I already know, on a napkin and hands it to me.

Christ! What a place to live, junkies' paradise, though there are decent people living there as well, who, I'm sure would love to sell their houses and move to somewhere decent.

I take the napkin and put it into my pocket and get up.

'Got to go, perhaps we can meet again soon.'

'I don't give my address to any old person you know, come and see me tomorrow.'

'I'll try but I can't promise, I might win the pools and then I'm gone.' I tell her.

I start walking towards the door when she shouts,

'Alan!

Yes' I reply,

'Try.'

I wave and walk out of the Café. Fucking Hell! She is one hell of an ugly bitch and she stink too.

CHAPTER TWENTY ONE

Having left Martin in the café I make my way to a book shop and look out of the window. A few minutes later, Martin comes along and enters Boots the Chemist right opposite me.

After about 5 minutes, Martin comes back out carrying a white bag. I presume it is her drugs prescription. She walks towards the town hall. I leave the book shop and follow her at a discrete distance.

She stops by a very scruffy individual who is sitting on a bench wearing a very dirty anorak and starts talking to him. He pulls from under his anorak some items which I can't distinguish, probably stuff stolen from a store. Martin sits alongside him and puts the items inside her coat, hands him some money and gets up and walks off leaving scruffy still sitting on the bench. No money for grub she told me, but has plenty for stolen property.

I follow her and as she is walking along, she pulls out a plastic bag with Asda written on it and proceeds to put the items from her coat into the bag. She has obviously bought some stolen goods.

Martin continues along Russell Road, when all of a sudden, anorak boy runs by me with a police officer in pursuit.

'Stop him.' Shouts the copper, but anorak boy is already past Martin who immediately goes into a shop.

A big guy is getting out of his car and as he turns knocks anorak boy to the ground, whereby the policeman now reaches him sprawled on the ground.

'Thanks mate.' The policeman says to the guy, 'He was getting away from me.'

'Always ready to help the police.' Says the guy,

'You okay with him now?'

'No problem.' The policeman says as he is handcuffing anorak boy. Definitely shop lifting I say to myself.

Martin comes out of the shop and looks up the street just as a police car arrives and she sees her mate being bundled into it. She sees me and comes over.

'Did you see what happened?' she asked.

'No, I was in the hairdressers making an appointment to get a haircut tomorrow, what has been going on?' I ask.

'I think my mate Chris has got lifted for thieving from some shops.'

'Shouldn't have got caught should he, silly sod. Mind you, I got caught a few times. I remember once when I was throwing the stuff away as a security guard was chasing me. I was too busy getting rid of the stuff when I went straight over the bonnet of a parked panda car. I got 3 months for that one.'

'You are a right little villain aren't you, fancy coming back to my place?' She asks.

'I only wish I could Mary, but I have to meet a mate, perhaps, I will, see you tomorrow evening, I've got your address.'

'Come round about 7 o'clock, I'll be in by then.' She replies.

'Okay, I'll see you then.' I say to her as I walk off in the opposite direction. Christ! I hope I haven't blown it. I hope she hasn't seen through me.

I wait till she walks away and then double back and observe her from a distance. As if by arrangement, she is stopped by a guy wearing a black bomber jacket. She hands him the plastic bag and he slips something into her hand and walks off. I bet he is her drug dealer. Martin then walks off.

I follow her for a bit but she is making for her house, presumably to inject the drugs. I go back to my car and return to the Fort and inform the Reception Officer of the inside contact she has at Greenham.

'I'll pass it on immediately.' He replies.

Today has been very eventful, I have now made contact with the, shall we say, the victim. It was a good stroke of luck bumping into her in the café. I hope I was convincing enough for her to believe me. Ever since working for the Firm, I have somehow met my intended victim by default. Will it always be like this? I doubt it. I must get my hair cut otherwise she might smell a rat.

The rest of the day is very boring. I walk round the grounds of the Fort and watch some people playing golf. On one of the parapets a guy is fishing. Bloody heck, he's about 40 feet up, I hope he has got plenty of line. I finish my stroll, and go over to the mess for tea. The evening is spent listening to a lecture and the wash up of the surveillance team who had gone out on the streets of Brandon this morning. Very interesting!!!!!!

Dinner is going to be late tonight as a team is still out, so I bang on

Richards door to see if he would like to go for a drink. There is no answer. Another chap informs me that Richards's team is the late ones. That explains why he is not answering. I thank the chap and go to my room.

As dinner is going to be late, I drive into town and have meal in a Chinese restaurant in the precinct. Boy! Could I do with seeing Anna and the kids? After the meal, I drive back to the Fort and turn in. Sleep comes easy, I am absolutely bushed.

Morning comes and I whip down to the local hairdressers and have my hair cut. I don't want her getting suspicious. I spend the rest of the day in the library looking up my ancestors. The Languard Library has a wonderful section on old Languard history. It has lots of information concerning people who used to live or in fact still live in the borough of Languard. I look up my dad's details and see he has lots of relatives. This whiles away a few hours. I must start a family tree. A lot of the information required is here in the library.

I return to the Fort and have something to eat. I have arranged a late dinner as I want to go and see Mary. I drive to Grand Avenue and park my car in a street close by. If I left the car in Grand Avenue, it wouldn't have any wheels on when I went to pick it up.

I walk to the house. The garden looks pretty overgrown. As I walk up the path the curtains twitch. Someone is watching me from the upstairs room. I can't see if it is male or female.

The bell doesn't work so I bang the door. A few minutes go by when the door opens and the most horrendous stink hits me. Fucking Hell! The pong is awful.

'Come in Alan, I'm glad you could make it.'

I enter and try not to throw up. I produce a bottle of vodka and hand it to her. Jesus! The place is a tip. Then, I suppose, junkies don't think to tidy their place up. She takes the vodka and shows me into a room, presumably the lounge. Crap is littered everywhere.

'Sorry the place is a mess, some friends have been dosing down, sit in that chair it is the tidiest.' She says showing me the chair.

I notice some tin foil which is blackened She puts the bottle of vodka in front of it hoping I suppose, to hide it.

'I told you yesterday that it would be to your advantage, I have someone staying here who can get you into Agent Orange.'

With that an extremely ugly guy comes into the room. He holds out his hand which is filthy.

'I'm Ralph; I understand you want to join the group?'

'Can you get me in then?'

He asks me a lot of questions and Mary suddenly says, 'Ralph! I wouldn't have asked him here if I didn't think he was genuine, he's okay.'

'Calm down Mary, okay, if you say he is alright then we will leave it at that.'

'Alan, you haven't got a couple of quid have you, my giro didn't turn up, I'll pay you back as soon as it does, that's a promise.'

I pull out a fiver and hand it to her (not my money, it's the Firms, 'keep it, I did a job yesterday.'

I can't stay in the house a minute longer, the smell is absolutely awful.

'As you have got company Mary, I'll see you tomorrow, okay.'

She nods and lets me out.

'I will be in at about 6 o'clock, come round then Alan.'

'Okay, see you tomorrow.'

She kisses me on the cheek, 'Thanks for the loan, I will, pay you back, I promise.'

Fucking hell! She's a right dog and she really stinks. The junkie bastard.

I make my way back to the car and drive back to the Fort. Once outside my room I strip off and make for the shower, I need to get rid of the smell of that house and to think I have to go back there, she has definitely got to go.

Having showered, I go to the laundry room and bung my clothes into the washing machine. Smell gone. I have my late dinner and get my head down. I wish I was at home with the girls and Anna.

This job is getting to me. I wake and drive into Languard and visit the library again. I don't bother going back to the Fort for lunch as I am totally engrossed in the records section concerning families who live in the borough.

The hours fly by when the librarian comes up to me and tells me that the library will be closing in 30 minutes. I look at my watch. Shit! It is nearly 1830hrs. I have been in the library nearly 9 hours.

I run to my car and within 12 minutes, I am again walking up Martin's path. In my pocket I have the plastic tube with the syringe in. Again the curtains twitch; I think it is Ralph up there.

Before I can bang the door, Mary opens it. She looks totally out of it.

'Come in Alan.' She says in a slurred sort of way.

I take a deep breath and enter and go into the same room as yesterday.

'You all right Mary?' I ask.

'Sure just a bit tired that's all.'

'Guess what I have got here.' I say as I pull the syringe out of the plastic tube.

'What is it?' She asks.

'It's liquid heroin, I nick it from the medical centre at the dockyard, they have it in the trauma kits. I lied when I said I got clean, I have been using this stuff for about 10 months. It's pretty powerful shit, and boy, is it good stuff. You want to try some?'

'Give me a hit, let's try it out.'

I pretend to inject myself and she comes over.

'Put it in there.' She says holding out her arm.

I gently squeeze a small amount into her arm. She winches and within seconds collapses and I carry her over to the sofa just as Ralph comes in.

'What's going on?' He asks, pointing at Mary.

'She has just tried out some new drugs I have brought over its powerful man.'

'Where's mine then?'

I inject a small amount into his arm and he too collapses. I check his pulse, none. I go over to Mary; she looks asleep, I check her pulse, none, both are dead.

Before I put the cyanide syringe back into the tube, I look for an old syringe and fill it with some of the contents. I then stick the syringe into Ralph's arm and put my cyanide syringe back into the plastic tube and put it into my trouser pocket. My heart rate has increased by 100 per cent.

It has to look as if they have overdosed. I start wiping my fingerprints from everything that I have touched, and check outside through the window. There is no-one about, but I bet the neighbour's keep a check on the place.

I need to look like one of these freaks, so I go upstairs and look in a bedroom. I find a jacket which looks just like the one Chris had and put it on, shit! Does it stink, but it will have to do. I also find a bobble hat and put that on as well. I just hope I don't catch anything. The bedroom is worse than the room down stairs.

Now, suitably disguised, I go back down and slowly open the front door. There is still no-one about, and it is raining. I then leave, leaving the door open. If the police are called, they will think they were too stoned to close it. The roads are deserted as I walk back to where I had parked the car. It would seem that no-one wants to come out in the rain.

Before I get into my car, I check all around to see if anyone is watching me. There isn't anyone about, thank goodness. I then remove the jacket and hat and put them in a plastic bag I keep in the car.

Now back to the Fort for a shower and clean clothes, but before I do, I drive to a telephone box and ring the number memorized from the "write up." A dull voice answers. I then say, 'God here, job done, looks like a drug overdose, two bodies in the house.'

All I get as a reply is, 'Thank you.' And the phone goes dead.

I still have the smell of the house in my nostrils. I can smell it on my clothes due to wearing that awful jacket and hat. I remove the tube from my pocket and put it in the bag with the clothing. I don't want it jabbing me, it's bloody lethal.

Back at the Fort I hand the bag to the reception officer and go for a shower. Then I chuck my clothes in the washing machine.

As I am coming out of the wash room, I bump into Richard.

'What have you been up to then?' He asks.

'Nothing much mate, just a recce on a military base down the road, pretty boring stuff really and I got soaked into the bargain. What have you been up to then?' I ask him.

'Surveillance exercise in Brandon, lost the bloody target twice in an hour, I'm off to bed, see you in the morning.'

'That is exactly where I am going to mate, catch you later.' I reply as I open my room door.

I write up my report and seal it in an envelope, and then climb into bed. That's another job done for the Firm but this time, I feel nothing, and I hate junkies.

CHAPTER TWENTY TWO

A week goes by and I hear nothing about the killings. I presume the bodies have been taken away to the local crematorium by the sweepers. The Firm uses crematoriums whenever they want to dispose of bodies, usually late at night or very early in the mornings, before normal work at them resumes for the day.

With nothing to do for the rest of the day, I drive into the town and buy the local Evening News. On the front page in big black letters I read,

"TWO DRUG ADDICTS MURDERED IN A LANGUARD HOUSE"

"A male and Female were found dead in a house in Grand Avenue, Languard. An autopsy revealed that they died from drugs laced with a very powerful poison. Death was diagnosed as instantaneous. The female a Mary Martin aged 25, unemployed. She had no living relatives. The male was named as Ralph Willis aged 27, also unemployed. Willis also has no living relatives. A friend raised the alarm when he went to visit them. Hampshire Police have started a murder investigation. A police spokesman has said that they have issued warnings to known drug users to be on their guard concerning drugs which could possibly be laced with poison. The spokesman also stated that they did not want this to happen to any other drug user. Neighbour's were spoken to, who all wanted to remain anonymous, said that they knew the house was a drugs den as there were far too many odd looking people coming and going, but never reported the matter to the police for fear of reprisals."

The article went on to say that both were members of Agent Orange, a notorious faction who had murdered and caused mayhem up and down the country. More information will be forthcoming as and when it is revealed by the police. Deep down, I bet the spokesman thought, that's another two off the scene.

Now I know why the firm did not contact me. What I had done must have been enough for them not to do anything about it. The authorities will think that Martin and Willis had purchased the drugs from their supplier, and would never have known that the drugs were contaminated. The police will be pulling in anyone known to them who might be suspected of supplying drugs. Half heartily, I expect.

On returning to the Fort, I have to report to the Reception Officer.

'You are free to return to your family, collect your things and hand in your key. You will be contacted later.'

I go to my room and pack my things. The course if you could call it that is now at an end for me. As I leave the room I bump into Richard and say goodbye and wish him luck with the rest of his course.

'Perhaps we will meet again.' He says as we shake hands.

'You never know mate, Bye.' I reply closing my door.

I carry my case down to my car and throw it in and then go to the Reception Office and hand in my key. I then drive out of the Fort. Free at last. I will be glad to get home to Anna and the kids.

CHAPTER TWENTY THREE

It is great being back home with Anna and the children. I hate being away from them. It was bad enough when I was in the Forces, I didn't think it would happen again once I had left.

I'm sitting at home waiting for the postman when the telephone rings. It is the Firm.

'Jason will meet you at the lake Friday at 0900hrs.'

Before I can tell them that I wouldn't be able to make it, the phone goes dead. The Firm must have been waiting to find out if anything would be forthcoming from the police over the deaths of the two junkies. I doubt if they will do much investigating, its two junkies off the scene.

If only I could have told them that I was taking my daughter to the doctors, she isn't well. She had come out in a very red rash all over her body. Our normal doctor said it was a heat rash; you don't puff up with a heat rash. My family comes first; the Firm comes a very distant second.

Friday arrives and I take Caroline to the pediatrician at Hamber Hospital. As soon as he sees her, he immediately gives her an injection.

'She's had a violent reaction to penicillin, lucky you brought her to me, another day and she could have died, what idiot said she had a heat rash?'

I immediately make a formal complaint against the doctor in question. He should have known about the reaction to penicillin, he prescribed it. Caroline starts to feel better and I take her home. As we are going by the Lake, I check to see if Jason is there. I don't see him and we continue on home.

On opening the front door, I hear the telephone ringing. I pick it up and a very irate Jason is screaming at me. My answer is to slam the phone down. No-one and I mean no-one talks to me like that. I don't give a toss who they are.

I ring a number only known to me and speak to Deputy "C." I inform him that I couldn't meet Jason because I had to take my daughter to the hospital as she could have died, I also tell him of the way Jason spoke to me.

'I will contact him for you and tell him of the reason for not being at the meet.'

'Thanks but tell him that if he talks to me like that again, he won't be seeing Christmas.' I then put the phone down and get Caroline some lunch.

One evening whilst I'm out in the garden with Bob my next door neighbour, he informs me that he has seen a cat digging up the lettuces and has made a moveable catapult to get rid of him.

'It's accurate to the end of the garden and with one of these, (showing me a round lead ball) in the back of his head, we won't get any more bother.'

We go to his shed and there on the bench is the device in question.

'Have you tried it out then?' I ask him.

'Put this tin on the box at the bottom of the garden and watch.'

I duly place the tin on the box and stand out of the way.

Whack.

The tin flies in the air. I go and pick it up and find a neat round hole in it.

'It's accurate,' I tell Bob.

'No more cats.' Bob replies.

We go back into the shed and blow me down, if a ginger cat doesn't come into the garden and start to dig a hole, obviously to have a crap. Bob loads the catapult and as the cat starts to squat.

Wham.

A lead ball hits the cat square between the eyes. We go and look at the cat. Its head has nearly gone.

'That's one less.'

He picks the cat up by the tail and starts to throw it over the fence. In doing so the cat is separated from its tail and the body flies through the air straight at the fence. Bob still has the tail in his hand.

At this point our neighbour, Joan, comes along her path.

'Evening lads,' she says, 'Hello! What's that cat doing trying to get through the fence?'

She goes up to the cat and says, 'It's dead, it must have died trying to get through the fence.'

Bob hides the tail behind his back.

'Stupid things, cats,' says Bob.

We go over her fence and retrieve the dead cat and bury it in her garden.

'Well the catapult works mate.' I tell him.

'Never doubted it for one second.' He replies.

Bob is one of the fittest men I have ever known. He swims in the sea every morning and exercises in his bedroom every day. He takes part in the winter dip at Christmas ie: a swim in the sea. He says he is looking forward to retiring.

I always think of Bob as the mad professor as he is always tinkering with something. I remember once when he put an engine on his wife's rotary washing line as there wasn't any wind in the garden, and as he was telling me about it, it took off with Jackie's sheets on it.

'It makes a fine helicopter.' I tell him pointing up in the air.

'Fuck me! Jackie's new sheets are on that, what the hell is she going to say if I don't get them back.'

I start laughing.

'It's no laughing matter, she will kill me.'

Jackie is Scottish and Bob is Welsh. Great combination.

A few weeks go by and Bob comes into the house.

'I've ordered a new car it's a Rover Metro Vander Plas, I thought I would buy a new one now that I am going to retire.'

'Good on you mate, may as well use your money for something you need.'

The weeks go by and one day I find Bob in his shed, he is complaining of pains in the stomach.

'I'll get you some stuff for that.' I tell him.

I go into the house and return with a bottle of jollop.

'Here try this.'

He takes a swig and after a few minutes says,

'Blimey it worked.'

Bob never did see retirement. On the day he was supposed to retire he died. He was the fittest man I have ever seen, but still died of stomach cancer. He never did drive the car he ordered. It arrived on the day of his funeral.

When in the garden I believed I could still see him, so I lawned the lot, I enjoyed our friendship. We use to make wine together. I made five gallons of martini once and asked him to try it. He liked it so much that he took the five gallons back to his house. Never saw the going of it, so it must have been good. I could tell many stories about Bob, but I like to keep them to myself. I still miss him to this day; he was one hell of a likeable man.

I am watching the TV one evening with Anna when the telephone rings. I answer it and blow me down it is Ronnie.

'Can you meet me?'

'When?' I ask him.

'You name the day the time and the place.' He replies.

I put my hand over the mouthpiece and ask Anna if we are doing anything on Tuesday.

'Not that I know of, why?'

I take my hand from the mouthpiece and say,

'Tuesday next at ten o'clock in the Forces Gardens in Languard.'

'I'll be there.' The phone goes dead.

'What was that about Dave?' Anna asks.

'Are you in trouble?'

'No, the Firm wants to see me, so I have arranged a meet.'

'I hate it when you have to work for them, can't you find a better job?'

'I wish I could, but they have me over a barrel.'

'Just what do you do for the Firm Dave; you have only told me that you do jobs for them, what jobs?'

'I was hoping you would never ask that question. I kill people for them.'

'Stop mucking about, what do you really do for them?'

'As I have just told you, I kill people for them. I am the governments assassin or if you put it another way, their hit man.'

'Oh my god, you are serious aren't you?'

'Yes I am and by the way, "God" is my code name.'

I explain in detail all the jobs I have done so far and the reasons behind the hits. Anna does not like this one little bit. Her placid husband is a killer.

'If anything goes wrong what will happen to us?'

'You will be taken care of, so don't worry, forget we have had this little talk.'

'How the fuck can I forget this, I really don't know you do I.'

'Darling nothing will happen, as long as you say nothing to anyone, this must remain secret. You have had a bodyguard with you all the time I have been working with the Firm so have the girls. Our security is top of the range. The house is bugged and cameras have been installed. No-one can get in without them knowing.'

'So that is why we had that alarm installed.'

'Yes, the phone is bugged but we don't have a bug in our bedroom, if we did, we would scare the pants off of them.'

I start to laugh, but Anna doesn't see the funny side. I then show her where the cameras are.

'Nobody is to know about this. If we drive anywhere we will be followed, but darling, no-one can come to the house, not even one of your friends from work.'

'What is the name of this government department you work for?'

'MI6, it's also called the Secret Intelligence Service, but we call it the Firm.'

'Oh my fucking Christ!'

This is the second time I have ever heard Anna swear. Anna never swears.

Anna is certainly not very pleased with me. I don't think she can comprehend the situation.

'Please remember darling, no-one is to know about me.'

'Do you honestly think I will tell anyone, Oh my husband kills people for a living, come off it, even I don't want to know, I wish you hadn't told me now.'

'No secrets remember.'

Nothing more is said and the rest of the evening is in silence.

CHAPTER TWENTY FOUR

Tuesday the 20th of October, 1000hrs, in the Forces gardens, Languard. Ronnie is walking around the gardens looking at the flowers. I have been waiting in the small car park since 0900hrs. I wanted to make sure he had come alone. As Ronnie had come from the ferry, he must have come down from London by train. I can't see anyone following him or anyone doing anything out of the ordinary, so assume he is alone. (Remember – never ever assume – Old training manual)

I get out of my car and walk towards Ronnie.

'Morning Ronnie, nice to see you.'

We shake hands and sit down on a bench donated by some military association.

'It has been quite some time since we last met, how are things?' Ronnie asks.

'I had to tell Anna about my work with you, she won't say anything.'

'I thought you might tell her, not to worry, as long as no-one else is told.'

'What was wrong with Jason, why did he shout at me, I thought we were friends?'

'I have spoken to him and he wants me to apologies for him, he didn't know the circumstances.'

'He would have done if he had allowed me to get a word in.'

'Anyway, water under the bridge, how is your daughter?'

'She is fine now, the problem was that she is allergic to penicillin and we didn't know, though, you would have though our doctor would have known especially with the symptoms she had.'

'Well, I am glad she is okay.' Ronnie replies.

'We couldn't reach Jason after you rang in, his radio phone went down and we had no means of getting in touch with him until he returned to the office. So much for modern technology.'

We talk over the good times we had when we were in the army and how things have gone since we left.

'I want to say that the department is very impressed with your quick thinking. You have now done two jobs for us and I am to inform you that you are now working for "K" department as the government's assassin. You have been promoted to the rank of Major. No-one in SIS can tell you what to do. You come under my direct control. "C" will not know you exist nor will he be informed of what you do. (It might be "M" in the James Bond films but in real life it is "C") The reason why he will not be informed of your tasks is so that he will not be able to answer any embarrassing questions, when asked by the government.'

'Do I get any money for working for you?'

'Have you checked your bank statement lately?'

'So my services are not free then.'

'I knew you were the right person for the job, we can't get over how quick thinking you are.'

'Well, I have had the best training in the world.' I reply.

'Another job will be coming up shortly, I have to iron out some details first and then I will send you a file.'

'You know Ronnie; I thought you were going to bin me after the Jason episode.'

'What! You must be joking, you are thought very highly of, why do you think you got the rank of major, think of the doors that will open.'

'Yeah, more like crematorium doors.'

'Bollocks you prat come on let's get a cup of coffee before I go back to London.'

We find a little coffee house in Jacobs Lane and talk about all things not army or SIS.

After drinking gallons of coffee, Ronnie says,

'It's been great coming here and talking over old times and as much as I would like to stay, I must return to London, so I will bid you goodbye till next time. I will keep in touch and Dave, thanks.'

He shakes my hand and we go back to the ferry. I wait for him to board the ferry to Brandon and return to my car.

What a two faced prat I am, I was hoping to get binned, but then, what would have happened, a dum dum bullet in the head and a trip to the local burning factory probably. Ugh! Don't bear thinking about.

It was really nice meeting Ronnie, just to be able to talk without the need to worry about work. I wish he could have stayed longer but in his job that could never happen. He is always required for something or other.

A few weeks go by when out of the blue I receive an invite to Vauxhall

Cross. Stone the crows an invite to the inner sanctum. They even send the tickets for the train journey. Now what do they want I wonder.

'How would you like a day out in London at the Firms expense?' I ask Anna over dinner.

'Who is the Firm?' asks Caroline.

'No-one you need to know about.' Anna replies sharply.

'No need to bite my head off, I was only asking.' Caroline counters.

'If you girls have finished your dinner, then off to your rooms and do your homework.' Anna replies in a stern manner.

The girls leave the table and as they go up the stairs, Karen says to Caroline,

'What's got into mum, she certainly flew of the handle when you mentioned dad's firm.'

'Well, how would you like a day in London,' I ask Anna.

'No thank you, the less I hear about them the better. I can't have my friends round, I have a guy following me everywhere I go, why can't they just leave me alone.' Anna replies nearly in tears.

'You know he is there for a reason darling. I will ask my controller if the Firm will relent to letting people come to the house, but don't hold your hopes up.'

The evening is again spent in silence. I feel sorry for Anna, she comes from a family that oozes happiness, and friends in the house all the time, this is alien to her, and she should not be put into this situation, and I shouldn't allow it. If it carries on like this, I fear she may have a nervous breakdown. I must try and change the minds of SIS on this matter. For her sake as well as mine.

CHAPTER TWENTY FIVE

The Secret Intelligence Service (SIS) or MI6 as they are usually known have now come out of the closet so to speak, they have their own act of parliament and are subject to law. (They have always been subject to the laws of the land, though with what they get up to, you wouldn't think it.)

SIS came into being in 1909 under the control of Mansfield Cummings, a one legged Officer. He was known a "C" because of the way he signed his letters and memo's. Cummings died in the job in 1923. Since then MI6 has been commanded by several "C's" some good and some bad, some really bad. Most agents are attached to British Embassies around the world gathering intelligence necessary to protect Great Britain. Well that is what they are supposed to do, but I know different.

Some agents work for 2 countries, ours and another. They are called double agents and have an extremely dangerous life style. Most double agents could never be trusted and quite rightly so. Some were very good and had a preference for the security of this country. Some agents used DLB's (dead letter boxes) to pass on information. How it worked was, you both found a particular place and to let each other know that information had been stashed, you put something you both agreed on near the DLB and removed it after the information had been collected. Each agent would state a time that they should visit the DLB. This was usually a good way of passing information, but you had to be very careful that no-one knew about them. Double agents were usually retired early in their careers when their usefulness began to wane. ie: killed.

One such double agent who worked for us and the Russians was a knight of the realm, who looked after the Queens paintings. When he was found out he was stripped of his title and sacked, and quite rightly so to. There are still double agents working inside MI6 and for that matter MI5. They are all on borrowed time, as people like me will get to know who they are and will retire them.

Many books have been written about double agents. One who springs to mind was Kim Philby. He worked for the Russians and us; he later escaped to Russia and lived a life of luxury on a fat pension given to him by his Russian masters. There were even allegation against a "C" once, but nothing came of it. Everyone in the department thought he was working for the Russians and many people tried to prove it with little success.

MI6, SIS, Firm, or Box some of the names used, moved from run down offices in Curzon Street and then on to Gower Street. They are now at 85 Vauxhall Cross a very impressive modern building. MI5 are at Thames House just up from the London Eye.

(If you have seen "Spooks" on the TV, the building they use as Thames House is in fact the London Lodge of the Masons)

Would you believe that this Security department had darkening film put on their windows so that they could not be seen from the London Eye? (Snipers!!!!) The mind boggles.

I get the train to London and a taxi to Vauxhall Cross (usually known as just 85); I couldn't persuade Anna to come with me. My day is spent in the department that controls my actions.

I am informed that I will be enrolled in the Ministry of Defence Police to carry out a job that will take quite a long time to complete. It will be extremely dangerous. The task assigned to me is the misuse of Polonium 210, a radioactive isotope used in special munitions. Polonium 210 is a very stable product. The radiation it produces cannot go through anything solid. It can be put into paper envelopes and will not cause any problems whilst in the envelope. But a hundredth part of milligram ingested into the body will kill all tissues around its path through the body to a depth of 2 inches. You will be dead in a few days or a few weeks, depending on the dosage. It is very doubtful if it would be detected in time to issue an antidote.

'Why do I need to join the MOD Police, I thought my job was terminating undesirables.' I ask Jason, my controller.

'It still is and someone will be once you have found out who is stealing this bloody dangerous substance.'

I just cannot see myself as a Mod Plod. It isn't my style, but they are paying the money, who am I, to argue.

I arrive back home late in the evening and tell Anna that I am joining the MOD Police.

'Good heavens, are you serious?'

'Yep.'

'But what about the Firm, does that mean that all the security is now lifted and we can start having a normal life at last?'

'Ah No, the Firm has told me I will be a copper and have an interview on Tuesday at the dockyard.'

'So you are still doing things for the Firm then?'

'Nothing has changed.' I tell her.

Tuesday arrives and I go for the interview at Ellington. I am shown into the office of the Superintendent MOD Police.

'My name is Superintendent George Halpern; I control all the police officers that work in the confines of Ellington. Before we carry on I should inform you that our powers are exactly the same as the Home Office Forces except we only use them on government property or against government personnel, anywhere else we have only the power accorded to a citizen.'

He doesn't ask me any questions. It would seem that it is a foregone conclusion that I will be accepted. He continues telling me about the MOD Police and how they were formed from the three service Constabularies, which were the Army Department Constabulary, the Air Force Department Constabulary and the Admiralty Department Constabulary, and before them, government property was policed by the Metropolitan Police and that is why all their equipment and uniform is based on the Met. The pay and conditions are identical to any Home Office force.

(Today's MOD Police is a Force to be reckoned with, they are experts in terrorism, and they have the most up-to-date equipment, more so than Home Office Forces. The MOD Police were given the new MP5's before the Home Office Forces, and the Force are used on many occasions because of their expertise. The MOD Police were used on the London Bombings. They have sniper teams, CID and scenes of crime officers, police dog handlers, just like the Home Office Forces, in fact anything the Home Office Forces have, so do the MOD Police.)

Gone are the days when you would see an MOD Policeman manning gates at government sites. That is now done by the MOD Guarding Department. This leaves the MOD Police to carry out their proper role of protecting the countries government establishments. The MOD Police are an armed police force. Anyone wanting a Police career would be hard put to find a better force. Their entrance exams are no different than the Home Office Police exams.)

He then shows me some photos of a suspected suicide they are dealing with. They are pretty gruesome to say the least.

'Would you like a cup of tea?' He asks.

'That's very kind of you.' I reply.

After the tea ceremony, he informs me that I will be posted to Limfield for a start and then to an Air Station where the real work is. How the hell am I going to get to the Armament place to do the job they want me to do, I wonder. Halpern still doesn't ask me any questions. It is obvious that the beings on high have said something. It is all very strange.

'You have come very highly recommended, you seem to be just the right person for the MOD Police, and so it is with great pleasure that I welcome you into the fold. I will arrange for you to get sworn in at a Magistrate's Court on Thursday, I wish you luck in your new career with the MOD Police.'

Career my arse, I don't intend being with this lot longer than I have to.

On returning home I inform Anna of the interview.

'Did he ask you any questions Dave?'

'No, not one, he explained how they were formed and showed me some photos of a death they were investigating and apart from telling me that I will be sworn in on Thursday, I will be going to Limfield, wherever that is. I will know more when I have been sworn in. I must be the first person to be given a cup of tea by a Superintendent.'

Nothing more is said and we have a very cosy evening in front of the TV. The kids have gone to bed. Peace rains.

CHAPTER TWENTY SIX

I have now been sworn in as a Constable in the Ministry of Defence Police and posted to a government establishment at Limfield. There are 3 Sergeants and 10 Constables to police the place doing 3 shifts of 8 hours. I am teamed up with a new recruit called Sam who joined the same day as me.

'I think I'm going to like this place.' He says as we are walking around.

We are in civilian clothes as our uniforms haven't turned up. We get an extra 10p a day for wearing civilian clothes

The sooner I get out of here the better. We return to the Police station and I am called into the Station Inspectors office.

'What do they want with you at Vauxhall Cross then?' He asks.

'I have no idea Sir, what's Vauxhall Cross?'

'The headquarters of MI6.' He replied.

'Then I haven't got a clue Sir, why would I be needed there, have they got problems or something?'

'I don't question HQ any more, I just do what they tell me, you have to go up there on Wednesday, I've asked for a train warrant to be issued to you. It should arrive in time for you to go.'

'Do I come in for my shift that day Sir?'

'No, treat the day out as your shift, we will cope, there isn't a lot going on and one less won't make any difference to the shift.'

I leave the office and the first person to say anything is Sam.

'What did he want Dave?'

'Just to tell me that I am on a detached duty at a site in London for the day.'

'Blimey detached duties already, lucky bugger, think of the overtime.'

If only he knew.

The rest of the week flies by and I get the train to London. On arrival at Vauxhall Cross, I'm checked in by a policeman; at least I think he is a policeman. He tells me how to get to the 3rd floor. This is the office of my controller.

'Hello Dave, come in and take a seat, I will be with you in a minute, I just want to finish this report, and it won't take long. Do you want a coffee?'

'Thanks, I'll get it.' I go over to the coffee pot which seems to be on the go all the time.

'Right that's that, now Dave, we want you to do a job for us.' Jason says putting the report into a draw of his desk.

'Crumbs, so soon after the last one.'

'This one is so secret, only "K" Department knows about it, and 3 very senior top people whose names you do not need to know.'

'Who have I got to kill, the Prime Minister?' I say laughing.

If looks could kill I would be dead.

'Take this file and read it over, do not leave the building with it, there is a rest room along the passage, use that, once digested return it to me. Is that clear?'

'Keep your hair on, I'm sorry if my little quip upset you.'

'Just read the file.'

I take the file and proceed to the rest room.

I undo the envelope and pull out the usual papers and photograph. Bloody Hell! It's a Labour MP. What the hell has he done! I read the splurge. He's head of a terror group, who usually target testing centres. How can a prat like this be a member of parliament? Trust him to be body guarded by an armed policeman. This job isn't going to be easy. It will either be long range or very close up. I seal the envelope and take it back to Jason who puts it through the shredder.

'Well now you have read the file, and you now know who it is, you will appreciate this has got to be handled carefully.'

'Don't I know it, but it will be done that I can assure you.'

'The trouble is Dave; you have only 12 days to do it in.'

'I will have to get in close for this owing to him having an armed Police Officer.'

'Have a word with Walter Greenslade in the basement; he may be able to help you.'

I go off to the basement and seek out the "Professor." I find him testing some sort of gas.

'Walter, I need a terminal poison that is not instantaneous, but has an affect after about 4 hours. Have you got anything like it in your empire?'

'You want a Ricin compound in a pellet form, once in the body it will take about 3 to 4 hours before it takes instant effect.'

'How will I get it into the body?'

'Oh, that's easy, you use a device that will shoot it in, and it will feel like a pin prick to the person, he will never know what hit him.'

'But what if he is wearing heavy clothing?'

'No problem, this device is pretty powerful.'

He then shows me a small hand held device which is stuck to the palm of your hand and triggered by pressing it against a person thereby releasing a miniscule sized pellet through clothing and into the body at speed.

'He will feel a bit ill after about 30 minutes, the full effect won't happen for a few hours then bingo, dead. It is very effective; it has been used on several occasions in the Far East with great success, so it is just the thing you will be wanting.'

(I have a funny idea that "Q" of James Bond fame is based on Greenslade)

I thank the "Professor" and return to Jason's office.

'Can you get me an itinerary of the MP's movements over the next few days and also get me a detachment order to be in London from the MOD Police.'

'Already done, they have been informed that you are on a course to further your career, there won't be any problems, and here are his movements up until next Thursday.'

This guy seems to have a very full calendar, what with opening department stores in his constituency and going to events in and around London. Being escorted everywhere by his police officer is going to be extremely hard to get near him. Looking at his movements, I notice that he will be at the museum of art's opening a new section dedicated to landscape artists. Now this may give me the opportunity to get near him and administer the poison. It's worth a try.

'Jason, I'm off back to Languard, the job will be done once I have worked out a way to get near him, see you later.'

'Just remember Dave, no-one is to know and that means your wife, no-one, understand.'

'Don't you worry on that score; I don't want to talk about this one ever.'

I leave Vauxhall Cross and make my way home. I arrive home just in time to say goodnight to the kids.

'Well how did your day go Dave?'

'Anna you do not want to know, I met the wackiest person I have ever seen in my life today. Talk about a fruitcake, boy have they got some funny people there.'

The rest of the evening is a bit fraught. Anna hates what I do.

I return to duty at Limfield and the first person I meet is Sam.

'Well how did your detached duty go? Was it anything interesting?'

'It was bloody boring, it was on anti-terrorism, and since when do we get terrorists at Limfield. The place is so quiet, they wouldn't know where the place was, let alone cause any problems.'

The Inspector comes on duty and goes to his office. All of a sudden there is a roar.

'Hammond! get your arse in here.'

Sergeant Hammond looks at us and says, 'Oh bugger, he's found the hole in the book.'

'What hole?' I mouth at Sam.

Sam shrugs is shoulders and mouths 'I don't know.'

We hear the rants and raves, who wouldn't they are loud enough.

'I thought I told you no smoking whilst on duty in the office, look at the Occurrence Book, a bloody big burn hole right in the middle of it, what have you got to say about it?'

'The ash must have fallen out of my pipe Sir, it won't happen again.'

'Damn right it won't, you do it again and I will suspend you, now get out of my office.'

Hammond comes out with a smile on his face.

'Pratt, his teeth fell out when he was ranting.'

Hammond goes off to the toilet, pipe between his teeth and a paper under his arm. So much for a bollocking on smoking in the station office. Jesus H Christ, I'm surrounded by loonies.

The Inspector comes out and hands me a new occurrence book.

'I don't want to see any damage done to this one.' He says thrusting it into my hands.

I take the book and put it in the station office. Pinned to it is a hand written note. **"DO NOT DEFACE"** What an outfit I have joined.

I'm just going in for refreshments when the Inspector calls me into his office.

'Constable Stubbs, you are on further detached duties to Vauxhall Cross, I understand that you will be the anti-terrorist officer for this area. What do you know about terrorism then?'

'Not a lot Sir, only what they taught me on the course yesterday. I did ask the Superintendent when I had my interview to join the MOD Police if there were any course going that would suit me, he must have put me in for it Sir.'

'Well my friend, you leave tomorrow for a week, don't let the side down and good luck.'

I'll bloody need it. I say to myself.

Sam comes into the station.

'What's this I hear, you going on detached duties again, you got friends in high places or something?'

'I don't think so; I reckon it was when I asked the Super if there were any courses going, he must have put me in for this.'

'Good on you mate, anything is better than listening to the Inspector and old Hammond having a go.'

My shift has finished and I jump on my Suzuki pop pop and head off home. Boy! Will I be glad when I leave Limfield?

CHAPTER TWENTY SEVEN

I arrive at the digs in Pimlico that have been arranged for me and sort out my kit. I spend a few days shadowing the minister, and learning about his habits etc., I find a chink in his armour. He has a knack of holding the arm of the person he is talking to. I believe this is the way to get close to him and administer the poison pellet. He is due to open a section in the arts museum containing "Immoral Art" on Thursday.

I contact my controller and ask him to get me an invitation to the opening.

'No problem, consider it done.' He replies.

'Thanks.' I say in return and the conversation is ended.

Well that's got me into the museum. I have decided to go as an art critique. That should get me close to him. I hope. Now to check out the device.

I drive out to a nature reserve and park in the small car park at the entrance. As I am walking down a track I fit the device into the palm of my hand. It fits very snugly. To prime it I have to pull a small cord. I feel it puff up. It is now ready to do business. I move over to a small silver birch tree and push my palm against the bark. I feel the device deflate. Using my penknife I dig into the bark. Sap starts to pour out of the wound. About an inch down I find the minute pellet. It has not dissolved yet. If it can go this far into wood it will definitely go further through clothing and flesh.

The minister, Henry Porter lives with his aging parents just outside Cobham but has a bed sit in the city which he uses during the week. It would be impossible to assassinate him there. I can find no information as to a girlfriend; he seems to prefer the company of men. Homosexual! I have no idea, and it isn't my problem anyway. Parliament and churches are full of them, and, for that matter, so is the department. They do say "If you haven't tried it..........." Yuk!!!!

I cannot understand why he has a police bodyguard. He isn't that high up in the cabinet. All that I have read about him points me to believe he is a right disgruntled bastard. I now have to work out how I will get close to him. It isn't going to be easy.

Thursday arrives and I am in the museum talking to the curator. He explains to me the reason why the section is now open to the public. Not knowing anything about art let alone immoral art, I bluff out my expertise.

'Would you like to meet the minister?' He asks.

'I'd be honoured, thank you.'

He explains that all those who will be presented to the minister will be standing by the entrance. The minister would be arriving at about 1100hrs.

I have a look round the section. Bloody heck some of the pictures are virtually pornographic. A whistle blows. Playtime has finished.

'All those meeting the minister, please make your way to the entrance.' The deputy curator shouts.

We all move and make a line along the left hand side of the entrance to the section.

Dead on 1100hrs the minister and his entourage are being led into the section. The curator is introducing each person in turn to the minister. Fuck! I have the device in my right palm. I quickly change the device over to my left palm behind my back, and pull the little bit of cotton. The device starts to inflate. Let's hope nothing goes wrong.

As the minister comes in front of me, the curator says, 'This is Mr David Stubbs, an art critique who is writing an article on the new section.'

He reaches out and shakes my hand and in doing so, places his left hand on my right arm. I move my left hand to his shoulder and feel the device deflate. I squeeze his hand tightly, which will, with a bit of luck, take his mind off of the pin prick. He doesn't show anything on his face.

The minister then moves on to the next person in line. Job done, I hope. I remove the device and put it in my pocket. No one has seen me do it.

After the introductions the minister and his entourage move off around the section to view the pictures. We then go for drinks and small triangle sarnies in a room just to the left of the entrance. I can see the minister is sweating profusely. He starts to talk to his detective and then the curator.

'I'm afraid we will have to leave you as I have another appointment shortly. Thank you for allowing me to open this section. I hope it will be successful.'

With that they leave the museum. I tell the curator that I too must leave and thank him for his help.

'Please write a good article, we really do not want adverse criticism before we open the collection to the public.'

'Don't worry; I am really impressed, once again, thank you.'

He shakes my hand and I leave the museum.

On the drive back to my digs I turn the radio on to Radio 3 and listen to the classical programme. It is very soothing.

At my digs I start to pack my things into my case. There is no need for me to stay here any longer. The job is done. I think. I walk down the road and have a coffee in the café I have been using since being in London.

'I'm leaving Paddy, got a job up North, can you make me some sarnies for the journey mate.'

'Of course I can, cheese and pickle okay?'

'Great, thanks mate.'

I drink my coffee and pay for the sandwiches.

'Perhaps I'll see you again, next time I'm down this way, thanks for the great food, see you Paddy.'

'Bye, Bye I will look forward to it.' He replies.

I go back to my digs collect my case and throw it into the car and head off back to Languard.

As I reach the A3, I turn the radio on and hear the end of a news break.

"…..the Arts minister collapsed and died whilst opening a department store in the city. A spokesman said that the minister suffered from heart trouble and had not been feeling very well for some time and it is believed he died of a heart attack."

At Winchfield, I telephone my controller and inform him that the job had been completed.

'Yes, I know, I have just heard it on the radio, get back to your job as a copper, I'll contact you later.'

The telephone goes dead. Nothing. No thank you for doing a good job. Nothing. These people are like robots. Still as old Freddie use to say, "Another one bites the dust………."

On arrival home the girls greet me with,

'Hi dad, come and see what we have been doing.'

It is great to be home.

CHAPTER TWENTY EIGHT

Obituary – The Times – 8th November 1977

"The death has occurred on the 14th of September 1977 of Henry Joshua Porter, born 8th of August 1932. Henry Porter was the Member of Parliament for Tower Hamlets and Minister for the Arts. Porter suffered a fatal heart attack whilst conducting the opening of a large department store in the city.

Henry Porter was a board member of 5 companies which included the RSPCA. He came into politics late in life when he stood and won the Tower Hamlets seat from the late Desmond O'Connor. Porter will be remembered for his sometimes acidic arguments in the Chambers when animal testing was debated.

Henry Ported never married. He once confided that he was far too busy to take a wife as work always came first. Lord and Lady Porter have requested family flowers only. Donations in Henries name may be sent to the RSPCA, c/o Jones and Lambert, Solicitors, 1a Jeremy Street, WC6 if so desired."

If people only knew what this prat really got up to when he was away from parliament or bumming free lunches. He was an ardent member of Agent Orange, the notorious faction that caused death and havoc to personnel and property of Government backed animal testing sites, the length and breadth of the country. He will be no loss to the country, let alone the Arts.

It was luck that he suffered from heart trouble; no autopsy will be carried out as he was under a doctor. The only people who know he did not die of a heart attack are me and the selected few in the department. No-one else will know that he was murdered. "DON'T REST IN PEACE, YOU WANKER." I say to myself.

Going back to being a copper at Limfield is going to be a pain. The place is so quiet you could hear a pin drop. That is, if you discounted the arguments between Sergeant Hammond and the Inspector. It is rumoured that the Inspector, who I think is a bit of a drip, lives in a Police married quarter on his own. He has about 5 locks on each door. These are to keep people out especially women. He had a bad experience once (sexually) when a girl took advantage of him. It scared and scarred him for life. If anyone in his company started talking about women, he would storm off in a huff.

The rest of the guys are okay. They are very helpful in explaining the way things are done at Limfield. **(Now an industrial park)**

CHAPTER TWENTY NINE

Limfield is a typical military establishment. The site isn't very big but the compliment is. Why, I have no idea. The daily routine is either working at the front desk with a Sergeant or patrolling the site. Up on the ramparts is a derelict building which once housed the luminating works. This place use to put the luminous paint on compasses and watches, only in those days it was pure radium. Nobody knew then, how dangerous it was.

One day I am asked to take a scientist up to the building because it is going to be demolished. To get to it we have to walk along the top of the rampart. As we approach, we both see that it has been vandalised. All the windows except three have been smashed out. The doors are hanging off.

'Bloody Hell!' Says the scientist scratching his balding head.

'It looks as if the buggers have totally wrecked the place.'

He takes from his bag a Polaroid camera.

'I'll just take some pictures from inside the building.' He says going through a door which is held on by one hinge. He clicks away and asks me to hold the prints whilst they develop. He takes about 10 pictures but none of them come out.

'Damn!' he retorts, 'The film must be duff.'

'Does that happen often?' I ask him.

'Never happened before, I'll go and get another film from my case.'

He returns a few minutes later with his briefcase and loads a new film into the camera and proceeds to retake the pictures. We wait for the prints to develop. Nothing happens.

'There is something wrong here, hang on while I get my Geiger counter out.' He switches on a small hand held piece of equipment. The needle of the meter shoots over to the right.

'Fuck me! Let's get out of here. This fucking place is radioactive.'

I radio the police office and talk to the desk sergeant.

'The scientist wants to talk to you.'

'Put him on the radio.' Says sergeant Goodbody.

'Hello sergeant can you ring this number urgently 023337684, I require a decontamination unit here immediately if not sooner, we cannot come back from here until it arrives, the area must be cordoned off immediately. This area is very radioactive.'

'I will get onto it straight away, is Stubbs okay?'

'We both are at the moment, but we are moving back from the building until the decontamination unit arrives, keep everyone away from here.'

A few hours pass bye when the radio bursts into life.

'The decontamination unit is here where do you want it put?'

'Position it at the steps and let us know as soon as it is up and running.'

Another hour goes by and the radio again bursts into life.

'It is all up and running.'

'Thanks Sergeant, okay Dave, let's go down and get decontaminated.'

At the bottom of the steps are three caravans all humming away. As we reach the first one, there is a guy dressed in a white suit with a head covering.

'Strip off your clothes and put them in these bags.'

Bloody hell! All this for going into an old building. I think all the coppers use to go up there for a skive.

We are then ushered into the next caravan that has jets of warm water. We are given some liquid soap and told to wash every part of our bodies.

Gosh! Two showers in one day. After we have showered we end up in the last caravan where we are given the once over with a Geiger counter.

'You are both clear, put these on.'

The guy gives us some paper coveralls.

'Your clothing is being checked and if safe will be returned to you.'

After what seems like hours but is only minutes our clothes are return to us and we get dressed.

'I have to get in touch with my department to have the area of the building checked. I think there may be radiation in the ground, and if that is the case we will have to start digging massive holes and have the soil removed in secure containers.' The scientist tells me.

'I think you had better check all the guys in the police station, as they use to walk along the ramparts by the building.'

'I have already put that into being, a unit will be checking them as we speak.'

'How are they going to do that?' I ask him.

'Everyone will have a blood test and the results will be given to them, if they require medication, they will be referred to their doctors.'

'That quick eh!'

'Things move very swiftly when you are dealing with anything radioactive, especially if you have been exposed to it for any length of time, it will, kill you and in a horrible way.'

'Thank you for those kind words, enough said.' I reply.

Returning to the Station Office, Sgt Goodbody says, 'Well done Stubbs, but quick thinking by that scientist, he certainly knows his stuff.'

CHAPTER THIRTY

Having endured the rigors of decontamination, things get back to normal. The radioactive soil removed from the site of the building has been put into 40 gallon metal drums and weld sealed.

The drums were then taken to a council tip at Languard and buried under many tons of house hold waste. It seemed strange that the Lorries carrying the drums left the site very early in the mornings. Was that so no-one saw them, thereby, not getting any dodgy questions being raised. All I hope is that when the drums disintegrate in a few years' time, the soil is deactivated. But I doubt it.

Now that the soil has been removed, the building is demolished and put into drums and taken to the tip at Languard. If people only knew that this stuff was radioactive, I dread to think what the public would have said.

Over the next few weeks the moat is dredged and further phials of Radium are found. Some are still sealed and complete, others are broken. It could be assumed that the broken ones have leaked into the water.

Anglers have been finding fish with sores on them for quite a lot of years. They put it down to a fungus in the water. These sores must be attributed to the Radium in the water and not a fungus.

If you go down the motorway to Brandon, look to the left and you will see a break in the trees. That is the place the scientist dug out the bank and found the Radium. I bet the water is still radioactive.

I remember a place in the North that had a Nuclear Power Station on its beach. At certain times of the month, fish were washed up onto the beach covered in sores. The fish had obviously swum through the outflow of the Power Station.

One day I took a Geiger counter onto the beach to measure any radiation coming from the Power Station. The needle went straight off the scale. I was eating Iodine tablets for days.

The beach was very radioactive. Off course the authorities denied this. (Beach is now okay)

A lady who lived near the Power Station used to take her dog for a walk and always found dead fish on the beach. She reported it to the authorities, who told her there was nothing wrong with the Power Station outflow. She kept on ringing and writing to the Nuclear Energy Authority and even spoke to the media.

She had lived in the same bungalow for over 40 years and never had any problems. She was suddenly burgled, but nothing was taken. She still kept badgering the Nuclear Authorities.

Her friend called on her one day and found her dead. She had been murdered. (Not by me) To this day the murderer has never been caught. The government works in mysterious ways. Nothing ever came of her complaints but the papers had a field day.

Radiation is extremely dangerous and weird and lasts hundreds of years. You use it in one place and it will creep to another. A Power Station on the East coast had patrolling police dogs. Their patrolling beat was a long way from the reactor. All died from nose and throat cancer. The authorities again played the problem down.

Dosimeters issued to employees never read a fatal dose of radiation as they were set far too high. Employees getting a fatal dose of radiation poisoning, never knew it, because it was always diagnosed as Leukaemia by the medical doctor on site.

The surrounding population had the highest rate of leukaemia and various other cancers in the country. Certainly higher than the national average. Is radiation involved? I think so.

The media carried the story of high cancer deaths for months and then it all died down and no paper carried a story about it. It has never been reported by the media since. Enough said.

I have still to find out who is stealing Polonium 210 from the Ammunition Depot. I am sure this should be investigated by a department of the Security Service and not "K" department of the SIS, because I am getting nowhere fast at present. At this rate I could be a Mod Plod for years. Boy! Oh Boy!

CHAPTER THIRTY ONE

1400hrs on a Tuesday morning, I'm walking around the Ammunition Depot Bunker area when I see a Jamaican, I know by sight named Belusha in the vicinity of Bunker 68A. He should not be in this area because I know he works in the Test Bed department. No-one is allowed to be in an area they are not employed in. He has a bunch of keys in his hand. He comes round the Bunker and I say to him,

'What are you doing here?'

He replies, 'Christ man, you gave me a fright.'

I again ask him why he is here.

He replies, 'I've been checking this bunker because we are taking it over to store missile nose cones.'

I let him go but I am not happy with his answer so I go and check out the Bunker. The lock is covered with cobwebs and so are the hinges. He certainly hasn't used a key on this lock nor has it been opened. I check out the rest of the Bunkers in the area. None have been used for ages.

I return to the Station Office and ring the Test Bed Laboratory.

'Hi Mate, it's Dave. I understand your department is taking over some Bunkers to store missile parts, is that correct?'

'I don't think so Dave but hang fire; I'll check with the Boss, he may have forgotten to tell us. Give me 10 minutes, you still on 5643?'

'Sure am, there is a reason for asking.'

'Leave it with me; I'll get back to you.'

20 minutes go by when the phone rings.

'Hi Dave, sorry for the delay, we are definitely not using the Bunkers, and never will. We test things and don't have anything to store. Where did you get your information?'

'I stopped an employee near the Bunkers who said the Test Bed Department was going to use the Bunkers to store missile cones.'

'Can you remember his name?'

'Yes, he's a Jamaican called Belusha.'

'He don't work for us anymore, he was fired last week for disciplinary reasons.'

'What! Are you telling me he shouldn't be on site?'

'That's correct mate.'

'Thanks Phil, I owe you one.'

Now this is serious, heads will roll for this. I go into the Inspectors office and inform him of the incident.

'I'll inform HQ, send the Duty Sergeant in, I want every gate investigated. I want to know how this bastard is getting into the Depot. This is bloody serious.'

Now is this one of the people I am after or is it just a coincidence. I need to find out. I tell the Duty Sergeant that I will go back and patrol the Bunker area.

'Any problems, get on the radio immediately, don't take any chances, is that clear?'

'Okay Sarge'

Let's hope Belusha is one of my men, this could be the break I need. I hope so anyway.

As I round Bunker 60B, I see at Bunker 68A, Belusha. He is opening the Bunker door. Now what is he up to? Just as I am about to move towards the Bunker, my radio activates.

'Dave, a chap by the name of Scott has been arrested for letting Belusha into the Depot. There are a lot of offences, return to the Office soonest, over.'

Fuck! Belusha has heard the broadcast; I forgot to turn the radio down. Do I inform the Office that I have Belusha or do I go for him on my own? The answer is made for me. Belusha runs out of the Bunker, sees me and pulls a pistol with what looks like a silencer on it. He fires and the earth spurts up about 4 feet from me. Shit! I then radio the office.

'This is Dave, Belusha is on site I need help, and I have just been fired on by Belusha. He has a silenced gun, I need help.'

'Armed Officers on way, what's your location?'

'Bunker 68A, hurry.'

I move round to the side of the Bunker and see Belusha crouched by the Bunker door. He sees me and takes aim and fires. The gun just clicks. I run at him and knock the gun from his hand. We scuffle and I knock him to the floor. I then run over to the gun. I can hear the Police siren; the team will be here in seconds. I point the gun at him.

'You are involved with the stealing of Polonium 210, who are you working with?'

'Fuck off spook, I will never talk.'

'Really, I jamb his gun in his mouth and pull the trigger. The bullet flies out of the back of his head and he drops to the floor. I wipe my prints from the gun and put it in his hand and I then run to the side of the Bunker.

I get onto the radio and shout down the mike, 'Belusha has shot himself.' Just as the armed team turn up. They pour from the van.

'You okay Stubbs? Now weren't you told to ring for backup if you had a problem?'

'I did Sarge, but this all happened so quickly.'

'Right cordon off the area, Mathews, get onto Languard Constabulary and inform them. You Morris stay here and stop anyone from coming anywhere near the scene. Stubbs, back to the office, I want a full report. The Home Office bobbies will want to talk to you as well.'

CHAPTER THIRTY TWO

Back at the Station Office I make a statement about the incident. I am then interviewed by Languard Constabulary Crime Squad, who also takes a statement. I hope they don't find anything at the scene that will incriminate me.

The first opportunity I get, I inform SIS of the incident.

'Have you found the others who are involved?'

'A guy who let Belusha onto the site is down at Languard nick, I haven't been able to interview him but he may be involved.'

'Leave that to us, you are known to the local police due to them visiting the site when they make social calls, so we can't involve you, we will let you know if we get any evidence of his involvement, what's his name?'

'James Scott.'

'Okay, but you will have to leave the Depot, we don't want you there anymore, and it may not be safe for you or your family.'

'What do you mean, not safe for me or my family?'

'Just do as you are told, we have an office in Boldcroft near Darlington, you are posted there forthwith, start packing.'

I don't believe what is happening, and Anna isn't going to like this one little bit.

My shift is finished and I go home. It has been a long day.

Anna is in the Kitchen making me a sandwich. The kids are in bed asleep.

'Anna leave the sandwich come in here will you, I have something to tell you.'

'What's the matter? You sound very serious.'

'We have to move to Boldcroft in County Durham like yesterday. Languard is not safe for us, something happened today that has spooked the Firm, they don't want us to be here anymore.'

'I knew something like this would happen, why can't you just leave the Firm?'

'You know why.'

It looks like another evening of doom and gloom and silence.

CHAPTER THIRTY THREE

My posting with the MOD Police has come to a fast end, and a lorry turns up to take our stuff to Durham. Anna and the children are about to get into our car when my phone activates. It is the Firm. I have been given a contract in Northern Ireland and will be away for about four days. Anna is fuming, but there is nothing she can do except divorce me, and she won't do that. After a shouting match she drives off to Durham with the children. I make my way to Gatwick airport.

At the airport, I am met by one of the Firm who hands me a folder and a ticket to Belfast and a return ticket to Manchester.

'You will be met at Belfast airport, have a good trip.' He then left.

The flight doesn't take long and I am not enjoying it, in fact I am pretty pissed off. I don't need all this especially as Anna will have to move into the new place bought by the Firm on her own.

As I am walking through arrivals, I see my name being held up by a chap dressed in a black leather jacket. 'You must be waiting for me, I'm Stubbs.'

We shake hands and he informs me that a car is outside at my disposal. 'It is yours for the duration you are in Belfast. You have your equipment in the boot, read this and destroy it.' He says handing me a file. He never tells me his name.

Outside the airport he shows me a beaten up wreck of a car. 'It's all yours, see you.' With that he leaves. And I still don't know his name.

I see a traffic warden coming towards me, so I jump into the car and take off toward the A1. In a layby I stop and read the files. Boy! Is this one hell of a mother fucker I'll get this job over as soon as I can, I don't want to be here any longer than I have to.

I drive to the area and park the car in a car park used by the people in the flats. No one will take any notice of it; it is too much of a wreck. I take the box from the boot and proceed into the flats and up to the top floor which for some reason is not occupied. I push open the door leading onto the roof just as it starts to rain. Shit! I check where the contracts flat is by orientating the drawing. It is about 100 yards away and I can see it through a hole made in the side of the wall. No one will be able to see me. Rather convenient this hole!

I change into the Gortex coveralls and assemble my rifle. The rain has stopped. I move onto the roof and lay down and put the barrel of the rifle in the hole in the wall facing towards the flat in question.

After about an hour the rain really starts pouring down, not a light trickle but a downpour. Large puddles are beginning to form all around me. I have now been lying on top of the Broadbent flats for 6 hours. What I wouldn't give for a lovely hot drink right now. Thank goodness for the Gortex coveralls, they are doing a great job of keeping the cold and rain out. My right eye is beginning to see double from the constant looking into the rifle scope. 'Come on you bastard show yourself.' I say to myself for the hundredth time. The only person I have seen so far is a blonde headed git with a beard. He doesn't look anything like the guy in the photo I studied in the car. I know his details off by heart. Sean O'Patrick, aged 23, height 5 foot 3 inches tall, brown hair, blue eyes, and no distinguishing marks, but sometimes wears a silver cross ear ring in his left ear. He is the youngest Commander in the IRA, Belfast East Division.

The window I am looking at is about 100 yards away from me. With the rifle scope I can see right into the room even to the statue of the Virgin Mary standing on a shelf over the fireplace. Christ! This scope is brilliant. I refocus the scope for the umpteenth time when all of a sudden, Blondie opens the window and looks out. This is the first time he has done this since I have been in position. Now is a good time to get a good description of him to give to control when I get back.

I line the scope on his head and then staring at me is a tiny silver cross in his left ear. Boof! I let loose a silenced 7.62mm ceramic headed round which hits Blondie right between the eyes. A small hole appears, and the back of his head explodes sending a blonde wig, blood and brains into the room. For a millionth of a second he stands there and then shits himself, a look of bewilderment on his face. He then falls to the floor. He has died not knowing where the bullet had come from. The room will smell of shit and copper. Shit because that is what you do when you are killed violently and copper, that's the smell of blood.

I quickly pack away the rifle and equipment and whilst doing so, remember the old Freddie Mercury song, 'another one bites the dust.............'

This is what the Firm call "Deniable Operations." They can deny any involvement with the Operation and any involvement with the person if he is caught by the power that be. Deniable Operations my arse, murder more like.

I drive to a secluded spot and scrape a hole in the ground and set fire to the files. I then cover the ashes with the soil. I inform control that the job has been completed and that I will leave the car in the airport car park. Now I make my way to the airport where I leave the car with the key under the seat. Someone will pick it up I'm sure especially with what is in the boot. I then get the plane to Manchester and the train to Durham.

The Operation has taken a day. Why! Because I'm pissed off. I can't wait to get home.

THIS STORY CONTINUES IN
"GOVERNMENT ASSASSIN"
WHICH WILL BE PUBLISHED DURING
2011, WATCH OUT FOR IT.

Milton Keynes UK
Ingram Content Group UK Ltd.
UKHW020425120424
441015UK00001B/124

9 781456 770372